Editor: Caroline Palmier—Love & Edits

Cover Designer: Melissa Doughty—Mel D. Designs

Proofreading: April Editorial

Formatting: Cathryn Carter—Format by CC

PASS RUSH

BOOK FOUR OF THE
OUT OF BOUNDS
SERIES

If you've ever had the strength to start over when it would've been easier to stay complacent. If you've ever chosen to leave chaos and step into the unknown, even if you stumbled a bit to find your footing. I hope you know it's not failure.
You're allowed to begin again.

If you've ever been made to feel inadequate or unworthy. If your success could never be enjoyed because of someone claiming it to be theirs. I hope you understand their insecurities are not yours.
You get to choose who you are in this life. So be nothing like them.

A NOTE FROM THE AUTHOR

Hi Friends,

I wanted to take a moment to express my gratitude before you dive into this book. It's a bittersweet feeling having this series come to an end, but Demi and Liam are so special and round out this series in the most loving and beautiful way.

Sports feel like home to me in a lot of ways, especially football. It's where I feel a lot of memories with my dad and ultimately something that brings me so much happiness. I thoroughly love everything about a sports romance, but the found family aspect is something that's unmatched. I have loved writing this entire series and while it wasn't always easy, I can wrap this up saying I'm truly proud of these stories.

I knew years ago that I wanted Liam's love interest to be someone in his world of sports. Someone who could go toe to toe with him, challenge him, but also be a soft place for him to land. Demi fits the bill and in turn he's exactly what she needs, too. I love this story and this world and I'm sad to leave it behind, but always excited for what's to come.

Please note this is fiction, so I understand that there are many circumstances a sports reporter would not get involved with an athlete they work with professionally.

Hope you enjoy Pass Rush!

Content Warnings

Discussion of verbal abuse, cheating, divorce, drunk driving accident (details talked about on page), discussion of having children, infertility, depression and anger/emotional distress (therapy session on page) and a toxic parent relationship.

PROLOGUE

LIAM

"God, you look good." My eyes sweep over my date standing next to me.

She's a tiny thing, maybe five foot three if I had to guess, and I tower over her as we stand on this red carpet waiting to go inside.

She smiles up at me, tucking her purse under her arm. Her light brown eyes sparkle, and I notice the bright pink shade on her cheeks. I honestly can't tell if it's makeup or if she's blushing. But I don't care, she's keeping me company for this charity event.

"Thank you," she says. "You clean up nicely too." Her eyelashes flutter my way.

I follow behind her—unabashedly distracted by the sway of her hips as she walks into the downtown hall.

When I asked Lacy to come with me tonight, I knew it would be a yes. She's fun company on nights I just don't feel like being alone.

This charity event is packed to the brim with athletes from

around the city. It's always really cool to see how everyone rallies behind a good cause.

There's soft music coming from a band in the back corner, and I can spot the basketball players right away—giant mother-fuckers they are. Tampa's team recently signed a new power forward and it's been the talk of the town since it happened, considering how awful they are. Well, it *was* the talk of the town until two days ago when the Knights officially named me the starting quarterback going forward. And the spotlight shifted to that.

Funny how fast news moves and how quickly the next best thing pops up.

"This is our table," Lacy says, reaching for my hand and gently tugging me to the right.

I pull out her chair, and she sits before I take my own seat, leaving the table with four other open chairs. I recognize Connor Hughes's name right away—he plays for Tampa's baseball team. One other name is that of a hockey player, the other two chairs are on the opposite side—too far for me to read the names.

"What's up, man?" Connor palms my shoulders from behind, and I tilt my chin up at him with a smile.

"Hell yeah, good to see you."

"You too," he says, taking a seat to my left. "Congratulations on becoming the starter, don't fuck it up." He quickly tips his head as he laughs.

"I'll do my best," I answer, just as I feel Lacy's hand on my thigh. Her delicate fingers create circles over my black suit pants, and I knock my head back just the slightest, the physical touch feels good.

From across the room, I notice a crowd gathering around a few people, one sticking out amongst the rest.

Connor's chin tilts up. "That's Brandon Nells, new power forward for the Wildcats. That's who they're hoping can turn the franchise around."

"He's fucking massive."

"Six foot eight." Connor scoffs, shaking his head just before taking a sip of his drink.

A small crowd of people begin making their way toward our table, and I'm starting to think one of the name tags on the opposite side says Brandon Nells.

"Hey," Connor says, and both of us stand.

Maybe with both of us standing upright we'll each appear taller—two guys around six foot two should balance out one at six foot eight, right?

"Hey, man, welcome to Tampa." I extend my hand.

"You're Evans," he says. His voice is fucking deep, and I don't know if he's making it deeper on purpose or if he actually sounds like Thor in real life.

"I am," I say with a grin. "Liam Evans. Nice to meet you."

Connor introduces himself, and I watch as the people behind Brandon fan out. A few of the planned speeches are about to begin—I know a *quiet down* gesture when I see one as the lights lower.

"Brandon," he says as he takes a seat at the table. I give Connor a quick side-eye as we both notice how much fucking space he takes up.

The Wildcats are expecting big things from him—and honestly, they should.

I take a sip of my drink, feeling the burn as it coats my throat, and turn my head toward the bar to see if I can make it there and back for another before anyone starts talking. But there's commotion on the other side of the table and I quickly glance that way.

"Sorry, I was trying to network a little with my new boss," a woman whispers to Brandon.

Well, it's not exactly a whisper, I can hear her pretty clearly, but I think *she* thinks she's whispering.

Whoever this woman is, Brandon doesn't give her the time of

day as he simply nods and continues to do whatever the hell he's doing on his phone.

I watch as she pulls out her own chair and takes a seat with a glass of vodka in her hand. Unless it's water? You've got to be pretty fucking brave to drink a tall glass of vodka on the rocks, so maybe it's water. I feel far too invested in her beverage.

She brushes a wave of hair over her shoulder, and I tilt my head slightly, watching each movement she makes. She's beautiful. In that *I shouldn't be staring, but I can't stop* kind of way. The way that makes you do a double take and stop what you're doing to pay attention. I wish she was closer so I could see more of her features.

I've never seen her before—or if I have, I've never noticed—and I hate how that makes me feel. Because a woman like her deserves to be noticed. But she's definitely got my attention now.

Her hair is in dark curls and she's wearing a black floor-length dress—both are my kryptonite. Which is interesting, since Lacy is blonde and in a pink dress.

I feel Lacy's fingers on my thigh again when the lights dim even farther, practically reminding me she's there, but this time I subtly brush them away. Lacy's beautiful, and on any other night, having her hands on me would be something I crave, but the air completely shifted when I saw this woman across the table.

Though I make sure to give Lacy's hand a quick squeeze while offering a brief smile. I like her—we've been friends for a couple years, and I don't want to be rude. Plus, I'm not a dick.

There are a handful of speeches being made by guests of honor and a founder of one of the charities just wrapped up his speech, ending on a cheesy joke that only made me, Connor, and the woman I've been catching glimpses of all night laugh.

"I'm going to grab a refill. Can I get you anything?" I ask Lacy, my hand on her shoulder as I stand.

"I'm okay, thank you." She grins up at me and then continues her conversation with Connor.

"Old fashioned, please." I raise my index finger to the bartender once I lean my elbows against the bar top.

"Oh, Liam, we could've come to take your order," one of the bartenders says.

"No, that's not necessary. I like coming up to the bar and cataloging all the expensive bottles you have displayed up here." I grin at her as she's making my drink.

She's a little older if I had to guess, and has that very sweet, small-town demeanor about her. I decide pretty quickly she'll be getting a good tip from me.

"You've got some nice whiskey on display here," I say as I take in the top-shelf liquor. "Macallan is one of the best drinks I've ever had."

She smiles and slides my drink to me on a napkin.

"Can I just have vodka cranberry and a water, please?" The voice I hear to my left pulls me in. It's identical to the one I heard earlier when she was speaking well above a whisper.

"Vodka cranberry, wow. Can't remember the last time I had that."

She turns to face me—a few barstools are between us—but it's brighter here than it was at the table, and I can see her face more clearly.

You can stick a fucking fork in me this very second. The darkest—and most stunning—eyes I've ever seen roll my way. And I genuinely mean they roll my way. A big fucking eye roll. And dammit, I probably shouldn't love that as much as I do.

I watch as she takes a seat, following her every movement.

"Too cool for a vodka cran and moved onto a harsher drink with that old fashioned?" she bites back, but there's a tiny smirk that plays on her lips. "The alcohol isn't mine," she says.

She smiles down at the sticky bar top. Ah, so the drink I saw her with earlier must've been water. Kind of relieved, to be honest. Seems dangerous to allow someone that much vodka.

I glance over my shoulder at the table. Lacy is still talking to

Connor, and Brandon is talking to a couple of gentlemen who've approached the table—no one's paying any mind to the bar.

"So you're the water. Smart. Stay hydrated." I tip my drink before taking a sip, and I hear her laugh.

I swear to god, my knees feel like they might buckle at the sound of her laugh. It's the best thing I've ever heard, and I'd pay to hear it again. I catch a dimple on her cheek that's facing me, and I can't help but wonder if she has a matching one on the left.

"I'm just grabbing my—" There's a brief pause in the flow of her sentence, but then she continues, "Fiancé a drink."

Fiancé?

My attention snaps to her left hand. I know I would've noticed a ring. Engagement rings are hard to miss, aren't they? Women usually become left-handed for everything once they have a rock on their finger.

But her right hand nervously cups over her left as she notices me looking at her bare finger, and I avert my eyes somewhere else. I don't want to make her uncomfortable. Although, it's kind of a douchebag move to make your fiancée go to the bar to get your drink. Docking a few points from this guy.

"It's…a long story." She sighs as the bartender puts both of her requested drinks down in front of her.

My lips turn down as I shake my head. "No need to explain."

She nods and tucks a stray strand of hair behind her ear, and it's then that I get a glimpse of the ink on her wrist.

The letter B.

B, as in Brandon? Based on her hesitancy to admit they are engaged, I find myself wondering if the tattoo is for him or something else.

"Well, congratulations on the engagement." I turn my back to the bar, looking out over the tables full of people.

I usually only come to these events as a reason to bring a date. And then a reason to take them out afterward. Admittedly,

Lacy and I couldn't be more different, but she's hot and a good time. Which is really all I'm looking for right now.

"Congratulations to you too, Evans."

My pulse jumps at the sound of my name coming off her lips. Logically, I understand she knows who I am because of the speech by one of my buddies earlier on stage, but I wasn't expecting her to talk to me tonight—let alone say my name. I make a mental reminder to thank Ford for shouting me out on stage.

I turn to thank her, but all I can do is stare at her. Stare like some teenage boy who just saw a woman for the first time. Her eyes, her hair, the way the dress seems to fit her like a glove. And the spark in her? The wit and sass took my goddamn breath away.

She moves to get up, but slightly stumbles.

"Oh shit." I extend my hand to help, but she seems to catch herself and avoids taking my hand. "Good thing you've switched to water," I joke.

"Stupid heel," she mutters. "That was embarrassing, I feel dumb that you just saw that."

It looked like the heel of her shoe got caught on the footrest of the stool.

"If it makes you feel any better, I think you're smart."

Her eyes narrow at me and I casually grin her way. "We just met four minutes ago."

"I'm a quick study." I shrug. "And technically, we didn't meet. You know my name, but I don't know yours."

"Demi," she says, standing up straighter. "And I actually don't drink." She grabs both glasses from the bar, regaining her composure before she takes a step forward and then stops. "Have a good evening."

"You too," I say, watching her walk away.

I've been on my fair share of dates. I've interacted with plenty of women. But even the best sex I've ever had doesn't compare to the five-minute conversation I just had with that woman.

Training camp starts today, and to say I'm excited is an understatement. I'm over the fucking moon to be back at this place, getting to do what I love.

There are only so many puzzles and boat days I can take before I start to go a little stir crazy, missing my home away from home.

Freshly cleaned dark wood floors and the smell of new leather greet me as I enter the building. Perfectly placed red and black flags with the Knights logo hang from every corner of the lobby when I make my way in. A round wooden desk is centered in the middle with Tampa Bay Knights on the front, along with previous and current team jerseys lining the walls. There are two different shrines on either end of the far wall, one highlighting Ring of Honor players and the other holds memories of the last time this team won a championship. That was over a decade ago.

A lot of the staff are already in the building—a surprise since I'm notoriously one of the first ones here every morning. The allure of sleeping in doesn't do anything for me, so nine in the morning might as well be noon to me.

"Good morning," I say with a smile to Greg as I pass him.

He's the head of our media team. Our social media has really blown up in the last couple seasons since he joined, letting a few of the more trendy interns take the reins on the accounts. Apparently, people are really interested in knowing which teammate we'd all let date our sisters.

"Morning, morning. I have a new reporter starting today. I'm sure you'll meet her, she's already here somewhere…I think saying hello to Coach Aarons."

"Awesome, I'll be sure to say hello."

I've made it a point to always be lighthearted and playful with the staff—coaches, medical, athletic trainers, reporters—their job in this organization is just as important, maybe even more so than mine. It makes it easier when we have a mutual respect for each other's role.

Walking toward Coach Aarons's office, I hear a laugh that sounds all too familiar. A series of sounds that have been living rent-free in my mind since I heard it a week ago.

Down the hall, I see a tall figure leave his office. Dark hair spills over her shoulders and a large brown bag is on one of her arms. She's smiling down at her phone and then looks up—as if she could feel me staring at her.

"It's you," I say—in probably the softest, most pathetic voice I've ever used.

"Hi," she says.

"W-what are you doing here?"

"I'm your new sideline reporter."

No way. *No fucking way.* I haven't stopped thinking about this woman since she rolled her eyes at me last weekend, and now I'm supposed to work with her, knowing she's engaged to a mediocre man?

I guess I could spin it. I *get* to work with her. I *get* to see her. Even if she can't ever be mine. At least I get to be around her. That'll take some getting used to, but I'm nothing if not a team player and excellent colleague.

"Oh wow, congratulations. You didn't mention it last weekend," I admit.

She shrugs, pulling the shoulder of her gray cardigan up over her skin as it keeps falling, and I notice a small red and blue flag keychain dangling from the strap of her bag. I take a mental picture of it so I can look up which flag it is later.

"That night wasn't about me."

Jesus, she's pretty, smart, *and* humble? This must be what they mean when they say God gives his hardest battles to his strongest soldiers. Because how the hell am I supposed to stop thinking about her?

"I've got to run. But I'll see you around, I guess." Her shoulders rise and fall as she softly smiles.

"Sure," I say, stepping to the side as she begins to walk away. Because sure is the only word I can form as I melt at the sight of her dimples.

I keep heading down the long hallway to Coach's office, but hear her call out before she approaches the elevators.

"Hey, Twelve?"

I turn around at the sound of her voice.

"I've watched your film." Her head nods up and down and she turns her lips up into a soft smile. "Pretty good for a third-rounder."

And my chest swells.

CHAPTER ONE

LIAM

"Sorry, could you repeat that?"

The press conference today is full of reporters wanting to get the scoop on how training camp is going.

The reporter in a gray polo sighs as I ask him to repeat his question, and this time I force myself to pay attention to him instead of the high ponytail at the back of the room. The one attached to a woman who will barely make eye contact with me. The one with pouty lips who loves to roll those beautiful brown eyes at me any chance she gets.

"With Graham Turner announcing his retirement in the offseason, how do you suppose that'll impact your season?" He speaks louder this time, noticeably annoyed he had to repeat himself to begin with. I can't blame him.

"Graham's retiring?" I let the joke fly out of my mouth and wait for anyone in the room to laugh, but it seems to fall flat. *Tough crowd.*

After a few seconds there are a handful of low pity chuckles, and at the back of the crowd I catch her shaking her head at my attempt. If I didn't know any better, I'd swear she's biting back a smile as a flash of red tints her cheeks. And making Demi Sanchez blush is still on my life's bucket list.

"I'm kidding." I assure the dozen people sitting in front of me that I'm not completely oblivious to the happenings around me. "I'll miss him, but he deserves the time off now. He's done a lot for this team and this is part of the business. I've been tempted to bribe him into staying…" The crowd lets out a laugh. "But I completely respect his decision. He's given everything to this organization for a long time. Now it's his time to do something else."

My palms rub the edge of the podium as I scan the room for the next voice I hear. Sweat is dripping down my temples, and I'm itching to get inside. But another reporter speaks up as I take a deep breath.

"Liam, Willa from *Hello, Tampa,*" she introduces herself. "How has camp been so far? There are a lot of new faces out there. Seeing anything special?"

I nod. "Everyone is working really hard and bringing something great to practice every day. Listen, it's not ideal out here—the heat and humidity all day is a really hard thing to adjust to…" I pause. "But everyone's giving it their all. They're showing up and busting their butts. We have a lot of special players out there, and I couldn't ask for a better group to be around."

"Last question," the head of our PR team mutters from my left as another reporter speaks up.

"Hi, Liam," Jan from one of the local outlets says. She's been at this for years, and I always appreciate seeing her front and center.

"Hi, Jan." I offer her my biggest smile yet today.

"Liam, how have you been feeling in camp? You've been at this a while. Any tips you're giving to the new guys?"

I feel my neck stiffen. "I've felt great. You know, it's a tough game and every day I get to do it I feel blessed. It's just about seizing opportunities—that's really what camp is for. It's an opportunity for everyone to come in and show what they've got. Thanks, everyone," I say before I leave the podium and step out from under the tent back into the sun.

Nate Campbell, our running back, is eyeing me with a raised brow as he walks over.

"You want to be more obvious next time, or what?"

A grin twitches at the corner of my mouth. "I don't know what you're talking about."

"Right." Nate laughs as our strides sync up.

I'm always distracted by Demi. For years, I've been getting distracted by her. Staring at her isn't new, and honestly I've never made much of an effort to hide it. It's crazy to think when we first met she was engaged and then, shortly after, she got married. But now, she's single. And for the first time, it doesn't feel wrong to look at her the way I do. I don't feel a sour pit of jealousy over knowing someone else is falling asleep next to her or holding her hand.

My crush on Demi was instant, and only grew as time went on and I got bits and pieces of her time over the course of our careers. But I knew it could only ever be just that—a crush—because she wasn't available. I hated it, but I respected it.

It's hard to pull my gaze from Demi anytime I'm around her, but today, seeing her in that outfit she was wearing, I wouldn't be surprised if the cameras saw me drool. Black washed jeans and a fitted T-shirt with a pair of sneakers. It's my favorite thing she wears. Probably because I can tell she's most comfortable in it.

There's a loud sigh from Nate as we walk side by side. "Did you still want to play poker next week?"

I hear Nate's words, but don't reply as I catch Demi walking out of the tent in my peripheral vision. She stops to talk with one of the producers, and when she glances our way I give her a playful wave, wiggling my fingers with a cocky grin. It's like I'm begging for an eye roll or something.

Nate's voice echoes around me, but I don't hear a damn thing he's saying. My attention is fixed on her again. Like some kind of hypnosis, I swear I'd do anything this woman asks me to.

"I appreciate the dedication you have to the one woman on earth who seems to be unfazed by you, but we were talking, you know. Can you pay attention to our conversation?" Nate jabs my rib with his elbow as he chuckles.

"I'm a man in love, what can I say?" I tilt my head to him, grinning as I do.

Demi's hands move as she speaks. Whatever she's talking about is exciting to her. I can tell by how big her gestures are. They're spacious and open. When she's pissed off, she's sharper, more rigid.

"Yeah," Nate mutters as we walk through the doors that head to the locker room. "So you've mentioned. That woman would chew you up and spit you out."

"And I'd say thank you." I shrug, pulling my jersey off once we're inside, but I glance back toward the doors one more time. "She's just unlike anyone I've ever met, man. I can't believe Brandon was dumb enough to lose her. But him fucking up means I might have a chance."

Hope swells in my chest every time I think about the possibility.

Nate nods just as Chase Hunt approaches. He's one of our defensive captains—and a real tight ass, but our little group wouldn't be the same without him.

"Some guys don't know what they have." Nate shakes his head, glancing at his lock screen with a picture of Mia and their boys. "Luckily, I'm well the fuck aware." He grins.

"Well aware of what?" Chase asks.

"How lucky he is that Mia puts up with him," I joke. "I just mentioned I can't believe Brandon fumbled Demi." I shrug, and Chase scoffs under his breath.

I glance over as he's fastening the top button on his shirt.

"Yeah, he fucked up there." Chase says as my memory shows me a picture of her from earlier today. It's impossible to get her out of my mind.

"I just want to be around her all the time," I admit.

"But would she want to be around you all the time, that's the question." Chase smirks, palming my shoulder lovingly.

"Hey, let's not forget who encouraged both of you to have some balls and go after your girls," I reply.

Chase points at me as he nods toward Nate. "He's not wrong."

"I would've said something to Mia sooner or later."

"Nah, you would've waited too long. She'd have taken that date with Hughes, had a great time—because, let's be honest, he's cool as hell. Then, when he got traded last year, she probably would've moved with him. So I saved you the heartbreak, you're fucking welcome."

"I—no—you're—"

"Let it go," Chase says, palming Nate's shoulder before he turns to me.

"Demi doesn't tolerate bullshit, Liam. She's a grown woman with a big career I'm sure she worked her ass off for. Plus, a marriage and a divorce under her belt. I can't see her being interested in anything right now. And especially something that could fuck with her job."

"It's not forbidden for reporters and players to date. I've looked it up."

"Of course you have." Nate shakes his head and lets out a low chuckle.

"I'm sure it's also not praised, either."

My hands dig into my hips as I face Chase. "Are you trying to hurt me?" I tuck Chase's words away. I'm not so naive to believe that a reporter getting involved with a player they work with wouldn't lead to questions.

Chase has always felt like an older brother to me. He's level-headed and responsible, it helps balance me out sometimes I think.

He slaps my back. "I'm heading out," he says. "There's a painting class CeCe wants to go to today, and Summer just bought a new dress I'd like to see in private before I need to go do dad things."

Nate takes a seat on the chair near his locker, just a few down from mine.

"You know we all want to see you happy. But you know he's right though on some level, she's newly divorced and probably not looking for someone like—"

"Someone like me?" I cut him off.

"I think I'd just assume whoever she dates next wouldn't be someone in the sports world. I'd guess she wants someone less flashy, less spotlight, less reputation."

He winces as he spills the last word. It's no secret I've been coined as a serial dater. But they've never been serious. Plus, with Demi being single now, I have no interest in anyone else. No more random hookups, no more dates or photos with "mystery women."

For the longest time, I never thought I'd have a shot with Demi, and now that she's single, I just want a chance to prove to her I'm more than whatever the tabloids want to box me in as. I know she's seen media outlets and their gaudy headlines over my dating life whether they've been true or not—I never cared enough about what people assumed to correct them, until lately.

I make my way closer to him. "If you must know, I haven't actually been with a woman in…almost a year." The realization surprises even me. "She's single for the first time since I've known her, I'd be a fucking idiot to blow that shot."

I still have no idea what really caused the divorce. There was speculation, and I heard whispers here and there. A gossip column made some accusations that pissed me off thinking of her being hurt, but unless I hear the story from Demi, it's all just hearsay.

"Yeah, guess you would be," Nate taunts with a teasing grin.

"She needs to see that I'm serious about her, that I've *been* serious about her since the day I met her. But I just need time to show her who I really am. All she knows is what she hears."

Nate sighs. "Well, I'm rooting for you."

Teammates have been passing by throughout this conversation, none chiming in but nearly all giving me a shake of their head with a laugh or a smile. My stance—that Demi Sanchez is the best reporter and person in existence—is something I'm always very vocal about.

"As far as I'm concerned, I'm not available to anyone else. Not for PR, not for events, none of it. I only want Demi."

As we're wrapping up getting changed and ready to leave for the day, I hear Coach Aarons before I see him. "Listen up!" he calls. "Take it easy this weekend. No screwing around." His gaze slides to me with a stern look, and I just raise my hands in front of me. "Great day today, guys. We need a lot more days like today before preseason begins. If you're scheduled for any interviews, don't be late. Be professional. Show up and do what's expected of you." He sighs, pulling his red baseball cap from his head and wiping his brow. He scans the room one more time before moving again. "Have a good night, fellas," he adds before walking out.

Having extra cameras around during training camp this season is new. But something I'm thankful for. Demi typically only works our regular season games from the sidelines or does feature interviews when needed. It's rare that I get to see her this often during camp. So, while everyone else is moaning and groaning over the cameras, I've never been better.

With the locker room clearing out, most guys are gone,

heading home to their families for the night. That's not the case for me, though. I can't remember the last time I had someone to end my day with. I really am just the guy who has never actually had a serious relationship.

It's not like I'm going home completely alone though. Birdie is always happy to see me and has dinner with me almost every night. Granted, she's covered in fur, pees in a box, and hisses every time there's a bird out the window. But I found her on the golf course a few months ago, and despite my best efforts of shooing her away, she nuzzled up against my golf bag and I couldn't say no. I'll never forget driving home from the golf course, her purring in my lap as the realization hit that I just became a member of the reluctant Cat Dad club.

I'd never considered myself a cat guy; I figured if I ever had a pet, it'd be a dog. Man's best friend. But no, I had to be the guy who falls for a cat that knocks over everything and looks me dead in the eye while doing it.

Nate's palm cups my shoulder as he walks by. "Heading out, I'll see you later."

"Later, man," I reply as I fasten the string on my athletic shorts.

Ford Anderson, our tight end and another close friend of mine, gives me a nod from across the locker room as he exits, and I take a seat on the black cushioned chair next to my duffle bag.

"Hey, Liam, can I bother you to sign something for my son?" I glance up to see Ian Marx—one of my newer tackles—standing over my shoulder holding one of my jerseys in his hands.

"Hell, I should be asking for yours. Are you kidding me?" I smile, reaching for the jersey and marker. "What's your son's name?"

"Brody." He smiles from ear to ear when he sees no hesitation in me agreeing.

I sign my name on the jersey and reach into my locker to grab a pair of gloves.

"Give him these too."

Ian's eyes widen and he tries to thank me, but I cut in, "I need one of your jerseys. Signed. Think you can spare one for me?"

"Really? You want my jersey?"

"You're here doing great things. Hell yeah, I want your jersey."

He lets out a surprised chuckle as he bobs his head up and down. "Yeah. I'll get you one. Thank you."

When he leaves, I pull a white T-shirt with the Knights logo over my head and stand before grabbing my notebook from the seat beside me.

Today was grueling, but it's not over yet. I have some notes I want to go over before calling it a day. I've been so conditioned to operate like this from such a young age, it's just second nature now to spend extra time studying plays. It's pretty much the one thing my father made sure of.

Growing up with a two-time league MVP and Super Bowl-winning father wasn't the dream most people think it would be.

There are only a few people outside of my brother who know the ins and outs of my childhood. I never talk about my father. Even in interviews when I'm asked about him, I keep it as brief as I possibly can and keep the narrative going—that he's a great guy.

Landyn Evans Sr. is a name that's famous no matter which team you root for. People don't forget the quarterback who had back-to-back Super Bowl wins. The guy who threw for over three hundred yards in a game with two feet of snow. The guy who had comeback after comeback, proving he was resilient on the field.

Everyone knows that version of my father. I'm not here to

tarnish the image people have of him. To them, as a player, he was great.

Unfortunately, as a father, he wasn't.

I grew up with the guy who pushed his eight-year-old son to play a flag football game in the dead of summer when he had the stomach flu. I puked between almost every play. I begged to go home. Begged him to let me sit out this one game.

"Don't embarrass me," he said. And so I played.

Away games meant I didn't have to see him for at least twenty-four hours. God, I fucking lived for those away games. How my sweet mother ever married him, I'll never understand. But at the end of the day, she knew how hard he was on me and rarely got involved to ask him to stop. I try not to ever blame her —I think in a lot of ways he was doing the same thing to her as he was to me. Belittling her, making her feel like without him she'd be nothing. Turning a blind eye was her way of surviving, and while it wasn't right, I try not to dwell on her decisions.

Sometimes, I think he tried to be fatherly, but it was always short-lived. There's one thing that has stuck with me, though.

He always reminded me how rare big opportunities are. Second chances are so few and far between, so you have to make the most out of your first. Study. Stay late. Wake up early. Become obsessed with greatness.

It's what has always pushed me to work as hard as I do.

Truthfully, there are quarterbacks who are more talented than I am. They're bigger, they're faster, they might have a stronger arm, but talent like that only gets you so far. You have to take it to the next level to be successful.

So I became consistent. I became resilient. I don't take my time on the field for granted, and I *don't* like to lose.

CHAPTER TWO

DEMI

The manilla folder on this coffee table has been staring at me for the last hour. It's a thin folder, only a few papers inside the clasp, yet it carries so much weight.

It's an ending. And a beginning.

Filing for divorce isn't something I ever thought I'd be doing, but life is full of countless moments we never expected.

It's a surreal feeling, considering I was raised in a home where divorce wasn't a word that was spoken. Marriage is sacred and forever. A lifelong commitment you make to someone, for better or worse, in sickness and health, until death do you part.

Except, I learned that sometimes the "'til death do you part" tidbit doesn't have to be literally kicking the bucket. There are many ways to die in a relationship.

I cherished my marriage. I fought for it when things got tough. And then, silently, I grieved the loss while still wearing the ring.

The last year has taught me that I'm a hell of a lot stronger than I ever gave myself credit for. I've always been independent and confident, but the ways my soul shattered in recent months showed me a strength I didn't realize I had.

My coffee is getting cold as I sit in this little cafe downtown. I can practically hear the echoes of Brandon's raised voice from countless arguments swirling over people's chatter and the whirring of the espresso machines.

I'm trying to keep busy, procrastinating watching game footage on my laptop, as if I'm on a deadline.

I am—except I have four more days to finish watching sixty minutes of game play for an upcoming interview, and I don't need four days for that. I'm stalling. Avoiding the inevitable because even though there's relief in this part of my story, I can't help the feeling of sadness in my chest. And there's a nauseous feeling in the pit of my stomach, something that feels so heavy I can't physically leave this stupid chair.

I inhale a deep breath, in through my nose for four seconds, hold for four seconds and out through my mouth for four seconds. The aroma of coffee fills my senses, and I instantly relax my shoulders.

A thousand memories play in my mind.

Brandon and I fell in love at twenty-two the moment we met. God, it was *instant*. And it was consuming. But looking at it now…maybe it was reckless and forced. There was no friendship beforehand, nothing to build on. No taking things slow. No late nights up talking. No tender moments that felt like home.

We jumped and we soared. But rose-colored glasses only work for so long until they eventually become distorted. We outgrew each other in all the ways that mattered. And now he's someone I don't even recognize.

I sigh, leaning back against the chair and close my laptop before placing it back into my tote.

Get up, Demi, I internally shout at myself.

Just because it's the end of my marriage, doesn't mean it's the end of the world.

Endings can be beautiful too.

I repeat the words in my head over and over until I can breathe without my eyes watering. I hate that I feel sad. Because I shouldn't. He sure as hell doesn't. And not because I'm upset about being thirty-five and single—it's something much deeper. A different level of heartache. Even though I know this is the right decision, it's still there.

Failure.

I feel like I failed. Like *we* failed. Like I let everyone down by ending my marriage. Because even though he was the one who initiated our downfall—I'm the one who left, the one who filed for divorce, and after today I'll be the one who serves him the paperwork.

My phone dings with a text from Greg, my boss at the network. He's letting me know I'll be assigned to cover the interviews for the Tampa Bay Knights training camp next season and the corners of my mouth tip up. I've always enjoyed working with the Knights, and it's definitely a chance to continue proving why I deserve more large-scale interviews—maybe even a broadcast position for the prime-time games.

Just get up, Demi. There it is again.

"Are you doing okay over here?" A petite blonde girl with glasses and a sleeve of cups in her hand pulls my attention away from my phone.

I stare at her blankly for a few seconds, noticing the ring on her left hand.

I've let this marriage make me feel small for long enough. I've begged for the bare minimum. I bent over backward trying to please him for longer than I needed to. I bit my tongue when things bothered me just to keep the peace. How fucking silly of me to think his voice meant more than mine.

"I'm good, thank you. Just packing up," I say, offering the barista a smile.

Just get up, Demi.

And this time, I do.

PRESENT

Being one of the only women in a male-dominated field is a challenge—add in the fact that I'm a Dominican woman talking about sports in a highly competitive field, and I really chose the path with the most resistance. But it's a challenge I'm always up for. The crew I work with for the Knights is amazing, but I still see comments online where people question me and the other female broadcasters. When I first started, I was the only woman in the room during meetings, but now, at least there's two of us.

My job as a sideline reporter is something I take a lot of pride in. I've worked really hard to get where I am—harder than most. But I still have goals I'm trying to achieve and people I'm trying to prove wrong. Women are important in sports, and I only hope that my presence can somehow inspire others.

Teenage Demi would be screaming if she knew this was her life. Traveling to amazing cities, reporting on a sport I truly love, attending award shows and community events—this career is everything I used to dream of, more even.

I can still recall the first interview I did in high school with the running back during my sophomore year. I stumbled over words at the start, but about halfway through something clicked and it was as if everything in me—in my bones, in my soul— knew I wanted to do this, *had* to do this. And I've been tangled up in this world ever since.

Women belong in this space, and I'm not going to stop pushing for that.

While professionally I'm flourishing, my personal life has been an up-and-down roller coaster for the last year and a half.

I flow through days where I'm happy and so proud of myself,

but then there are days where I feel that hurt all over again. That stinging feeling of failure. But as much disappointment as I ultimately felt when I drove away from the person I thought I'd grow old with, there was also a push of confidence. A swell of something within me whispering, *you're doing the right thing.*

Two things can be true. And two feelings can coexist. It's okay to be sad about something ending, while knowing it's the right decision. The best thing I ever did for myself was leave that marriage, even if I stumbled a little on the way out.

Sun gleams through the windows of this hotel building next to the Knights facility. Floor-to-ceiling glass overlooking the bay as light glistens on the water, and I get lost in thought staring at it.

"Demi, Ford's on his way in."

Greg's words bring me back to the present, and I tuck my loose curls behind my ear as I close the notebook on my lap. When I do, I get a quick glimpse of my fingers, noticing the naked one on my left hand. I'm still getting used to it being bare after wearing a ring for so many years. But there's no time to feel anything or let my mind wander as Ford Anderson strides into the room.

His big, bright smile lights up the room the second he steps through the door, and I watch as he says hello to every single person on his way to me. Ford's tall and lean, but full of muscle. As a tight end, he's not as slender as a wide receiver, but still has an incredible athletic build.

I haven't spoken with him since last season ended, and it's obvious as he comes to give me a hug hello that he wants to say something about my divorce. I can see in his eyes that he's silently telling me he's sorry.

Although, he doesn't need to tell me he's sorry. One man can't possibly carry the burden of apologizing on behalf of the entire male species being crap. Present company excluded. Anderson's a great guy.

Ford's sigh carries across the space between us as we both take a seat just feet apart in these dark brown leather chairs. His denim-clad legs extend in front of him coupled with his black T-shirt that showcases the sleeve of tattoos. It looks like they've grown to start covering his hand now too.

"Long time no chat," I begin.

"It has been a long time."

I want to jump right into the conversation, there's always so much to discuss with these guys and no use in wasting time with any small talk. Nodding at Greg again, I let him give us the go ahead on cameras and we get started.

"Another season on the horizon. How are we feeling? The last time we spoke, you were coming off a really great year. Seems pretty routine for you, though. I feel like every time we turn around, there's someone talking about Ford Anderson."

"I'm excited every season. Even if we ended on the losing side of things. I'm always going to walk back into this building with my head high and just ready to go."

"The fans down here love you and that's probably a big reason why. I think it's so obvious to this city how much *you* love the game and the whole spirit of football. Let's run through that final game of the season last year. Where was your head at when you decided to make that impressive hurdle over the defender? We don't see that often from six-foot-four tight ends."

Ford drops his head back with a laugh and runs a hand through his hair.

"Oh man, Coach Aarons did not love me doing that. Neither did my wife. Might be a first and a last, but I just…I saw the safety coming toward me and had the split-second thought of maybe I can clear him, so I jumped. Thankfully, it worked out."

I chuckle as I nod. It was impressive, that's for sure. "You didn't have the ending you were expecting, but still closed the season at ten and seven last year. Not a bad record, but not the best you guys have seen. What's the thought process going into this year?"

"Win." His chuckle vibrates. "We want to win. I feel like I'm still playing good ball, a lot of the guys are. Plus, we've got a strong group of new players coming in and they're hungry too. Which is always good. All in all, I love playing and being out there with my teammates, and I'm going to have a good time regardless, but the goal is to win."

Ford is a leader, it's very easy to see why so many of the young guys look up to him.

I've been covering the Knights for years now in some capacity, whether that's been player interviews, in-game reporting or speaking at foundations and charities they are a part of. They're a good team, a fun one. They're incredibly close off the field, and I think that translates to their in-game chemistry.

"Speaking of teammates, you've played your entire career with the same core group of offensive players. Which in itself is unheard of and honestly, really impressive." He nods. "I know Graham Turner just announced his retirement. What's he going to do now that he's not blocking the line for you guys?" I smile, crossing my right leg over my knee.

Ford rubs his hands together in front of him. "Oh man, Turner's about to go back to the farm." He laughs as he lowers his voice a bit. "Graham's great. I've loved playing with him, and I know he really took this decision seriously. He's done a lot for us, so now he deserves some time to relax and hang out with the goats he always shows us pictures of."

My face twists in confusion, but I laugh at his statement. "Graham has goats?"

"Graham has goats," he echoes.

With wide eyes, I nod at him, somehow not shocked at all that the kindhearted Graham Turner would be returning to a small-town life after football.

"Speaking of goats, we have to talk about your quarterback.

He's got to be in that greatest-of-all-time conversation. Some of the plays he's able to make I think leaves all of us scratching our heads wondering how the heck that just happened."

I watch as Ford sits up straighter and leans forward a bit. His dark features soften as he begins to speak about his friend and teammate.

"Liam's the best. He kind of had this chip on his shoulder when he entered the league, right? High expectations and a shadow he really wanted to get out from underneath. I think a lot of people doubted him, and sometimes they still do. But he'll go down as one of the greatest quarterbacks of all time. When he was drafted and we started camp together, I remember he wasn't the quickest guy or the biggest. But he had a good arm. Everything this league likes to see physically from a quarterback, Liam didn't have at first. Now, he's exactly what every coach wants."

Ford smiles to himself and it causes me to picture a younger Liam, a kid who simply loved the game of football and had a dream of being in the NFL and kept running with it.

"He's so smart. He fools people, though, because everyone sees this flashy guy who goes out and has a good time, but anyone who knows him can tell you what kind of man he really is. He's so fucking—oh sorry, can I curse here?" He covers his mouth and the crew laughs.

"Technically, no, but go on." My lips curve up.

"I've just never known someone who knows the game the way he does. We all know how much he likes the spotlight, he has that cool guy swagger, the game day fits, all that extra stuff...I mean, you see how he carries himself. Liam won't shy away from a chance to joke around or a moment in front of the cameras. But ask any one of the guys in that locker room and they'll tell you how his switch flips for game time. He's smarter than I think people realize."

Ford doesn't mince words when he sings his praises for Liam. None of the guys I've ever talked to about him do. The respect, admiration, and just overall commitment they have for their quarterback shines through in the way they speak about him.

Although, if someone were to judge Liam based off what's in the press or how they see him through a small lens on social media or in the tabloids, they'd probably never believe a word any of them say about his work ethic and maturity on the field.

Liam screams playboy. He screams everything about the fast life that so many people think would be a distraction. But regardless of how he spends his time off the field, he doesn't let any of it affect how he performs on the field. I've watched him on film and in games for years.

On the gridiron, he's magic. But off it? There's no telling who he really is.

CHAPTER THREE

LIAM

"Hey, Birdie girl," I say through a yawn as I reach for my phone on the nightstand.

I feel her tiny paws kneading on the comforter by my thigh. "Making biscuits this morning, are we?"

She faintly meows as I sit up, lean against the headboard, and take a deep breath. There's rain gently hitting the window outside, and I can hear a low rumble of thunder as I sit there staring at an email from my agent. It's short, but I'm hung up on the words "after this season" because I didn't realize how quickly we were approaching the end of my contract.

Playing anywhere other than Tampa seems fucking crazy to me. I can't picture it. And I'm sure the fans would feel the same way. But I shake my head out of the looming thoughts, I can't let any of that cloud my mind and distract me from the season at hand.

Tonight is Ford's surprise party, and I've been tasked with helping Nate set up this afternoon. The girls have given me crumbs on party details. Something I'm told was intentional because of a surprise I ruined a few years ago. How the hell was I supposed to know that Summer would use her icy blue eyes to trick me into telling her about the celebratory dinner Abby was throwing her after landing a nursing job here?

Birdie follows me from the bedroom to the living room, making her presence known the entire way with small meows and little sprints between my strides. As I'm making coffee, I hear the same knocking sound I've been hearing for a week straight, and I almost lose it.

"There it is again, Birdie. What are we going to do about this guy?" I motion her to the window where there's a bird pounding its beak into the eaves of my building.

It feels like this fucking bird has been trying to become my new neighbor ever since the apartment next to mine became empty.

Taking a seat at my breakfast nook, I watch as Birdie paws at the sliding glass door. Her tiny body pounces and makes sounds at the bird beyond the glass as I sip my coffee and scroll through my phone. This has practically become routine at seven in the morning these days.

Coffee—black. Bird—annoying. Kitten—rambunctious.

A post from the Tampa Wildcats pops up, and I stop my scroll to look. It's a carousel of the top ten most iconic plays in recent history from the team. The Wildcats are Tampa's less than stellar basketball team. Sure, they've got talent, but their management has no fucking idea how to run a team, and it shows.

A highlight of Brandon Nells, the team's power forward—and Demi's ex-husband—drills a slam dunk over two opponents after a sweet rebound. He's talented. And someone six foot eight should be, considering he was the talk of the town when he first got drafted. It's a shame he's such a piece of shit human, otherwise I could've been a fan of his.

Shaking my head, I scroll past and put my phone down so I can get myself ready for the day.

"Keep at it," I say to Birdie as I head into my bedroom.

"Are we sure about the quiche?"

Abby, Mia, and Summer all turn their heads slowly in my direction as I close the oven in Ford and Abby's kitchen after peeking my head in.

"Yes. For the third time, I'm sure about the quiche," Abby clips.

"Do you even know what quiche is? Your continuous questions make me think you don't understand how popular of a dish it is." Summer's ring-clad fist taps me in the chest as she walks by.

"Of course I do." Shrugging, I take a piece of cheese from the platter on the counter. "I know food."

I break the piece of cheese in half, popping one in my mouth and handing the other half to Nate and Mia's son, Luke, as he rolls by on some toy car and into the living room where his brother and CeCe, Chase's daughter, are playing.

"Oh." My eyes light up when I notice the tray Abby pulls out of a giant white box. "Can I have one of these donuts or are they for later? What's inside?"

"As much as we are *loving* all your questions…" Abby walks to my side and rubs my arm. "I think Nate could probably use your help now with those folding tables outside."

I feel a subtle nudge as she tries to move me toward the door.

"It feels like I'm being kicked out of the kitchen."

"No—"

"You are," Summer cuts in, speaking over Abby.

"Fine."

Taking the not-so-subtle hint, I make my way outside, expecting to find Nate hard at work setting up tables, but I couldn't be more wrong.

As I close the door behind me, I let it slam a little, startling Nate awake as he's lying on the chair next to the pool.

"Sleeping on the job. Abby is going to kill you."

"I wasn't sleeping. I just needed to rest my eyes."

I shake my head and take a seat on the empty chair beside him.

"The girls are ruthless." I pout, nudging my chin toward the house.

Nate barks out a laugh before pulling himself up to a seated position.

"You normally like when women are mean to you."

"Well, not these women." I brush nothing off my shoulder.

"You love them and you know it. Quit your bitching." He shakes his head at me, and I smile to myself.

"Yeah, yeah." I nod and slap Nate's outstretched hand as we both stand to our feet.

"All right, let's set up these tables before they yell at us."

Nodding, I point to him. "If they do, I'm telling them you fell asleep on the job. Take some of the heat off me."

"Fine." Nate sighs.

Between the two of us, we set up several tables, chairs, and two large white tents in the backyard of Ford and Abby's house. The pool has a volleyball net set up in it along with an inflatable beer pong table and beach balls are floating all around.

"I'm fucking sweating. And I'm hungry. I'm going to run home to shower and change real quick, then I'll be back." I pull my T-shirt from my body and wipe the sweat from my face.

"Mia had me bring clothes to change into," Nate says, pulling his T-shirt off before he makes a splash in the pool. "And this will be my shower," he says after popping up.

"Yeah, wish I would've thought of that," I grit out as I turn toward the house.

It's loud and chaotic when I re-enter through the sliding glass door. Mia is sitting on the floor with one baby attached to her chest and two toddlers rolling around in front of her. CeCe has crayons and coloring sheets scattered all over the coffee table, and Abby and Summer are going back and forth about an episode of *Love Island* they saw last night.

"I'm going to head home to change. I'll be back," I say into the noise, barely expecting anyone to hear me.

But all three of them stop what they're doing and look at me.

"Okay, don't be late," Abby urges.

"And don't talk to Ford in the next hour and forty-seven minutes," Mia adds.

"I'm not going to ruin the surprise."

There's a thud from the door behind me as Nate walks in with wet hair, holding up a bleeding thumb.

"Abby, your pool thermometer is the fucking worst. I'll buy you a new one," Nate whines, and confusion covers Abby's face.

Mia stands and walks over to him with a loud sigh.

"Did you break their thermometer? There's a Band-Aid in the diaper bag. Go," she orders, pointing down the hall, and like an obedient puppy, Nate abides, kissing the top of her head.

Mia mouths, *sorry*, to Abby as he passes.

"He'd never survive without you." I raise my eyebrows at Mia as I'm about to walk toward the front door.

"Oh, please. None of you would," Summer chimes in, perched on one of the barstools with a glass of champagne in her hand. Her blue eyes staring me down.

"I'd be okay," I say, knowing it's probably not true. These women have become some of my favorite people in my life. They're badass, but soft and gentle. I admire the hell out of them. "Three less people being mean to me."

Mia chokes out a laugh. "Would a mean friend invite the woman you're obsessed with to this party?"

My head whips around to Mia as she stands there and smirks when she realizes she has my attention.

"Demi's coming?" I smile as my pulse begins to race.

"Yes," Abby confirms.

Unless it's been a work related event, I've rarely interacted with Demi outside of the football field or the facility. She attends charity events and dinners that are put on by the team or by the community, but she's always in work mode. And most of the time, she had her plus one with her. Something that she definitely won't have if she comes tonight. It could be my only shot to actually talk to her about something other than work, and it's a good chance to see how she's doing.

"Cool," I say, knowing the girls see right through my nonchalant demeanor.

No way in fucking hell I'd just be cool knowing I might get the chance to hang out with Demi tonight. Even just being in the same room as her outside of work is enough to excite me.

"You can rush home now and freak out. Get yourself all dolled up and handsome for her. We know you want to." Summer grins, sipping her champagne.

I take a few steps back around the kitchen, ruffling the hair on top of Summer's head with one hand and pulling Abby in for a hug with the other.

"God, you stink." Abby shoves at my ribs, pushing me away from her.

"Maybe I'll just freshen up a bit, yeah." I smirk, giving Mia a kiss on the top of her head as I pass by.

"Mm-hmm," Summer hums. "Wear something pretty," she teases as I'm already at the front door.

"I always look pretty," I shout, as it closes behind me.

CHAPTER FOUR

DEMI

A year ago I wouldn't have said yes to attending a birthday party for an athlete I work with. I love the Andersons, but I don't make a habit of socializing with the players outside of work related events. Not that it's something I'd get in trouble for; there's no rule against it. I guess it's just a personal preference I've had since I started in this industry. The fear of not being taken seriously in sports started early, and my ex was always quick to remind me that spending offseason time with the players gives the wrong impression. Although, now I want to attend everything and anything just to give him a giant *fuck you.*

Even still, I think there will always be the unspoken differences for women in sports. While my male colleagues can hang out with whoever they want, whenever they want—women will still field the stupid ass comments about choosing this job just so we can date the players.

I've had an athlete, and believe me, they really aren't all they're cracked up to be.

So, finally saying yes felt good. Even if I did reread my response seventeen times before sending it and then three more for good measure after it said delivered. Overanalyzing and over-thinking are just part of my charm.

I run my hands over the thighs of my jeans as I stare at myself in this bathroom mirror. It's so much smaller than the one in my old house. There's barely any room in here. A toilet, shower, and sink with a small piece of counter space, and I can basically reach everything without even moving my feet.

This isn't even my house—or apartment, I should say. I've been staying with one of the interns, and while I appreciate her hospitality, I desperately need to get my own place for the season before I reevaluate my long-term living situation. Her lease is almost up anyway, so I'm on the clock.

"Are you ready?" Alyssa's voice on the other side of the door stirs me out of my thoughts.

Alyssa is young and cool and very much new to the world of professional sports, but she's taking it in stride. She's eager to learn and doesn't seem to know how to say no to anyone. A nice trait to have—the former, that is. The latter could use some work, especially if she plans on making a career in the sports world. Being kind is good, but being a people pleaser won't help your career. In some ways I've been taking her under my wing when I can, explaining the ins and outs to her, how to talk with the coaches and owners and not let them run all over her with their mansplaining and egos.

"Yeah, I'll be right out," I call back.

I decided to invite her to come with me. She's a people person and she always invites me out with her friends, though I never go.

"Think they'll have a coffee bar along with the alcohol bar?" I ask, swinging the door open to find her on the other side, bobby pin between her teeth as she places another one in her hair.

"Mmm, my guess is no, but we can grab one on the way out."

Her fingers run along her slicked back hair that she has

perfectly placed in a low ponytail, and I do a full scan of her outfit from head to toe. A pair of jeans and a white flowy tank top with a red lip. She's a classic.

"Eh, it's fine. We can get going, I don't think it's far." I shrug as I walk by and give myself one last look in the mirror in the living room.

I can't tell if this outfit is working for me, but after trying on three other things and finally being too tired to change again, I just left this one on. It's a pair of light wash denim with a plain black cropped T-shirt and a pair of sneakers.

We both grab our bags, and I brush a dark wave of hair off my shoulder, tucking it behind my ear once, then twice, just before we head out.

Walking up to the Andersons, I'm quickly reminded that Ford is one of the highest paid tight ends in the league. Their home sits right on the water with what looks to be their own private beach access behind it. The large palm trees near the entrance make it feel like I'm about to walk into a tropical paradise.

Tapping lightly on the door, I can see Abby from beyond the glass, waving her hand at us.

"God, look how cute she is." Alyssa giggles as Abby opens the door.

Abby's smile is contagious as she greets us and welcomes us in. This foyer belongs in a *Better Homes and Gardens* magazine. The way she's thought of the smallest details for the decor has me adding everything to a mental Pinterest board.

"I'm so glad you could make it, thank you for coming. Hi, I'm Abby," she says, beaming at Alyssa. "Chase is on his way now with Ford so you're just in time."

Alyssa introduces herself, and Abby leads us to the living room where there are people scattered around the large space.

Many seated on the couches, some on the barstools along the kitchen island that backs right into the living room. And beyond the living room, I can see out the sliding glass doors and into their backyard. And it sure is dreamy. With a small golfing green, a large pool with a slide, and a full sunbathing deck. Not to mention a killer view of the water.

I catch glimpses of a handful of Knights players as I make my way to the back of the crowd, following idly behind Alyssa. I knew her socialite ways would take over the moment she was in a crowd. Nate Campbell and Graham Turner both smile my way as I look around while walking in.

Other athletes are also in attendance too. A few baseball players from the Angels, some players from Tampa's hockey team and even two actors are here. I'm not often starstruck, but I'm getting butterflies being in the same room as the guy who was a television heartthrob growing up. To my surprise—and relief—not a single basketball player is here.

I breathe a silent sigh of reassurance knowing I don't have to pretend not to notice anyone from my ex-husband's life.

My attention is still lingering on my teenage crush as I take one more step behind Alyssa, reimagining my bedroom growing up, knowing his poster was *definitely* on my wall. When I shift my focus, it lands on a pair of hazel eyes—a set of deep mossy forests that find me every single time we're in the same room.

Liam doesn't seem too interested in the birthday boy who just arrived, instead he grins at me with a cocky smirk, and I watch the word "surprise" leave his lips all too effortlessly. It's a word meant for Ford, but it's easy to see he's saying it to me.

"Hey, Dem." The greeting rolls off his lips as I get closer. He says my name like it's his favorite word. "Can I get you a drink?" I don't miss the gleam in his stare.

"I don't—"

"You don't drink alcohol, I know."

I feel the tension I was holding in my shoulders fall as I look at the sincere smile on his face. He's charming.

"They have plenty of drinks other than alcohol," he begins as if he's the waiter listing off a beverage menu. "Want a tea? There's lemonade too. Unless you want a virgin drink, the bartender will make anything."

Cheers erupt around us as Ford makes his way through to say hi to everyone who came to the party, getting louder every time he sees someone that he "can't believe is here."

Liam leans his back against the counter and places the palms of his hands on the marble as he waits for me to answer him or to say anything at all really. He's in a black T-shirt with dark jeans and black boots. His look is effortless and yet he still looks so good. So annoyingly—good.

He tilts his head with a stupid, cocky smirk as he raises his brow. Feels like he just caught me giving him a once over, although I was *not* checking him out, if that's what he's grinning about. Merely becoming aware of my surroundings.

"I'm…thinking," I nearly stutter, propping a hand on my hip.

Liam staring at me with his pretty hazel eyes and giving me that flirty little grin isn't new. Although, the fact that I haven't turned him down already for the simple drink offer is making alarms ring in my ears. Normally I'd be on the other side of those sliding glass doors by now.

"Take as much time as you need. I know this is a big decision." He runs his tongue over his bottom lip as he stares before smiling again, and I bite the inside of my cheek so hard I'm shocked I don't taste blood.

Brandon made a comment once years ago that he didn't like the way Liam looked at me. Funny, considering I can't recall a time Brandon looked at me with half the adoration that Liam does.

"Coffee," I finally huff out.

"Iced or hot?"

The shock on my face comes from the fact that he's not questioning me asking for a coffee at almost six in the evening and instead just wants to know how I want it, although I doubt they have café con leche, so I'll happily take an iced coffee.

"Iced."

"Stay here." He pushes himself from the counter and disappears beyond the door and onto the patio, leaving a rich woodland scent in his wake. He kind of smells like a forest during Christmas time. I can't explain it, but it's comforting.

I can see him talking with a bartender and then he ushers Abby to his side and asks something close to her ear.

I thought I'd feel a little more out of place here considering I don't socialize like this, but oddly enough, the five minutes I just had with Liam are the most comfortable I've felt in a while. Realistically speaking, he is one of the first people I actually met when I started with the Knights all those years ago, so maybe I subconsciously created a small soft spot for him.

"Now, Demi, what are you doing without a mic attached to you?" Graham Turner gently places his hand on my arm as he comes to my side. "Nice to see you," he says with a smile.

"Hi, good to see you. Congratulations on your retirement."

"Oh, thank you. Can I get you anything?" he asks with a contagious smile.

I shake my head, knowing Liam has already made his way outside. "No, thank you. Liam's grabbing me something."

Graham's brows raise slightly as he nods with a grin. "What a gentleman," he says, lowering his voice as he begins to move. "I better go see what the birthday boy is up to."

Graham tips his hat at me before he walks away, and I take in a deep breath, doing a quick scan of my surroundings.

This entire house is full of people. Something that definitely overwhelms me a bit, but it's nice when I see familiar faces in nearly every corner. And it's clear to see how well loved Ford is by the amount of people here to celebrate with him.

When I glance back to the patio, it's easy to find Liam right away. He's still standing next to the outdoor bar, but he has his arm around a small silver-haired elderly woman. I've seen her before at the Recreation Center downtown. I'm pretty sure she's one of the people who help run it.

I watch as he pulls her in, kissing her near her temple and keeping her close under his arm. She smiles at him and he grabs a drink for her before walking her to a chair at the patio table.

I'm glued to the interaction. He's so attentive with her, so genuine, and it's a very sweet and tender moment I seem to have barged in on.

Shaking my head, I turn my attention to the food on the counter in front of me as I blow out a sigh.

Lots of men help elderly women. This isn't something new and profound that Liam Evans is discovering. But it does make me smile.

CHAPTER FIVE

LIAM

"Here you go, Doll. One gin and tonic." I grab the glass from the bartender and place it in Dolly's free hand just before I help her take a seat on one of the comfortable patio chairs.

"Oh thank you." She brushes me off as I grab her a napkin and place it on the table in front of her.

"Anything for you."

She offers me a smile and cocks her head to the side.

"Go have fun," she says in a sweet, low tone.

Dolly is one of those women who has made taking care of other people her life's work. She doesn't have children, and since I've known her has put all her time, energy, and good spirits into helping kids downtown. She's one of the best people I've met since living here.

When I turn back to the bartender, I see he's placed the coffees I ordered on the bar top. I nod in his direction and place a tip in his jar before grabbing the drinks and walking back inside.

My eyes land on Demi immediately. Goddamn, she's pretty. How anyone fucked up big enough to lose her is beyond my understanding. Aside from being the most beautiful woman I know, she's got this grit about her. This relentlessness and strength I've always admired. She's sure of herself and what she's capable of. It's also always turned me on that she seems about 30 percent annoyed with everything I say.

I hang back a second, watching as she glances around before taking a seat on a barstool that just opened up at the kitchen island. There are finger foods in front of her, and she doesn't shy away from grabbing a bit of everything and placing it on a plate in front of her. She bites into the quiche, and I notice the smallest tilt of her head as she leans it back before grabbing two more, her shoulders doing a subtle wiggle as she chews.

So fucking cute.

I make my way toward her, placing the coffee down.

"Hang on one more second," I say.

Abby told me she has an assortment of milk, creamer, and sweeteners so I grab everything I can find and bring it over to the small free space left in front of Demi.

"I know it isn't the type of coffee you usually drink."

Her eyes narrow at me in question. And honestly, I'm surprised *she's* surprised I know she usually likes her coffee hot.

She doesn't say anything, just keeps her eyes on me.

"So…" I sigh. "Iced coffee. How do you like it?"

She finally smirks. "Are you going to play barista?"

"Play? I worked in a coffee shop for a bit in college. I'm a seasoned professional."

Her lips curl up and it's so close to a smile I can nearly taste it. I'd do anything to see her dimples right now.

Her eyes flit between the beverages in front of us. And everything in me is just hoping I can hang out with her for as long as she'll let me tonight.

"Why two?" she asks, gesturing to both drinks.

"Well, I got myself one."

"Aren't you drinking a beer? I swear you had one in front of you when I walked up to you earlier."

"You mean when our eyes locked across the room? I

remember the moment well. But I don't drink much during the season. One, maybe two, if I'm out. Tonight I had one, and now I'm switching to have coffee with you."

Her teeth pull on her bottom lip, and I get a glimpse of the whites of them as she parts her lips.

"Okay." She inhales and then reaches down to her plate, picking up another piece of quiche. "Almond milk." She takes a bite and moves the carton of milk closer to me. "And this," she says after finishing her bite and points to the white mocha syrup on the counter.

"Iced coffee, splash of almond milk with white mocha syrup. Easy." I stare at the thick wave of hair over her shoulder as I'm grabbing what I need.

She settles into the chair and sits up a little straighter, both elbows resting on the white marble. "So, do you just order drinks for any woman you talk to?"

I crack a smile at that comment, and I can't seem to wipe it away as I look at her. Her brown, nearly black eyes narrow in my direction as she stares at me confidently, very aware of how much I'm enjoying this moment.

"Jealous, Dem?"

Her head shakes slowly as she dips her chin and replies. "Oh, please."

She turns to hide her face, but there it is. Without effort. Without prompting.

She smiles.

And it's something else. *She's* something else. Just being around her makes me want to freeze time so I can stay in these moments with her for as long as possible.

Her head moves back and forth as she pulls her lips in.

"I love when you do that." My voice is raspy as I speak.

"Do what?"

My head dips down as I smile to myself, opening the drawer

where the spoons are, and I grab two, placing one in her coffee and another in mine.

"Smile like that," I say, looking directly at her. "Your face… it just—it lights up. I don't know, Dem. It's literally one of my favorite things." The admission falls so simply from my lips, but it's just skimming the surface of everything I want to say to her. I can't properly explain right now how crazy I am about everything when it comes to her.

The two of us hold eye contact for what feels like an eternity, neither bothering to take a sip of the drinks or make any movements. Looking at her, I can see there are a million things running through her mind. Her eyes are full of walls, boundaries, and things she wants to keep to herself.

I've never asked about her divorce from Brandon. I never felt it was my business. When some things came out last year, I had many thoughts running through my mind about what I'd do if I ever saw him out. The questions I'd want to ask him. The pain I'd like to inflict on him. But unless Demi ever opens the door and wants to discuss it, it's off the table as far as I'm concerned.

In the space between us, Summer reaches for the milk carton. "I love your makeup, Demi."

Demi quickly clears her throat as she pivots her attention to Summer. "Oh, thank you. I'm not very good at it. Thank god for online tutorials." She tips her coffee toward Summer, but her eyes flick back to me.

"Anyone who can draw on a cat eye deserves a standing ovation." Summer pours the milk into three small cups before adding chocolate syrup.

What the fuck is a cat eye? My brows crease as I stare at Demi's face. I have no clue what they're talking about.

From the corner of my eye, I see Demi tilt her head down with a faint smile. She gives me a subtle nod as she stands.

"I'm going to do a lap, see if I know anyone else here. Thanks for the coffee." Her dark eyes hold mine for an instant before she walks around the island toward the sliding glass door, and my head falls back.

"She looks really pretty," Summer says, stating the absolute fucking obvious.

My head turns slowly to her as she stirs the cups of chocolate milk for the kids.

"Tell me something I don't know, Kincaid." I pull my hand through my hair as a low groan leaves my chest.

Summer shakes her head as she laughs to herself. "Hey, Siri, play 'Sucker' by the Jonas Brothers."

"You think you're making fun of me, but joke's on you. I love the Jonas Brothers, and I *am* a sucker for her." My arms cross over my chest as I smirk.

"You ask her out yet?"

"Well, someone interrupted our conversation." I glare down at her before softening my stare. "But don't worry, I will," I add, staring at Demi through the glass.

Summer pats my forearm. "Don't dilly-dally. Looking like that, she's definitely going to have some suitors."

"Some *suitors*? What fucking year is it?"

She laughs before grabbing all three cups, carefully holding them in her hands. I motion to take one from her to help, but she shakes her head.

"Also, what the fuck is a cat eye?"

"Oh, Liam." She sighs with a smile. "Why don't you go ask her?" Summer wiggles her eyebrows at me as she turns to walk out of the kitchen.

There are muffled conversations happening around me as I back away from the kitchen with my coffee in hand. I usually drink my coffee black, but decided to add whatever Demi liked in hers to mine too. I don't even know why the fuck I drink it black to begin with. Probably some bullshit my dad drilled into me about not needing the extra stuff.

The dark leather loveseat in the living room is filled with

kids. Chase's daughter is sitting on one cushion while Nate and Mia's twin boys are sprawled out on the other. All three arguing over what to watch.

"Scoot over. Make some room for Uncle Liam."

As soon as I sit down, all three of them pile on top of me.

"Wrestle?" Luke puts both fists in the air.

"We don't wrestle with fists. What's your daddy teaching you?" I joke, pulling his arm lightly and knocking it to the side. "I'm sure you've got a mean right hook, big man, but save it for your dad."

He laughs and jumps on me as CeCe rests her head on my shoulder and changes the television to something she wants to watch.

"Smart girl," I whisper to her as the boys continue rough housing.

Just beyond the sliding glass door, I catch a glimpse of Demi at the patio table. Not shocking at all—I feel like I could spot that woman in a three-hundred-person flash mob. But it looks like she's playing a game when I notice a few glasses in the middle of the table with more than a handful of guests around it.

I pull myself from the couch, the kids seemingly unbothered by my departure, and make my way outside as I take a sip of the iced coffee in my hand.

"This is a case of beginner's luck. I'm not usually this good at party games." Demi aims before bouncing the quarter off the table, but it just misses the glass in the center.

"Quarters?" I ask as I stride up on her left.

"What are you drinking?" Chase cocks his head back as he pulls my arm down to get a better look at the cup. "Is that coffee?" he questions.

"Sure as hell beats the hangover you're all going to have."

"I've decided I'm okay with it," Ford blurts out, focusing his attention on the glass before making the quarter plop right in the center, sending beer sloshing to the sides.

I take the empty seat next to Demi and watch a couple more rounds go by. Truthfully, I have zero interest in playing this game, but every interest in sitting this close to her.

"Not a quarters fan?" she asks, when nearly everyone else leaves the table.

"Oh, I'm a fan. I'm *very* good at quarters, but it's Ford's birthday so I needed to let him win."

I see her eyes roll with my response and she blows out a deep breath from puckered lips. To my surprise, she doesn't leave her seat and instead seems to settle in more comfortably.

"So…" Before I can say anything else, Demi pulls the glass closer to us and tucks a stray dark brown wave behind her ear. Once, then twice.

"Play me." Her chin is set in a stubborn, yet confident line. "Let's see this '*very good at quarters*' in action."

I scoff at her request and rub my hands together. "I always knew you liked seeing me win, just never thought it was at your own expense."

"Tone it down, Twelve." Her words are flat, but there's a glimmer of something in her eyes. A challenge, maybe?

"Care to make it interesting, Dem?"

She narrows her stare as she studies my face, and a smirk lifts on my lips. "Let's make a bet."

CHAPTER SIX

DEMI

This is probably a bad idea, but I've been having fun tonight. Something I can't exactly say for the last few months.

Liam's flirty smirk makes me hesitate, but I nod anyway.

"I win and I take you out for coffee," he suggests.

"We just had coffee," I say, shaking my nearly empty cup at him.

"You know what I mean." He leans in closer to me.

"Liam, I'm not going out for coffee with you."

"It's the most innocent type of outing, Dem. Three shots—if I make all three, we get coffee."

"Awfully confident, thinking you'll make all three shots."

He gives me a cheeky grin and places both hands on the surface of the table as he stands to reach for the cup. This party is filled with people, but somehow Liam makes me feel like I'm the only person here with the way his attention is so laser focused on me and our conversation.

"I'm determined to spend as much time with you as you'll let me. All my focus will go into making these three shots."

"I think we spend enough time together." I shrug, twisting my earring with two fingers.

"Hardly," he mutters under his breath, but I catch it.

His eyes are leaning toward a bluish hazel tonight and I don't miss every time he runs them across me. But it doesn't feel invasive when he does. I don't feel the need to shift myself in my seat when they linger on my lips. It's like, in my bones, I know he's a safe person.

Aside from his player stats, the only things I truly know about Liam are the bits and pieces I see on social media or things I hear from other people. He dates around. He likes attention. Commitment isn't a word he's interested in. I respect Liam, I always have. But there's a reason I've always brushed off his endless flirting—aside from being married.

Liam Evans is a thrill-seeker. I see it every week. The extravagant plays. The *"how the hell did he pull that off"* wins. He likes chasing those highs, and it's easy to see his little crush on me is nothing more than just that. Something to chase.

"And if you miss even one, there's no more talk of coffee dates or any other kind of date, right?"

"No more talk ever? Or just tonight? Be specific."

I roll my eyes. "You know what I mean."

"You roll your eyes at me a lot, and I've been meaning to tell you I like it."

I pull my mouth into a firm line, biting the inside of my bottom lip as I do. "This party is packed with other women you could be flirting with."

Sparring with Liam is fun, I'll give him that. Although I don't think I should enjoy it as much as I do, but Liam's a good distraction from everything my mind has been wandering to lately.

"Is it?" He doesn't bother looking around when he shrugs his shoulders. "I guess I'm only interested in flirting with you."

With barely any aim, I watch as he tosses the quarter against the table at the perfect angle. Causing the coin to land right in the beverage and it quickly floats to the bottom.

"One down." His stare becomes playful as his teeth bite his bottom lip.

"Fine. Harmless coffee," I concede. "*If* you get all three in."

"*When* I make them, where should we go? And when? There's a new cafe where the old diner used to be right over here by Harris Island. Sundays are hard for both of us, as you know, but I'll make anything work for you."

"Liam," I say his name with a sigh and a chuckle.

He's insufferable sometimes, but it's also entertaining, I suppose.

Leaning myself back in the seat with my arms over my chest, I cross my right leg over my left knee and watch as he sinks quarter number two in the glass.

I'm waiting for him to make a comment, but my attention snaps to the sound of his chair scooting back against the patio flooring. When I look back toward him, his index and middle fingers are waving back and forth in that *come here* motion as he gestures to my shoes.

"Lift your foot."

"Huh?" I ask as I glance down again.

When I see the untied shoelace, Liam's hand is already outstretched. His hand palms the back of my ankle in a possessive gesture and he rests my foot on his knee.

"Oh, you don't have—" I begin, but he cuts me off.

"I like these. They look good." His smile widens as he loops the bunny ears and finishes tying the laces.

"They seem like your style." He taps the side of my shoe twice with his left hand, but doesn't let my leg go as he keeps his hand firmly on my ankle. I can feel his warmth on the exposed skin of leg, and I glance up at him at the same time he closes one eye and holds the quarter up with his right hand, carefully focusing on the glass.

Liam turns his focus from the glass and looks directly at me as he bounces the quarter on the table and a boastful smile spreads across his face when he hears the sound of it dropping into the glass.

Never bet against an NFL quarterback in an aiming contest, Demi. You know this.

Pulling my ankle off his knee, I swiftly stand.

"Well, look at that," I state in a more chipper tone than normal. "Three for three."

Pulling the waist of my jeans up, I fluff the bottom of my top as he stands to face me.

"Hey, Dem." His finger gently grazes the back of my hand. He doesn't hold it there, but I feel the heat from his touch even after they're gone. "I'd actually love to get coffee with you. I know this was a fun little wager, but I'd really love to, if you're up for it."

"We made a deal. I'll honor it. But it's *not* a date. It's just coffee."

His lips form a firm line as he nods and dips his chin.

"Well, I'm ready for our 'not a date' whenever you are."

The people around us became nothing but muffled noise during that little game and it isn't until Alyssa approaches me that I fully hear the noise from the party again. Like I was in some kind of bubble with Liam just now.

"You have to see this cake that Abby just brought out." She pulls at my arm. "Oh, hey, Liam. Sorry, can I borrow her for a minute?"

Liam grins at me and then moves his attention to Alyssa. "She's all yours."

I walk closely next to her as everyone from the party is making their way into the dining room where Abby just lit the candles on this extravagant cake. It's in the shape of Captain America and looks like it's an actual statue of Steve Rogers himself.

"I take it he's a superhero fan," Alyssa whispers to me as we stand with everyone.

I hear her, but don't answer because all I can think about is if agreeing to go out for coffee with Liam was a huge mistake.

CHAPTER SEVEN

DEMI

My stomach grumbles as I pull into the parking lot this morning. I rushed out the door and didn't have time to eat before I left, and my insides are reminding me. I barely had time to tie my curls back in a messy bun before hurrying to button up my oversized flannel. Thankfully, I can at least get dressed here today since I have a stylist for media and interview days. It's still the craziest thing to say out loud. I have a stylist. Who the hell am I? Either way, she's a saving grace on days like today where choosing an outfit is the last thing I want to do.

Rushing around in the mornings isn't a normal occurrence for me. I tend to wake up when the alarm blares—exhausted or not—and move about my day, but I didn't sleep well last night, or the night before actually. I've always been envious of people who can shut their brain off and fall asleep the second their head hits the pillow. It's something I've frequently brought up in therapy, actually. My anxious mind works overtime as soon as the silence sets in.

Sometimes it's me envisioning scenarios that haven't happened, working myself up over what ifs. And other times, more often lately, it's reliving a tragedy. Reliving things that broke me down and brought me to my knees.

The clock ticked on for three hours after I laid down last night before I was able to fall asleep, and then when I did, my subconscious thought I needed to be reminded of the worst day of my life. Replaying it for me to see again in the form of a nightmare. I felt myself clawing to wake up. I was screaming at myself, but I couldn't open my eyes, I couldn't break free from it. By the time I finally did, I was sobbing into my pillow.

As I make my way down the hall and toward the hair and makeup room, I hear voices up ahead, somewhere around the corner. I recognize one right away.

My first interview this morning is with none other than Mr. Liam "not a date" Evans.

When I round the corner, I see him standing in the threshold of one of the offices. His head tilts back with a laugh, and I continue on my way, picking up my pace.

He sees me dart by, and I hear him excuse himself from his conversation as he scurries to catch up with me.

"Hey, Dem. In a rush for our coffee date? We haven't even picked a day yet, but now works for me."

I stop at the sound of his voice.

"Not a date." I stare at him unamused. "I'm running late and —" Mid-sentence my stomach makes the most obnoxious sound, and I know he hears it as his eyes widen, trailing my face and head toward my stomach. A playful smile spreads across his lips.

"Hungry?"

"No time. I don't like eating while Cheryl does my makeup. I think it's rude and it makes her job harder." I offer him a smile in return, noticing his hazel eyes fixed on me.

Staring. Judging. Probably looking at the dark circles under my eyes and thinking I look like shit.

But his head tilts softly and he stares at me for a quick

moment. His rich dark hair is trimmed and styled perfectly, the hard-set shape of his jaw loosens. His entire face softens.

"Are you okay?"

His question catches me off guard as his voice lowers and loses its sarcastic tone, becoming mellow and sincere. The answer "no" flashes in my mind, but I blink my eyes and swallow the word.

"I'm fine, just in a rush this morning."

His lips press together into a line and he doesn't blink as he nods, moving to the side and extending his arm out for me to pass him.

Clutching my notebook under my arm, I pivot past him, but not without one more glance back as I hear his voice again. He could tell something was bothering me. And he didn't press it. I appreciate that.

"Breakfast is the most important meal of the day, you should eat," I hear him say as I'm already a dozen paces down the hall.

But I don't answer.

I still can't believe I agreed to get coffee with him. There's a version of me that wouldn't have agreed to that if my hair was on fire, but something about the way our conversation flowed that night. The ease of it. The care he took with his attention. His words. I've always known about his little crush, but something about his presence at the party helped me feel so safe and calm—two feelings that have been hard to come by lately.

Alyssa apologized for interrupting us, but I brushed it off. It's not like we were discussing anything monumental, although I can admit I did enjoy our conversation.

I haven't had a deep conversation with someone in months. My mom has asked me a few times recently if I plan to start dating again anytime soon. My answer has been no every single time. But I will admit I miss having someone to talk to all the time. A constant ear at the end of the day. I guess I lost that long before I actually got divorced, though.

Despite the ever-present uninterested look on my face, I really do enjoy talking to people. I crave it, I think. But that isn't the vibe I give off and I realize that.

I've had a fair share of people—particularly, men—tell me I look intimidating.

I guess looking unapproachable is nice when I don't want to be bothered. But apparently I look unapproachable to everyone except Liam.

Once hair and makeup are done, I quickly get dressed. Pulling the black pants over my thighs and buttoning the white blouse. A black and white combination is my favorite and I'm thankful my stylist knows me so well.

"This hair is every girl's dream." Cheryl approaches on my left as she examines my curls one final time.

"That's definitely not what I thought at fifteen. I ran a hair straightener over this for so long." I pull at a curl between my fingers. "I'm surprised they're still around."

She takes the makeup poof and gently pats it against my chin, careful not to let anything drop on the white blouse I'm wearing.

As I'm standing in front of Cheryl as she takes one more look over my face, the door of the conference room opens, and a deep, charismatic voice instantly greets everyone.

Glancing over, I smile professionally, but Liam makes a beeline directly for me and extends a small brown bag. His forearm flexes as he holds it up, and I tilt my head in confusion.

"What's this?" I take the bag from his outstretched hand, and he shoots me a quick, direct reply before he shifts his attention to my producer.

"Eat."

My fingers grip the bag as I stare blankly at the back of Liam now that he's turned away. He brought me food?

I peek in the bag, smiling down at the empanada and cup of fruit along with a smiley face on the sticky note. It's very sweet.

But I pull my lips in, tuck my shoulders back and regain my composure—except not before I pop one of the giant green grapes in my mouth.

He catches my eye from the corner of his, and I mouth a silent *thank you* as he nods. I probably seemed awkward two minutes ago when he first walked in, but to be fair, who expects the quarterback to show up to an interview with a brown bag of food for the reporter about to conduct their interview?

"Are we ready?" I ask, confidently placing myself between all the men in the room.

"I'm ready." Liam's deep voice runs through me.

A grin spreads across his face the moment I turn toward him, and it's incredibly obvious that he knew my question wasn't directed at him based on the twinkle in his eye. I'm tempted to roll my eyes at him, but remember I'm standing in front of seven other men as well.

"Well, we're here to talk about you." I turn to him and whisper, "And I know that's your favorite subject."

Greg gives me a nod, and both Liam and I take our respective seats in the room.

Interviews with Liam are always really well received by fans. There's a lot of interest in a thirty-something quarterback with stats like his. He's exciting to watch and fans love his story.

Liam hums to himself as he sits. His long legs spread slightly and his hands come together in his lap. The dark blue pants and white polo he chose today are complementing him and his sun-kissed skin well. There's a mossy green to his eyes today, and I'm starting to think I'm getting a different version of them every time I look lately.

"Would you like to hear about other subjects I'm interested in?" He leans toward me with a whisper.

I fan myself quickly with the papers in my hand. "No, thank—"

But he rattles some things off.

"Puzzles. Anatomy. The Roman Empire. Anything Demi related, really…"

I huff, sitting back in my chair as I shake my head at him spewing off a list.

"Anatomy. Really?" It's hard to hide my facial expressions on a normal day, but I skip right over the last thing he said.

"Well…" I watch as his eyes scan my face. But *just* my face. He doesn't move to my chest or roam my body at all like most— all other men would have. "I like *Grey's Anatomy*," he says.

A laugh rises from my chest at that. It's such an unexpected response, such a quick, truly genuine reply that makes me laugh like I haven't in months. Maybe aside from the weekend, when he was also using his witty charms in a very obvious effort to get me to laugh.

His eyes soften as he smiles at me with a lazy grin. I see why the girls love him. Honestly, he's very charming and has the good looks to put him at the top of anyone's most attractive athlete list. But if it's not football, I really don't think he takes anything seriously.

"*Grey's Anatomy*, huh?" I cross my arms. I too have been known to binge some Grey's in my spare time.

He nods. "When O'Malley died, I lost it." I watch his hand pull at his jaw.

Noticing the sports watch on his wrist. The veins on his forearm. The gold ring on his pinky finger.

My teeth sink into the inside of my bottom lip as I look at him.

The clapper board slaps in between us. "Camera three, ready."

My attention snaps to Greg, and I nod.

Talking with Liam in any interview I've done with him, it's so clear he's going to be one of those athletes who will be talked about years after he's left the game. Other quarterbacks will be compared to him, he'll end up as a first ballot hall of famer when the time comes, and kids will be watching his highlights and studying his plays for years.

It's true what Ford mentioned about his switch flipping. Liam came in here high on sarcasm and wit, but the moment we begin talking football he speaks so carefully. So thoughtfully and with so much intelligence and passion. He's still himself, but you can tell he wants to be taken seriously in the world of football.

"Liam, let's jump back to last season for a second. You guys had some injuries that hit a few of your starters late in the season. Chase Hunt goes down right before the playoffs. I know that was really tough."

Liam's head shakes back and forth in a slow, steady motion as he exhales. "Yeah, that was hard, but things are going to happen that we just can't really prepare for. So we adjust, and some guys need to step up when starters go down."

"It seems like few things really affect you on the field. The way you handled that loss, the uncertainty of your offensive line when Graham took a nasty hit. But you seem to work really well under pressure." I smile at him, really meaning that as a compliment. "I think I can count on one hand the times I've done an interview where the starting quarterback was the guy with the most rush yards in a playoff game. You just adapt, and it's crazy, but you get things done."

"Well, if I can't get it done in the air, I need to find other ways. I've got guys who depend on me. So I'll do anything to get things done, and it feels good to accomplish it for the team."

"Ultimate teammate." I lightly laugh as I move a piece of hair from my shoulder and I don't miss how Liam follows my movement. "Training camp is underway. Lots of new faces, but still a lot of the same guys. How's it been?"

"I love this time of the year. Everyone's so hungry and ready to go. New guys, veterans, coaches, there's really just something special and probably underrated about this time of the season. I've always thought that, and I've always really soaked up this time at camp, doesn't matter if it's year one or year ten. I need this time just as much as the next guy."

With my shoulders back, I take a quick glance at the paper in front of me.

"Chasing greatness? I'd have to imagine some of your dad's records are on your mind. You have the weapons this year on offense to really take a shot at that single season passing yards' record."

Liam is very tight-lipped whenever his father is mentioned in interviews. I've never known why. Typically, I figured it's due to the constant comparison or possible shadow he's always been in.

His throat clears. "He's a legend."

I stay silent for a moment, allowing space for him to elaborate, but there isn't anything more he adds before he makes eye contact with me and smiles. It's not his usual giant lights-up-a-room kind of smile. It's close-lipped, not exactly forced, but hardly effortless.

It's the first time I've seen this reaction from him, and I've interviewed Liam plenty of times. Sure, this is maybe the second time it's been a formal sit-down interview—they're usually sideline recaps after a big win or tough loss—but something in his reaction almost pains me. I'm finding myself wanting to know more. But I shake my head to clear the thought and move on.

There's a few more minutes of discussion on the rookies before we end the interview and his shoulders relax. He glances at the brown bag on the barstool a few feet away and motions toward it.

"Don't forget to eat," he says for only me to hear as both of us stand.

All the energy in this room moves with Liam. When he walks toward the window, every eye follows him, every camera points in his direction and every person's next breath is practically hanging onto his next word.

But he stands and stares over the city beyond the glass and

pulls out his phone, snapping a picture of whatever he sees below from the floor we're on. It's a really small moment that in some ways reminds me he's just a normal guy, taking pictures of things he finds beautiful.

I grab the brown bag to put it near my purse, but see my phone light up when I do.

It's Alyssa letting me know that the landlord is giving her another two weeks in her apartment. Originally, me staying with her was supposed to be short-term—a couple weeks, maybe a month. But that somehow turned into multiple months.

She offered to let me just take over her lease since she is moving in with some of the other interns, but I want my own place. Somewhere fresh and one that's just mine. Unfortunately for me, I've unintentionally been putting off the apartment search, and now that the season is about to start my free time will be even harder to come by.

Time to go apartment hunting. *Today.*

CHAPTER EIGHT

LIAM

"Hey, Dem." I stroll past her on the sideline as practice is getting started this morning.

We've been busy now that camp is officially underway. Meetings in the mornings, then practice, followed by film and playbook study. Although that last bit is mainly just me.

"Twelve," she says sweetly, tipping her chin in my direction.

I fucking love when she calls me by my number. It does something to me. Sends a burst of electricity down to my damn bones.

Without thinking, I turn on my heel and walk back to her. I can tell that my sudden appearance in front of her is startling by the way she widens her eyes.

"You're very close to me." She crosses her arms over her chest as her eyebrows raise.

"I really want to say something in response to that, but I'm going to remain a gentleman." I offer her a charming smile. "How are you today?"

"Well, apartments are astronomically priced and the book I was reading ended on a cliffhanger. But I love my job and my coffee tasted so good this morning, so who am I to complain?" She exhales, smiling.

"If you need a place to stay—"

"No," she cuts me off before I can finish, and I can't help but laugh. "Don't finish that sentence."

I nod and raise my hands in front of my chest, taking a step back with a chuckle before glancing up at the sky, noticing bright blue for miles without a cloud in sight.

Fuck, it's going to be a brutal one today.

"Well, it's a beautiful day for football."

"It is."

"So, I'm thinking our 'not a date' date should be soon. We're both going to be getting busier in a couple weeks, so why don't we just pencil something in right now?"

She flips through the handful of papers between her fingers and thinks I don't see her fighting back a smile, but I do. I wish she would quit pretending to be so annoyed with me, it's becoming obvious she isn't as annoyed as she wants to seem.

"Your new receivers are all waiting on you." She dramatically wiggles her pointer finger toward the field.

I see the guys on the sidelines, but Coach isn't out here yet. I've got a few minutes.

"I'm in the middle of a very important conversation, and I give my full, undivided attention to people I'm speaking with. They can wait."

"Liam," she says my name with a shake of her head. "You probably say that to all the girls."

I step closer, just a hair. "Don't you know by now that I only see you."

Her throat bobs, and I sense a tiny bit of hesitancy in her body, but she remains still and doesn't step back.

Her eyes narrow. They look slightly lighter when the sun hits them. "Okay." She sighs. "You'll probably be done with camp around three tomorrow afternoon, right? Why don't we grab coffee then? Sips Coffee House."

My eyes light up and my body wants to jump up and down, pumping my fist in the air. Every cell feels like it's raging with electricity at this simple sentence.

"I see you know my schedule," I reply, trying to play it cool.

"Part of my job description."

"Fair." I chuckle, grinning like a teen with a crush. "Tomorrow is perfect. Have a nice day, Dem."

She playfully brushes the papers in her hand against my arm as I'm backing away. "You too."

"You've got to run that route better!" I shout to Ford after he comes up empty for the second time in a row.

"I'm running it like I always do."

Placing both hands on my hips, I tilt my face up to the blazing sun. I hear him sigh as he comes up next to me after the play.

"I've run this route a dozen times that exact way. Your throw is off."

I gape in his direction. "*My* throw is off?"

"You're hitting me after I've already crossed mid-field, man. I'm having to reach back every time. Get it out sooner. Hit me in the chest with it." He slaps my shoulder and jogs away from me.

Get it out sooner.

I'd like to hit him in the chest with something, all right.

My hands clap together with the ball in between them, feeling the rough exterior of the leather on my palms.

Make sure your timing is right. Every time.

Words my dad would tell me in high school ring in my ears.

I sling the ball again, this time like a bullet the second I drop back and watch as it drills Ford between the numbers on his jersey. His laugh is loud and he shouts excitedly as he slows his pace.

"That's it, baby." He points to me with a wide grin.

"I think he liked that one," Nate says, shaking his head with a smile. And I do the same.

Nate and I walk over to the sidelines where there's already an assistant standing with an ice-cold soaked sponge ready to wring it out over my neck. I lean forward, ready to welcome the cold water in this heat. It's hot as hell out today. I'm thankful for all the resources our team has available for us, though, when it comes to our safety in this heat.

There's a cooling trailer on the practice field to help drop our temperature after being out in the heat and humidity all day for practice. The trailers are set around eighteen degrees—frigid, but something to look forward to after a long day. Ice benches are used during practice and in game days when needed too. Plus, good old fashioned ice caps we can just place on our neck or wrap around our head to help bring our temperature down.

The cameras are all around the field, and Demi is on the far end doing an interview with Chase. I try not to stare, but I think that ship has sailed. My eyes always find her.

She's in simple black jeans with a white T-shirt as she stands on the sidelines holding a mic, forcing Chase to do the one thing he hates. Talk.

I watch her mannerisms. Her facial expressions and her body language. She's full of strength and grace today. And it's fucking beautiful to see. Although I can't help but wonder why she's looking for an apartment now when I thought she had moved in with that intern from Ford's party. At least that's what Abby told me.

"Hundred bucks says he comes over here and bitches about being interviewed." Nate tilts his chin as he sees Chase nonchalantly walking our way.

I bark out a laugh, knowing there's no way I'm taking that bet.

"At least she's quick." Chase runs a hand through his hair as he groans.

"Pay up." Nate looks at me, extending a hand.

"I knew better than to take that bet."

Chase looks between the two of us. "What bet?"

"That you'd come over here and immediately complain about being interviewed."

"That was hardly a complaint. More like a compliment toward Demi," he replies to Nate. "How about you pay me?"

Ford jogs over to us, wiping his hands on a towel hanging out of his shorts.

"Any chance Coach won't notice if I just go sit in the cooling trailer early? I'm fucking dying out here."

"I definitely wouldn't point it out to him that you were missing," Nate teases, smiling at Ford.

"Yeah right." Ford chuckles.

Coach waves us over for a quick huddle post practice as the final drills are wrapping up.

"Gentlemen, we know how important these moments are. Nice day today. We've got to challenge one another, keep each other accountable and focused. Make sure we keep these connections we're building strong." Coach Aarons looks around at the men standing before him. Not everyone on this practice field will make the fifty-three-man roster. It's a tough reality, but part of the business. "Compete your asses off. Not just amongst one another, but compete with yourself. Make yourself better for your teammates. There's an old saying, 'If you want to go fast, go alone. If you want to go far, go together.' We go far on this team. We work together on this team. There's not just one guy on this field who is going to do it all for us. Every one of you needs to be prepared and in shape. Meet with the trainers, they're here to help. Get some rest and we'll be back at it tomorrow."

There's a collective "yes, sir" among the guys as Coach Aarons nods in my direction and begins to move away from the huddle.

"All right, boys, bring it in," I say, raising an arm. "One goal every year, fellas. Bring home the championship. For each other and for the city. Everything we're doing from now until the end of the season becomes intentional. We need that mindset on this field so it translates to those sixty minutes every game. Like Coach said, let's keep competing our fucking asses off. Let's stay committed to one another, to the team. Yeah? Family on three—one, two, three, *family*!"

The huddle breaks apart, and I run a hand through my sweat-soaked hair. The guys start filtering out and walking toward the facility, getting ready to head home for the day.

Except today, I don't go right home. Because today is a therapy day.

A few years ago, I finally admitted to myself what I think I had been suspecting for a while. I needed an outlet. A place to get some of the things I harbor off my chest. My childhood was anything but a childhood, and as an adult I now see how that affected who I became.

It took the team therapist, Dana, two sessions to tell me the symptoms I was experiencing were depression. And four sessions for me to break down in her office. Something I never, *ever* thought I'd fucking do. I didn't realize how lost I was until she created the space for me to talk about everything. Now, these biweekly appointments are like a damn cleanse for my soul.

I've never publicly shared that I go to therapy, but my closest friends and my brother know. Truthfully, I probably never would have even started if Mia didn't have me researching a bunch of shit for Nate a few years ago before he started his foundation for mental health. It's been cool as hell seeing that small idea of his turn into such a big movement for athletes all over the country.

Summer was the first person I told that I wanted to go talk to someone, and she's been who I've shared the most with since. I'm not entirely sure how, but fiery Summer Kincaid somehow ended up as my ear for a lot of hard days, and I cherish that woman so much for it.

Therapy days always lead to my best night's rest too. Something about getting all the bullshit off my chest is freeing.

And I'll definitely need a good night's rest; I've got a big day tomorrow.

CHAPTER NINE

DEMI

I'm no closer to finding an apartment. Are they incredibly expensive on purpose? Alyssa offered again for me to stay, but I need my own space.

Something I vowed to myself after my divorce was the promise of being selfish. In the right way, of course—doing what I felt was best for me, speaking my truth and removing myself from people or places that no longer felt right. And that's exactly what I'm choosing to do here. I'm so appreciative of Alyssa helping me a few months ago, but I need to find my own place anyway, and this kind of pushes me to do it sooner.

But at this moment, all of my energy is going into this coffee with Liam. I've been thinking about it since I woke up this morning.

And not in the obsessive kind of way people might assume if I said this out loud. More so, why did I agree to go get coffee with him? I have nothing against Liam. But hanging out with him one-on-one could very easily give him, and anyone who happens to see, the wrong impression. The last thing I ever want is someone to assume I didn't earn my spot in my career. But I overthink normal everyday interactions, so I shouldn't be surprised I'm nearly spiraling over coffee with the quarterback.

But it's just that. It's coffee. And we're just friends.

So that's why I'm sitting at Sips Coffee House, at a table in the corner with a baseball hat tipped down over my face.

"Excuse me." A shaky teenage voice grabs my attention, and I glance up to see a barista holding a cup of coffee in front of me. He looks genuinely nervous as he places it down on the table. "This is, uh, from Liam Evans." He looks behind him and then back to me as he swallows and steps back.

I tilt my head and see Liam near the counter. Leaning against it with a sly grin spread across his face. His tanned biceps on display as they cross his chest and the light gray shirt hugging every ridge of his shoulders. The perfectly messy, but not so messy, look to his hair paired with black denim jeans. He may as well be holding a sign that says LOOK AT ME, I'M VERY ATTRACTIVE. He isn't trying to hide being here one bit. Living up to his love for attention in all areas of his life apparently.

"Sending me coffee?" I slide the cup closer to me as he takes a seat across from me.

"What's with the hat? Afraid to be seen with me?" The left side of his mouth tilts into a grin. He doesn't acknowledge my question, and I don't follow up.

I take a slow sip of the drink, letting its warmth coat my throat and exhale a deep breath.

"I've had enough gossip around my name to last a lifetime. So, yes, I'd really rather not be seen right now." I sigh. "Although, I did agree to meet you, so what does that say about my decision-making skills?" My eyes widen at my own state-ment. I'm talking to myself at this point.

A throaty chuckle bellows out of his chest and he takes a sip of his coffee before rubbing the back of his neck.

"I think your decision-making skills are impeccable."

"That's debatable." I laugh to myself, shaking my head back and forth.

"Why do you say that?" He leans in closer, as if he's genuinely curious.

"Forget I said it. I'm still just looking for an apartment and feeling stressed out over it, I think."

Liam's eyes shift down, looking at the table and then back up to me.

"Can I offer a genuine suggestion?"

"You can…" I hesitate in my response, but he's probably going to offer it regardless.

He lightly laughs.

"The apartment next to mine is empty."

I cough out a laugh, drawing a couple head turns in our direction. I wait for him to make a comment, something sarcastic or witty at my outburst, but nothing comes. Is he actually serious? He thinks I should move into his building? Be his neighbor? I pull my lips together to avoid another laugh.

"You're…serious?"

"I said I had a genuine suggestion, yes."

I don't even know where he lives, but I already feel like it's a bad idea.

"It's downtown. Not far from the stadium. There's a dog park, a gym, a doorman, and the floor I'm on has a private elevator. There are only four apartments on the floor, so not a lot of foot traffic. You'd be high up and safe."

I don't know why the mention of the word safe makes me feel so calm. It's almost like Liam somehow knows the chaos and recklessness I've dealt with and how all I want in this next chapter of my life is to feel at peace.

"Well, I appreciate it. But I don't know if I can swing living on the same private floor as the NFL's hotshot quarterback"

"Think about it." He shrugs, offering up one of his postcard smiles. "Is your coffee okay?"

I nod, thankful for the subject change as I take another sip. "It's perfect, thank you."

"I have a Demi-graphic memory." He smiles with pride as he sits back in the chair.

I watch as people stare at him when they walk in and there are two men standing in line who look like they could freak out like twelve-year-old girls at any moment.

"A what?" I scoff with a laugh.

"Once I learn something about you, it's here forever." He taps his temple with two fingers before he finally notices the guys in line gawking at him.

He doesn't get up, but he nods in their direction, and that seems to be enough for the men to be satisfied.

"So you have a photographic memory? Makes sense, you study plays and stuff like that all the time."

"No." He laughs. "I don't have a photographic memory. My memory as a whole probably isn't the best. But I'm good at remembering things I care about." He pauses. "I'm good at remembering things about you."

I stare at him blankly, my mouth slightly open as he takes another sip from his drink and smiles at me again. He's so honest. And it's easy to let his charms chip away at my defenses.

But it's also hard to look at Liam and truly see beyond his flirtatious personality. If I ever gave in to his very obvious crush, would all the kindness fade out? Not that I ever plan to cross that line with him, but his charms would leave any girl guessing if it's sincere or just a tactic.

"You look pretty today."

Another compliment catches me off guard, and I quietly clear my throat.

"Is it the matted hair under a baseball hat? Or the oversized T-shirt and jeans that give that impression?" I chuckle.

I'm not used to all the compliments Liam slings my way, and

while they're very kind, I feel like I don't know how to receive them and it makes me say stupid shit like that.

He shakes his head and leans forward—he's practically halfway across the table at this point. Both elbows resting on the surface.

"It's this," he says in a smooth voice as he slowly reaches across the space between us and tucks a tiny piece of stray hair under my hat. "These too." He points to the dimples on my cheeks, darting his tongue between his lips. "And I like those. A lot." He emphasizes as he points to his eyes and then back to mine, and my stomach drops.

Liam lets out a low sound of amusement as he notices me inhaling.

"Well…" I collect myself. "That's very forward of you." My shoulders straighten and I stare at the corner of his mouth as it tilts up.

"Just telling the truth."

My indecisiveness can't determine if I want to let this play out or thank him for the drink and leave. I run my index finger along the inside of my thumb as I weigh the options. All the while, Liam's sitting across from me, leaning back in the too small chair as his hand works its way over his jaw. He's just staring at me and looking far too handsome for someone who had a grueling football practice less than an hour ago.

He looks so comfortable. And not that I'm necessarily *uncomfortable*, I guess.

I sigh, confusion swirling in my mind. Where's the flashy guy with women on rotation? That's who he's supposed to be, right? I've seen him at events and parties—he's a joker, the life of the party, but every time I'm alone with him, he's so settled and secure. It makes being annoyed with him incredibly difficult. Before I can actually make a decision myself about leaving, he scoots himself closer into the edge of the table.

"Please don't leave." His mossy eyes focus on mine, a plea, almost. "I know that's what you're thinking."

"No, it isn't," I rush out. I'm a terrible liar, my facial expressions screw me every single time.

Both of his eyebrows arch as he dips his head.

"You're a really bad liar, Dem."

I gently pull myself back in my chair, letting out a sigh as I do.

"How was practice?" I finally ask after a moment of contemplation.

"I don't want to talk about work."

"Well then, what should we talk about?"

The contemporary music in this coffee shop is playing at a soft, low volume as the song changes, and I feel a shift in the entire atmosphere. There is greenery that hangs on the brick wall beside us in this back corner and a sign behind Liam that reads SIP & YAP. It's cute. I could sit here all day and inhale the smell of coffee beans and pastries.

No one is in line at the counter anymore. There are only two other people in this entire little place on the opposite side of the cafe, and I see one barista cleaning some of the coffee appliances behind the counter. Their mid-afternoon rush seems to have slowed and it's that time of the day where people are thinking about switching to a cocktail, not grabbing a latte.

"Anything else," he says. "Tell me something new with you."

"Fine. There's a prime-time reporter slot opening up next season—no one is leaving, they're just adding one more to the crew—and I want it." I haven't actually said that out loud to anyone other than my boss, yet I just said it to Liam with so much joy in my chest it has me pulling back briefly in shock at how easily that news left my lips.

"You'll get it." He nods, no sarcasm in his words. "I believe in you."

A phrase no man has ever said to me, and it makes my stomach drop.

My index finger picks at the nail polish on my thumb as I stare at him. His lips lift into a smile as he brings his cup to his lips. "You found a loophole into talking about work. Smart." He takes a sip and then clears his throat, placing the cup on the table. "You know I'd listen to you talk about anything."

"It's probably best to stick to work topics."

"Seriously?"

"Liam, aside from work there isn't anything for us to talk about."

His head shakes back and forth. "That's not true. There are a million things to talk about."

My shoulders slouch slightly as I watch his Adam's apple bob through the words and I'm staring too intently, I can feel it.

"Tell me about the last book you read." The corner of his mouth lifting.

"Do you read?"

"No, but I've seen you on the sidelines a time or two with a book sticking out of your bag."

"Observant." I drag my gaze to his before taking another sip of coffee. "Sometimes they have dragons, sometimes they're like reading a rom-com movie, it just depends on my mood." I shrug, thinking to myself how odd it is having him ask me that. No one has ever asked about the books I read.

"Would I like them?"

I draw circles on the table between us, sighing. "I don't know. Are you into dragons or rom-coms?"

"What would you classify *Grey's Anatomy* as?"

"An emotional roller coaster medical drama where everyone you love leaves or dies. Oh, with a very well curated playlist and highly attractive people."

Liam's mouth opens and a loud laugh follows. "I wasn't

expecting that," he admits, palm clenching his chest. "That's pretty damn spot on."

He smiles again and it's a nice smile. One that feels like it should be contagious, but I'm too in my own head right now to mirror him, so I simply nod and use my coffee as a buffer and take a sip.

"Can I ask you something? I don't want you to take this the wrong way, because I don't want to invade your private life, but I've known you a while and…" He trails off.

My eyes narrow suspiciously, but I find it endearing that Liam always tries to be as respectful as possible.

"Suuuuure." The word drags.

"Are you happy?" Well, there was no beating around the bush there.

"I know you've gone through a lot of shit recently, and while I don't know or need to know specifics, I just want to make sure you're okay. You lied the other morning when you said you were fine. I could tell, but it's okay. I figure there are a lot of things you're still working through and processing, and maybe you still have bad days…but…" He sighs, and I can't help but just sit back and stare.

It's such a loaded question to ask someone if they're happy. It could go so many different ways, even backfire, but I feel my shield lower the tiniest bit at his question because no one ever asks if I'm happy. It's a question that catches me off guard, but maybe it's one I need to be asked every now and then to let myself say it out loud.

Despite the hard days, I am happy.

"I guess I just want to make sure you're okay."

"We all have bad days," I say in nearly a whisper. "But a bad day doesn't mean a bad life."

He nods as he takes a sip of his drink, his eyes focused on mine.

"So, yes, I'm happy."

I feel warmth run through me. So much comfort and safety that it almost feels wrong. I haven't felt this way in god knows how long.

"That's all I need to know."

I appreciate Liam's tenderness. It's a different side to him than I normally see. He's typically full of sarcasm and wit, a true goofball in every sense of the meaning. But lately, I've been seeing his more mature side, the one I've only heard about through his friends and teammates, and I'm not quite sure what to think of it yet.

CHAPTER TEN

LIAM

The sun hits Demi at the perfect angle, giving her an angelic glow as we sit across from each other in this coffee house. I can't stop fucking staring. I can't stop internally freaking out that she's actually sitting here with me, and I want to keep asking her a million questions to make this afternoon last as long as I possibly can.

This may have only happened because of a bet, but she didn't have to follow through. I gave her an out, and she still wanted to come. Whether that was her need to keep her word or maybe that she actually wanted to, I'll probably never know for sure. But I'm sure as hell thankful nonetheless.

"It's kind of an up and down thing," she says after a bout of silence between us.

I nod, not knowing her exact situation, but understanding what she means. I know what it's like to look happy on the outside and want so badly to feel it on the inside, but you hide behind all the darkness with a smile and positive attitude.

"Yeah, I get it. Emotions ebb and flow…been there," I admit, without sharing too much of my own experience.

Her lips part ever so slightly, if I hadn't been staring at them so closely I may have missed it.

"Right." She shifts her eyes to the other side of the cafe.

Demi's walls are so fucking high. It's obvious she doesn't want to let a soul into her mind—or heart right now. She goes quiet for a moment again, and I don't want to let her get too in her head, so I perk up.

"About those books." I smirk, watching her eyes refocus on me instead of zoning out. "What are your three deserted island books?"

She takes a sip of her coffee, and my gaze is stuck on her lips as she coats them with her tongue, tasting the remnants of her drink. It's a quick swipe, but I don't miss it.

"Oh god." She chuckles, shaking her head. "I don't even know. There are so many books I love. Asking me to pick three is a crime."

"I'd bring a survival book."

"Oh yeah?" she questions, her voice laced with amusement.

"Of course. I'd want something to read that could potentially help me get off that island."

"Is there a book for that?"

"I'm sure if I were to google *how to survive on a deserted island*, something would come up."

Demi's laugh makes me smile and I don't miss her tuck the stray hair back under her hat after it falls on her cheek.

When I look at her, I see a woman with so much strength. So much goddamn beauty, it hurts. And I wish I could tell her that. But something tells me she doesn't want to hear how strong she is, because I get the feeling she's tired of having to be.

"Do you want another coffee?" I ask.

"I shouldn't," she says, chuckling to herself as she seemingly glances at the time on her phone. "I already have a hard enough time sleeping, I don't need to add to that."

Without missing a beat, I ask, "Why do you have a hard time sleeping?"

"Oh, you know…" She trails off, waving her hand in the air.

"I don't. Enlighten me."

"Let me guess, you're one of those people who falls asleep the second your head hits the pillow?"

Not exactly.

"Why can't you sleep, Dem?" My words feel more direct this time. They hold more curiosity than before.

"Little of this, little of that. I have a lot of baggage." She sighs heavily on the last word.

My chest tightens at her answer, but whenever I'm around her I feel this urge to be a safety net. Someone she can talk to without judgment or ridicule. "Well…" I sigh. "Lucky for you, I love unpacking."

She tilts her head in what I think is an attempt to hide a smile, but it's hard to tell when she returns her face toward mine and looks indifferent.

But then her eyes narrow almost playfully. "It's highly suspicious that you're this interested in my sleep."

Knocking my head back, I let out a rough sigh. It drives me fucking nuts she can't seem to believe anyone is genuinely interested in her wellbeing. What the hell kind of husband was Nells?

"You have to know by now that I'm interested in anything you want to tell me, Dem. I don't have stipulations or requirements, nothing is conditional. I want to know everything you want to tell me."

She breathes in and out, those dark eyes staring at me with uncertainty. I can tell she's weighing out the options right now. "I just have a hard time sleeping more often than not. It's nothing." Her head does a quick little shake back and forth as she clears her throat. "My mind messes with me. I know how stupid that probably sounds to you. But I just have a hard time turning it off."

"You aren't alone, you know. Just because my issues might not look the same as yours doesn't mean I can't understand and empathize with you. Don't assume my life is all rainbows and butterflies. Do you actually think I have *no* issues? No baggage myself?"

Her brown eyes look anywhere but at me. She fidgets with the coffee stirrer between her fingers and it's like I can see what she's referring to at this very second. Without her saying anything, I can see how her mind is spinning, how it's causing her to spiral and probably overthink this entire conversation and interaction.

"You're right. That was unfair," she answers. "Baggage for baggage," she offers, and I nod. "Why'd you tense up when your dad was mentioned the other day?"

I choke back a cough as that's the last thing I expect her to ask me. I didn't even think I made it that obvious about my desire to talk about *anything* else.

"Going for the throat right out of the gates, okay."

Her black nails mindlessly draw circles on the table between us as she stares at me. She never stares at me. At least not like I stare at her, and *fuck*. I like it. Her attention. Her gaze. Her interest.

"I saw the way you reacted when I brought him up."

"Yeah." I shrug. "We just have a complicated relationship. That's the long and short of it."

She blinks a few times, watching me carefully as she decides if the information I just gave her is enough to satisfy her before she speaks.

"I have nightmares sometimes, and other times I just can't fall asleep at all," she admits, head down, voice hushed. As if she wants as few people as possible to know.

I notice how Demi picks at her fingernails, and I'm starting to realize I don't think she's sat completely still this entire time.

"Nightmares where you can't fall asleep, or they wake you

up at night?" I'm no stranger to sleepless nights. Only Dana, my therapist, knows about that, though.

"Both," she says, clearing her throat with a small chuckle.

I nod as she stares at me and she returns the gesture. Somehow both of us seeming to feel a little relieved for this admission of hers. It's kind of nice to know I'm not the only one who often sees pain when I close my eyes, even if we don't know exactly what the other is referring to.

The sound of shoes scuffing the floor grabs my attention. "Oh shit, Liam Evans." The eager voice of a male interrupts the silence between us, and I turn my head to see a man and woman standing at the counter waiting on drinks.

"And you're Demi Sanchez." The woman with him perks up.

Demi smiles as if we weren't just in the middle of a heavy moment and nods as she greets the woman.

"I'm so sorry, I didn't mean to interrupt your—"

"Business meeting," Demi cuts in before the woman can place any labels on today.

I scoff under my breath as I stand and shake the guy's hand. They both ask for pictures, and I can see how hesitant Demi is to be photographed with me, so I take the asshole card for the day and decline as politely as possible.

Thankfully, the couple seems to understand, and I catch a closed lips smile from Demi.

"We should go," Demi says in a hushed voice, scooting her chair back.

I nod, extending my hand out in front of me to follow her lead.

It's warm once we're on the sidewalk and the sun is glowing in the sky. Humid, even in the evening, it feels like a summer out on the water. Like I should be pulling in the anchor and loading up the boat from the island to head back to the dock.

The curve of Demi's hips distracts me when I take a few steps after her.

"I…" She pauses when she turns to face me. "Your dad will be off-limits. In interviews with me, I mean. I won't bring him up, and if I see anything on the media sheets I'll decline."

She has no explanation of the circumstances. Not even the smallest morsel of information. For all she knows, the "it's complicated" could mean something as simple as we don't like the same music. She has no idea why, but it doesn't matter. She's still telling me she won't ask about him, and fuck. This woman has no goddamn clue what that means to me.

I swallow the lump in my throat and feel my jaw tick as I nod.

"Thank you for the coffee. And I shouldn't have made that fan interaction so weird for you. I'm sorry about that, I just…" She doesn't finish the thought as she takes a few steps toward me. "I appreciate your friendship, Liam."

"Friends." I nod as I repeat the word.

"Think you can handle that?" Her voice holds a little amusement as she smirks at me.

I've been handling it for years. I can do it easily, even though I don't want to. But I'm curious to know if she can, now that circumstances are different. I'm also not going to rest easy until I know she's found a new place to live—whether it's by me or not.

I smile, tilting my head down to her as I hold my hand out, gesturing my index and middle finger for the phone she's holding. "What?" Her hip pops as she stands in front of me, her eyes curiously glaring in my direction.

"*I* can be your friend, Dem. But it's not me I'm worried about." My fingertips graze her wrist near the tattoo I've always wondered about as she hands me her phone.

I hold it up to her face, unlocking the screen so I can add my number.

"What are you—"

"Let me know when you want to come see the empty apartment. It's got a great view. Friendly neighbors." I wink, and she gapes at me as I hand her phone back to her. "You're welcome for the coffee, Dem."

CHAPTER ELEVEN

LIAM

I should be awarded for my willpower right now, because it's taken everything in me not to beg one of the girls for Demi's number so I can check in on her. I'm pretty certain Abby has it.

"Hey, Jules, is there any way you could tell me if the apartment next to mine has any interested renters or if it's still just sitting on the market? You can call me back or just send a text, whatever is easier…thanks." I leave a quick voicemail for my business manager.

My management team is the fucking best. When I started in the league, my dad tried to force his way into handling things for me, but every single person I spoke to advised against that. Although I didn't need their warnings—I already knew that would've been a fucking nightmare.

My agent, Kat, is the president of football operations at her agency and has a team of talented, badass women who work with her. I've never had a single complaint. From contracts to my brand deals, public relations or overall business management—these women have it covered.

Jules handles a lot of business tasks for me, so she was my first call this morning when I couldn't get Demi out of my head. She thinks the apartment is too expensive so I'm going to do just about whatever I can to make it in her price range.

I place my phone on the bathroom counter facing up, just in case Jules calls me back while I'm in the shower I'll see her name.

I close my eyes the moment the water streams down my face. It feels so damn good. I've shamelessly spent plenty of time in this exact shower picturing Demi. Thinking of her in all the ways I shouldn't. I want her so fucking badly, it's enough to make me crazy some days.

The sound of a text tone goes off, and I peek my head out of the glass door to get a better look at the screen, except it isn't Jules texting me back. It's a number I don't have saved in my phone and something tells me to get out and check it.

UNKNOWN NUMBER

Really? You saved your number in my phone as Hotshot Quarterback??? Do you realize it took me ten minutes to find your number?

I bark out a laugh and can't help but smile from ear to goddamn ear.

> Of course I did. I believe Hotshot Quarterback were your exact words.

UNKNOWN NUMBER

You're insane.

> You have no idea.

> What do I owe the pleasure?

UNKNOWN NUMBER

Against my better judgment, I'm curious about that apartment you mentioned. I need a place to live and don't want to spend a ton of time looking.

> The Grove, 9 South Lancer Ave. Text me when you're here, I'll come down and get you.

UNKNOWN NUMBER

I won't need an escort up.

> Who else is going to give you the full tour? Text me

There's no hiding my smile. Today is about to be a good one.

Before Demi gets here, I head down to the lobby once I finish the quickest shower of my life. Rob is standing at the desk and waves to me when he sees me exit the private elevator.

"Hey, my man. I have a question for the leasing department. Any way I can get in touch with someone right now?"

My phone vibrates in my pocket while Rob is taking a look at his computer for me, but I tell him never mind when I see it's Jules calling.

"Hey," I answer.

"I have some information from the leasing director for that apartment building. I just emailed you the numbers, along with a snapshot of some of your financials if you're thinking of doing anything. Let me know if any paperwork needs to get done today or if things can wait until Monday."

"Ah, thanks, Jules. You're the best."

I take in my surroundings before moving over to a corner where I can talk more freely without any eavesdroppers.

"Full disclosure, I want to rent the apartment. I know it sounds crazy, but I'm trying to help someone out. Whatever the rent is monthly, I want to cover half." I can't exactly tell Demi this place is just free, she won't buy it, but fudging the numbers can't hurt, right?

"You're willing to pay your full rent, plus half the rent for your new neighbor?" She sighs into the receiver.

I know it can be done, there has to be a way.

"Exactly," I confirm.

This feels like the right call. It doesn't feel as impulsive as it probably sounds. Demi needs a place to stay, and I want to help. Simple as that. It just so happens to work out that my previous neighbor left last spring. The apartment has been sitting empty for months and it's a place I know Demi will be safe.

"And this is a stat situation?"

"I think so, Jules. If anyone can make this happen, I know you can."

She laughs. "Liam, you don't need to gas me up. I know I can get it done."

"You're the best," I say one more time before we end the call.

Now, I just need to sell this place enough so Demi wants to move in.

GIRL OF MY DREAMS

I'm about to walk into the building.

I've been hanging out in the lobby with Rob for the last thirty minutes so I'm already here when she walks in. I see her hesitate before she walks through the automatic doors. Her head instantly tilts up as she looks at the high ceilings and artwork on the walls.

Her lips are pulled together when she sees me, and she shakes her head back and forth as we walk toward one another. Demi's dark brown hair is pulled back away from her face and her sunglasses are sitting in her hair. My eyes shoot to her waist, not missing the way the shorts hug her hips, and then I smile at the band T-shirt she's wearing. blink-182.

"Nice music taste," I say when we're within earshot, gesturing to the black shirt hanging off her shoulder. Demi wears black and white exclusively, I'm not sure I've ever seen her in something different—maybe gray.

"Just walking in here I can tell this is going to be a look, don't buy situation. Like when I browse the candle section at the store, or stumble into a model home just for fun."

"Ah, I think you'll be surprised." I motion my hand to have her step in front of me. "Before we start the tour, anything you need? Coffee, water, restroom?"

"Are you a realtor now?" She laughs. "First a barista, then this. I'm starting to think you're prepping for life after retirement."

"I'm a jack-of-all-trades, honey."

Demi huffs out a chuckle as she passes by me, and god, she smells like Valentine's Day. It's all sweet fresh flowers as I let myself linger for a moment.

"Is this the elevator?" She jerks her thumb to the corridor to the left that says private access, and I nod.

My throat bobs as I finally move my feet toward her.

"Sure is, you'd just enter these doors here with the keypad," I say, punching in my code.

Once the door unlocks and we walk through, there's a set of elevators that goes directly up to the fifth floor. It's not the highest in the building, and I'm thankful for that considering I'm not too keen on heights.

"Rob works at the front desk. He'll make sure you don't have any issues getting in, and of course the code is different for each resident on our floor."

"*Our* floor?" she says, raising a brow at me as the elevator is rising.

I just smile. I'll let the building speak for itself. I haven't been in the apartment next to mine in well over a year, but I remember the ins and outs of it. The old tenants were a couple who owned some kind of gym franchise around the area, and I'd played poker with the husband there a handful of times.

"It's probably nice having a private elevator. No one can come up without you knowing."

"It has its perks."

She glances at me from the corner of her eye before shifting her observant gaze back to the touchscreen where it shows us moving up.

The elevator dings and the doors slide open, making a killer first impression with the giant windows overlooking the water. Demi's eyes widen, and I smile seeing her body perk up.

"Wow," she breathes out.

Wow, indeed.

CHAPTER TWELVE

DEMI

I've lived in nice places before. I mean, my ex-husband plays in the NBA and has the most high-end taste of anyone I've ever met, but this building I've been in for the last ten minutes feels like I'm in a resort.

And not because of the architecture, although it's very fancy on the outside with fountains and valet. But it's everything inside the building that feels so welcoming—despite my internal protest —Liam is making it feel like home already.

"Two apartments down to the right, and we're over here on the left." He points to the long hallway to his right and then tilts his head to the left.

I roll my eyes at his constant word choices. *Us, we, ours.* But I follow him down the hall, along the hardwood flooring that looks sparkling clean and smells like citrus.

"I'm right here," Liam says, stopping in front of a black door. "So, you know, if you ever need anything. Eggs, milk, a movie companion. I don't do bugs, though, we can call Rob for that."

He grins at me, staying in place longer than I thought he would. He stalls for a moment, and I watch the sharp edge of his jaw twist.

"No one knows where I live. I mean, my friends and my brother do. But that's about six people." His eyes dart to the floor beneath his feet. His crisp white sneakers taking the smallest step back, as if he's working on letting me into his space.

It's surprising behavior from him. Before the last few days I probably would've made some comment about him bringing all his female guests here, but it doesn't seem appropriate now.

"And yet you're telling me where you live. Showing me, in fact," I say softly, my eyes eagerly searching his for whatever reason.

Liam has a pull that constantly makes me want to know more about him, and I keep having to stop myself.

"I guess I trust you." He shoves his hands into the pockets of his black athletic shorts, and I don't miss his forearms flex as I glance down.

It feels like Liam has layers no one even knows about. I can't help but wonder if it relates back to his childhood or what. His throat clears, shaking me out of the curiosity spinning. I'm a reporter after all, and it's hard for me not to want the whole story.

"All right, and now for your new humble abode," he says, gesturing to the last door at the end of the hall.

"We'll see about that."

"Rob gave me the master key for this instance. I don't just have a key to this place," he says as he twists the handle on the door and it swings open.

Holy shit. I mean, holy *fucking* shit. This apartment is amazing. I expected to walk into a place that was gaudy and had too much space for just one person, but somehow it's exactly what I need.

There's a sliding glass door that's the first thing you see when you enter the apartment with a small patio area just beyond it. The kitchen is off to the left with a spacious island and great light fixtures hanging from the ceiling. There isn't a big dining room space, but I'm thankful for that. I was never the one who liked to entertain in my last house—all the entertainment spaces were Brandon's needs.

"I know it has two bedrooms and two bathrooms. What else do you want to know?"

I laugh to myself, peeking my head around the corner to a short hallway where I spot a bedroom and bathroom right away.

"Thought you were trying to sell me this place," I tease, looking back at him with a quick smile.

"I just needed to get you in the door. I knew it would speak for itself."

I nod, but he doesn't see me as I'm walking in and out of bedrooms because he's still in the common area. I can't believe I love this apartment. I also hate that I love it because it means Liam would be my neighbor. That alone should be a reason to turn it down, but for some reason all it does is end up in the pros column. I want to feel safe in my own home again. And as much as I hate admitting it, I've always felt safe near Liam.

The master bedroom has one big window that has a partial view of the city, and the rest shows off the glistening water of the bay. It looks like I can see a small portion of a handrail on another balcony too.

There's a good size walk-in closet and a gorgeous bathroom with a giant bathtub as the focal point.

The sound of knocking grabs my attention, and I twist my head back and forth trying to determine where it's coming from.

"Yeah, that's Walt." Liam's deep voice pulls me toward him.

He's standing against the doorframe, leaning with both hands in his pockets and one foot casually placed over the other.

"And Walt is?" I ask.

He blows out a loud breath, lifting himself from the frame and strolls over to the window.

"A fucking menace, that's what." He peers out the window and then lightly pounds on the wall beside it. "I was hoping he would've waited to introduce himself to you until after you were already moved in."

I still don't know if Walt is a ghost, a rodent, or something else. My eyes widen at him, an urge for more information.

"It's a bird. Knocks on the building sometimes." He pauses. "Okay, all the fucking time he knocks on the building. Kind of surprised you hear it here, though, actually. I can see him from my bedroom window so I thought he was closer to my place."

"I love birds."

"Really?" The look of confusion and slight concern rises on his face.

"Yeah. I grew up with birds as a kid, I've always liked them." Shrugging, I continue walking around as I head back to the common area. "I'm just glad it's not a rodent of any kind," I call out behind me. "A bird is fine with me."

I've officially seen all that I need to see and now have to ask the soul crushing question of how much it costs.

"All right, so I'll admit the apartment is great. But let me down easy with the price, okay?" I lean against the island in the kitchen, studying the beige and gray swirls in the marble.

"Take a guess." Liam nods his chin in my direction as he's walking toward the kitchen. He leans his back against the counter next to me and stares down.

"Is everything a game to you?" I scoff, with a laugh.

"Not *everything*."

I roll my eyes as I consider the pricing. It's almost twelve-hundred square feet, two bedrooms and bathrooms, private floor in a fancy downtown building, with security and water views. I nearly choke on the amount as it leaves my chest.

"Easy five-grand a month."

The smile on his face grows, and I know that look. He's just dying to prove me wrong.

"And how would you like it for an easy two a month?"

"Liam, there is no way in hell this apartment goes for two

grand a month. The place I'm staying now is two grand a month and it's smaller, older, and uglier."

"Two grand, that's the price."

I narrow my eyes at him suspiciously.

"What did you do?"

"I found a place for a friend to stay and made sure it was affordable for her. That's all I did."

There's a part of my brain yelling at me to stop asking questions and just accept the very nice offer that's currently in front of me on a silver fucking platter.

There's a knock at the front door just before it opens and a man with jet-black hair and glasses walks in, holding a packet of paper as he smiles at Liam and then me.

"Hi, I'm glad you were able to look around. I'm the leasing director, Marcus."

"Hey, Marcus. Thanks for letting me show her around a bit. I think she likes it," Liam replies, giving me a quick wink. He's not wrong, though. I love it. Dammit.

"If you have any questions, I'd be happy to answer them." Marcus steps closer to me, placing the paperwork on the counter in front of him. He smells like baked goods, and it has me craving a nice warm chocolate chip cookie.

"I have to run to a meeting, but glad you like it, Dem. And again, thanks, Marcus, for all your help." Liam's hand grazes the small of my back when he passes by and the hair on the back of my neck immediately stands up.

I watch as Liam leaves the apartment, practically memorizing his steps. I know he made some kind of arrangement for me to be able to move in here, and as annoyed as I want to be by that, I'm tired of looking for a place, tired of living where I'm living, and ready to be somewhere new. I want a fresh start. I need it.

I think of the promise I made to myself after my divorce. This new chapter I'm starting is about *me*. Doing what I need to do for *me*. I need to live on my own—I've never done that. I need to live somewhere out of my comfort zone—never done that either. Both admissions feel pathetic at thirty-five, but that's what happened when I went from living at home, to college roommates, to getting married.

I tagged along with Brandon for years as we moved where we needed to, based on where he was playing. And now I finally have the chance to make my own decisions about my life—every single part of it. And I want to say yes to this apartment. I'll talk with Liam about whatever he pulled for the rent another time, but for now I'm going to be selfish.

"This place is great, Marcus. I'd love to sign a lease."

CHAPTER THIRTEEN

DEMI

My alarm sounds on my phone, but I've been up for an hour now. Tomorrow I'm officially moving into my new apartment, and I can't wait to have a fresh slate. A place that's just mine. Furniture that's mine. No other profiles on my streaming apps. Food I like in the fridge. God, there are a million other things, and I'm excited just thinking about it.

I've spent the last thirty minutes browsing Liam's social media page. After many clicks, I somehow landed here and my attention has been fixated on his posts since.

Shirtless. Football games. Events. His boat. A cat. A *lot* of a cat, actually. In every picture he's smiling so big. Like he's actually the happiest man on the planet, but I'm not sure I actually believe it. And I linger on that thought for a second.

The only pictures of Liam's family are the ones he's posted with his brother, Landyn. Nothing with his parents at all.

As reporters, we're generally made aware of any topics that are off-limits when we're speaking with an athlete or someone within an organization. It's pretty common knowledge to respect personal matters, especially if it's something that isn't directly related to their athletic career.

But I get why Liam's never told anyone he doesn't like speaking about his father. Once he says it, the questions come. The whispers and the people who are just downright nosy, wanting to know why he isn't a huge fan of his Super Bowl-winning father. So he keeps it politically correct. He gives the standard answer people expect without giving his father too much praise.

It's smart, honestly.

I swipe off his profile before locking my phone and tossing it on the bed beside me. Time to get up and get ready for family day. It's usually one of the busiest days at training camp, but also one of the most fun. A lot of the players have kids who get to come out to the field and play games, see their dads, and of course watch a practice take place. Everyone seems to love it.

⊏⊐

"Oh, who have we got here?"

As I'm finishing a quick on-field interview with Mason Baker, four kids approach the back of the chair he's sitting on.

Two girls and two boys come running up, all wearing his jersey, and he pulls two of the smaller children onto his lap.

"This is the team," he says proudly, kissing the tops of their heads.

Mason's wife stands off to the side, just outside of the tent we're under, and smiles as he waves her over.

We chat for a moment before he's needed on the field, and I get a small window for a break.

The practice field that is normally wide open space is now filled with vendors, picnic tables, and strollers. The Knights mascot is running around too, taking pictures with the kids and having fun with the media crew.

As I'm making my way over to the far end of the field by the street where the food trucks are located, I notice a large group of kids and families in a grassy area near one of the sidelines. A familiar laugh causes me to stop in my tracks and focus on where it's coming from.

"So close, try again!" I hear Liam shout to a young boy about twenty yards from him.

The quarterback throwing net is out and Liam seems to be working with the kids on their throws. I watch as he jogs over to the boy, taking the ball from his hands and showing him how to properly hold it with the laces for a spiral.

He takes a knee, getting right at the kid's level, looking him in the eye when he speaks, and palms his shoulder before he walks away, back to where the net is.

The boy launches the ball again, and this time it lands perfectly in the center net. Liam's arms both fly in the air as he yells and runs toward the kid.

"Yeah!" he shouts. "That was a great throw, Brody!"

My smile reluctantly widens as I watch him interact with the kids and families. He doesn't have to be out here for this. It's not like he has kids of his own out here running around, he could easily be taking a break like a lot of the other guys—cooling off under the mist tents. But he seems so in his element hanging out and teaching these kids.

Glancing at my phone, I only have about twenty minutes until I have another quick interview. Today is filled with a handful of small chats with the guys. Days where fans are in attendance for practices seem to be more for fun than anything else, even though they still give it their all—you can easily tell the team just loves playing for an audience. Even if it's their wives, neighbors, or seven-month-old babies. Having someone on the sidelines is an extra rush of adrenaline for them.

I notice Mia Campbell, Nate's wife, on the sideline gently pushing a stroller back and forth as her two toddlers seem to be playing tag with one another on the field. When she spots me, she gives me a smile and a wave.

I mimic the greeting and walk over to her.

"Is he sleeping?" I whisper as I approach the stroller before peeking in.

She nods. "Finally. He was getting a little restless, so I'm glad he fell asleep. I'll rock this stroller for as long as I need to if it helps keep him comfortable."

"They're beautiful," I say, gesturing to the three little boys who all look exactly like Nate.

"Thank you." She smiles, looking at the two older boys in front of her.

Nate and Liam stride up to where the two of us are talking. Liam's hair is caked in sweat, but he runs a hand through it nonetheless. The guys are in full pads today under their uniforms, making them look even bigger than they already are.

I'm sweating everywhere in this heat today. It's stagnant and uncomfortable for someone dressed for it, I can't even imagine how they feel. I wore an athletic skirt with an NFL tank top today thinking that would help, and while it does help with the heat I suppose, it doesn't stop the sweat from dripping between my thighs as I stand here.

When Nate approaches, he pulls Mia by the waist and kisses her as if she's going to put the air back into his tired lungs. When they finally break apart, he turns to acknowledge me with a hello.

"I did that," Liam says, smirking as he points to the two of them.

"You did not," Nate retorts, leaning into the stroller to peek at the baby.

"I did," Liam whispers to me, swiping his tongue between his lips with a teasing smile.

I shake my head back and forth, looking away from him as I do.

"How are you today?" Liam directs his attention to me.

"Good," I say as I watch the boys run around. "A little tired from packing."

"When's move-in day?" He grins.

Pulling my shoulders back, I open my mouth slightly, taking a look at Nate and Mia beside us before answering.

"Tomorrow," I finally say with a smile.

Liam's hand forms a fist by his side and he pulls it back the slightest bit. A subtle fist-pump.

"Well, as I've mentioned, I love unpacking, so just come knock if you need help." He smirks.

"Where was this enthusiasm when we moved into our house?" Nate teases, looking at Liam.

"Stop," Mia says to him, reaching to pinch his side, but Nate catches her hand first, and they smile at each other. Jesus, they're cute.

"I'm going to get back to the tent," I say, turning to walk away.

"I'll walk with you," Liam says.

"That really isn't necessary," I say, but he's already by my side.

"Those ribs smell fucking good," he says, pointing up ahead to the food truck.

"I thought the same," I admit, shyly tucking a piece of hair behind my ear. "Messy food seems to always taste better."

"Agree." He chuckles before he stops walking.

Without realizing it, we're already back at the tent. He stands just on the outside as if he's dropping me off at work or something.

"Save some good questions for me." He runs a hand in his hair, and it slicks back with all the sweat.

"Oh, that's right. You're my final interview today."

"Stop. I know you didn't forget." His smirk pulls me a fraction of a step toward him.

"Maybe I did, maybe I didn't." I shrug as he walks backward

to the field, still facing me. "Guess we'll never know," I shout out to him as he turns.

I'm shocked at my own decision to be playful with him. If I were in this situation even a month ago, I wouldn't even entertain him.

As I'm standing with the crew watching them practice, I see the offense huddle together. Liam stands out amongst the players and not just due to his bright red no-contact jersey either.

He commands them in a way that requires so much respect. The usual playful tone Liam brings to conversations is sharper on the field, even in just a practice. He's intense, while still throwing out a joke or two to his linemen.

I hear his series of play calls before he yells "hut" and a wide receiver runs down the field to catch the pass that's already in the air.

Liam's release time is incredible. It's probably why his sack rate has been so low over the last few seasons. Although a lot of that is credit to his offensive line. He doesn't feel pressure in the pocket because of them, not a lot of quarterbacks in this league can say the same.

He's so good at scanning the field too, looking at all his options in what has to be record timing before he chooses the route he believes will have the best outcome. I've actually started thinking that the way he studies a defense should be taught to all rookies.

Not to say he doesn't go for the big moments, because he has his fair share of those. But great quarterbacks are smart. They know when to use their arms and when to take the yards. And Liam's one of the smartest in the league right now.

It's time for Liam's interview, and I do a quick look at my phone camera and flatten out one of the stray pieces of hair going rogue in this heat.

"Saved the best for last." Liam comes up behind me.

I see him in the camera of my phone as it's still forward facing.

He grins from ear to ear and secures a baseball hat on his head, checking himself out in my camera before I close it.

When I turn around, I get a good look—and whiff—of him. It's clearly been a tough day out there. I brush my hands off as I finish taking a bite of my mozzarella stick.

"Glad to see you eating before your interviews this time," he says as he takes a seat in the chair.

"For the record, I didn't purposely not eat last time. I had no time. Trust me, I love to eat." I sway my free hand in front of my body in a proud display. I love food. And I love my body.

"What's—" He imitates my motion.

"Does this look like someone who doesn't like food?"

His shoulders shake with a chuckle. "Oh, Dem," he says, leaning closer to me. "It looks like a lot of things I can't say if I want you to still think of me as a gentleman."

My eyes roll slowly. "You sure like to play with the line, though, don't you? You get pretty close to crossing it almost every time we talk." I place my notebook on the small table beside my chair and adjust my skirt before I take a seat.

When I thought an athletic skirt would be best for today, I didn't consider that they were made with slits and not the most suitable for women with thicker thighs or someone who is going to be alternating between standing and sitting all day.

"All I'm hearing is that you remember our conversations," he says in a hushed voice.

I give him major side-eye and don't miss the wicked grin on his face as we sit beside each other waiting for a post-practice interview to begin.

The interview itself lasts a total of three minutes as Liam is quick to answer the questions, and I don't waste time with any other side questions or off topic remarks. He's the last of the afternoon for me, and I can tell he's tired too. His eyes look heavy. Maybe even like he didn't sleep great last night either, but I brush that thought off. He's probably just exhausted. But he still speaks with excitement and charisma and makes sure to include the entire team in every answer he gives.

Every time I shift in this chair, I feel the skirt ride up on my thigh and I find myself practically keeping my left hand in place to make sure it doesn't go to an unprofessional or uncomfortable height up my leg.

Mental note for next time—don't wear the damn skirt.

"Thanks, Liam," I say, glancing at him and then back to the camera in front of us, offering a smile into the lens.

He nods and smiles as well. The perfect media presence. Not that I'm surprised—he's got a face made for television.

I stay seated and place my notebook on my lap, my fingers tugging at the fabric of my skirt when Liam stands from his chair and plants himself directly in front of me. Close enough to see the beads of sweat near his temple, but with just enough space between us for me to stand.

He takes his hat, flipping it backward on his head as his tongue coats his lips.

"Stand up." He stills, blocking the front of me from anyone's view, including his own as his eyes stay focused on mine. "Go ahead, Dem. I'm here, you can stand."

I swallow, tugging at my skirt one last time before I scoot myself off the chair to a standing position. All day, I've been getting creative with how I get down from this higher than normal chair. My go-to has been keeping my notebook over my legs. Not once today has someone noticed, let alone helped.

"Thank you," I say as I stand before him.

He backpedals a few steps and smiles with a cocky shrug as he's about to leave the tent. "Gentleman. Remember?"

CHAPTER FOURTEEN

LIAM

I heard the sound of voices coming from the hallway early this morning. It makes me wonder who Demi may have recruited to help her move, but I guess it'd be pretty fucking stupid of me to assume she doesn't have friends of her own she can call.

Birdie's pouncing all over the end of my bed, chasing her own tail as I make my way into the closet. I reach for an easy outfit, something I can wear for a quick run down by the water— or help someone move, whichever presents itself first.

NATE

Charity golf tourney coming up, you still playing?

Yeah I planned on it. When is it again?

NATE

Next weekend.

I'll be there baby

The charity golf events are always a good time and a place where we see a lot of other athletes too. In my younger years, it used to be one big party to me—a time to play golf, drink beer, and have a good time. I still enjoy doing all three of those things, but I don't try to turn a day's event into a whole weekend ordeal anymore.

After throwing on a pair of running shoes, I grab my keys, give Birdie a few behind the ear scratches, and head out the door. There are two men walking toward me in the hallway, and I hear music coming from Demi's new apartment. It's like a fucking siren song, I can't resist it, and instead of heading to the elevator I take the handful of steps toward her open front door.

Demi's facing away from me, a large moving box sits on the coffee table as she's slightly bent over pulling things out. I watch as she pulls out a book, and then another book and…is that entire box just books? I look at the six boxes lined up behind that one.

There's a clear bin on the floor near the kitchen island that looks to be filled with kitchen appliances. I scan what I can, noticing an air fryer and something that looks like a coffee maker or an espresso machine, except it looks like something that's maybe used on the stovetop. On the floor next to the bin is her brown bag with the Dominican flag keychain dangling on the side. A piece of knowledge I committed to memory after seeing that keychain on her bag in the hall outside of Coach Aarons's office. I've never googled something so fast in my life.

Her hair is up in a bun, but some of her curls are falling out from the sides. She's probably been at this for hours, based on how early I heard things this morning. Her feet are bare, she shuffles between boxes, and I notice she's just sorting books around within the boxes, not actually unpacking them.

"Excuse me." A rough voice sounds behind me. It's one of the guys from the hallway. His unruly brown hair spilling over his forehead. It isn't until he walks past me that I see the back of his shirt says Heff and Son's Moving. So these aren't friends of hers.

"Hey, should I expect you to just be lurking in my doorway and stuff now that I live here?"

I move my attention from the mover to the sound of Demi's voice walking toward me. She has a paper towel roll in her hands, and I slowly let my eyes roam over her. I smile at the black leggings and acid washed T-shirt she's wearing, proving my point that she doesn't wear color.

"We have a noise policy here," I say, tipping my chin toward her Bluetooth speaker on the counter. "I was just, uh, checking on that volume."

"Ah." She grins, turning away from me. She unrolls a couple pieces of the paper towel and begins wiping down the counter. "I like my music at a reasonable volume, not to worry." She clicks her tongue, and I follow her hands as they move in circles on the counter.

"That's good to hear." I cross my arms over my chest before taking my hat and flipping it backward on my head.

Demi's chocolate-coated eyes give me a not-so-subtle roam as she crumples up the paper towel and tosses it into a garbage bag hanging on one of the cabinet knobs.

I feel dumb as fuck standing in the doorway like this, but it also doesn't feel right to just walk into her apartment.

She reaches into a brown paper bag and pulls out a giant chocolate chip cookie, taking a bite and tossing her head back, clearly enjoying the flavor.

Cookies at ten in the morning, huh? Who am I to judge?

I clear my throat, working up the courage to find any way I can to stay near her. "Can I come in?"

She stares at me, cookie in one hand and the other propped on her hip.

I almost repeat myself based on the amount of time that's passed, but I give her my most charming smile instead.

Demi finishes off the cookie and wipes the corners of her mouth with her thumb and index finger before licking them, and I've never been into food play before but fuck, that was hot.

"No," she says, smiling as she does.

My shoulders pull back a bit and I almost choke on a laugh as I nod. Honestly, it's even hotter that she said no.

"Smart," I say. "No boys allowed."

"Have a good day, Twelve." She turns around without a second glance and goes back to her box—or boxes—of books.

"You too, Dem," I say, palming the doorframe just before I leave.

I guess no better time than the present to go for a quick run. Burn off some of this *energy* I've developed in the last ten minutes. Demi being my neighbor is fucking awesome...but, man, is it going to test my willpower.

I haven't seen Demi in two days. I thought living next to her would increase the time I see her, not the opposite. But her schedule at training camp hasn't involved me since a lot of her interviews are already wrapped up and we've been busy prepping for preseason.

"Morning, you beautiful gentlemen." I tip my hat to Ford and Nate as I pull up beside them on the golf cart.

We're participating in the Par for the Course charity today. It's a big golf tournament that helps benefit the children's hospital in the area—athletes from all Florida sports teams come together for this one.

"Did you know the temperature is supposed to feel like 107 today?" Ford jabs both hands into his hips like a pouting child.

"Cry me a river." I get out of the golf cart and walk over to see who else is here at the check-in tent.

"West is here," Nate says, motioning up the hill.

"Is he?" I'm eager to see West Hendricks. He's on Tampa's baseball team—he and I work out together whenever we're able to. His sister is a professional volleyball player, and I always love giving him shit about his little sister being more talented than him. "I'm going to go say hi to him real quick. I'll be right back."

I toss Nate the keys to the golf cart as I head toward the tent, passing crowds of people as I do. To my disdain, when I see West, he's talking to the one guy I want to punch more than anyone else.

Brandon Nells stands tall, towering over basically every other person here today.

"Hey, Evans!" West shouts, slapping my hand and pulling my shoulder for a hug.

"How's it going, man?"

"Hey, I'm just happy to be here. How's it looking this season?"

Brandon doesn't say anything to me but doesn't completely ignore my presence as I notice his body straighten in an effort to appear bigger—a gesture he doesn't need to make. *You're a fucking giant, no comparison needed, man.*

"We'll see, we'll see. So far things are looking great. It's been a fun camp so far."

Brandon scoffs under his breath, but he should know nothing he does goes unnoticed when you take up that much space.

"What's up, Nells?" I finally say, taking a step in his direction.

His size doesn't intimidate me. It never has. But he doesn't stick around for conversation.

"Nice seeing you, West." Brandon extends his hand to West, turning his attention from me.

"Have a great day!" I wave to him as he's already a handful of steps away.

"The fuck was that about?" West laughs.

I stare in Brandon's direction. I wish he'd turn around and say something to me. I wish he'd just give me a reason to unleash on him. I don't even need to know what happened with him and Demi to know it was his fault.

His piss-poor attitude toward me started well before they divorced, though. I wouldn't be completely shocked if he knew about my crush on Demi, but it's not like I ever acted on it while they were together. I'm not a fucking scumbag.

"Nothing," I mutter. "Glad I got to see you, bro. Leah still making you look bad at family functions?"

"Always," he says with a laugh and a shake of his head. "Let's work out next time we can. Have a good day out there."

We shake hands, and I head back down the hill where Ford and Nate are waiting. The tournament is about to start and I'm looking forward to my last golf day for a while.

CHAPTER FIFTEEN

DEMI

"Hi, Mom." I smile as I answer the phone.

I've been missing my parents a lot lately, and haven't seen them since last Christmas when everything was going to shit.

"Hi, honey. How'd your move go?" My mother is fiery and straight forward, but she's also soothing and so wise.

"I'm still getting some furniture delivered, but aside from that everything has been really smooth. It's nice having my own place."

"Well, you know we worry about you living on your own."

"I have pepper spray and a mean right hook."

"Ay Dios mío, Demetria," she says with a soft sigh.

I can hear my dad in the background.

"What's Dad up to?"

"Oh, your father." She hums. "He's doing okay, stubborn as ever still."

My parents have been married for decades. She's lively and he's the one grumbling in the corner as she's salsa dancing in the middle of a restaurant, but he never shies away from telling someone she's his wife.

Telling them I was getting a divorce was probably one of

the scariest things I've ever had to do. I'd expected them—specifically my mom—to talk me into staying. To see if we could work it out. Or even to tell me that maybe I should change my mind on certain things and give Brandon what he wanted.

But she didn't.

She told me I could come home if I needed to. She asked what I wanted to do and if I wanted to stay with him. When I told her I had no intention of staying married to him, she smiled on FaceTime and simply said okay.

Truthfully, moving back to Arizona where I grew up was appealing. The weather, being close to my parents again, the amazing food, and close proximity to mountains if I was feeling athletic and wanted to take a hike, were all things that briefly—*very* briefly—crossed my mind.

"But he's doing good. I'm making some empanadas, and he's in the other room watching a show."

"Tell him hi." I smile to myself.

"Oh, I meant to tell you, I saw MJ's mother at the grocery store the other day. I think she's going to be moving back to Phoenix. A bad breakup, apparently. You should text her. You two were so close growing up."

MJ was my childhood friend. We were close as kids until her family moved, causing her school district to change and we kind of lost touch.

"Hmm, maybe I will."

"It's been so long…you should make sure she's okay."

My lips pucker as I breathe out. "Yeah, I'll see if I still have her number," I say, staring out my sliding glass door. The view here is so calming, even being downtown.

"Your empanadas sound so good right now." I groan, missing my mom's cooking. My abuela too. Between the two of them, I hit the jackpot in the food department.

She lightly chuckles into the phone.

"The offer to come back here for a while still stands, although I know you did just sign a lease."

My lease is for six months. I wanted to give myself the freedom to choose after this football season. Do I want to stay in the city? Buy a house somewhere else? Plus, if I get this promotion I've been eyeing, that means I can stay here if I want to or move. The choice is mine.

Mine. And that's what I focus on.

"Yeah, I did," I say.

"Well, honey, I'll let you go, I just wanted to check in. I know you're very busy keeping those athletes in check." She sighs, and I laugh.

"I love you," I say, smiling.

My mom is my best friend—she has been for years. I didn't have a ton of girlfriends growing up. MJ was it for a lot of my childhood, then came high school where I met Brianna.

Bri and I clicked immediately our freshman year in English Honors. One of the guys tried to pull a "name five players" on her when she mentioned being a hockey fan and she rattled off over two dozen with a few years of Stanley Cup winners included.

It was at that moment I knew I found my person. For four years we were inseparable. I know people talk about soulmates as a romantic partner usually, but I'm pretty convinced my best friend was mine.

The sound of Walt breaks up the silence after I end the call. I still find it hilarious Liam named the random bird that bangs on the building. I peek my head toward the window, trying to see if I can get a glimpse of him, but I'm distracted when I notice a hand on the railing of the balcony beside me.

The curve of my balcony doesn't allow viewers—I asked Marcus before I signed—but I didn't think to ask if I could see anyone else's balcony from my window.

I recognize the hand right away from the gold ring on his

pinky finger. It's Liam. He moves closer to the railing, his abdomen right up against it, and I avert my eyes away. It feels invasive looking at him shirtless standing on his own balcony. I'd hate it if someone were staring at me like that. I have to give him the same courtesy I'd want, right?

Sometimes I wish I hadn't met Liam the way we did when I first started here. I enjoy working with him, but my first impression of him was as a kind, stupidly handsome stranger at the charity dinner who made me laugh. I often wish I would've met him the same way I met the rest of the offense. In a conference room as they were scarfing down food. I really think that would've helped.

Because Liam's a playboy. He's the league's hotshot who gets pretty much whatever he asks for in terms of perks and royalty. But knowing he's also kind and caring is really a pain in my ass.

My eyes betray me as they lift back to the window, and I watch him stand oddly still. Like statue-type still, actually, and it's freaking me out a little. I almost want to tap the window to see if he moves like he's in some kind of zoo enclosure and I'm the child on the other side of the glass.

But I notice his breathing. And then he digs his fingers into his eyes before shaking his head. I wish I could see his face clearer. He runs a hand through his hair roughly, it makes me concerned he actually yanked some out. His body language doesn't say mad, though. I feel my body relax as I stare at him. He inhales before his head dips and his elbows hit the rail, holding him up.

Pain stings at my chest—is he *crying*? The shake of his shoulders seems to answer my internal question, and right then and there my heart breaks for the hotshot quarterback, who appears to have it all, but it's so clear he's struggling too. And it makes me feel like absolute fucking garbage thinking of our coffee outing, where I was less than compassionate in assuming he lived a perfect life.

But it's inappropriate to be staring at him, especially in this private moment, so I pull myself away from the window and drag myself to the kitchen. On the counter is a basket of muffins from Marcus—a welcome home gift—and I take the biggest bite from a chocolate chip one.

Seeing Liam in that moment, however brief it may have been, made him seem a little more human. He almost seems too good to be true usually, but emotions like that looked real and raw. While I don't know exactly what he was upset about, maybe I needed to see it. Maybe just to remind me that we're all going through something.

The sidelines are filled with rookies this evening, second and third string players all trying to secure their spot on the roster. Liam isn't in uniform, he's wearing a pair of athletic shorts, a hat, and a long sleeve dry fit shirt with the Knights logo. Similar to the other starters who are also sitting back tonight.

Fans pile into the stadium, although it's less than a regular season game—much less. But the smaller crowd still brings as much energy as possible to preseason. It's a good chance to see what the new rookies have to offer, and it's definitely a time that helps the coaches see what everyone brings to the table.

I watch as Liam lingers on the bench with the other quarterbacks, he's got his hand on one of their shoulders, and I assume that's the guy who is going to start the game in seven minutes. It looks like he's giving him a pep talk of sorts, and I stare harder than I should at his body language. He's encouraging, even without hearing a word he's saying I can tell in his mannerisms. He taps the rookie's shoulder, smiles at him, and claps the moment he begins to back away. It's so clear he wants everyone to do well, he's not at all threatened by someone else coming in and competing for his job and it's—against the part of my brain that knows better—*hot*.

This first half is flying by when I somehow hear my name through the crowd.

"Demi!" I'm standing close to the tunnel watching the game when I look in the direction it came from, I see Abby, Ford's wife, waving to me from the stands.

Her field access badge swings from her neck under her long brown hair, and I wave back.

"Hi, why aren't you down here?" I shout, and she leans closer to me as the sounds of the game nearly muffle her voice.

"I was down there earlier. I almost didn't come at all since Ford isn't playing, but I didn't want to sit at home alone."

"No Summer or Mia tonight?"

Abby tilts her head sweetly, smiling with her pretty green eyes. "Kids," she says. "They're with the kids and don't usually go through the trouble of finding sitters for preseason."

I nod. "Well, you're welcome to come down here if you'd like." I shrug, pointing to her pass. I've never actually hung out with her, but she's always so kind whenever she sees me.

Within a few minutes Abby is tiptoeing toward me. Her slender frame is swallowed by one of Ford's jersey's that she's wearing like a dress with a pair of Converse.

"You're allowed to be here," I say, giggling at her attempt to be stealth.

"I know. This handy thing grants me all kinds of access." She points to her pass and smiles. "I'm just never down here during the game, but it's kind of cool." She wiggles her shoulders and then yells with the rest of the fans to make noise on a third down.

"How have you been?" I ask when things calm down.

"Good, you know, gearing up for Ford's busy time of year, but I know this doesn't last forever, so soaking it in. How about you?"

I nod. She's so right. "Good too. Finally settled into the new place."

"Oh, you moved?" She raises her voice to speak over her own clapping.

"Yeah…" My reply is hesitant, I'm a little surprised she doesn't know. "I actually just moved into Liam's building." I sigh. "Right next door, to be exact."

"Oh my god, you're kidding." There's genuine surprise on her features and there's no way she could be faking this reaction. "Bet he loves that." She smiles. "But it's a great place. I've always loved his apartment."

"Kind of shocked he didn't tell the guys, considering I'm pretty sure he's pulling some strings to have me live there." I know there's a hint of sarcasm in my reply and I quickly adjust my face to make sure I don't look as snappy as I just came off.

But Abby doesn't seem to notice—or care if she does—and just grins at me as the two-minute warning for halftime stops the game.

"Liam's not really in the business of sharing other people's business…even if he probably wishes he could run through the halls screaming that you're his neighbor."

My head turns from our conversation over to the sidelines, but Liam is already walking toward us to head into the tunnel for halftime, and I need to do a quick interview with Coach Aarons before he heads into the locker room.

Every time I learn something new about who Liam truly is, it makes my soft spot for him grow, and I haven't figured out if that's a good thing yet or a bad one.

CHAPTER SIXTEEN

LIAM

We're seven minutes into the first preseason game, and I've already got the itch to hop on the field. And not because the backups are royally screwing up, it's because I love this game so fucking much and all I want to do is play it.

"See that move by Daniels?" Nate elbows me as he steps to my side. "Looks like a little Evans 2.0 in the making."

I smile to myself, nodding at the rookie getting a few snaps and making me proud.

The rest of the offense is playing well too. Preseason is a good time to be able to see how these guys bring what we've been doing in practice to a live game. Stakes are higher and hits are harder, but so far they seem to be taking it in stride.

During a quick game break, my eyes leave the field and scan the perimeter, looking for the pair of eyes I've missed this week.

"There she is," I say to myself, smiling as my eyes land on Demi.

Is it possible for someone to get prettier every time you lay eyes on them? She's standing near the tunnel, a stack of papers in one hand, and the other propped on her hip in true Demi fashion as she talks with Abby.

Her hair is up in a ponytail and her curls bounce every time she moves her head. She's in a black skirt and sneakers with a blazer over a white shirt.

I sigh, my tongue darting between my lips as I inhale a deep breath.

Every time I see her, I just can't believe there's someone *this* beautiful alive at the same time as me and I get to even be in her presence, let alone be her friend.

Within seconds, my view is blocked as Chase steps in front of me, Ford and Nate join him a moment later, and we've now created a four-person square on the sidelines. We probably look like we're gossiping with how close we're all standing, but to be fair it's loud in here.

"Have you guys watched *Love is Blind*?"

Chase's question throws me for a loop. Reality television, really?

Nate's the first to ask what we're all thinking. "Have *you*?"

"I've seen it." Ford grabs his hat from his head, shaking his hair a bit before putting it back on.

"I've never watched it, but I've heard of it," I admit. "You've sat and watched it?" I turn to Ford.

"Yeah." He's so nonchalant in his answer as he shrugs. "Abby watches it, sometimes I catch an episode or two. It's entertaining, don't knock it until you try it."

"And you?" I ask Nate.

"I've never watched it. I only learned about it maybe two weeks ago from my sisters."

The perk of no sisters is being completely unaware of anything trending, ever.

"Are you about to tell us you're an avid watcher, big daddy?" I direct my attention to Chase, smirking as I do.

"If Summer has it on, I'll watch it. And he's right," he says, gesturing to Ford.

"Yeah?" Ford perks up. "What season are you on?" The energy coming from Ford makes me pull back as I look at him.

"Is it any good?" Nate asks.

"No fucking clue what season we're on." Chase's face contorts. I get the feeling he didn't even know there were multiple seasons. "Summer has been watching it, and I originally told her I thought it looked stupid, but it fucking sucks you in."

"They get married without seeing each other, right?" I ask.

"They get *engaged* without seeing each other," Ford emphasizes.

"Really?" Nate sounds intrigued.

"Yeah, it's wild. I don't know if I could do that," Ford continues. "Not that someone's appearance is everything, but I just think it would be really hard to ask someone to marry me if I've never been face-to-face with them."

"The concept is cool," Chase says. "Forces you to really get to know someone."

"So, you're really into it then?" Nate asks.

"Kind of. It's reality television, so take that for what it's worth." Chase shrugs.

The clock has been ticking, and our offense hasn't scored anything so far this half, but neither has the other team so it's still anyone's game. The two-minute warning is about to hit, and I'll take that as my go-ahead to start toward the locker room when it does.

"Well, I'm really happy for you." My hand palms Chase's shoulder. "It sounds like Summer is really adding some spice to your life. There's more on television than just the animal documentaries you watch." I smile, taking myself two steps away from them.

"Hey." He points at me. "Those are educational *and* fun."

Along with a few other starters, I begin making my way toward the tunnel. I can't fucking wait for this season to start and to be out there playing, but for these couple weeks I give my body the additional time before I'm having to scramble away from three-hundred-pound guys who want to throw me to the ground.

Demi's busy in conversation with Abby, and I see one of the sideline photographers staring at both of them. He's clearly not interested in the game happening to his right as his focus is on the girls. I watch him the entire time I'm walking. He finally turns back toward the field and crouches down near the end zone where he's ready to snap a photo if something happens.

But this guy must be new—either that, or he's just a fucking creep with zero decency or respect. I don't miss when he pivots on his bent knee, moving the camera in the direction of Abby and Demi.

What the hell? I speed up so I'm a little closer, and it hits me that both of them are wearing skirts. Or at least Abby's in some kind of jersey dress thing.

"Hey!" I yell, grabbing his attention, the girl's attention, and anyone within a ten-yard earshot to be quite honest. "Get up," I demand, throwing my thumb in the air as I approach him. "Camera faces that way," I say, pointing toward the field.

He's standing and his eyes nervously dart between the tunnel and the field, barely making contact with mine.

"Hey, yeah, of course." His words are muffled and rushed.

"Point your camera at *any* woman like that again, and I'll make sure you never hold one again."

He doesn't work for the league, but he's local media, and I can see the lanyard hanging around his neck that he was given credentials to be down on the field tonight. I'll make sure that's *swiftly* revoked.

"Hey, man, I think you have the wrong idea. I wasn't doing anything." His words are hurried.

"Your camera was angled up and pointed at two women ten yards away from you. The game is in the opposite direction.

Let's remember why you're here, shall we?" I gesture toward the field.

Men who don't respect women are the most despicable fuckers on earth. It really makes me want to take a fist to his face, but I know that isn't the answer, so I land on a different kind of blow.

"I hope you enjoyed the first half, buddy. You won't be around for the second." I sneer at him, walking away. I'm just steps away from Demi and Abby now.

"*What* was that?" Abby charges me, all five foot seven of her, and I peer down.

"Me saving your husband and brother from a suspension and a fine at the least. Charges at most. You're welcome."

My hands grip the sides of Abby's arms lightly and I kiss the top of her head as I pivot past. Demi doesn't say anything to me, but she watches me as I walk by, and I don't miss the subtle nod and faint smile she hands me as I do.

I can bounce back from a bad call, a bad mood, or even a bad day pretty quickly. I think it's part of some coping mechanism I learned as a kid. Letting myself sit in any kind of emotion was frowned upon—heavily. Even with success, when I'd win games or have a great day on the field, I was always told not to linger in the moments.

The text from my dad has sat unanswered for days now.

DAD

> If you think another passer rating like last year is going to get you where you want to be, you've got another thing coming. Work harder, Liam.

My dad has no fucking idea the personal work I've been

doing in the last few years to undo all the terrible shit he made me believe growing up. Now I try really hard to allow myself space for the emotions I feel. I still can bounce back and turn things around quickly, but if something upsets me, I'm learning to let myself understand the emotion instead of just tucking it away like it doesn't belong. Because what I feel is valid, even if I was raised to think the opposite.

I rarely complained as a kid, mostly because I knew that I was more fortunate than most. We had a nice home, fancy cars, any kind of toy we wanted, and the best resources at our fingertips. That's the shit I used to think meant you were rich.

Now, as an adult, I realize how little a fancy house and car mean.

There was no compassion in my home. No love, aside from the conditional type. Landyn would've been my dad's pride and joy on the football field if he hadn't broken his collarbone in high school. After that, my dad focused all his energy on me. For a while I resented my brother for it, but it wasn't his fault our dad was a fucking dick.

Any time I feel aggression over something, the years of frustration toward him come up too. It's like I want something else to be able to blame an outburst on, when in reality it's just thirty years of a shitty parent who needs the blame.

The bullshit at the game last night has been bothering me since. I just can't fucking believe there are men out there like that. I didn't hesitate in making sure that jerk lost his access, and I made a strong case for why he should lose his right to cameras too.

This morning, it's just me and Birdie. Just the two of us on the couch as the sun comes up and I sip my coffee. No television, no music, no Walt. She's purring as she lies on my abdomen, and I can feel the tickle of her whisker when she twitches.

I place my coffee on the end table to my right as I rub the back of her head by her ears. Somehow this little thing has weaseled her way right into my heart. She's like a comfort I never saw coming, but now feel so damn thankful to have.

My phone vibrates on the cushion beside me, and I glance at the screen only to be shocked by the name that pops up. Especially at seven in the morning.

GIRL OF MY DREAMS

I don't know if this is appropriate or not, but I feel the need to thank you for last night. You didn't have to say anything, but you did and I appreciate it.

Little does this woman know, I'd do absolutely anything for her.

CHAPTER SEVENTEEN

DEMI

I've reread my text to Liam six times in the last minute since I sent it. Should I have even sent it? Why the hell did I? I shouldn't actually want to talk to this man outside of my work requirements, yet here I am up for an hour contemplating whether or not to send it before I just said fuck it.

Something tells me, though, that Liam would've done that for anyone, it just happened to be me and one of his closest friends.

HOTSHOT QUARTERBACK

I just did what any gentleman should. No need to thank me, but come to think of it, I do enjoy cake.

I roll my eyes at his name coming up as Hotshot Quarterback. I should change it to his name, or something a little less ego boosting for him.

your nutrition plan calls for cake?

Liam's ability to make me shake my head while simultaneously blushing should be studied. Because what the actual *fuck*, Demi? I should really quit while I'm ahead here, but Liam is proving to be my blind spot when it comes to good choices.

Before I can reply, he sends another text.

I pull the comforter up to my chest as I nestle into the warmth of my bed. It's weird texting with Liam knowing he's right next door to me.

He's right, though, I couldn't sleep. I've been in and out of it all night, and for no particular reason other than I just couldn't settle myself.

My thoughts kept playing ping-pong and bouncing from one thing to the next. I hate when my nights are spent that way.

His body. God, I should not be picturing Liam's body. The man is handsome, like abnormally handsome. But it still doesn't mean I should be spending time thinking about him.

What I should be doing is getting up and making myself a well-balanced breakfast. I've been eating pastries for too long, and I just know what my sweet mother would tell me about needing to eat something healthier in the mornings. She's right, but it doesn't mean I want to hear her say it.

> I don't sleep in much either. Solidarity.

Before he can say anything to continue the conversation, I double text.

> I should find something for breakfast though.
> Have a good day 12.

I get up and pull my closet door open, flicking the light on inside. One eye scrunches shut to help adjust to the brightness and I let my head fall back, stretching my neck. My arms fan out on either side of me before I link them behind my back and pull for another stretch.

No work today, but I have a ton of emails I need to answer, and I really want to try the flan recipe I asked my mom to send me the other day. So at least I can be comfortable on my first full day of not having to leave the house.

I pull a pair of sweats on and opt to stay braless in my tank top. No one is seeing me today so there's no point in putting one on.

Leaving my closet, I grab my phone from the bed and peek at the screen, there's another text from Liam.

HOTSHOT QUARTERBACK

> can I borrow two eggs?

I huff out a laugh as I make my way to the kitchen. *Become my neighbor,* he said.

> Sure.

HOTSHOT QUARTERBACK

> Is it ok to come grab them now?

I tilt my head down at my braless tank and sigh. That was short-lived. Reaching for my sweater on the barstool, I pull it over my head and send him a thumbs-up text as I'm making myself some café con leche. It smells so good, and I swear it's an instant mood booster.

There's a rhythmic knocking on my door. Not a quick one, two, three. More like a beat. It's one, then a quick two, and another one. I wonder if he even knows he knocks like that.

I quickly glance in the mirror by my front door. Gray sweats, an oversized NFL sweater, and three-day old hair is about as good as it's getting this morning. I blow out a raspberry from my lips and unlock both locks on my door before opening it.

"You don't ask who's at your door before you answer it?" He arches a brow. No good morning. No hello. No type of pleasantry at all.

Liam, on the other hand, looks criminally good for just waking up. He too is in gray sweatpants, a treat for all women, honestly, paired with a light blue T-shirt with some fish in the top left corner. My stomach does that annoying flip when I make eye contact with him. His stupidly beautiful hazel eyes look so soft this morning. Nothing like the intensity they showed last night.

His hand pulls at his jaw, and I catch the way his forearm flexes as he does. He genuinely looks concerned that I opened the door without asking who was on the other side and it's equally sweet and annoying.

"I'm not expecting any visitors today so I knew it was you," I say as I pull the door open and walk back toward the fridge, grabbing the egg carton. "Plus, I don't know anyone else who wouldn't just knock like a normal *knock, knock, knock.*"

I hear a faint laugh as I'm in the kitchen, but I don't see him which means he's still standing outside my door.

"You should ask who's at your door. Even if it's a secure place, you should ask. Or have a doorbell camera." He projects his voice, another sign he's not actually in my apartment.

"You can come in," I say, taking two eggs from the carton and placing them on a napkin.

When I look up, Liam's waltzing around the corner, and I hear the door shut behind him.

"Do you have a doorbell camera?" I ask.

He nods, looking around. He hasn't been here since I've moved in.

"It smells so good in here." He inhales twice in a row, and I smile.

"It's probably this," I say, lifting my coffee cup to his nose. "My coffee."

"Wow, that's the coffee you're always drinking, isn't it? I recognize the smell."

I step back and feel my cheeks heat at those words. He recognizes the smell of my coffee. I place my cup on the counter and I don't miss how his eyes scan over me. There's a hint of a smile when he fully takes in my outfit and I place both hands on my hips and clear my throat.

"Yes." I smile. "Café con leche. Here are the eggs," I say, handing him the napkin gently.

"Oh," Liam replies, allowing me to place the eggs in his cupped hands. He inhales one more time like he's literally trying to hang on to the scent. "Thank you. I'll bring them back."

His mouth curves into a lazy, beautiful smile, and out of nowhere the next five words fly out of my mouth as if I'm not in control of my own actions.

"Do you want a cup?"

He seems just as shocked as me when he tilts his head and stares my way. *Dammit, Demi, what are you doing?* He was about to leave.

"Can I take it to go?"

I'm kicking myself for even offering. Of course he can't stay. This man probably has a million better things to do than slum it in my apartment with me this morning. But why does that bother me all of a sudden? On a normal day I'd never have even offered.

"I don't want you to think I don't want to stay. I do, *really*." He takes a step toward me. "It's just—" He raises his hand with the eggs.

"Right, of course, you're in the middle of something."

I shake my head, embarrassment creeping up my spine as I make him a quick cup to go.

"It's hot," I warn as I give him the cup. Both eggs are cradled in one hand, and I hate how my mind wonders how many more he could hold with the size of it.

"Thanks." He smiles as he walks toward the door and I open it.

There's a small, but likely, chance I curl up into a ball the rest of the day and replay this whole interaction, questioning my decisions because *what the actual fuck* was the last ten minutes?

Once Liam is out the door, I lock the door behind him and hear him say "thank you" from the hallway. His obsession with home security makes me laugh.

When I make my way back into the kitchen, I turn the dimmed lights up all the way, and I reach into the fridge to pull out the eggs again. Gathering all the ingredients I need for flan based on the list my mom sent me. She makes cooking seem so easy, but it's never been something I took much interest in. I'm sure something she wished was different, considering how much she loves this. But I've never been too much into the same things as my family. I'm proud of who I am and where my family comes from, but after thirty-five years, I've really come to be okay with the fact that I'm not like my mom in a lot of ways. Something that, at first, was hard on both of us, but now we've never been closer.

As I'm whipping the eggs, my thoughts drift to what Liam needed his eggs for. Is he baking? Does he cook? I sigh to myself and refocus on the bowl in front of me. The text from my mom says not to whip the eggs too much and I need to focus on that, not Liam. I should *not* care about his life outside of football.

It's been easy to find myself so comfortable with him though, a feeling I've not had in so long. Maybe that's why something internally is wanting to be around him more. I've been in fight or flight mode for so long and my nervous system has been craving peace and calm for years.

I just can't fucking believe I feel it most with Liam Evans.

CHAPTER EIGHTEEN

LIAM

I finally hear Demi's lock click on her door after standing in the hallway for a handful of seconds waiting. Having her so close to me has my protective instincts working on overdrive, and I'm tempted to do something crazy like buy her a doorbell camera.

The thought lingers in my mind before I close and lock my own door, placing the eggs and coffee from Demi on the counter.

Jesus, she looked beautiful this morning, but I could tell she thought the opposite. I can read Demi so fucking well, it surprises even me sometimes. Sweatpants, no makeup, hair up in a messy bun, and the sweater swallowing her whole. A fancy dress is great, but a low-key, just woke up on a Sunday morning kind of look stirs something inside of me.

When Demi texted that she needed to find something to eat for breakfast, I immediately thought of making her my signature omelet. I don't cook often, and it isn't because I don't like to cook—I simply don't like cooking for one.

Most of my meals are from delivery services—single-serve meals and snacks packed with protein and all the things I need for whatever current plan I'm on. But I'd love to have a reason to cook more. I'm no Nate in the kitchen, but I fucking love food and have always enjoyed trying out new things.

Birdie is perched on the small table I put next to the sliding glass door. It gives her a good view of the outside while also making her feel bigger—I think—when she's facing off with the bird. I realized the moment I moved the table that I'm way too invested in my cat's life, but I can't have her feeling inferior when they're having a standoff.

I take a sip from the coffee Demi sent me home with and let my head fall back after I swallow. I've never had coffee like this and it's fucking insane how good it is. My black coffee is getting some serious competition lately.

Rummaging through my fridge, I take out all the things I need for this omelet. Green peppers, ham, and onions, along with cheese and all the spices I know work well together. It's been forever since I've had one of these myself, but the Denver omelet is something I've been eating and making since I was a kid.

I take five minutes to chop up the peppers, ham, and onions, and then toss them into the skillet to let it all cook together before adding the eggs. It's literally the easiest kind of food to make, but also easy to fuck up.

After a few moments, it's done and plated, and I add a piece of toasted sourdough bread to the dish before heading back to my door.

"I'll be right back again," I say to Birdie as the door shuts behind me.

When I was at Demi's thirty minutes ago, I noticed some baking items on her counter, but nothing looked omelet related so I think I'm in the clear bringing this over. At least, I hope I am. I've been paying attention to Demi for years. I've seen her eat egg sandwiches, different pastries, and plenty of cookies that have eggs in them so there's no concern about any allergies.

I tap on her door in a rhythm and hear music coming from

the other side. I can't really make out what type of music it is, but it sounds upbeat so that's a good sign. There's a shuffle on the other side of the door, and I open my mouth to speak, but she beats me to it.

"Who is it?" she asks in a teasing tone, and my smile instantly spreads.

"Your neighbor."

Demi pulls the door open with a smile of her own. She's still wearing the same thing she had on earlier, except now I see the sleeves of her sweater are rolled up. Her hands are ring-free and polish-free—a difference from the black nail polish she usually wears.

"I knew it was you. I checked the peephole this time," she says as she looks up at me and then notices the plate in my hand covered with Saran Wrap. "Oh." She pauses, tilting her head as she stares at the food.

"Told you I'd bring the eggs back." I shrug, stuffing my free hand into the pocket of my sweats.

"You…you made me an omelet?" The shock in her voice burns a hole in my chest. This woman is constantly surprised when someone does a nice thing for her, and it makes me want to run a fist into anyone who ever made her feel like doing something as simple as making her an omelet was a burden.

"Yeah, I'm known for my omelets."

She smirks and I lower the dish to hand it to her.

"Oh yeah? By who?"

"The great state of Colorado."

Demi nods as she smiles, looking down at the plate.

"I hope you like green peppers. That was the one thing I wasn't completely confident in."

Her head snaps up and she softly narrows her eyes at me. She tilts her chin down and then nods as if to say yes while the corner of her lip curves up.

She doesn't invite me in and honestly, I don't need her to. I just wanted to do something for her. I take a step away from her doorway. "Don't let it get cold, Dem. Go eat."

"Thank you, Liam." Her words are practically a whisper.

"Welcome to the building." I smile, walking away.

I've only seen Demi in passing around the facility a couple of times since last weekend. She's been busy and so have I.

"Look at that fancy new watch," I call out to Alex Farr, one of my teammates. "Someone's using their extension money wisely." I wink.

"Almost bought a boat, but ended up with a watch. I'd say that's a smart financial decision."

"I don't know, man. I love my boat."

"Exactly." He chuckles, buttoning his shirt after practice. "*You* have a boat. Why spend my own money when my quarterback has one?"

"That's my philosophy," Ford chimes in as he strides up with a towel around his waist.

"Get dressed, no one else is walking around like this. What do you think this is?" I tease.

Ford flips me the finger, and Alex walks past me as he's heading out.

"Mind if I leave a jersey for my niece?" he asks, motioning to the spare black chair next to mine.

I glance at it, noting another couple jerseys, a few hats, pictures, and an array of other objects scattered around.

"Go for it."

"Thanks, man. She's been bugging me. I figure I need some cool uncle points."

I laugh. "I got you, big man."

He palms my shoulder before he walks out, and I take my time changing while the rest of the team hurries out of the locker room. Today was our last practice before the regular season and in all the years I've been playing, I don't think I've ever been hungrier to get into a game.

The adrenaline. The noise. The stadium and the fans. It rips through me in the best way possible. No matter what's been going on in my life I've always felt the most alive under the lights and I'm ready for that feeling again.

I usually get bored during the offseason. I'd spend time going on meaningless dates, vacations for no reason other than to pass the time. But these last few months I haven't wanted to do any of that.

It's nearly five, and more than half of the guys are already gone, with the remaining few about to leave. Practice ended around three thirty, and between conversations, social media shenanigans, and outfit changes it usually takes the guys around an hour to clear out.

One afternoon last year, I had a teammate ask me to sign some hats for his kids, and I asked him to just put them on the empty chair near mine. Somehow that ended up becoming "the chair," and now every so often I'll have a teammate or a staff member leave something there they want signed for someone. I joke about it sometimes, but honestly? It kind of chokes me up thinking that I get to do this—I'm just a kid from Boulder who likes to play football.

I play hard and I work hard, and I'm fucking honored that anyone even wants my autograph, let alone enough people to have me set aside time every now and then to sign it all. I'm blessed, and I know that. But I also know I put in the work and I take a lot of pride in that.

No one outside this locker room knows I do this. Not my dad, not the media, no one. I don't do it for any superficial attention or a pat on the back for signing autographs. It's literally part of what I signed up for when I took this job, I don't need a thank you for that.

I hit shuffle on my phone, letting the playlist shuffle through everything from blink-182 to Britney Spears. A song hums into the AirPod I have in one ear, and I pull the first thing that catches my eye to sign.

It's one of my college football jerseys. Talk about a blast from the past. I hold it up in front of me as I stand, admiring the gold and green colors with the number twelve on the chest. Fuck, I loved playing college football. I think my time in college is what really solidified it for me. I got to play with a coach outside of my dad. Someone who truly made the game feel fun again.

Before I can spend too much time on nostalgia, I take a seat and grab the Sharpie from my duffle bag and sign it. I easily work my way through a handful of things from jerseys, photos, and a couple of hats, keeping myself focused on the task at hand.

"Oh god, I'm sorry." Demi's calming voice pulls my attention from the music, and I turn my head up to her. "I'm looking for Kelsea. I was told she was back here, I'm so sorry for intruding, they said all the players were gone," she says.

Kelsea is the athletic trainer, but she left hours ago.

"Hey, Dem." I grin. "Kelsea already left for the day, something I can help you with?" I position my entire body toward her as I stand.

Her dark brown curls cascading down both sides of her collarbone with the prettiest brown eyes I've ever seen popping as she stares at me.

"Why are you still here?" She seems to put two and two together as her eyes shift to the marker in my hand and the pile of items to my right. "Are you signing things?"

I nod, swaying my hand in the air like it's nothing. "I stay late sometimes and do it for the guys. It's no big deal."

Demi's shoulder dips, and I watch her body nearly slouch as she hears what I'm saying.

"You're staying late to sign things for the guys?"

"Despite you calling me a hotshot quarterback, I do have a heart you know, and am happy to do things for people."

"I never assumed you didn't have a heart," she says, her voice barely above a whisper. "I'm just..." The pause in her reply has me taking a step toward her.

"Just what?"

"I'm constantly surprised by you, Liam."

CHAPTER NINETEEN

DEMI

My eyes can't focus long enough on one thing as my mind jumps back and forth between the signed items, the spare chair, the grin on Liam's face, and his massive hand making the Sharpie look like something Santa's tiny elves would use.

"Happy to keep you on your toes." He smiles again before he turns back to what he was doing.

"Yeah." I let out a soft chuckle. "Okay, well, sorry to bother you," I say, ushering myself out.

"Never a bother, Dem."

I quickly dart down the hall and as far from the locker room as possible. In looking for the athletic trainer, I stumbled upon Liam doing another kind thing that resulted in butterflies in my stomach. A man being a generous, decent human shouldn't turn me into a pile of mush—but lately that's how every interaction with Liam is ending.

He seriously stays late to sign things for his teammates? Disbelief wants to cloud my mind, but I saw it firsthand. He had a pile—a large one—of things with his quick signature.

I've learned over the years that Liam is a team player, but there's absolutely *nothing* that says the athletes have to sign autographs. In fact, there are often cases where the players have to be mindful of what they're signing. Sometimes if they have contractual obligations—that often limits their ability.

With every step I take, the pain in my hip intensifies. Who knows what the hell happened, but that was my reason for needing to see Kelsea today. I just got back from a quick forty-eight-hour trip to Los Angeles, and when I woke up this morning —insanely jetlagged, might I add—it was killing me. The internet was helpful in some remedies, but I figured chatting with an actual professional, rather than just people on the internet, might be best.

Plus, I try to limit my time online anyway. I understand it's part of life now and it isn't going anywhere, but I still hate that it can take up so much of our time.

Blocking out the noise and comments from strangers online is easier said than done. The comments that make me laugh the most, though, are those that come from men bitching about the game recaps I do. Little do they know, I'm just repeating—word for word, usually—what the coach has told me.

One of my favorite comments I've ever seen was about how terrible my broadcast was, but my outfit was "pretty good." Cheryl and I had a laugh about that one.

Being in reporting can be hard. Being a woman in reporting is even harder. But being a woman in sports reporting? I might as well have a sign on my chest that says PLEASE QUESTION EVERY-THING I SAY.

I love my job and I always have. My team is incredible, and every single player and coach I work with are wonderful. But you'll always have the people on the outside who hate every-thing you do, especially when you do it well. And to those people, I raise my perfectly polished middle finger.

I watch the final play of the game as Mason Baker drills a forty-one-yard field goal to break the tie and secure the first win of the season for the Knights.

Holy shit, what a game that was. Talk about a season-opener.

The time winds down, and I make sure I'm prepped and ready to grab Liam on the field for a quick postgame report. I spot him as he's walking away from the sidelines, hands clapping together before pointing at his kicker and smiling.

His pads make him look so much bulkier than he truly is. He doesn't seem that tall from a distance, but when he gets closer, his six-foot-two frame starts to show. He has a towel in one hand that he wipes his brow with once he approaches me.

We have a minute before we're live, and instead of standing in silence, I opt for a quick compliment. Because, honestly? His finesse on the field today was damn near magical. He's got to be feeling good after those stats.

"Feeling good today, Twelve?" A smile passes over my face as I ask.

Liam closes some of the professional distance between us with an easy step forward, leaning down just the slightest bit toward my ear. "Always good with you, baby."

Baby? I swivel my head in his direction and notice he's already back to his three-feet buffer stance.

Why'd he call me baby? And why'd I kind of enjoy it?

It wouldn't be my first pick as a term of endearment, but rolling off his lips it actually makes me like it.

But it's adrenaline. That has to be it. Full-fledged, great win kind of adrenaline that's coursing through his veins. Because in no universe would Liam call me baby on a football field, moments before I need to conduct an interview. I'm thankful he didn't do it while we were live—I can only imagine the color my cheeks turned after that exchange.

One of the guys on the camera crew points to me, giving the go ahead, and I begin.

"And there you have it. A wild one to start the season, what a back and forth game that was. After starting your first two possessions three and out, what'd you say to the guys to get them fired up?"

Liam's eye black is smeared almost down to his chin from sweat. But he stands next to me in a red and black jersey with a smile as guys come up behind him during the interview and slap his shoulders. He doesn't take his focus off our conversation, and I note the small scrape on his throwing hand when he runs it through his sweat-soaked hair. A battle wound, I'm sure.

"Four quarters, sixty minutes. Plenty of time to hang in there and fight, and that's exactly what this team did. I'm so proud of our guys. Everyone stepped up when we needed them to." Liam's tongue quickly coats his lips and he gives someone on the field a quick nod.

"Do you think this game kind of sets the tone for the season? It was a tough-fought battle."

"Yeah, I mean, our mission here is to win. It's what we want to do and something we know we're capable of. It wasn't perfect, I'm sure when we get into the tape on Monday we'll see plenty of things to clean up. I know a few of my reads could have been better. But it's a good day when we win the game."

"For sure. Congrats, Liam. Thank you."

"Thank you," he says as he pivots away from me.

As if he knows my eyes are still on him, he turns quickly, giving me a quick smile and a wink.

What the hell is happening? First, he makes me breakfast—which was actually incredible and I even looked up how to remake it myself—then he calls me baby, and now he's winking at me?

How am I supposed to be annoyed by him in these conditions?

As I'm walking away from the field and to the exit, all I'm thinking is at least I don't have to see him tomorrow.

But then the reminder that he's my neighbor creeps in, and I blow out a very, very audible sigh.

CHAPTER TWENTY

LIAM

Time moves fast during the season, and it feels like the only time I really sit with nothing going on is early in the morning. Or in Dana's office.

She just redid the interior, giving the whole space so much more light with the retractable shades she keeps open. The view isn't anything to write home about, but natural light will boost my mood any day of the week.

Every piece of furniture looks new, down to the wastebasket in the corner of the room.

"Like what you've done with the place," I say, offering a smile as I take a seat.

"Thank you. This room was overdue for a makeover." She gathers her notebook from her desk and comes to sit at the large beige chair beside the couch I'm seated on.

The room smells like cinnamon, and I notice a candle warmer on one of the bookshelves, likely the culprit.

"What a nice start to the season too. How have you been since we last saw each other?" Her right leg crosses over her left knee and she sits up straighter in the chair.

Where the fuck do I begin?

My dream girl moved in next door. My dad is still sending me aggressive text messages. The bird is still fucking with my cat. And the deli on Fourth discontinued my favorite sandwich, claiming it was just seasonal for the summer.

"I've been busy," I say. It's the truth. "I'm still working on a few things we talked about last month. With…you know, emotions and stuff like that." I sway my hand in the air with a shake of my head.

"Processing them." She nods. "And allowing yourself to feel those emotions without them consuming you. Most importantly, knowing that it's okay to feel things."

She jots something quick in the notebook, and I lean back on the cushion, pulling both hands behind my neck in a stretch.

"Right," I reply.

"What else?"

Dana is a nice woman, but she's no fucking nonsense. She hears me out and offers her guidance, but she isn't here to let me skate around what's going on. I appreciate her approach now more than I did in the beginning.

"I have a new neighbor," I say, adjusting in my seat again.

"That's great news."

"It's a…colleague." The words are hesitant. It isn't up to me to share where Demi lives so I leave out the specifics.

"Oh. Is that a problem for you?"

Technically, no. But emotionally, yes.

Because I *want* Demi. I want her on a level I know isn't widely accepted, and I don't even know what to do about it.

"Can I be honest here?"

"I'd prefer it if you were," she says with a light chuckle.

"I'm having a hard time, uh, emotionally, I guess?" I shake my head back and forth and lean forward—elbows to knees. "I don't have a lot of people in my personal life that I share things with. I mean, I have my friends, but they really don't know *everything*. The thoughts that swirl in my head sometimes, the hopelessness, and then just complete...sadness. It's—I don't even know what it is, but I feel like I can't tell anybody. Which feels crazy, because normally I don't shut up." I sit in silence, thinking of how I want to formulate the next few sentences. I've been having this new feeling the last few weeks when it comes to Demi.

Reliance is the word that comes to mind.

I've known her a long time, but never deep enough to gauge how she might handle my past. The last few weeks have given me a glimpse, and it's like something in my bones just knows that every ugly secret and skeleton would be safe with her. And it makes me want to open up to her. To tell her things I don't tell anyone else.

I talk to Chase and Summer about a lot of things. Summer probably knows the most, but still not everything. I don't really know how that happened—especially because when we first met, I was absolutely hitting on her. She turned me down quickly and it was clear her intentions were set on Chase from the get-go.

"There was an incident at one of the preseason games." I clear my throat. "Well, an almost incident, I guess. Anyway, I wanted to just unload my emotions on this little piece of crap photographer who was on the sidelines. I reined it in and kept my cool as best I could, given the situation and where we were. I knew I was bothered by what was going on, but it's like the second I feel any kind of frustration, I know part of the feeling is misdirected. I hold onto so much repressed bull-shit from my dad that I think it comes out any time something upsets me."

Dana takes her notebook from her lap and places it on the table. She leans a little farther in.

"You're learning how to process emotions in a healthy way, Liam. You haven't mastered it yet. You're allowed to be angry, bothered, upset—all those things. Learning how to regulate your emotions is part of generational healing."

I nod, feeling a lump the size of a basketball forming in my throat.

"You've mentioned in the past that you've typically dealt with your sadness or frustrations by completely shutting down, pushing the feeling away at the first sign of being upset."

I nod again.

"You are allowed to be frustrated. You are allowed to be sad. Those are natural feelings. And you're learning that it's okay to show them in a healthy way. It's progress." Dana nods, lifting the corners of her mouth into a soft, sincere smile.

Her eye contact is steady and her voice is too.

The rest of the session creeps by. It feels like the longest hour of my life any time I have to talk about my feelings and emotions, and I'm completely drained when I leave, but I also feel like the biggest weight has been lifted.

<hr>

"Toasty one out there," I say in a huff to Rob.

I decided to take a walk this evening, thinking it might be a good way to get some fresh air, forgetting there's no such thing as a nice evening walk during a Florida summer.

"Got that right." He tilts back in his chair with the shake of his head. "If ya hurry, you'll be able to catch a ride so you don't have to wait."

"Wait for what?"

He tips his chin, and I see the private access door swing shut.

"Demi?" My eyes light up and I've forgotten all about the exhaustion I was just feeling from the heat.

He gives me a knowing nod, and I make a beeline for the door. Even stepping it up to a little jog.

I haven't seen Demi all week. I was in Philadelphia, but this week we're home, and boy oh boy, am I excited to have her in the crowd. Even if she's contractually obligated to be there.

I hear the elevator doors open as I'm briskly walking toward them and pick up my pace slightly again. There's a scent of coffee trailing her, and I can't help but smile, knowing she's probably got a coffee in her hand at four in the afternoon again.

The doors begin to close, and I can see her frame tightly in the corner of the elevator looking down at her phone as I quickly place my hand between the two doors and they begin to backtrack.

Her head lifts up and her eyes connect with mine, confusion and surprise written all over her face.

"Hey, Dem," I say as the doors open up the space between us.

CHAPTER TWENTY-ONE

DEMI

I'm exhausted. Completely and utterly exhausted. There's still no real excuse for getting a coffee this late in the day, when I could just go to sleep in a couple hours and get some rest. But when I have a craving, I have this rule about giving in.

It applies to everything in my life. Well—*almost* everything.

I've been trying to avoid seeing Liam outside of work obligations lately. The last two interactions we've had have left me with silly butterflies and confused brain fog, and I refuse to let his kindness and charms cloud my judgment.

This past weekend, I reactivated the dating app I had downloaded out of spite right after my divorce. I still doubt I'll actually go on any dates, but swiping left and right on whether or not I'd let random men take me to dinner helped clear my mind of the Liam-sized thoughts I kept finding myself having. Maybe if I didn't keep finding him doing kind and generous things, I wouldn't have been betrayed by my own mind with thoughts of him.

The walk back to the apartment is quick, and I smile at Rob as I walk through the doors.

"Here you go, I added some cold foam to the top this time. I think you'll like it," I say as I hand a coffee to him.

He's been so gracious since I've moved into the building, always asking about my day, how things are going. He even shared some of his wife's chocolate chip cookies with me when I mentioned they're my favorite.

He works the overnight shift a couple times a week, so when I'm able, I've been bringing him coffee and stopping to chat for a few minutes.

"Look at that," he says, grinning at the cup. "Is that a little sprinkle of cinnamon on the top? Thank you."

"Sure is." I tap the counter between us a couple times as I smile back at him.

His blue-gray eyes meet mine as he takes a sip and hums. The pocket of his collared shirt has a pin on it that I always notice. It's different every time he's working. Sometimes it's something silly, like a banana wearing sunglasses. Others, it's a team—like the Knights. Today, it's a goose that says "silly," and I can't help but smile.

"Silly goose, I love it." I point to his pin.

He chuckles. "Oh, my granddaughter gave me this. She won it from some school fundraiser and gifted it to me."

"It's amazing," I say. "Have a good night, Rob."

"You too," he calls back as I make my way toward the elevators.

I enter the hallway and make my way down the short stretch. The doors to the elevators open right away and I step in, taking a sip from my drink. I don't anticipate anyone else in the hallway and I reach toward the buttons, pressing the close door option, and take a step back into the corner.

My phone dings as I do and I pull it out to see a notification from one of those apps I reinstalled. Before I have time to read the entire notification, I feel the abrupt stop of the doors and watch as they reopen, noticing a gold ring on a familiar pinky finger as the doors spread apart.

Liam.

"Hey, Dem." The greeting rolls off his lips in a smooth tone.

I feel myself swallow as I look at him for a beat. He's infuriatingly beautiful. And not only that, he's charming and he's full of life. He's quite the opposite of everything I think I emulate these days. Maybe that's why I'm drawn to him more and more lately. Although that's not something I'm very interested in admitting outside of my own thoughts.

"Liam, hi," I rush out.

His large body moves into the elevator, taking up half of the space and apparently all the air as my lungs instantly feel constricted.

I inhale a shaky breath as he stands beside me, hands placed over one another in front of him. He smirks as he catches me with a sly side eye and I clench my jaw. Can't believe I just let him see me react that way.

"How are you?"

I take a tiny step back, forcing myself even more into the corner. "I'm good, how are you?"

A slow smile builds on his face.

"I'm great, thank you," he says, not looking directly at me.

My fingers fidget on the hem of my shirt as I attempt conversation. "How's your elbow?"

I saw a recap where he took a nasty sack, and it looked like his elbow took the brunt of the hit.

He turns toward me, hazel eyes staring directly into mine. The white shirt on his back hugging his shoulders and biceps like a perfectly-sized glove. He extends his arm to the side, an obvious way to showcase how toned he is, and twists his arm. He bends it and rubs the outer part of his forearm near the elbow.

"Working great. Thank you for asking," he says, lifting the corner of his mouth into another smile.

I nod, glancing at the elevator screen. Should I be concerned we haven't reached our floor yet? I mean, what the hell is taking this thing so long? It doesn't ever take this long.

"Almost there," he coos as if he read my thoughts.

"Yeah, doesn't it seem like it's taking a long time?" I blurt out.

Liam's Adam's apple bobs as he tilts his head down with a chuckle.

"Can't stand being alone in an elevator with me, Dem?"

Alone in a closed box with the way my brain has been playing dumb when it comes to him—yeah, probably not the place I should be.

"No, this is awful." I tilt my head at him.

His hand clenches his chest as he makes a pained—yet sarcastic—sound.

My phone dings in my hand, and I attempt to silence it, but it doesn't deter Liam from darting his eyes to my hand.

He says nothing as it dings for a second time, and I shove it into my bag on my shoulder.

"Popular," he finally says.

He would be physically unable to say nothing.

I shake my head at him. "You have no idea."

His scoff is cut short by the sound of the elevator doors opening on our floor.

"After you." He extends his hand, gesturing for me to walk out first.

"Thank you."

His footsteps are heavy behind me, and I do my best to walk at a pace that keeps up with his long strides so I'm not holding him up. I pass his apartment on the way to mine, and just before I'm at my door I hear him call my name.

I turn my head to see him standing outside his door, keys in his hands as he looks down at them and then up at me.

"What are you doing for dinner?"

My eyes widen and I freeze in place.

"Uh, I hadn't gotten that far yet. My train of thought ended here." I hold up the cup of hot coffee in my hand.

Liam shifts on his feet, taking a few slow steps my way.

"Let me get us dinner." He tips his chin up in my direction. "You have no plans. I have no plans. Sounds like we need each other."

"Um." I nearly stutter the simplest word. "Y-yeah, that would be okay," I say, scratching a non-existent itch on my neck.

His tongue darts between his lips before he smiles, backpedaling a few steps.

"Have you had Alba's Kitchen?"

My eyebrows crease. "What?"

"Alba's Kitchen—have you had their food before?"

"Yes." I tilt my head.

Honestly, I'm surprised *he's* even familiar with Alba's. It's a small family-owned Dominican restaurant a few blocks down from here. Incredible mangú and their tostones are so good. Almost as good as my mom's.

He smiles as he nods. "Meet me on the roof in an hour." He moves toward his door. "Please," he says as a follow up.

"Okay. Sure."

I just agreed to have a rooftop dinner with Liam—from one of my favorite restaurants no less. So much for trying to avoid thinking about him.

CHAPTER TWENTY-TWO

LIAM

Every time I pass Alba's Kitchen on a walk or a run, I think of Demi. I've thought about taking her here a thousand times. And it's the first place that popped into my mind when I suggested we have dinner tonight.

Pulling up the menu on my phone, I skim through the section labeled *Alba's Favorites* and decide to order a handful of different things to try. I haven't had a lot of the food I just ordered, but I definitely love to try everything at least once. Plus, I know I've seen Demi with an empanada in her hand on multiple occasions, and really, you can't go wrong with an empanada.

After placing the order, I grab two giant blankets from the hall closet and as many pillows as I can carry, shove my phone into my pocket along with my keys, and make my way to the roof.

I come up here a lot in the summer—especially lately. With all my friends coupled up, a lot of my evenings are spent alone. It would be easy to find company, but I don't want just *any* company. I stopped wanting something casual, meaningless, and unfulfilling. Seeing all the people I love the most find a partner to spend their time with made me realize that's actually something I want too.

Don't get me wrong, I am thrilled for Ford and Abby—even though she took my number one wingman away from me. And with Nate and Mia, it was only a matter of time for them to get their heads out of their asses. Summer really could've had just about any man she laid her eyes on, but I watched how she tirelessly loved Chase—and CeCe—for years, before Chase finally came to his fucking senses.

I've sat back for the last few years watching all my friends fall in love. I didn't think I was ready for it for a while. A long while, to be honest. The only woman I ever really wanted to see me—couldn't.

But I feel like I have a second chance. A window of time to prove to her that I'm not who people think I am—and I really don't want to blow it.

"Thank you so much, I'll be right down." I end the call after Rob tells me my food is here.

He offered to bring it up, but there's no way I'm having that man trek up the elevator and then hike up stairs and out here when I'm perfectly capable.

When I glance at my watch, I have about ten minutes until Demi should be up here. That is, unless she completely ghosts me. I hadn't considered that until this very second, and now I'm fucking spiraling as I head down to the lobby.

"Awful lot of food you've got here. Is this what they call carb-loading before a big game?" Rob chuckles when he sees me walking toward him.

I smile, reaching for the bags on the counter and begin hanging them from my forearm so I don't have to make multiple trips.

"She likes this place," he says softly, tipping his chin down as he moves back around to the center of his desk. "I've seen her order it a couple of times. You did good."

I'm silent for a moment before he speaks again.

"I'm an old man, Mr. Evans. I can recognize a man enamored by a woman the way you are from a mile away."

I don't try to hide the smile as he takes a seat in his chair, leaning back.

"Go on," he says, flipping his hand at me. "Have a good night, Mr. Evans."

"Call me Liam." I nod graciously at him.

He smiles, lifting his glasses from the end of his nose, and directs his attention back to the door.

I swallow hard as I'm standing over the blankets and pillows I've set up in the shady corner up here when my phone dings.

GIRL OF MY DREAMS

Just to clarify… you're actually on the roof?

I let out a laugh, knowing she's probably just making sure I wasn't fucking with her. Instead of a simple yes, I pull up my camera and take a selfie with the downtown skyline in the background and send it to her. The moment it says *Read*, I imagine her rolling her eyes, and damn, if that doesn't get me going.

A few moments later I hear the door close and turn to see Demi walking toward me.

She's so pretty. The kind of pretty that owns a room whenever she walks in—no matter where she is.

It's the first thing that crosses my mind the second I see her. She's changed into a pair of black leggings and a dark gray T-shirt with a distressed dragon on the front. Likely a nod to some of the books she says she reads.

"Hi," I say, taking a few steps closer to her.

"Oh, wow." She looks around at the setup behind me.

Take-out containers set up on the blanket next to a couple of waters and pillows.

"Just a few things."

She stammers a little as she sits on one of the pillows. "A few?" She laughs. "Looks like you ordered one of everything." I smile, taking a seat opposite her. "Also, feels worth noting that a yes or even a thumbs-up emoji would suffice. You didn't need to send a selfie."

"Yeah, but now you have a picture of me on your phone whenever you want to see my face. I gave you my best smile."

"Your face is on the building I work at." She opens the take-out container and grabs something to add to her plate of food. "I could do without the selfie, no matter how nice the scenery was."

"Thank you."

She sighs as she holds back a smile with her teeth. "I meant the skyline, the—the view *behind* you."

My head tilts back slightly. "Oh, you hurt me, Dem," I say, staring directly at her as I smirk. "I love it."

"Unbelievable," she mutters, but I see her fighting the smile.

I'm still shocked she agreed to meet me up here, but I've decided the best way for Demi to get to know me is by spending time with me, and what better way to do that than over food?

"I've never had this before." I lift up the toston in my hand and take another bite. And I've been missing out, because this shit is good.

"They're good, right? This place makes them perfectly. They're one of my favorite foods."

I nod as I take another one from the container. "Really fucking good. That's good too," I say, gesturing to the box to her right.

"Mm-hmm," she says between bites. "I love how flavorful the chicken is."

We pass around a few containers, each taking more than

enough food to feed us, and just watch the clouds move in the sky.

It's warm, but this part of the rooftop is well shaded, and since our floor is private access from other tenants, the roof is too. For someone who isn't too big on heights, the roof has never really bothered me.

"Thanks for getting all of this." Demi wipes the corner of her mouth with a napkin after taking a sip of water. "What do I owe you? I can send it now or do cash."

"Nothing."

"I don't expect you to buy me dinner."

"I know you don't."

"So, can I please pay you? I'm able to pay my half."

I brush my hands off and lean back into one of the pillows against the wall.

"Dem, I know you're able to. I offered to grab dinner, let me do one nice thing for you."

"You've done a lot of nice things for me lately, Liam." Her voice is low.

"That a bad thing?"

I watch the wind rustle the wisps of her hair that frame her face and she tucks them behind her ear, but it's no use with the breeze.

"Undecided," she says firmly.

"I like doing things for people, especially you." I shrug and lean a little closer to her.

There isn't much space between us on this blanket, but I swear it feels like she's miles away from me.

A moment of silence passes and then another as I watch Demi battle her inner turmoil over me refusing to take her money. I don't know all the reasons she's so fucking guarded and reluctant to let me do anything nice for her, but I'm sure it has a lot to do with her divorce.

"Have you ever had flan?" She finally breaks the silence, and I don't miss her scoot a bit closer.

"I have, it's great."

She nods, a soft smile spreading over her lips. "I'll repay you in flan. I make it. Well, I've made it before. It's my mom's recipe so it isn't *as* good as hers, but it's still pretty good. I like to try her recipes whenever I can—which isn't often, but this is one my mom and abuela both made often growing up."

"Did your mom cook a lot when you were growing up?"

She nods again. "All the time. I really think making us food was her love language."

"That's awesome," I admit.

"Did yours?"

I shake my head, noticeably crinkling my face together. "My mom wasn't a big cook. She had a couple dishes that she made on rotation every so often, but for the most part, there was a chef who cooked, and it was very much catered to my dad's wants."

Memory flashes of a pan of lemon pepper chicken with roasted potatoes and ears of corn. My favorite thing my mom used to make, even if it wasn't anything groundbreaking. I fucking loved it. But it wasn't something we had too often. Our lives were so busy when we were young. Between my dad's career and my sports, it was rare we spent more than two nights a week together as a family for dinner.

"Well, still, I bet those few dishes were amazing." Demi smiles at me with a tiny look of pity, and I hate it.

The pity part, not the smile. Because goddamn, I'd do anything to see those dimples on display like that.

"So are you all settled in?" I haven't seen the inside of her apartment since the day I borrowed eggs.

"Yeah, I think so. I should probably get some more glasses and plates, things like that. But honestly I don't host anything, and—as pathetic as it sounds—I don't really have friends around here that I'd invite over, so I guess maybe I don't need them."

She chuckles, and this time it's me who offers the smile laced with a small amount of pity.

"It isn't pathetic. I hate hosting. I'll be someone's dinner guest every night of the week, but I want my space to be…I don't know, *mine*." I shrug, feeling a little odd I just said all that out loud.

"At least you have friends you can hang out with, though."

"You want 'em?" I laugh. "Seriously, take the girls."

"Wow." Her eyes shine as she laughs. "How would they feel knowing you're so easily giving them away?"

"They'd understand."

We exchange smiles again, and I feel like she finally settles. There's no stiffness to her anymore, no pauses to make carefully thought-out sentences. She's just *being*.

"That's kind of how I've always felt, though—going back to your last point about your home just being your space. I've always been a homebody, and I mean, I love socializing when I feel like it, but being able to come home to a quiet house is so good for me."

"Right?"

"Kind of surprised you aren't the one hosting all your gatherings, though." She raises a brow to me.

"At this point, it's probably easier for my friends to host, especially those with kids. But even before that—Chase always did the poker nights, Ford did a lot of the barbeques, and Nate and I kind of rotated for chill hangouts. I've never had a party here. Despite whatever the rumor mill might like to say about me, I'm not actually a wild party animal."

She eyes me intently, seemingly surprised we're so alike on this topic.

"So, you didn't have the idea to throw two footballs at the same time to two separate moving Jet Skis over the summer? Or was that one just a crazy rumor?"

"No." I laugh, and she starts to shake her head as she smirks. "That was all me." I proudly grin.

CHAPTER TWENTY-THREE

DEMI

Liam's cheeks turn a light shade of pink as he smiles proudly over his summer moment that was somehow deemed newsworthy, ending up on a few sites.

I'll admit I watched the video a couple of times. For the throw. Not for the footage of him shirtless on a boat in the sun.

"I've got good ball placement with a moving target." He runs a hand over his jaw, and I follow the movement, but shake my head out of it.

I refuse to let myself get caught up in the beautiful exterior. He is handsome. I let myself admit that—daily, it seems. But I can't let that distract me.

"It would appear you do."

He smiles at me. Again. And it cuts me deeper every single time. It'd be easier to stay annoyed with him if he wasn't also one of the nicest humans on the planet.

His smiles are genuine. They're intentional. He doesn't half-ass them. He's all in when he's showing you his joy, and it pulls me in a little more every time.

"So, you're happy living here, though? That's great." He circles back to our original topic.

"I am. I actually really like it."

"Actually?" He laughs. "Did you expect to hate it?"

"I just didn't know what to expect, honestly. Moving in here included a lot of..." I inhale a deep breath and hold it in for a few seconds before finishing. "Firsts," I finally say.

Pulling my legs into a crisscross position, I lean back on my palms.

Liam's outstretched leg is almost touching my knee. He takes up so much space and rather than it feeling invading, it feels secure. It makes *me* feel secure.

"What kind of firsts?" he asks.

I find myself staring at his legs. He's more muscular than I ever thought. In all fairness, I don't see many of the athletes I work with in shorts. But his thighs are thick and defined.

"Only if you want to," he assures me.

"It's fine," I say. "I've never lived alone." Embarrassment wants to creep down my spine. Thirty-five and never lived alone, is that normal? But the way Liam's looking at me makes me think—hope, almost—that I'd be able to say anything and he'd never judge me.

It's a major contrast to how I began feeling in my marriage. My feelings felt like a burden. My wants felt unimportant. I questioned myself way more often as time went on and somehow began to feel inadequate with Brandon. Like I was no longer enough for him.

"It's a big step," Liam says as he looks to face me.

"I went from my parents, to college, then with Brandon, and then Alyssa for a little while...and I never truly got to choose where I wanted to be. I went to college where I was accepted—I mean, yes, it was one of my choice schools, but then afterward, I moved here because Brandon was drafted and then...well, you know the last bit."

A look of guilt washes over his face as he shakes his head.

"And you didn't exactly get to pick this apartment either. I'm sorry," he says, his voice nearly a whisper.

"Just because you suggested the place doesn't mean I didn't choose to rent it. I love this apartment. I really love it."

"I'm glad. It's nice having you close by. Even if I'm certain you're avoiding me half the time."

His hand playfully reaches for my arm and the tips of his fingers gently make contact, sending goose bumps through my body, and instead of pulling away or even rolling my eyes, I softly smile.

The least I can do is be kind to him. Liam's always kind to me. He's always thinking of me and always willing to help.

"Choosing where to live and doing it on my own were big steps for me personally. I've spent the last nine months as a single woman for the first time in my adult life, and you know what?"

"Hmm?"

"I love it."

"Good. You deserve to live life on your terms. You should be happy." He smiles.

Liam's feelings for me aside, I can feel—genuinely feel—he means that. And I hate that he's making me second guess everything I thought I knew.

I'm flustered at how attractive he is. And not only physically —because, wow, yes. But everything. Lately, *everything*.

There's a burst of sunlight peeking through two of the buildings that were previously blocking it from my line of sight, and I squint one of my eyes to adjust.

"We can switch spots."

I shake my head. "Oh no, that's okay. I'm fine. It'll pass."

But Liam's already up and standing beside me as I peer up at him.

Black shorts, a white T-shirt, and a backward hat. I'm fully aware of the position I'm in and how many, *many,* women would kill for this view.

I feel myself swallow hard as I stare up at him.

"Dem?" He says my name, stirring me out of my daze. And I don't miss the way he smirks when he takes a step back.

"Oh, please," I mumble.

"No, no, by all means continue staring at me like that."

"I wasn't staring at you," I lie to save face, but I'm certain he sees right through me.

"Okay," he says, nodding at me sarcastically as he gives me a thumbs-up, and it makes me want to shove his thumbs-up into his eyes.

His really pretty, sparkly hazel eyes.

"Scoot over." He bends down, motioning his hand toward the shadier part and he sits where the sun is literally cooking his face.

"Liam," I urge. "You're directly in the sun—"

"Dem, I'm fine. It'll go down soon and I'll do just about anything to keep this conversation going."

My eyes glance his way, and I'm suddenly wondering how it might feel to lean closer to him. To be closer to him. With the way his eyes are scanning my body, I'm curious if he's also thinking the same thing.

But anything more than what we're already doing would be reckless on my part and quite honestly, unfair to him. Except my body's reacting to him in ways I hadn't expected and most certainly can't handle right now.

His gaze is shamelessly rotating between my eyes and my mouth, and I can't say that I'm bothered by it. I've never been in this intimate of a setting with Liam, even though we're literally just on the damn roof having a conversation. It's quiet. It's secluded. It's just us, and it's calm. It's like the second I stepped out here my nervous system could feel the relief.

"Should we keep talking, or are you really into this staring contest? Just a hunch, though, but I'd probably win," he quips, shifting his weight more to one side.

"Well, you've had a lot more practice than I have." I say the response without thinking it through, and he starts to laugh at my admission.

"I knew you were staring," he whispers.

"That's…not what I meant."

Electricity feels like it bolts through me as he plants his hand on the blanket next to mine, our pinkies grazing.

I've shaken his hand before. Hugged him even. But this? I feel pathetic and hopeless knowing how this small touch makes me feel.

"I like talking to you." He stills.

And I like this side of Liam.

"Me too," I let myself admit.

My phone chirps as it's beside me and it's just another notification from those stupid dating apps. Note to self: turn off the notifications.

"You can take that if you need to," he says, looking away from my phone.

"No, it's okay."

The noise starts to pick up from the street, and I watch as Liam stands. The flutter in my stomach comes unexpectedly as he extends his hand to help me up as well.

"It'll be a nice sunset tonight," he says on an exhale.

The sky is already starting to change color, adding more pink and purple into its display. I cross my arms over my chest and look around at the city below us. It's not that busy, nothing compared to somewhere like New York City, but it's still enough to make me retreat a few steps back.

"You okay?" he asks, turning to me.

"Yeah," I reply, his eyes locked on me, and I smile. "Sometimes I look into a crowd of people and think I'll see Brandon. I don't know why." I shrug, keeping my arms over my chest.

"Are you afraid to see him or something?"

"No, definitely not afraid. Just more like I could do the rest of my life without having to."

I've never said that out loud. I've barely formed the words together in my head before, but here I am spilling it to Liam.

I can feel the warmth of his body closing in on me and instead of forcing it away, I'm staying put, welcoming the comfort of a friend.

"Baggage for baggage?" Liam smiles down at me and I nod.

The phrase seems to have become our own little way of saying, *you show me yours, I'll show you mine*. I tip my chin as an invitation to go ahead.

"I love playing football. I love the fans, this city, the adrenaline that comes with a two-minute drill, game on the line," he says in a quiet voice. "But sometimes my dad makes me hate it."

Something cracks in my chest at his confession. Because you'd never, *ever* know how strained their relationship is. You'd never guess Liam harbors so much internally.

He goes quiet for a moment, and I don't say anything either as he turns and we both face the sky.

I don't have anyone who I share things with like this. And I get the impression maybe Liam doesn't either.

He slowly tilts his head back, and I notice him shift his weight on his feet. I can only imagine the kind of beating his body takes every week. I'm someone who gets aches and pains if I sleep wrong, how these guys get hit over and over and still walk straight is forever a mystery to me. I press my fingers into my hip, thankful that somehow it's feeling so much better. Stretching really is helpful, who would've thought?

"You okay?" I lightly nudge my shoulder into him.

"Always." His head snaps toward me and he grins.

I want to believe him when he says it. That he's always okay. But I saw him the other day on the balcony—in a moment that felt too personal for my eyes. I bite the inside of my cheek, but can't hold back my words.

"Well, if you're ever *not* okay, you know, on the off chance, of course"—I tilt my head in his direction with a narrowed gaze—"you can talk to me." I shrug, my thumbs circling one another.

Our eyes connect and he simply nods, a quiet agreement—one I hope he knows I mean.

I don't know if it's the way the sun's hitting his face or the comfortable stupor I've been feeling up here, but he looks so innocent at this moment. So perfectly sculpted and beautiful.

"What about you? You okay? You got quiet," he says leaning against one of the pillars.

I sigh. "I am. I think a lot and that tends to make me quiet. I'm not a thinking out loud type of person."

"Hmm, you should try it, it's great."

"Just saying the first thought that pops into your mind without thinking about it for hours on end? Sounds terrifying."

A low chuckle escapes him. "Let's try it." He crosses his arms over his chest, and I internally curse at myself for the feeling that builds in my lower stomach.

"I don't know."

"Come on, Dem." His head tilts and there's a teasing spark in his eyes.

"Fine. What do you want me to do?"

He pulls himself from the pillar and takes a step closer to me.

"I'll say a word and you tell me the first word that comes to mind."

"I've seen this exercise before."

"Okay, good." He puts both hands in his pockets and leans slightly closer to me. "Ready?"

I nod, placing my hands on my hips as my hair blows into my face. Liam doesn't hesitate when he gently reaches forward and brushes it back away from my eyes.

"Family," he begins.

"Love."

"Holidays."

I scoff. "Stressful."

"Work."

"Good."

"To be happy."

I open my mouth to answer, but realize it's so much more than a one-word answer. It's like an essay. A whole full-length novel. I associate that word with so many different things from different parts of my life—there's not one word that encompasses all of it.

"Multiple avenues," I say, after scrambling my thoughts.

His brow twists in confusion but he doesn't ask me to elaborate and just continues with the game.

"To dance."

"Couples."

"Eat."

"Cookies."

He chuckles at that before continuing.

"Me."

My eyes dart to meet his. He's staring at me so wholly, like he's seeing so much of me right now, and I don't find myself wanting to shield anything. While at the same time feeling so exposed and unsure.

I pause and let myself take a step closer to him, very aware that another step from either of us would have us touching.

"Safe." I relax my shoulders as he stands in front of me.

I'm safe with him. I'm considered. I'm seen.

God, why do I have the urge to kiss him? Or let him kiss me? Why can't I stop staring at his face and his mouth and his Adam's apple? It goes against everything I stand for when it comes to professionalism in the workplace.

But Liam Evans looks really kissable right now.

No. I'm stronger than my urges. I'm totally unfazed. Unbothered.

I'll just repeat that in my head three hundred times until I'm convinced that's actually the case.

He swallows, and I notice his fingers flex as he makes a fist and opens his hand, repeating that motion a couple of times. It's like he's holding himself back from something—from doing something.

His gaze sharpens, and I replay the last hour we've had together in addition to the last five years.

I'm the chase for him. He's competitive by nature. He's a thrill-seeker. Don't give in.

I shout the words at myself internally. I can't let his sweet smiles and pretty eyes paired with kind words and gestures cloud my judgment.

I feel myself breathing heavily, taking long inhales and calm exhales. All those things about Liam may be true, but I can't shake this feeling with him—that he's genuine, that I can rely on him.

He drags his eyes over me, and unlike previous times I've noticed him do this, I feel more heat in his gaze than before. More want. More desire. More resistance.

"You're always safe with me." He reaches a hand toward me, but doesn't actually make contact. Yet somehow, I can *feel* him.

I retreat the tiniest bit. "You're a piece of work, you know that, Twelve?" I say with a heaviness in my voice. "You do all these things and say the right words. You make me feel—" I stop, shaking my head.

"Make you feel what?"

I shake my head, staring down at my sneakers.

It's time to go. I have to leave before I do something stupid. And right now, I feel like Liam has the capability to make me do something very stupid.

"Dem?" His voice forces me to look up at him.

Part of me wants to question whether this is just an itch. An itch that needs to be scratched to make the feeling go away. But there's another feeling gnawing at my chest—the fear that I'll catch feelings if I let myself open up to him.

"I'm not just blowing smoke," he says, inching closer, and I bring my arms over my chest.

"I think I wish you were," I whisper.

I hate telling him that, but it's the truth. I wish I knew with 100 percent certainty that this was a game for him. A box to check. It would be so much easier.

He brings his hand close to my face. "May I?" he asks, and I slowly nod.

My body sinks the moment his hand cups my cheek, his thumb lightly running across my cheekbone. My stomach swirls at the feeling of his touch—so warm and protective—and I let my eyes close as we stand facing each other for a brief moment before taking a step back just out of reach.

"I'm sorry," I blurt out.

"I'm not."

"It's just my body reacting."

"Is it?" he challenges, reaching one hand behind his neck.

"Y-yes, it's a reaction to human contact, that's all."

"Really, Dem?" He sighs. "I wish you'd stop acting like you can't stand me." His tone is almost sarcastic, but his face shows something softer. "When we both know that's not the case."

"Liam." I settle a shaky breath on his name.

"You're fighting it, and I can't really figure out why. I mean, I have my assumptions for your reasons. But if any of your reasons were actually good, you wouldn't still be standing here."

Is he right? There's such a heaviness in the air between us. He's pulling and I'm pushing, and I just want so badly to meet in the middle.

"I like our working relationship."

"I do too," he agrees.

He leans closer, and it causes me to back into the wall near the door. We're hanging onto threads of daylight as the sun is about to set.

All I can do is stare at him. Study him. I shouldn't want anything to happen between us, but I can't stop wondering.

"Are you curious where I stand at this exact moment? My intentions? Because I'll tell you."

I only shrug.

"I want to kiss you. I've wanted to kiss you every moment since the first day I met you. I'm pathetically hanging on your every word, all the time, because all I want to do is kiss you. But I will not touch you without knowing it's what you want."

I lower my hands to my sides.

"It could mess up what we have at work. And as friends." I chuckle, but there's no humor in it as I pull my shoulders back firmly.

This feels like a surefire way to make my life more difficult, but what if I just need to get it out of my system? Ease the burning, annoying itch and be done with it?

"But I can't stop thinking of your face and your silly grin. And how wonderful you are and—" I let out a frustrated sigh. "I don't know, maybe we just need to have a moment so we can move on. Fulfill a lifelong dream of yours and a momentary urge of mine?" I try to smile teasingly and he laughs.

"A lifelong dream, huh?"

I swallow, feeling my heart rate pick up but I do my best to mask how flushed I'm feeling.

"Exactly. One and done. I mean, we should just get it out of the way so we can go back to being coworkers and neighbors."

His eyes narrow as he tips his head down with a sly smirk and he clears his throat softly. I catch the heat in his eyes as our gazes meet.

Liam's thumb gently pulls at my bottom lip and he cradles my chin with his index finger.

We've both been playing with fire recently, and I'm tired of the constant battle I'm having over what's right and what's wrong. Tomorrow I can pretend this never happened and he can go back to being just another athlete I work with.

I slowly lean forward, letting him lead as his hand lands on the curve of my hip. His breath skims the shell of my ear as he gets closer.

"Tell me now if you want me to stop," he whispers.

But I'm sure as I reach my hand up to his shoulder and he pulls me closer. His grip on my waist tightens, and I feel my stomach drop at his commanding touch.

Liam's lips collide into mine in the most delicious motion. I feel the high immediately—the spark, the dizziness, the butterflies.

The absolute magic that is Liam Evans hums throughout my entire body.

And in that instant, I know I'm royally fucked.

CHAPTER TWENTY-FOUR

LIAM

Demi leans closer, and I feel her body sink into me. Giving up all that control she so fiercely holds onto all the time.

"Fuck," I moan as she pulls away slowly.

Her fingers touch her lips as soon as we part. She's breathing slowly, keeping her eyes trained on me as she lets out a slow breath through puckered lips.

Both of her hands frame her face as she moves to the side, closer to the door.

"I should really go." Demi reaches down to the floor, grabbing her phone and keys. "Thank you." She perks up—almost sounding shrill. "For the food and the conversation."

When she turns to leave, I reach for her hand and gently catch her wrist.

"For the record—you could never be just a moment, Dem."

Her shoulder falls, and I release her wrist, letting it slowly fall to her side as she stares at me for a moment.

I watch as she swallows through a soft smile, moving her attention back to the door, and I stuff both hands in my pockets. I glance around the empty roof with only a few streetlights keeping it lit.

She opens the door, but I call out to her before she's all the way through.

"Hey, Dem." She stops and turns back to me. Her plush red lips are so fucking teasing I already want more. "Delete the dating app."

I turn away before she does and begin cleaning up the blankets with a giant fucking smile on my face.

The last week has flown by with minimal Demi sightings—aside from seeing her on the sidelines at the game.

I saw her face after we kissed. The panic. The realization. The way she wanted to deny it being fucking magical.

Yeah. Magical. When the hell have I ever used that word to describe a kiss?

I don't really know where we go from here, but I do know I'm about to see her for the next few hours as she's covering our game today. I'll even get some extra moments with her since I'm being mic'd up for today's matchup. An opportunity I jumped at when Coach mentioned volunteers.

The weather is brutal today as I step out of my truck. There's a breeze, sure. But the strength of the sun is enough to make any logical person reconsider leaving their air conditioning. I'd bet the UV index is easily a nine or ten right now. Whatever it feels like in the stands or even on this sidewalk, it's ten times hotter on the field.

I feel my phone vibrate in the pocket of my pants and I sling my duffel bag over my shoulder before reaching to grab it. The social media team will be perched and ready to get a clip for content of whatever I'm wearing for our game, and lucky for them—I never disappoint.

Today, it's a burgundy suit and a crisp white T-shirt,

complete with all-white sneakers, and paired with my usual watch and my grandfather's ring.

I keep my sunglasses on as I walk toward the facility and peek at my phone to see who the text is from—thankful I did. Because my eyes roll in a dramatic Demi-fashion as I read the text preview on my screen.

DAD

I'll be at the game in a couple weeks with your brother. Was thinking we could...

I don't have the energy to open it right now—it's the last thing I need to see before getting ready to compete, so I lock my phone and stuff it into the side pocket of the bag. I'll deal with whatever that says later.

"Let's go to work, boys!" I make contact with every guy around me in the huddle—handshakes, a little rough housing—whatever it takes to get fired up.

Spotting Demi on the sidelines is easy. If she's within sight range, I'll find her. She's holding a mic and talking into the camera, likely doing some pregame reporting and any kind of injury update.

Her hair is up in a high ponytail with two curled pieces framing her face. But it's the dress she's wearing that stops me in my tracks. Black, sleeveless, with white detailing on the bottom. I know nothing about women's clothes, but I know that dress was made for her.

"God, she's beautiful." My hands land on my hips, and I do the only thing I can do right now—stare.

"You're mic'd up, man." Nate nudges my elbow with a shake of his head.

"I hope they heard me. Raise the volume." I laugh lightly, taking a step back toward the sideline. "Look at her."

There's a groaning sound coming from where Nate's standing, but I ignore him as I smile and finally pull my gaze from her.

The guys gather for a huddle, and I lock in the moment I'm surrounded by my teammates. It's a feeling like no other, the rush, the adrenaline. You just can't describe this to someone who hasn't played the game at this level. It's one of those rare "you had to be there" kind of moments, and I soak in every goddamn second I'm in this league, because I know how quickly it can change.

"Same energy as last week, my man." I slap Ford's shoulder before knocking helmets with Nate, ready to get this game going.

Except, as time goes by, this game is actually turning out to be frustrating as fuck.

Fourth down for the third time in a row, and I've yet to see past the forty-yard line. Today hasn't been our day yet, but I'm determined to turn it around. Our defense is taking the field again, and I give Chase a look before he leaves the sidelines.

"Hold 'em," I grumble, and he nods before he runs to the field.

We feel Graham's absence on the line; there's no way around that fact. I'm excited for the new guys and have faith that they'll only improve as the season goes on, but right now I'm getting fucking laid out on this grass.

"That's on me." Cribley, our new center, comes up in front of me as I'm sitting on the ice bench. "Ninety snuck by too many times. Sorry, man."

I extend my hand to slap his. "Hey." I lean forward, giving him my full attention. "We've got time to turn this around. Don't beat yourself up for plays that already happened. We'll get the ball back and do what we know how to do. Let's focus on the next drive."

He nods and walks back over to the bench he was previously seated on while I replay the last series on the tablet in my lap.

I get a glimpse of Demi from the corner of my eye, and she quickly looks away as soon as I lift my head.

Was she staring at me? Have the tables turned? Satisfaction builds in my chest at the possibility of her replaying our kiss over and over the last few days like I have been. It has me wondering if she too has spent a few evenings alone with thoughts of me the way I have her.

Her head hesitantly stutters back my way, and I take the chance to let her know I see her. I lift my hand, waving my fingers in her direction and sporting the biggest smile I can.

And she sees me. Oh, does she see me.

She pulls her bottom lip in by her teeth—no doubt fighting back a smile as she shakes her head. Both hands full with a microphone and a stack of papers as the first half is about to end and she'll be interviewing Coach Aarons.

As the second quarter comes to an end, I'm on my feet with the rest of the team heading into the locker room, and I take the opportunity to say hello to Demi as she's walking toward our sideline.

"Hey, Dem," I say in a low voice, stopping next to her.

"Twelve." She lifts her chin, papers in hand as she waits for my coach to be free.

"You look really pretty today," I whisper, and she jerks her head up at me. Her cheeks tint pink, her eyes widen—it's a look of pure embarrassment. But knowing I just made her blush makes my chest pound.

She knows I'm mic'd up.

"Thank you," she mumbles before rushing away.

And that almost-smile from her is enough to power me through the second half of this game.

The scoreboard reflects a tough-fought battle, but not a

victory. And it fucking sucks. Every time we don't win, I know there are a million things I could've done differently.

As the quarterback, there's a leadership aspect to my role. I'm a captain. A veteran. Someone every single guy on this roster looks to. When we lose, it feels like I've let them down and the last thing I want to do is a postgame interview, but it's my job.

There are a handful of reporters in the postgame wrap-up, and I step up to the podium, black Knights T-shirt and a backward hat. Still sweaty and banged up—but this is the way it goes.

"Liam, what's said on the sidelines when you're in that kind of position so late in the fourth quarter?"

I lean both hands on the wooden podium. "Yeah, we just needed to do more in the red zone today. And we didn't. You know, I always tell my guys to keep fighting until that clock runs out, and that's what they did. Our defense played lights-out football the whole game. I missed a few throws, too many throws, I think…and yeah. There's work to be done."

The same reporter speaks again. "What about Alex Farr? Any word on how bad his injury is?"

Alex went down on the first play of the third quarter. Best guess is a hamstring injury and he'll miss a handful of games, but it's not on me to tell the reporters.

"I'm not sure."

The head of PR points to a woman in a polka-dot blouse with big frame glasses and she begins another question.

"You guys had thirteen penalties today. That's more than any game last season, is the offensive line still getting accustomed to new roles?"

I want to roll my eyes. I want to be able to ignore questions like this. I'll never throw my guys under the bus—even if there were moments I was frustrated in the game.

"Yeah, listen, there have been a lot of moving parts offensively and those guys played great. There's work to be done across the board, we'll see that in tape."

She dips her head to write something down, and I field two more questions from the eager group seated in front of me before heading to the locker room.

My body is banged up today. I felt every hit, every bump, every fall. Thank god tomorrow's an off day.

Summer Kincaid has changed the name of your group chat to Liam's Angels.

SUMMER KINCAID

Hello!

What's with the name change?

SUMMER KINCAID

I needed an easy way to find the group text so it wouldn't get mixed up in my texts.

You have that many people texting you that ours gets lost?

CLARKY

She's very well liked Liam. People text her.

I'm very well liked too, but I don't need to name all my group chats.

LITTLE HUNT

Oh don't give me that. You named the one you're in with the guys The Avengers.

She isn't wrong. I did do that.

I chuckle to myself and take another sip from my coffee before placing it on my nightstand beside me. My hand runs over my jaw, feeling the stubble that likely needs a shave at some point today. There's a persistent ache coming from my left side and I'm afraid to even look, wondering if there might be bruising from yesterday's game.

The amount of hits I took felt record high. And it's only a matter of time before there's a follow up text—to the one I didn't answer—from my dad letting me know I played like shit yesterday.

I send an eye roll emoji in the group text and toss my phone on the bed next to me. I have to get up. I have to move around, otherwise the stinging pain will only get worse. A dip in the ice bath sounds good, and a possible Demi run-in sounds even better.

CHAPTER TWENTY-FIVE

DEMI

This last week would've been an ideal time to have a group of girlfriends—or even just one friend—that I could scream to about what happened with Liam. But I don't, and therefore, Walt the bird has been getting an earful from me whenever he makes his presence known.

I did tell my mom, but I tell her everything. I don't think I've gone more than two days in my life without speaking to her. And that has nothing to do with dependency and everything to do with her being my actual best friend.

But I guess I am needy when it comes to her. Proudly, though. Because she's the best woman I know.

I spared her details but let her know she'd be happy to hear I did spend time with someone recently and enjoyed myself. She asked an array of questions, and I answered as willingly as I wanted to, but she literally has no idea it's Liam Evans, and I'd like to keep it that way for the moment.

I'm still processing how the hell it happened. How I let it happen. But when I replay it in my mind, it was all me. I basically said *"please kiss me!"* to the one person who wouldn't have to think twice about it.

I just needed a moment to feel something. I'd been numb for months. Not exactly wanting to admit it, but knowing it nonetheless. And being around Liam makes me feel joy again.

Swinging the sliding glass door open, I take a step out onto the patio. The humid air makes me blow out a deep breath as I take a seat on the chair, watching the clouds slowly move.

It's only once I lean my head back and close my eyes that I hear the word "fuck" over and over in a hushed, deep tone. My brows crease and I look toward the sound of the voice, unable to see anything around the corner, but I hear moans and groans coming from a male voice before I hear something louder.

"Son of a bitch!" The words come shortly after there's a knocking sound on the side of the building.

My lips pull in and I do my best to stifle a laugh, knowing Walt the bird is making his appearance this morning and disrupting whatever it is Liam was doing.

The black silk tie on my robe blows into my open coffee cup as the wind suddenly picks up, and I too find myself yelling out a string of curses as it does.

"Dem?" Liam's deep voice carries around the corner.

We can't see each other out here, but we can definitely hear one another.

"Uh, yeah. Hi." I flick my hand to get the excess coffee off.

"You okay?"

"A little spilled coffee, that's it. I'm fine." I pause. "Are, uh, you okay?"

It sounded like someone could've been having sex with the way he was moaning a moment ago, and the thought of that unfortunately sends a flicker of jealousy through me.

"Sore ribs, ice bath." He makes a gasping sound, and I assume he's moving around at this point. "Come over for breakfast." He's definitely not one for subtle or beating around the bush.

"No," I firmly state.

"But I make great omelets."

I sigh quietly. He does, actually. And I owe him a flan. One that I actually made two days ago but haven't had the nerve to bring it to him. My repayment for his dinner the other night.

"You're quiet. Are you still there?"

I lightly chuckle to myself and feel my cheeks heat at the sweetness of his tone.

"Fine. I have to bring you your flan anyway."

"Yesss." He drags out the word, and I hear water sloshing around.

It causes me to picture him and make up my own image in my head of how he looks right now. Something I shouldn't be doing—but decide not to stop anyway.

Does he take ice baths naked? No, right? Especially on the balcony. He's at least in a swimsuit. But that doesn't stop my thoughts from swirling over what a bare chested Liam looks like with droplets of water dripping down his stomach.

"Okay. I'll get dressed and be over soon," I say, tugging at the collar of my robe.

"Whatever makes you comfortable." I can picture the grin on his lips as I slide the door open and then close it behind me.

A few moments after that exchange, I tap on his door a couple times, glancing down at my feet as I stand on the outside of his door holding a pan of flan. Black cardigan over a white tank top and a pair of black leggings. I'm nothing if not consistent with my color palette.

"Good morning." He beams as the door opens and sunlight comes streaming through his back window.

"Not taking your own advice I see," I tease, smirking up at him as I tilt my head. He creases his brows, and I avert my gaze from his wet hair and bare chest. "Answering the door without asking who it is. And you couldn't find a second to grab clothing."

His arm leans on the door as he steps back with a smile. His body is immaculate. Not that I'd expect otherwise.

"Come on in, Dem," he purrs. "I have a doorbell camera, remember? I saw you. And look—" He grabs a shirt from the small table near his entryway.

Convenient it was sitting there, but okay. He pulls it over his head at the same time he pushes the door shut behind me. I turn as it clicks and when I look back at him, he runs a hand through his hair before doing a little shake, letting some damp pieces fall wherever they please. And my stomach does seven thousand backflips in a row.

"Problem solved." He grins, tugging at the shirt he's wearing.

I give a thumbs-up and raise the dish in my other hand as something bumps into the back of my ankle and it startles me slightly.

"Oh," I gasp. "Right. You have a cat."

"That's Birdie. You aren't allergic, are you?"

I shake my head, offering him a smile as I see the genuine concern flash on his features. "No, not at all. I like cats."

I refer to the dish again as the playful kitten darts away from me. "Can I put this in your fridge?"

"You know you didn't really have to make it." He opens the fridge door, making some space on the top shelf toward the back.

"Yes, I did. And it was good practice anyway. It's one thing I crave. Well, I crave a lot of sweets." I lightly laugh at myself. "But this one's my favorite and I'd like to perfect it. So you'll have to tell me how it tastes."

Liam reaches into a drawer, grabbing two forks, and places them on the counter.

His apartment is cleaner than I anticipated it would be. I guess I didn't really know what to expect, but it looks like no one lives here. It's minimally decorated, but the things that are here are incredibly masculine. Dark colors, leather, rich scents.

"Let's taste it now."

"Uh, okay. Sure." I open the airtight container I've had it in.

"Dig in." He hands me a fork.

"Don't you want to cut a slice?"

"Nah," he says, sticking his fork into the dessert. "It's just us."

I'm somehow loving the fact that he'll just eat a dessert straight out of the container.

"Fuck," he moans as he tilts his head backward and goes in for a second bite.

"Good?"

"See for yourself. It's amazing." Taking his fork, he scoops up a giant piece and brings it to my mouth. "Try it." He licks his lips, and I hesitantly open my mouth.

I guess I'm going to let him feed me.

My tongue runs between my lips, tasting the sweet flavor and feeling pretty fucking proud I made that.

"It's good," I say, reaching for a paper towel on his counter.

He nods. "So fucking good."

He closes the container, my fork still in his hand, and his eyes firmly locked on me as he licks it clean.

There's a dance happening in my lower stomach that I have absolutely zero control over as I watch him suck on the fork before he places it in the sink. When he finally turns away, I let out the breath I've been holding and finally regain some of my composure.

"So I'm really only great at making omelets. I'm sure that comes as a shock to you since I'm so good at everything else." The corner of his mouth lifts and he gives me a knowing smirk.

One that I'd like to brush off his face. With my lips.

No.

I roll my eyes and take a seat at the counter. There's a wooden fruit bowl in the center, filled with apples, oranges, and bananas. They're so perfect they look fake.

"I'm fine with an omelet if that's what you planned on

making." My fingers skim the outside of the orange in front of me.

"You can have whatever you want," he says referring to the bowl. "I can peel that orange for you."

"Oh," I say, pulling my hand back. "I-I can peel an orange."

He nods, moving the paper towel closer to me. Liam begins to work on the omelets while there's music playing from his phone and a candle burning off in the distance. It smells like apple cider.

I instantly feel comforted in his apartment. For a space with so few decorations and photos, he's made it feel so homey.

"Can I have a slice?" He tips his head toward me, walking around his island so he's now at my side.

I look up at him standing over me. Piercing blue green eyes, a five-o'clock shadow, a few pieces of hair that went rogue falling onto his forehead.

"My hands are eggy." His mouth opens, and I take one of the pieces and bring it to his mouth. There's no hesitation in his bite as he takes the whole piece into his mouth and smiles with closed lips as he does. And, honest to god, why is that one of the cutest fucking things he's ever done?

"So…" I say on a sigh as I watch him walk back to the stove. "How are you feeling after the game? Pretty nice you own an ice bath."

"My body's beat up." He winces as he lifts his shirt and I can see a bruise already forming on his side. "I hate that we lost the game. But we didn't play at the level we're capable of, you saw it. There's a lot to work on." His shoulders shrug up and down and he shakes his head as he plates the omelet. "But I know it's early in the season. We'll clean up the things we need to clean up and things will get better."

He lifts his eyes to meet mine, placing the steaming hot breakfast right in front of me.

"This smells so good." I lean in closer to the dish and inhale.

"Oh, and yes"—he raises the spatula in his hand and points to the sliding glass doors—"I do have an ice bath. Want to try it?"

I swallow hard as I look at him once he turns back to face the stove, finishing up his own omelet. I study how the shirt on his back hugs his muscles, how he's stretching something at all times. His neck, a shoulder, his back, hips—he's constantly moving his body. It feels like a tactic to keep me staring, and I hate to admit it, but it's working.

CHAPTER TWENTY-SIX

LIAM

Am I freaking the fuck out that Demi is in my kitchen, eating my omelet, and peeling my oranges? You bet I am.

What a whirlwind morning it's been, but I somehow feel like I must've done something right in my lifetime to be experiencing this. A year ago, I would've done anything to spend time with Demi. I've been hopelessly, pathetically, crazy about her since the day I laid eyes on her, and any time I thought the feelings would pass or subside, that day just never came.

"I wouldn't last five seconds in an ice bath...you must be crazy." She chuckles to herself, a delicate hand covering her mouth as she chews.

"It's really just the initial moment. You get in and you're immediately thinking *this sucks, get me out*. But once you get past the first few seconds your body adapts. There are a ton of benefits to ice baths."

"Well, I believe you, but I know myself. I'd get in and hop out immediately."

I lift my shoulders in a shrug. Maybe one day I can convince her to take a dip in mine.

We both finish our omelets, and she leans back in the barstool as she crosses her leg over her knee.

"So, what are your plans today?" I ask, pulling our plates into the sink and leaning my back against the counter.

Her arms cross over her chest, and I subconsciously mimic the motion.

"I have today off, so…" she says, leaving her sentence open-ended.

"Me too."

We hold a stare for a few moments. A Yellowcard song streams in the background from my phone near the fridge, and I find myself internally toying with the idea of asking her to hang out. No expectations. Nothing unsavory. Just time together.

If I'm being honest with myself, that's really all I've ever wanted with her. More time to get to know her. To see what makes her tick, what makes her happy, to know what fills her cup, and even things that make her see red. I know there are layers to Demi outside of what she lets people see.

And I don't know if I'm right—I hope I am—but I just feel like she might let me in.

"Well, how do you feel about being off today—together?" I hold my breath at the end of that sentence.

"You want to spend your one day off with me?"

I push myself off the counter and circle the island, bringing myself to her side. God, I fucking love her hair like this. Her face. Her dimples when she smiles, and the depth in her eyes under those dark brown eyelashes.

"Dem, if I had only one hour off, I'd want to spend it with you."

Her gaze on me softens, and I see the tiniest sliver of hope behind her eyes. She moves off the barstool, both hands clasping together in front of her as she fidgets for a moment.

"Sure," she finally says as her shoulders relax. "Show me what an off day for you looks like."

I smile softly, taking two steps closer to her. I half expect her to step back, but she doesn't and I'm close enough to lean down and kiss her again. Something I've thought about doing again since the second the last one ended.

"I don't typically leave my apartment on off days."

"Starting off strong." She pulls at the sleeve of her cardigan.

"Honestly?" I chuckle, rubbing a hand over my jaw. "I'll couch rot all day if I'm able to. A movie, *Grey's* reruns, binge a new show, naps. If I need a break from that, I'll do a puzzle."

"I did read somewhere that you puzzle a lot in the offseason." She giggles, her cute nose scrunching as she does.

"You read right. You want to do one with me?"

She swallows and her eyes shift from locking with mine down to my mouth. She doesn't try to hide it at first. It isn't until she probably catches herself staring that she shakes herself out of it and takes a step to the side, placing a hand on the countertop and her other on her hip.

"I might need a second cup of coffee first."

"I can order us some," I offer. "Anywhere you want. I'll have some delivered."

"Or I can go next door and grab some café con leche from my kitchen."

"That sounds even better."

Demi slides past me, and I don't miss the way her arm brushes against mine as she does. Once she's out the door, I quickly splash some water on my face and grab a few puzzles from the top of my bedroom closet.

A few more moments pass as I'm clearing off the coffee table in the living room and opening the blinds on the sliding glass door. The sunlight has all but faded as the day has turned cloudier than I expected, but it somehow feels fitting for a day off.

There's a knock on the door, and I make quick strides to open it, taking both coffees out of her hands when I do.

"Thank you," she says.

"Thank you. I've been dreaming of this coffee since the last time I had it."

"Oh yeah?" She chuckles, pulling her cardigan off and placing it on the back of the barstool like she's more than comfortable here and it sends a warm feeling to my bones.

"I took out a few options." I gesture to the living room, where I have a few puzzles laid out on the couch.

"Oh, definitely this one," she says, pointing at the box with cats on the front. "Definitely the cats in hoodies puzzle. I can't believe you have this." She laughs, picking up the box. "We have to do this one."

"Yeah, that showed up in my mailbox the day after I brought Birdie home. Courtesy of Summer." I scoff, half-smiling.

Demi smiles as she takes her coffee from my outstretched hand and sits on the floor by the coffee table. I follow her lead, sitting opposite her as Birdie pounces onto my lap. Her residence there is short-lived, though, once she spots a toy under the couch and she's off.

"Kind of surprised you took me up on the offer to hang out," I casually say as we're both sorting pieces and working on the outer edges in silence.

"To be honest, me too."

We both look up at the same time, eyes meeting.

"What's an off day look like for you?" I ask.

She shrugs, gathering pieces that look the same in a corner of the table.

"I've been trying to get into cooking more. Especially any dishes my mom or abuela make. But otherwise, I'm content reading for twelve hours straight."

"I'll gladly be a taste-tester if you ever need someone. I like everything."

"Everything?" She eyes me, brow raised with a questioning smirk.

"Yep."

"Hmm," she ponders, her lips turning down slightly as she nods.

"Here you go." I hand her a piece of the section she's putting together.

We've got the four corners figured out, it's always where I start and she seemed to just follow my lead. But she's making good progress on the orange cat in a green hoodie now.

"Are you close with your family?" I ask and she smiles with a nod.

"I am. I miss them a lot. My abuela is the most amazing woman. I get to talk with her in Spanish—something I don't really do with many other people—since her English isn't the best. And it just makes me feel so close to her."

"So, what you're saying is I need to learn Spanish," I say, shifting my eyes toward her with a lazy smirk.

She's looking at me like I'm not serious. And I love it.

"Well, she *is* my favorite person. Brandon never bothered to learn much past '*hola*.'" She shrugs, and I let out a low sigh at just one more thing this guy fucked up.

But she glances over at me, offering a sweet smile before switching gears.

"How'd you get into puzzles?"

"My grandfather, actually. We'd do puzzles together all the time when I was a kid. It kind of took a backseat when football became so demanding and he went into one of those assisted living places. I'd go visit when I could during high school and we'd get a few small puzzles done in a couple hours. After he passed, I didn't touch one for a while, but a few years ago I needed something stimulating to do. I was..." I pause, not knowing how much she really cares to know about my personal life, but the warm look in her eyes makes me feel comfortable enough to continue.

"I was telling my therapist about some things I was struggling with, and mentioned I used to do puzzles. She suggested I try again, and that was that."

"I'm sorry about your grandfather."

"Ah," I say, tilting my head. "Thanks. This was his." I raise my hand, turning it to show the gold ring on my pinky finger. "He wore it his whole life. When he passed, I got it. It started on this finger," I say, smiling to myself and wiggling my index finger. "But when it was getting too small for that one, I moved it to my pinky. Seems like this is where it'll stay."

"That's really sweet," she whispers, reaching her hand toward mine.

Her fingers gently touch the ring, and I just watch her examine it.

"What's the F for?"

"Francine. My grandmother."

Demi nods, pulling her hand back to herself, she sits up on her knees. She leans over the coffee table, grabbing a few more puzzle pieces and quietly brings them back to her side of the table.

"It's beautiful." She pulls her eyes from the barely completed puzzle between us, and I swear to god there's a moment where time stops.

Being around Demi, being pulled into her orbit, sets my soul on fire. In the deepest, warmest, and most beautiful way.

"Thank you," I push out through a gravely tone.

"Can I have that piece?" She points to the one by my hand, and we both work in silence for another few moments on the puzzle before us.

"So can I ask what the B is for?" I point toward her wrist.

She looks down at her arm, staring for a moment, and I watch as her eyes glaze, but she smiles down at the ink on her wrist. On a blink she looks up, still smiling.

"Brianna." She swallows. "My best friend."

CHAPTER TWENTY-SEVEN

DEMI

I stare at the tattoo on my wrist. A movie flashing in my mind of our last summer together. The first day we met. The sleepovers. Parties. Boys. Mall trips. Random nights in a Taco Bell parking lot talking about everything and nothing. The memories are hard. They hit me in the chest like a ton of bricks when I let myself think of her for too long, sucking out all the air in my lungs.

"Brianna is—was—my best friend." I don't like referring to her in the past tense. I know it's technically correct, but it's like my brain can't handle the fact that she's a memory—no matter how long it's been.

My eyes are burning as I'm praying for the strength to not completely lose my shit in Liam's apartment.

"Was?" His forehead creases and he puts the puzzle piece down he was holding.

All his attention is focused on me and the next sentence that comes out of my mouth. My neck heats as I stare at Liam, and I want to cry. I want to let myself just have a moment. A moment to unleash all the sadness I still feel but keep under a mask of a strong cat eye and bold lip.

"She…" I pause briefly, feeling my fingers pick at my nail polish. "She died when we were nineteen."

He looks like he's just seen a ghost. Liam's lips part, his eyes showing the most sincere concern as they soften, and without hesitation he's on his knees scooting around the coffee table to sit closer to me.

My fingers don't stop moving in my lap as I sit there, hearing only the faint sound of an Ed Sheeran song and my own heartbeat in my ears.

One glance down at my shaking hands and Liam's warmth steadies me. He wraps his hand over mine, gently squeezing as his thumb rubs the outside of my hand. His eyes plead with me to open up. It's like he can see I want to be vulnerable, but I'm holding back. Though I've never felt safer to let myself fall apart.

"Sorry," I say on a shaky breath as I sniffle. "I wasn't expecting to talk about her."

"You don't have to," he assures me, hand still placed over mine.

"I know."

"But also, you can if you need to. This is a safe space—it's just you and me."

I lift my heavy eyes to look up at him. He makes it so easy to be soft and feel feminine. To lay everything at his feet and be sure he'll still be there when it's all said and done.

"It's been almost twenty years and I still remember it like it was yesterday. The phone call. The scream. The sobs that felt uncontrollable. I hate that the most frequent thing I remember is the day she died, when there were so many amazing moments we shared for years before it happened."

"Tell me a fun memory." Liam's hand is still cradling mine. I should pull away. I shouldn't let myself find comfort in him. But I can't help it.

I lightly laugh as I tuck a piece of hair behind my ear.

"Okay, our senior year of high school we thought we were slick. We had block periods, even and odd days, I'm not sure if you had something like that." He nods, and I continue, "Well we would go to first period, skip third, but then come back for fifth. We did that for almost two weeks before our fifth period teacher called us out." I shake my head, laughing internally at the memory. "He said, do you really think we're that stupid? We know you've been skipping third period for almost two weeks."

"I can't believe you skipped class," Liam says, his mouth curving into a lazy grin as he makes a mock gasping sound.

"It wasn't my idea, but Bri had this whole elaborate story she told him about how we had to skip to help her parents at the little shop they owned in town. Total bullshit," I say.

"Did he buy it?"

I shake my head as I smile. "Hell no. He knew we were just skipping our electives. The year was almost over, we were already checked out mentally and thinking of college."

"Damn. You rebel." He squeezes my hand and then slowly pulls his away, and I find myself longing for it back.

"He didn't rat us out to the principal, though, so we always deemed him our favorite teacher. He really was cool as hell. Nice too. He came to her funeral."

"That's a story I would've thought to be your lie for two truths and a lie." Liam pulls the coffee table with one hand a little closer to us, almost boxing us in, and my heart rate picks up.

"Sorry, I just wanted my coffee closer."

I quickly wave my hand. "You're fine."

"It sounds like she was really fun." He brings the coffee to his lips, taking a quick sip.

"She was amazing." My thoughts trail off and I find myself thinking of the days after her accident. The weeks and months I spent in a state of depression and sadness.

"Brianna was funny and fiery and such a great friend. Everybody loved her. She was so open-minded and accepting. She brought out so much good in me—in everyone around her. I don't know how I would've made it through high school without her. There are so many moments I play back, and I just…" My eyes well up and a lump forms in my throat. "I loved being her friend." My words are hushed.

"She was sunshine in its brightest form. I always wished I could be more like that. But she was also steady and resilient. She held my hand on graduation day and we ugly cried together when we tossed our caps in the air. Losing her was—*is* the biggest loss of my life."

The candle burning nearby cracks, and I don't hear anything else as I focus my eyes on Liam staring at me. His hand moves to rub the back of my neck in a comforting way that makes me want to slip into his embrace entirely.

"Her accident crushed me. It took me months to come out of the dark place it put me in. I had so much anger and sadness, I couldn't see past it. I couldn't see the light at the end of the terrible, terrible tunnel I was stuck in. I barely remember going to classes, to work. I honestly don't know how I managed to finish school and even just function. It was the worst time of my life. She was hit head-on one night while driving home from work. She worked at this cute little restaurant right on a mountainside. A middle-aged man—drunk off his ass—crossed the center line and…she never stood a chance. I'll never forget her sister's phone call, her cries, the bloodcurdling scream that left my chest, and the sobs that felt never-ending. I didn't think it was possible for a person to cry that much. It took a long time—too long—for him to be charged. But the day it finally happened, I made the choice to stay sober."

"Dem…I…god, I don't even know what to say. I'm sorry. I'm so sorry."

Wind whistles outside the sliding glass door, and I glance out to see palm trees swaying against dark skies.

"So that's what the B stands for. It's in her handwriting. It's just something small but"—I rotate my wrist, looking at the script—"I needed a way to still see her every day…otherwise I thought I might die," I whisper.

If Bri were here right now, she'd be asking me why I'm pretending I don't like being around this man. She'd ask why I keep making things hard for him and why I can't just let myself live and see where things go. We'd go back and forth about the pros and cons, what it might mean for my career, his career—but we'd land on her telling me to follow my heart. Because if nothing else, Bri was always following hers.

"I've wondered for years, I'm glad to know. Thanks for sharing her with me."

He smiles, lips pressed together softly and it forces the memory of our kiss to the forefront of my brain.

"She would've loved you." Reaching for a puzzle piece, I smile to myself.

"Yeah?"

"Mm-hmm," I hum. "You're kind of similar, I think."

"I take that as the highest compliment Demi Sanchez can give."

"It probably is."

He shifts in his seat, creating space between us and slides the outline of the puzzle closer.

"I'm going to stay on this side of the table, okay? Don't go scooting away from me," he teases, and I hold up my right hand.

"Hey, I like my spot. It's the perfect placement in the room I've learned."

"Yeah?" He chuckles. "How so?"

"Well"—I point to the sliding glass door—"I can see outside perfectly so I know what the weather is doing. I can hear the music, see the bathroom door down the hall, and I'm the perfect distance from the candle. I can still smell it, but it's not overpowering."

His shoulders shake as a low laugh rumbles in his chest. "You're very aware of your surroundings. Not sure if that's something you've had to learn or just a beautiful part of your brain."

His comment is interesting. Because, is it? Did I have to train myself to be aware of everything all the time because I could never feel relaxed? I'm so hyper-aware of the sounds, sights, and smells around me all the time. I never stopped to think if it's a survival tactic I learned over the last decade.

My silence causes him to nudge me with his shoulder.

"You got quiet. What's going on up there?" He gently taps my temple.

"Just thinking." I shrug. "And you've mentioned my brain twice in the last thirty seconds. That a thing for you?" I tease, nudging him lightly.

"Honestly? Yeah. You're smart, Dem, and it's hot."

A man interested in my brain and not just my body has to be the sexiest thing I've ever experienced.

My cheeks heat and I can feel the blush coating my entire face as I move my attention back to the puzzle, grabbing a random piece off the table, as if I have plans on where it goes.

Truthfully, though, I'm doing anything I can not to look at Liam right now. Because looking at him lately, especially today, has me wanting to kiss him. My free hand taps on the edge of the table while my other scrambles over the puzzle, frantically searching for the spot to put this piece. I press it lightly into a connection that looks like it fits.

"Nope," he says, leaning his back against the couch.

When I realize he's right, I gently yank it out and move my hand to another spot, but before I place it, he perks up again.

"Not there either."

"Would you like to try?" I bite back in a teasing tone.

He opens his hand. It's twice the size of mine. Well, maybe that's an exaggeration, but it's definitely not soft and dainty.

His fingers graze the inside of my hand as he picks up the piece and connects it with one of the top corner pieces. To be fair, I was barely trying earlier. And he does these regularly, he has a trained eye for it.

"We don't always get a match the first time we try, and that's okay. Eventually you find the piece that fits." His voice is velvet as he breathes the words into the space between us.

Music plays in the background, a song I know and love. It seems like Liam catches the lyrics too as he loses the sarcasm in his expression and his eyes soften. His hand reaches up, almost with hesitancy as he lightly brushes a piece of hair behind my ear and goose bumps erupt on my skin.

His hand lingers near my cheek, and I instinctively bring mine over his as his hand touches my skin.

"Liam," I whisper as I blink my eyes. "I shouldn't want this." He stares at me. "I've worked *so* hard to get where I am."

"I know you have," he says, nodding and slightly pulling back, letting silence settle in.

Staring at him like this would bring me to my knees if I wasn't already seated. He's beautiful. With a heart unlike anyone I've ever met before. His silence remains as he stares back at me. Eyes intensifying as he does, gold specks flickering against the green and blue hues in his eyes. I can tell he's leaving every decision up to me.

"But I..." My breath catches and I feel myself lean into him. He smells like I'm in the woods after it's been raining and my mind finds peace and comfort in that. I inhale a deep breath and slowly exhale. "I can't stop thinking about you," I admit, feeling freedom in those words.

"Dem, I haven't seen past you since the day we met." He leans back in, leaving only inches between us as his hand remains steady, cupping the side of my neck. "Back then, you were with someone else so I tried to stay away. Occupying myself with other women, comparing every last one of them to you. Since the second I learned you were divorced, I've just been desperately praying you'd finally notice me. I know what your career means to you. I know you've worked so hard, and I've been your biggest fan for the last five years. But this isn't spur of the moment for me. It's always been you."

The last time we kissed, he said if any of my reasons for not doing it made sense, then I would've already left. I just want to feel happy again. I want decisions to be mine. Liam always considers my feelings; he lets me choose.

He was right then. And it's true now too.

I *can* kiss him. I *want* to kiss him. And *fuck it*, I'm going to.

"Liam." His name leaves my lips breathlessly just before he lowers his lips to mine.

This kiss is different from last time. It's more commanding, more intentional, more everything. And my brain can't compute what's happening as I allow myself to sink into him. My god, he feels good. His lips are soft and his tongue sweeps against mine. It's not overpowering or sloppy, it's sexy and unhurried. His movements are gentle and comforting.

Liam's hands slide down to my waist, pulling me gently—but with intention—onto his lap, and I let myself melt into him.

Our kiss deepens as my legs straddle him as we sit on the floor in his living room. The sound that leaves his chest sounds more like a whimper than anything else and it sets something on fire within me. This man wants me. I mean, he really wants me. And I want him.

My mind can't help but wonder how it would feel to be with him. To feel his body against mine without the barrier of clothing between us. The knowledge of knowing how his tongue feels in my mouth sends a jolt to my lower stomach, imagining how it would feel between my thighs too. The thought makes my body rock against his, and he moans into my mouth as his hands glide up my back.

Both of his hands find their way into my hair, and I pull

back, allowing myself a good look at him. His lips are swollen and smirking as our eyes lock, and I see up close the tiny, faint freckles on the bridge of his nose. Our foreheads meet, and I let out a breath as I smile against him.

He's so soft in this moment, but still carries so much power it flips my insides upside down. His fingers pulse into my scalp and it causes my head to tilt back a little at how good it makes me feel.

"Jesus," I mutter under my breath.

He takes some of my hair into his hand and I feel the yank—gentle, yet commanding. I lean my head back even more, exposing my neck, and his lips find the spot just below my ear and I shudder as I let out a breathless gasp.

"Is this the spot?" he breathes out, his lips gently kissing my skin.

I nod feverishly as his hands find my thighs, holding me in place on his lap. And everything around me disappears. Time, logic, where I am—all of it.

It's only us. All I see is him.

CHAPTER TWENTY-EIGHT

LIAM

Demi pulls back slowly. Her lips are red with evidence of our kiss.

And fuck, what a kiss it was.

She's the epitome of everything I've ever wanted. The list begins and ends with Demi. I want more of her, all of her, but I won't do a damn thing I know she doesn't want as well. So whatever the hell this is, we do it on her terms. She can set the pace, the tone, and the rules if she needs to. I know she doesn't want anyone to think less of her for her personal choices, but honestly, fuck anyone who dares to question her integrity or place in our world. *Our* world, because sports belong to women too.

"You're stunning," I say, unable to keep it to myself any longer.

She laughs lightly, pulling herself off my lap and sits next to me on the floor. Her fingers tracing her lips. I glance out the window to notice the weather has completely changed in the last hour. Before we kissed, the sky was dark and moody. Now, there's nothing but sunshine and an actual rainbow outside my window.

"I'm not sure we'll finish this puzzle today." She stands and takes her cup to the counter.

"I'll leave it right here. We can finish it on our next day off."

"Your cat won't destroy it?" She gives me a pointed look as she knocks her head to the side.

"Birdie has manners." I lean against the couch, crossing my arms over my chest and forcing myself to focus on the conversation at hand to help the situation I still have going on from the time she spent in my lap. "She won't mess with our puzzle."

"Uh-huh, okay."

I smile at her.

"But I should go," she says, pulling her cardigan on. "We both work tomorrow, and I still need to do some laundry."

I make my way to the kitchen island where she's standing, arms crossed over her chest. My hands land on the outside of her arms, gently holding her in place as I look down at her.

She gazes up at me. And there are a million things I want to say about today, but she beats me to it.

"I hope I didn't come on too strong or...I don't know, awkward earlier. I'm just in this new phase of my life where I'm trying to do more of the things I want, and I've just really wanted to do that I suppose."

"Dem, I have zero issues with you kissing me."

Her head shakes as she smiles down at the floor.

"You know what I mean, though, right? I just don't want to ruin our friendship and our working relationship. I value both of those things."

I nod, pulling her into me for a hug. She nestles against my chest like it's exactly where she belongs.

"Can I be honest?" I clear my throat, still holding her, and she nods against my chest.

"I like our relationship at work—and as friends too—and I never want to put you in a bind, but I know I want more. If the options were to be only your friend or be the love of your life, you know I'm going to choose the latter. Every time."

Her head pulls away from my chest and she looks up at me, brow creasing and lips parted.

"The love of my life, huh?" Her lips pull together, trying to stifle a smile. "You're serious, aren't you?" Her words are broken by pauses between them. Like she's trying to wrap her head around the fact that I genuinely want her.

"Now I'm the one who doesn't want to come on too strong," I joke, taking a step back so we're face to face. "But…yeah. It isn't a question for me, I wouldn't need to think about what I want. It's really your call how we move forward from all of this. You want this to be it? I'll be bummed, but I respect it. Want to keep doing this in private, my lips are locked." I shrug. "I promise, Dem, this is all you."

Sometimes I look at Demi and think she's never actually been properly loved. Never been wholeheartedly chosen. Never been able to confidently feel secure in a relationship. And it makes my hatred for her ex grow stronger every time.

"I think I like kissing you…" she whispers across the space between us.

I smirk, rubbing a hand over my jaw. "Oh, I know you like kissing me."

"I need to stop complimenting you, it's only growing your ego." She sighs with an eye roll, and I approach her again, pressing my lips to the top of her head like it's the most natural response.

"Can I see you tomorrow?" I ask.

Her cheeks perk up, and I see those dimples as she nods with a smile.

"Yes."

She grabs her things and turns toward the door. I follow behind and reach my hand to the doorknob before she can, pulling it open for her.

"Get some rest, Dem." I lean against the doorframe as she walks into the hallway and stretch my neck to watch her leave.

She looks over her shoulder mid stride. "You too, Twelve."

Practice today fired me up. Although that's not entirely new. I'm a sucker for a rivalry game and that's exactly what we have coming up on Sunday night. A prime-time home game against a team we always battle hard with? Sign me the fuck up.

I sent Demi a text this morning before practice and then didn't check my phone until coming back into the locker room to change. A boyish grin spreads over my face when I see there isn't just one, but two missed texts from her.

GIRL OF MY DREAMS

Thank you for the chocolate chip cookies at my door this morning.

I appreciate that you feed into my obsession with sweets.

After she left yesterday, I did a quick grocery order and added some snacks I thought might be a good idea to have on hand for her if there's a possibility she'll be hanging out more. The pre-cut cookie dough looked like an easy enough thing to throw in the oven, so I grabbed a few packs of those and put some in a Tupperware this morning. It was really a fifty-fifty shot she hadn't left for the day yet, but most people aren't out their door before seven in the morning like I am, so I figured I was in the clear.

I was in the neighborhood

GIRL OF MY DREAMS

Is that so?

> There's more where that came from.

GIRL OF MY DREAMS

> Oh really?

> Yep, kitchen is stocked.

GIRL OF MY DREAMS

> Wow… good omelets and cookies? I don't know what to say.

> Say you'll have dinner with me tonight.

GIRL OF MY DREAMS

> Hmm sounds tempting.

> I'll cook. Whatever you want.

Bold of me to offer to cook for her, but I'd learn how to make a four-course meal if I needed to for her.

GIRL OF MY DREAMS

> Do you like seafood?

> I like everything.

GIRL OF MY DREAMS

> Right. Okay… I could go for some shrimp tacos. But maybe a bowl version? I can help cook.

Yeah, I'll need to look up a recipe or figure out what I need to make this, but I can do that. How hard can it be?

> Done. And nope. I'm cooking, just come over. 7:30 good?

GIRL OF MY DREAMS

> I'll be there.

I slide my phone into the pocket of my shorts. A grin the size of Texas on my face and I'm physically unable to stop smiling. I haven't shared a single detail about Demi with anyone—and not that I haven't wanted to, because god, have I. But I don't know how much Demi wants people knowing about her personal life, and somehow, I've become part of that personal life.

"Look at that smile." Ford's strides slow as he approaches me.

"Only one reason for a smile like that," Nate says as he pulls a shirt over his head.

The two of them stand before me, Ford's hands on his hips as he's smiling at me.

"Will you two leave me alone? Jesus Christ. Can't a guy just smile?"

"It's a big one, though. So, who's the girl?" Nate tips his chin my way.

"Oh. You know what? I know." Ford turns to Nate, whispering something in his ear like they're fucking kids.

"Just whatever you're saying, say it out loud." I grab my bag, slinging it over my shoulder and run my free hand over my hair.

The locker room has emptied out for the most part, just a few stragglers at the far end aside from the three of us.

"It's D-E-M-I," Nate whispers.

"I don't get why you just spelled her name. These are grown-ups around us, you know that, right? They can spell."

Ford's thumb jerks in Nate's direction. "Dad life."

"I'm not saying anything." I take a few steps toward the doors, both of them not far behind me as we all walk out into the hallway.

Not saying anything gives me away, but it's also not something I feel comfortable discussing until I know Demi is okay with it. The last thing I want is for her to feel judged or uncomfortable at work—not that these clowns would make her feel that way, but I know Demi. Unless she wants people to know, it's not up to me to share. She clearly told Abby we're neighbors, which is probably the only reason Ford suspected Demi to begin with. Well, and I suppose me spilling that we had coffee together might've tipped them off too.

The two of them change the subject as we're walking out. I hear mentions of different routes and screen plays, and I feel settled knowing they're now talking about practice and no longer my life. Although I want to fucking scream about how I've kissed her two times, I've been giving my best poker face for weeks.

Warm air greets us as the doors open and we head out to our trucks. Ford snagged a spot up front, and I wave as he hops in. Nate and I continue walking toward the patch of magnolia trees where we're parked.

"Doing anything with the kids tonight?"

His truck starts once we're close enough with a roaring sound. "Mia saw something online about a little league fundraiser happening, so I think she wants to do that and then go buy some Halloween decorations."

"It's September."

His hands raise in front of his chest. "Please. I know. But she loves it and I don't question the things she loves. Plus, the kids like when we take out all the spooky shit."

I nod, palming his shoulder before he gets in his truck and drives away. I do the same, plugging in my phone and pulling up the internet to find a good—but easy—recipe for shrimp tacos.

⬤

"Excuse me, where can I find your spices?" The basket in my hand is empty except for the list I jotted down in the car on the back of my receipt from the coffee shop.

Shrimp

Cumin

Rice—white rice, maybe Jasmine? Basmati?
Limes
Avocados
Sour Cream
Canned chipotle chiles
The recipe I found also called for cheese and corn, both of those I miraculously have at home already.

"Aisle seven," the teen employee replies.

I love food, but I don't cook things from scratch very often. Turns out, cooking for one is pretty fucking depressing, and I haven't actually wanted to make a huge mess in my kitchen just for me. That's why those pre-made meals have been my go-to.

Seriously? I mutter under my breath as I'm bent down looking at the spices. I see taco seasoning, but can't find ground cumin anywhere. Can I use taco seasoning and it'll taste the same?

Dammit.

I pull my phone from my shorts and hover over Nate's name before quickly pressing call.

"Hey," Nate answers followed by absolute chaos. Someone's crying and there's music playing and there's also someone asking him rapid-fire questions in the background.

"Can I use taco seasoning for the same effect as ground cumin?" I ask, cutting right to the chase. He clearly has his hands full, and I hate interrupting his family time as it is.

"Uh, I mean, cumin is in taco seasoning. But so is salt, paprika, stuff like that, so if you use taco seasoning I probably wouldn't add the other ingredients." He pauses. "Wait, what are you doing? Are you cooking?"

"I'm shopping and then cooking."

"Liam, you're grocery shopping?" I hear Mia's voice through the speaker and let out a heavy sigh.

"Yes, I'm grocery shopping. I do this sometimes."

"I think he has a lady friend coming over," I hear Nate say to her, and Mia lets out a gasp.

"Okay, well, thanks for the help, Campbells. Have a good night."

"Bye." It's a collective goodbye from everyone. My best guess is they were in the car and everyone heard the conversation.

I grab the taco seasoning and the rest of the things on my list, hustling through the aisles not letting myself browse. At the checkout counter, the older man ringing me up starts a casual conversation, one that ends with wishing me luck on Sunday, and I shoot him a smile and a thank you as I leave.

Spending time with Demi tonight has me excited. So fucking excited. And I refuse to let anything ruin that—even if my phone just buzzed with a text from my father.

CHAPTER TWENTY-NINE

DEMI

When I get to Liam's door, I can already hear music coming from his apartment. I straighten out my top, pulling at the bottom, and glance down at my jeans. I can't remember the last time I think I felt sexy, but every time I'm around Liam that's the word that pops in my mind.

I feel confident and good about myself most of the time, but he takes it to another level. The way he stares at me, longs for me almost—I always thought someone's attention like that would make me uncomfortable, but it's the complete opposite.

The door swings open before I can even knock, and I glance at the tiny camera near his door. He literally saw me coming.

I pause before I speak. Before I move or even breathe.

Because he looks perfect. And it's the first time I'm finally letting myself see him instead of rushing past the thought. He's absurdly handsome on a regular day. He takes on a hot, masculine approach in his uniform, but tonight there's a navy blue apron against his light gray T-shirt and black jeans. His hair is styled in that perfectly messy way where some pieces are in his face but you can tell they're supposed to be. His eyes are so pretty, and that smile—someone help me before I say screw dinner and just start kissing him again.

Because, of course, his lips are softer than a freaking pillow.

"Wow." He opens the door and the simple three letter word comes off his lips effortlessly.

"Hi," I say, smiling.

"You look really pretty, come in." He opens the door wider and steps to the side to let me pass.

"Thank you. It smells really good in here," I say, removing my shoes.

His apartment is becoming one of my favorite places to be, which is saying a lot since I've only been here twice. But I'm instantly comfortable. The same way I am around him in general.

"It'll be done in about five minutes. Grab yourself a drink if you want—there's some decaf coffee in the fridge and some other things too."

"You know, just because I don't drink doesn't mean you can't. I know you like a beer here and there, maybe even an old fashioned."

The fridge is stocked with beverages and food. A major contrast to what I previously knew about his empty fridge.

Liam's standing against the counter, two bowls in front of him as he starts plating the food. He layers things, beginning with the rice and then some corn, followed by everything else. He looks good in the kitchen. Almost as good as he looks on the football field.

"I know." He shrugs. "Honestly, I don't drink a lot during the season. But you're right, I do love to have one now and then."

I nod as I come up to his side. There's a mixture of aromas around me and it's making my stomach growl, it smells so fresh and so appetizing.

"I'll tell you what," he says, turning to me. There's a pair of tongs in his hand that he uses almost as a wand, waving it around when he speaks, and I pull my lips together to avoid laughing at the very cute gesture. "I'm not feeling a drink right now, but I promise not to hold back if I end up wanting one later."

"Go crazy," I tease, and his lips curl up as he finishes plating the meal.

He brings both bowls to the kitchen island, then grabs napkins and utensils before he pulls out one of the barstools for me.

"This looks really amazing, thanks for cooking."

Liam unties the apron, pulling it off his body and places it on the counter before he takes a seat next to me.

"Any time."

We eat in silence for the most part. Each looking at one another every so often, nodding our heads in agreement that this dish is fucking good. Like *good*, good. If I didn't walk into him actually cooking, there's a chance I would've given him shit about ordering takeout and pretending he made it.

Both of us clear our bowls and he even goes back for seconds after inhaling the first helping.

I can't help but notice his phone has been buzzing on and off for the last hour, and even though I'm trying to ignore it and be nonchalant...I am, in fact, very nosy about it.

"Should we finish our puzzle?" he asks just before it buzzes again.

"You don't have to avoid your calls or texts on my account, Liam. If someone needs you or something, just answer the phone."

There's a bite in my words. It's unintentional for the most part, but after all the bullshit I went through with my ex, I'd rather not be a fool again.

"No one needs me." He stares at his phone and then holds down the side button, completely powering it off. "It's the guys in the group chat discussing my life against my will." He chuckles. "I may have given them some fuel to work with and they're having an entire conversation about it. But the ones I'm actively avoiding are my dad's. His messages aren't important right now, or ever really. But especially tonight. I don't want to be bothered by him."

"Oh," I say, feeling a little silly for the jealous bone that poked out a little. I have no right to feel that way. No claim to him or whatever this is.

"Did you think another woman was texting me or something?"

"Or something." I shrug, feeling slightly embarrassed.

"Dem," he says, reaching for my hand, and I let him take my fingers into his. "I haven't texted a woman in over a year, except for my friends' wives or girlfriend. You're the first woman I've hung out with in a long time. I don't know how much clearer I can be when I tell you I'm all in on whatever this is. I'm happy to remind you every day if you need it—it won't bother me. But please know that it's you. It's only *you*."

It's weird that I believe him. He makes me question everything I thought I knew and thought I wanted after my divorce.

I nod, feeling his fingers lace through mine as we stand facing one another in his kitchen. The light above the stove is on, giving an almost somber glow to the evening. His thumb makes circles on the back of my hand, and I look at our hands together. The sheer size of his cover mine so seamlessly.

"So…" I smile, trying to lighten the mood. "I've seen a lot of interviews you've done when they've asked if you have someone special in your life. You know, any of those incredibly personal and—quite frankly, inappropriate—questions, and—"

Before I can continue, he cuts me off.

"You." He takes a step closer to me and his grip on my hand tightens slightly, but it's still gentle.

"Me what?"

"I was always talking about you. They're all about you."

When Liam stares at me the way he's staring right now, it could make my heart skip a beat. I feel so confident that every piece of me—the broken, battered, and bruised—would be unconditionally cared for with him. And I've never been that certain about anyone—even the man I married.

"What?"

"I mean, yeah, I didn't actually have you." He laughs, taking a step back, but his hand still wraps around mine, not letting go. "But I'd say it with you in mind."

I can't believe all these years, all those interviews and times I've seen him talk about a woman—he meant *me*. There has to be something to be said about a man who holds out hope for five years, right?

He jerks his head toward the living room and leads me to the couch, where I take a seat. There's a beige blanket on the corner that he hands me as I get settled before he grabs my drink from the kitchen island and brings it to the coffee table.

To my surprise, the puzzle looks like it's still in good shape, exactly as we left it. Consider my faith in Birdie restored.

"I—I don't know what to say to that," I admit.

"Is that weird?" He takes a seat on the couch near me and runs a hand through his hair. I watch as it falls back in place.

"It's…" I pause, shaking my head. "It isn't weird. I guess I'm just so taken aback by it. I mean, truthfully, Liam, I'm not naïve." I chuckle. "I've known, you know, about your crush or whatever you want to call it for a while, but I guess I never thought it was anything more than that. Certainly not as sincere as it apparently is."

"Well, you were married, Dem. Despite how it may seem to someone who doesn't know me, I am a respectful guy."

He's nothing like the picture I had painted of him in my mind. Emotionally, intellectually—it's almost enough to make me drop every wall and guard I have.

"Well, you're more respectful than he was," I mutter softly.

Liam's bicep flexes when he moves his arm to drape it over the back of the couch. I catch his eyes lingering on my lips and I allow myself to mirror him.

"If you ever want to talk about anything, you know you can, right? I mean, I fucking hate him, but if you need to vent, or whatever…" His hands tap his chest. "This is a safe space. It's just you and me."

"Just you and me." I repeat the words he said when I opened up about Brianna too. And I believe it. I feel it. "I guess I like the sound of that."

"Of you and me?" he asks, eyes flickering with hope.

I nod slowly, biting the inside of my cheek.

He reaches his hand out to me, and I bring my fingers up to his as he takes them and presses the softest kiss to my knuckles. My eyes watch the entire thing, my inhale hitching at the warmth of his breath against my skin.

"There isn't much to say." I take a quick sip of my drink. "Anymore, that is. I probably could've talked your ear off this time last year. Even a few months ago, but I've forgiven him— for my sanity, not because he deserves it. And I've moved on. Or, you know, I'm trying to."

"Did he ever apologize?"

My mind replays one of our final conversations the day I handed him the divorce papers. I was sad. I was hurt. I felt empty and lost. But I also felt sure. I knew it was the right thing.

"He did. We've had a lot of really mature conversations, and I think that's why when he does go through one of his immature moments I get so mad and upset. Because I know he can be rational, he just chooses not to be all the time."

"Yeah, that's hard. It's probably his way of dealing with it, right? Lashing out for no reason."

"Brandon's always had a temper. I knew that going into our relationship, but I always looked at his hotheaded personality about things as passion. I laugh at myself now for that."

"I promised I'd never ask about him and what happened—but I do need to know if he ever laid a hand on you. Please tell me if he touched you, Dem."

Liam's eyes plead with me for honesty.

"He never laid a hand on me. I promise. Our arguments were verbal—never physical."

He exhales a deep breath and nods. "Okay. I don't want to say that's good because, you know, fuck him for raising his voice at you, but I'm glad it never escalated."

Shaking my head, I scoot a little closer toward him on the couch.

"It didn't. When I—" I stop myself. "Never mind."

"No, what?"

"I don't want to make you sit through the downfall of my marriage. What a boring way to spend the evening."

His head tilts and he gives me an amused smirk. "I already said you can if you need to."

Moments like this remind me that I didn't have anyone to talk to during my separation and divorce. I worked through things with my therapist and I'd give my mom weekly updates on things, but neither of those are the same as having a person.

It just made me miss Brianna even more than I already do.

"The articles that came out last December about him cheating on me were true, but we were already having a hard time before any of that came out. Yes, he cheated." I sigh, unable to make eye contact with Liam. "But our issues started before that."

"It doesn't excuse him cheating."

"No," I say, shaking my head. "It doesn't."

"I'm sorry that happened to you, Dem. It pisses me off knowing the person who was supposed to love you the most hurt you in that way."

For a while I chose not to speak on things that happened. On how it all ended and what led up to it. It's no one's business. But, at the same time, all that does is protect the image of someone who I no longer respect. And how is that fair to me? I don't owe Brandon anything. Plus, is it really bad-mouthing someone if all I'm doing is explaining what they did to me?

CHAPTER THIRTY

DEMI

"You know what the craziest part about everything is?" I laugh to myself, finding actual humor in the whole situation now.

"Hmm?"

"Remember when you and I first met?"

His brow raises and his perfectly sharp jawline twitches as he grins.

"It was a Friday—"

"Okay," I say, interrupting him with a laugh.

"Of course I do."

"I wasn't wearing an engagement ring because we were working on things at that time."

"But you still called him your fiancé?" he questions, no judgment in his tone, just curiosity.

"Technically, we were engaged, but a week before that event I found out he kissed some random girl at a bar. He apologized left and right, cried, and begged me to forgive him for his mistake."

"Dammit," he mutters, lowering his head.

"So, like an idiot, I did, and we stayed engaged, then got married, only for him to do it all over again years later." I laugh as I shrug. "I should have known. But anyway, there were a lot of things we didn't agree on completely before we got married, and I should have been stronger and left sooner."

"Like what?" he hesitates.

I sigh, because bringing this up to anyone always makes people judge me.

"Kids," I whisper, fidgeting with my fingers. "We never really agreed on kids. I mean, I thought we did, but I was wrong."

"He didn't want kids?" Liam asks, and I softly chuckle. I don't blame him for assuming that's the case, most women want children.

"I don't think I want them." Saying this out loud used to cause me shame. I used to feel so unworthy as a woman knowing I didn't feel the urge for children. I love kids, but I've never pictured myself being a mom. Which was a very difficult conversation to have with my own mother. It took her time to understand, and I get it—having children is an important part of life the way she was raised. I think my abuela is still secretly holding out that I'll change my mind, though.

It was a conversation Brandon and I had early on, and I truly thought we were on the same page. Over the years, he changed his mind, and rather than telling me he changed his mind, he slept with someone else instead.

"Oh," Liam says. "I'm sorry for assuming the opposite, that was fucked up on my part."

I wave my hand, shaking it back and forth. "No, you're totally fine. I realize it's not the norm."

"So he cheated on you because he wanted kids and you didn't?"

I shrug. "I think that was part of it. We were on the same page at first, but he changed his mind. I don't blame him for changing his mind. But he handled it poorly."

"Understatement of the fucking year."

I grow silent, replaying one of our conversations we had before filing for divorce. I saw Brandon's remorse. He was sorry he cheated, but his mind changed and mine hadn't. Being together was no longer fair for either of us.

Liam's head tilts, his eyes searching for mine as he says, "Hey, Dem." He looks at me with a soft smile. So genuine and authentic.

"Your significance and worth isn't tied to becoming a mother or not. It doesn't define you or make you any less complete. It's nobody's business how you live your life, and if you decide kids aren't part of your story, then so be it."

My lips part and my eyes well up. No one has ever had that response to my admission. Not even my mother. Our biggest argument ever came from me telling her I didn't think I wanted children.

"You're perfect exactly as you are. Kids or no kids. And fuck anyone who is unkind to you over that very personal decision."

I don't know what to even say to him. I just nod, keeping eye contact.

"And say the word, I'll knock his teeth out. He might be taller than me, but I'm scrappy as hell."

That earns a laugh from me.

"Not necessary, but I really appreciate the offer. Honestly." I smile. "My marriage was a lesson, and lessons are good. So I'm good."

"Promise?"

The blanket spans over both of our legs at this point, and I feel his knee brush against mine as I'm sitting crisscross. I nudge his knee and he stills, looking at me before dipping his chin.

"Pinky promise," I reply, holding up my finger and he extends his hand, hooking his pinky with mine.

The last thing I want to continue doing right now is discussing my ex when I'm seated next to Liam. He's opposite Brandon in every way imaginable. My eyes linger on his hands, taking note of the size and strength before I trail up his forearms. I shouldn't be ogling over his body right now; it feels unprofessional, but I'm not at work. And I've already kissed him. I've already pictured him in various scenarios that don't involve a mic and a football field.

So any line I'm worried about crossing with my eyes, I've already crossed with my mind. My big, brilliant, horny mind.

This time it's my phone that vibrates on the coffee table, and I glance down to see my mom's picture coming up on the screen.

"It's my mom," I say as I reach over to silence the noise.

"You can answer it," he says as he rises from the couch. "I'll be right back."

I watch as he walks to a room at the end of the hall before shaking my head out of the daze.

"Hi, Mom," I answer, joy laced in my voice.

"Hi, mi amor, I haven't talked to you all day. I just wanted to see how you're doing."

Holding the phone between my ear and shoulder, I give her the briefest rundown on the last twenty-four hours, omitting the fact that I'm seated in Liam's apartment because I don't have time for all the questions I know will follow.

As she's telling me about something happening with one of their neighbors, Liam walks out of the room I assume is his bedroom. He's changed his clothes completely. And he looks just as hot. If not hotter than before. Gray joggers and a Spider-Man T-shirt. It's cute and a little nerdy, but I love everything about it.

My mom and I end the call as he's in the kitchen, and I get up to walk toward him.

"You changed." My eyes stutter on the joggers.

He nods. "Want to watch a movie or finish the puzzle? Or we can keep talking too."

"I assumed seeing you in your jammies means you're ready for me to leave so you can get to bed."

"I don't sleep in this," he says as he smirks, taking one of the cups from the sink and placing it in the dishwasher.

I roll my eyes at what he's insinuating and playfully push his arm.

"And I don't want to go to sleep yet. I want to spend time with you."

"Okay." My cheeks feel warm as I lean against the counter, watching him do the second most domestic thing I've seen all night.

Once he finishes loading the dishwasher, his attention turns to me. Eyes blazing as he works them up and down my frame.

"If you want to get more comfortable, you can change into some of my clothes," he offers.

"I live next door," I say, tipping my head toward my apartment. "I could always go grab something of mine."

"Or you could wear mine. You'd look hot in my clothes, Dem."

"Clothes are for overnight guests, Liam. I'm not your overnight guest. I'm your—"

"What? What are you? Finish that sentence." His voice is smooth as he crosses his arms over his chest. The Spider-Man logo popping out over his forearms.

"We're—I don't know exactly. Hanging out? I don't know, Liam. I've quite literally only been with one man my entire life so I don't actually know what to call someone who is my friend but I also like to kiss—even though I probably shouldn't."

With my back against the countertop, he comes closer, his body directly in front of mine and I look up to make eye contact with him. He drops his arms to his sides, and I want them on me. I want his touch. His taste. His warmth. I may not know what the hell to classify this as, but I don't think I care right now.

"A friend you like to kiss is often referred to as a friend with benefits," he whispers when he leans in and goose bumps overtake me. "Except, I'm not sure I like that term when it comes to you. It doesn't feel strong enough. Because with you, Dem, I feel it down to my bones. A longing, a connection, a desire that can't possibly be summed up as friends with benefits."

I swallow the lump in my throat. "Thank you for clearing that up," I whisper back, heart racing.

"I could kiss you right now—as an example. But only if you want." He inches closer, and I inhale his scent.

My breathing picks up and I can feel the heat building in my belly.

"I am a hands-on learner," I respond breathlessly.

Before I can think my next thought, his lips are on me. Hungry. Starved. His hands pull at my hips, bringing me closer to him as I moan into his mouth. His body pushes against mine and his tongue swipes over my lips in the most teasing way.

A desperate groan leaves his chest. The neediness. The desire. I feel every ounce of it as Liam's mouth moves against mine.

I'm aching for more. But too afraid to ask for it as I lightly suck the tip of his tongue, earning a low growl from his chest.

His hands rake over my body until they're cupping the back of my thighs and he lifts me onto the counter. I gasp when I hit the marble. He made that feel swift, effortless even. The aching only grows with each passing moment, and I don't know how to tell him I want more. I need more.

I'm almost certain he's holding himself back too. For someone who is frequently known as a 'gets what he wants play-boy' socially, Liam doesn't push anything on me. And at this moment, I find myself wishing maybe he wasn't such a gentleman after all.

He brings a hand to my hair, gripping as he glides it down the side of my neck and to the base of my throat. I feel his fingers against my skin as he leans in even more to deepen the kiss.

I can't control it any longer when I bring my hands to the

waistband of his joggers, dipping my fingers just underneath and pulling him even closer against me, my legs spread wider.

"Fuck," he breathes against my lips when he pulls away briefly.

"Liam," I whimper his name into his mouth, my breath heavy and arousal building.

Taking his thumb, he runs the pad of it over my bottom lip as he gives me a devilish smirk.

And then, he kneels.

CHAPTER THIRTY-ONE

LIAM

I'm a fool for this woman, a downright desperate man willing to do anything she wants. I don't think I'll ever get enough of her.

My name falls off her lips in a throaty whimper, and I watch her eyes burn when she looks at me. There's a hunger, a want, a desire bubbling behind those dark eyes that I haven't seen before tonight.

My hands work down her thighs, skimming the fabric of her jeans as I kneel. I grip the back of her knees and pull her to the end of the counter, and she gasps as her hands fall behind her to steady her body.

She's gorgeous. And I've waited years to experience Demi like this. Fuck, I never even thought I'd be able to, but here she is in my kitchen, on my counter, choosing to be here with me.

"Lean back a little, Dem," I grumble.

She does as I ask, reaching toward the button on her jeans to pull them down, but I place my hand over hers to stop her.

"No, no." I grin. "I want to do it."

Her cheeks tint pink and I watch as her lips part before I move my hands to replace hers.

Demi's skin is warm to the touch and each time my fingers

graze a new spot I notice goose bumps pop up. Her head tilts back slightly as she's breathing, and I slowly pull her jeans down, getting them completely off her body before placing my hands on her inner thighs, spreading her legs wider. What a goddamn sight she is.

"Oh, you forgot," she says quickly gesturing to her underwear that I purposely left in place.

"I didn't forget. Leave them," I say as I skim my thumb over her.

Her body jerks at the touch as she sharply inhales.

"I have years of filthy thoughts all trying to come to life at this very moment, Dem. You have no fucking idea how much I'm going to enjoy this."

She moans again, her hand resting on her lower stomach. I rise, bending over her body slightly as I press my lips near her belly button and trail down her stomach. I only hear her breathing. Her deep breaths and her labored gasps.

"Jesus, Liam." She squirms as I hook a finger into her underwear, moving it to the side.

Seeing her like this already has me so fucking hard. She's spread open for me and she's dripping wet. I want nothing more than my tongue between her thighs. To hear her cries and feel her body writhe against me, knowing she's coming undone because of me—of us.

I bring my lips to her center, kissing her gently. "*Fuuuck*, Dem," I breathe against her. "Look at you."

Without a single second of hesitation, I drag my tongue through her. If her reaction tells me anything, it's that she likes it. She really fucking likes it. Her body pulls back and her head drops. She lets out a gasp and then moans my name not once, but over and over as I continue to work my tongue over her.

I want to devour her. I want everything she has to offer.

With one hand on her inner thighs, I push her to open wider for me. My tongue pauses on her clit and I skim over her with my teeth before pulsing my tongue against her again. When I glance up at Demi, her chest is pounding, one hand is cupping her breast, and she's rocking her hips fiercely.

I run my tongue over her again. Slow and steady, sucking when I reach her clit.

Over and over.

Until she screams, and I feel my own body jerk at the feeling of her coming apart all over my tongue.

She writhes against my face, and I happily lick every inch, every drop that she has before laying my lips on her inner thighs. She has no words, just sighs and deep breaths when I glance up at her. She's sated and looks so fucking sexy.

I want one final taste as I work my tongue over her one last time before moving her underwear back in place.

"You tasted like you enjoyed that too." I stand, dragging my thumb over the corner of my mouth, and she stares at my face before working her eyes down my body, noticing my own mess. "Look what you did to me."

"I—" She stares, pausing as I adjust the waistband of my joggers.

I swear to god I could do this again. Right now if she wanted to.

"Seeing you like that, tasting you…" I blow out a breath, shaking my head. "I'm not shocked at all."

She sits up straighter on the counter, jeans still on the floor near my feet and I reach down to grab them for her. Bunching up one of the pant legs, I take her foot and gently bring it through, repeating the same motion for the other.

"That was…wow." Her chest is still moving up and down rapidly when I help her down. "I really don't know what to say. Which is kind of annoying." She laughs and I kiss the top of her head.

"I've rendered you—the reporter—speechless."

"I guess so." Her words are soft and teasing.

"Being with you like that…it was"—my hands cup her cheeks—"I loved every goddamn second."

Her brows crease as she looks up at me. "Really?"

The surprise on her face shocks me. "How could I not?"

Demi blinks slowly, nestling the side of her face into my hand against her cheek. And all I can do is hope like hell we can do this again.

"I guess you'll have to change again." Her hand motions toward my pants, but her finger grazes the fabric and she pulls her hand away. "Sorry," she adds quickly.

Looking down, I grin. "Please don't be sorry about that."

Her tongue coats her lips as she steps back and rolls her eyes with a smirk and she heads to the living room. Everything in me thought for sure that she would book it to the front door after what just happened. But she settles on the couch, pulling the blanket onto her lap and reaches for a puzzle piece.

I decide to change into a pair of shorts and then meet her in the living room where she already has a handful of new pieces put together. Puzzles don't usually take me this long, but I'm realizing how little I'm actually trying to complete the puzzle knowing it's something we've been having fun doing together.

"Baggage for baggage," I say as I take a seat on the floor right near where she's seated on the couch.

"Go ahead."

"My dad's been reaching out for weeks, and I haven't answered or returned any calls or texts. I just know whatever he has to say is going to piss me off."

She sets the piece in her hand into place and then leans down, elbows to knees to face me easier.

"Have you always had a rocky relationship?"

I can talk to her about this. I know I can. She trusted me enough to open up about Brianna and things with Brandon. She's a safe space.

"Yeah, actually. Certain years were better than others, but

once I really got into football and playing professionally was a real possibility, it got so much worse."

I feel Demi's hand on my shoulder and she squeezes lightly. My hand finds hers and I hold it in place there.

"Everything I've ever covered about you or read somewhere, you started playing football young. Like eight or nine, right?"

"Around seven I started."

"Jesus." She sighs. "That's just such a long time to have such a turbulent relationship with a parent."

"Fucking tell me about it." I blow out a breath. "He won the Super Bowl when I was ten, and that's when it got really bad. Just the pressure he put on my brother and me was ridiculous. I'll never understand how anyone can put their own child, or any kid, really, through that kind of mental boot camp. It was torture. I hated when he was at my games and practices for the most part."

"I understand why you don't share this publicly, but it really hurts me to know you've had to talk about him your entire career without anyone knowing these things."

Demi's fingers slide around my shoulder and to my neck, and I melt into the way it feels to have her hands on me. It's comforting and intimate and it's everything I've never felt with anyone else.

"Yeah." My throat clears and I lean my head back on the cushion of the couch, right next to where she's sitting. "My freshman year in high school, I wasn't a starter—not that I was bothered by it. I knew there were a lot of guys better than me. But my dad?" I blow out a breath with a shake of my head. "He embarrassed the fuck out of me with that coach. Almost made me not want to play. Of course he was charming in his way of going about it, basically making contributions to the team with new equipment, money, field help, anything he could do to butter them up. He made himself look like the world's best dad. But we'd get home, and I'd hear 'look at all the strings I have to pull for you.'"

I feel my nose burn as I relive that memory.

"He pushed me so much. Even making it to the NFL, after shitting on me for not going in the first round. He still found ways to make my success *his* success. I mean, yeah, he coached me, and I do believe in good genes, whatever. But *I* worked. *I* studied. *I* proved myself. The success I have in my career is *mine*." I don't see the room around me right now.

It's like I'm transported back to being fifteen, sitting in the locker room as the guys around me talked about my dad as if he was a superhero and I didn't have the fucking stones to tell them otherwise.

"Hey." I hear Demi's voice and then I feel her hands on my face, her fingers against my stubble as she runs her thumbs on my cheeks. "Hey," she whispers again, and I see her seated next to me on the floor. Worry written all over her face.

"Sorry." I shake my head and clear my throat.

"No, we're not apologizing right now. You have nothing to be sorry for. Okay?"

I nod, her hands still cupping my cheeks as I place my hands over hers, pulling her fingers into mine.

"It still gets me when I talk about it. Which isn't often. It's usually just with Dana."

"Well, it's only fair, right?" She chuckles lightly, leaning her head against my shoulder as we sit on the floor.

It's dark out. Pitch black, actually, and I don't even know what time it is since I haven't been bothered to check a clock since she got here.

"What?"

"I share about my crappy ex-husband, you share about your crappy dad. Baggage for baggage, right?"

I turn my head, planting a kiss to her forehead. "Right."

Sharing parts of my life with Demi feels so fucking easy.

Like it's the most natural thing I do all day long. Telling anyone about my dad—especially someone who has met him—would normally make me so fucking nervous and uneasy. I used to think people wouldn't even believe me if I shared all the mental bullshit he put me through. The things he would say to me were tailored to break me. To break my spirit and make me think that without him, I was nothing.

Opening up to Demi has given me this renewed belief in myself. She makes me feel seen and appreciated in ways I've never experienced simply by how she listens. Talking to her is easy and comforting—she's compassionate and has such a warmth about her, but also has a fierce way of reminding me exactly who I am. Something that's easy for me to forget when I end up on the wrong side of a bad day. It's easy to spiral and let my mindset become turbulent.

She's letting some of her walls down for me, yes, but she's taking a crack at mine too, and at this point I just want to let them crumble.

CHAPTER THIRTY-TWO

DEMI

Liam and I have been spending more time together than I ever thought we would. It's been easy and fun, and quite honestly, it's felt nourishing. His company fills something within me. He helps me feel seen—but not just seen, *understood*. Valued.

We kiss, sure. But we haven't shared any moments further than that aside from the one time he devoured me on the kitchen counter. I've thought about that often over the last couple weeks —and I'm not ashamed to admit it.

Right now, the way we spend time together feels like something we both kind of need, and when I left Liam the other night part of me wanted to turn right back around and knock on his door.

It's hard to ignore how he makes me feel when it's all I've ever wanted. I've felt cared for before, but Liam takes that simple word to a completely new level. He *wants* to know me. All of me.

My career is important to me, there's no way I'd say it isn't. Women are constantly put down in this profession, working ten times harder to be taken seriously and I've always been so proud of the strides I've made in this field. But for me, spending time with Liam doesn't diminish any of that. In a lot of ways, it feels like he helps me feel even stronger in this league.

He consistently makes sure the moments we spend together are of my own choosing. Sure, the first coffee meeting was the result of a bet he initiated, but he gave me an out immediately after he won. He values my job and my role, and I know that if tomorrow I said I couldn't see him anymore, he'd respect my decision.

Because Liam has always been about *my* decision.

Is it foolish to spend time with him? Maybe? Maybe not, though. I can't speak for everyone in this industry, but I know my heart, and I feel like I now have a pretty good grasp on who Liam is. This isn't just for show or for favoritism. Hell, no one even knows about us spending any time together and I've been singing his professional praises for years. I don't know exactly what any of this is, but I know right now I'm healing a part of me that has felt broken for a long time.

And I won't let anyone make me feel bad about that.

"Morning. The meeting starts in ten minutes, but Chris is going to grab coffees. Do you want one?" Kyle Long, one of the commentators on my crew, comes up beside me. He's wearing khaki pants and a dark blue polo. He's a colleague I've worked with for years and probably who I'm closest to. His wife and I have gotten dinner together a handful of times and we've connected over our love of books.

"Oh, that'd be great, thank you so much." I gather the papers from the table into the crook of my elbow. "Should I just text him, or do you have a running list on your phone and I'll just give you my order?"

Chris is one of the interns and easily the best one on our staff. He's quick, funny, and always so helpful. He's eager to be here and it reminds me of myself.

"Just put it on this list," he says, handing me the phone as two other colleagues walk in.

Tom and Michael approach Kyle, giving him a handshake as I'm typing my order into the phone. Tom is an older gentleman, he played football back in the seventies and he's so knowledgeable. I absolutely love working with him. Michael, on the other hand, can be a piece of work. He knows so much; he picks up on plays and penalties during games even before they're called, so for the network, he's a dream. And at the end of the day, he's a supportive colleague—but he has his moments.

"Demi, you taking coffee orders?" Michael's sarcastic tone goes in one ear and out the other, but my eyes sear into him. "I'm kidding," he retreats, attempting to seem playful.

"Chris is going to grab coffee." Kyle takes a seat in one of the gray chairs placed around the table in the conference room, and I hand him back his phone.

I don't give Michael the satisfaction of a reply, but I do say good morning and greet Tom who takes a seat to my left.

Chris pokes his head in a few minutes into the meeting, dropping the coffees off as Greg is going over some things for the upcoming schedule. It's hard to believe we're in week seven already. Mid-October got here in the blink of an eye.

Once Greg wraps up, Michael starts going over offensive plays on film. The Knights are playing Denver, Liam's dad's former team. And I'm pretty certain that's probably why his dad has been calling and texting him.

Michael stops and restarts the same clip of film over and over, examining every movement by the offensive line. It's interesting, and he definitely has everyone's attention, but all I'm really concentrating on is that Liam is probably going to be asked about his dad this weekend.

"Tess, you have the feature interview with Liam Evans. I'll probably want to give you some specific notes on what to talk about. There will be a stat sheet printed too, so you can look through that," Greg says to the only other woman at this table.

My eyes dart to Tess. Her pen is moving quickly across the

paper in front of her. She's very sweet and very good at her job. I really enjoy having her on the crew and think it's about damn time they added another incredibly talented female to our team.

She nods as Greg continues to spew off some information. Her bright blonde bob bouncing as she does.

"Yeah, I can absolutely do that," she says, referring to Greg's question about pulling some information on Landyn Evans Sr.

Dammit, I don't want anyone to ask him about his father. Why can't we just let him play his game without pulling him into it? *Because this is stuff fans enjoy.* I can hear Greg's voice in my head.

"We're going to grab lunch around one thirty, Demi. Do you want to join us?" Tom taps my shoulder as he rises from his seat.

I kind of want to hang around the facility to see if I can bump into Liam so I can give him a heads-up on what's coming this weekend. Although, he isn't naive and something tells me he's already anticipating this happening just based on the situation.

Grabbing lunch with my colleagues is probably a better idea than just awkwardly lurking around the building hoping I run into Liam when I know I can just see him later.

"Yeah, where are you guys going?" I ask, smiling up at Tom.

CHAPTER THIRTY-THREE

LIAM

If I don't reply to one of the seven text messages or three missed calls, I just know I'll never hear the fucking end of it. So even though I know there's a high chance I'll hang up this phone pissed off, I click on my dad's contact.

Demi didn't need to give me the heads up about the interview, I fully expected it. Although, having her come knocking on my door at nine last night was too fucking cute.

"About time you called me back. Jesus, Liam."

His voice is rough as he answers and full of that scolding tone I grew so used to as a kid.

"I've been busy, Dad. What do you need?"

"Did you not read any of my text messages?"

I roll my eyes as I sigh.

"I'm going to be at the game this weekend and I'm bringing your brother with me. Do you have a suite we can sit in or do I have to make arrangements on my own?"

Suites are not fucking free, and he knows that. The fact that he's asking if I'll have a suite just readily available for him should blow my mind, but I'm not even surprised.

"I don't have a suite, Dad. And don't have any plan on getting one."

"Doesn't your friend Ford have a suite?"

I scoff, shaking my head as I pull the phone from my ear. This man is acting like he's too good to sit in the stands, or that he can't afford to pay for a damn suite if he so desperately needs one.

"My friends split a suite because of all the kids."

"So because you don't have kids, you don't think it's important to have a suite? I had one when I was playing and you kids were in it all the time."

"Things were a lot less expensive back then."

"Are you having money issues?"

Of fucking course that's what he would zero in on.

"No," I firmly state. "I don't buy suites, end of story."

Nothing is easy with him. Even something as simple as a conversation. He drains so much out of me.

He hums, and I hear background noise. It's almost enough to make me ask where he is, but honestly I don't give a fuck.

"Denver's defense has the highest sack rate in the league right now. Make sure your O-line is intact and ready."

"Yep." I'm so mentally checked out of this conversation, but one thing I always told myself is I'd never give him the satisfaction of seeing how he gets to me. As badly as I want to tell him to fuck off and hang up the phone, I don't. Maybe that's a mistake on my part, but it's still part of the guilt he puts on me. *I'd be nothing without him.*

"I'll make some calls about a suite. I'd like to be comfortable as I watch my team make you work."

Not "good luck." Not "do your best." Not even a funny way of saying "hey, I'll always be a Denver fan, but you're my son and I'm rooting for you."

I hate how my nose stings and my eyes burn. I shouldn't pay

any mind to anything he says. But he's my fucking dad. He should care about how he makes me feel.

Once our phone call ends, I hop in the shower. I need to wash away the stress of this day. In addition to speaking with my dad, I had a meeting with my agent and we briefly touched on my contract. She said the Knights have been in touch with her, but haven't made any official offer yet for us to work with to extend me.

I'm not really surprised, I know these things are tedious and there are a lot of moving parts to make things happen, but I've done a lot for this organization since I've been here so to be almost halfway into this season and not have really any clue what's going to happen sucks. It's the business, but it still sucks.

Birdie meows at the bathroom door, and I hear her loud and clear as I'm drying off. The moment I close any door it's like she immediately needs to be in that specific room.

"What's the deal, Bird?" I poke my head out with my towel wrapped around my waist.

She scurries into the bathroom under my feet and then follows me right out as I'm walking toward my closet. I just shake my head at her need to be everywhere I am.

I'm starving and need to eat something. I wish Demi wasn't at a network dinner tonight. I'd order us some food from that Dominican restaurant again. I've been thinking about those fucking tostones since the first time we had them.

Pulling on boxers and a pair of joggers, I shake my hair a little to get excess water off and hear my phone chime three times in a row from my nightstand. I swear to god, if it's my father again I'm going to lose my fucking mind.

SUMMER KINCAID

Hi handsome!

Look who we ran into at Bricks!

Summer Kincaid has sent an image

The photo comes through of Abby, Summer, Mia, and then Demi on the far left. Holy fuck, she's gorgeous. Her smile gets me every goddamn time.

> **SUMMER KINCAID**
>
> She's literally stunning. I can't handle it!

I heart the photo and laugh at Summer's comment. Tell me about it, I know she is.

> **CLARKY**
>
> I'm in love with her makeup!
>
> **LITTLE HUNT**
>
> She was with a few people from the crew I guess, but we told her when they leave she should come sit with us!
>
> **SUMMER KINCAID**
>
> Impromptu girls night, don't wait up!

I laugh to myself before answering. I don't think Demi has ever hung out with the girls socially. I'd guess the football game was the first time she hung out with Abby.

> She doesn't drink so don't pressure her into a margarita Summer Kincaid.
>
> **SUMMER KINCAID**
>
> Ok dad, I know she doesn't drink. I already told her we'll have a crispy Diet Coke waiting for her if that's her thing.

I can't lose the smile on my face. The thought of Demi hanging out with my best friends makes me happy for her. In all our conversations, she's made it clear, without flat out saying it, that she doesn't really have anyone. And Demi deserves people in her corner. I have no problem sharing mine with her.

I haven't flat out told anyone we've been hanging out—believe me, it's killing me to keep quiet, but I'm leaving it up to Demi if she wants that out there. It wouldn't totally surprise me if Demi ended up trusting the girls enough to tell them. Especially Mia, she has a trusting face.

And here I was thinking my mood tonight would be sour because of that conversation with my dad. I'm still pissed at him, but even just the thought of Demi spending time with my friends adds some happiness to my evening. Hell, having Demi as part of my life lately has added a ton of happiness I didn't realize I was missing.

CHAPTER THIRTY-FOUR

DEMI

"Demi, I can walk you out to your car," Tom offers as I'm fishing my phone from my bag.

"Oh, no, thank you, Tom. I actually saw some friends so I'm going to sit with them for a few minutes before leaving. Have a good night."

He nods, and I head toward the ladies' room.

It was a pleasant surprise seeing Liam's friends earlier. Chase Hunt's girlfriend, Summer, is one of the funniest people I've ever met. She started talking to me immediately, and I just hope I wasn't awkward as hell at first just watching the three of them interact.

I found myself staring at Summer. Intrigued by her. She's beautiful, but she looks like the woman Brandon cheated on me with, and I hate that's the first place my mind went. I'd never been in the same room as that woman, but in looking at Summer they share a lot of the same physical features. Though, I feel confident Summer isn't a homewrecker.

Her long blonde hair, blue eyes, the curves that hit in the right places. I felt myself staring, and I just hope like hell she didn't notice, because it isn't Summer who deserves my look of disdain.

I head to where they said they were sitting and I spot the three of them at a high-top table in the bar area. Abby's in a black and white detail top with jeans, and Mia's wearing the cutest light blue dress with a pair of sandals. Summer's back is to me and her blonde hair flows down her shoulders, and I admire the black outfit she has on.

They did say to come find them when I was through, but I still feel a tad nervous approaching these women I've really only interacted with a handful of times. But they're Liam's friends, practically his sisters with the way he describes their relationship. And that nugget of knowledge alone eases my body a little.

"Hi," I say, coming up to the empty chair.

"Hey, oh my god, have a seat." Summer smiles.

"I'm so glad you came over," Abby says, beaming at me as she hands me a menu. "I know you probably already ate, but if you want to browse the drinks."

"We know you don't drink alcohol, though," Mia rushes out.

"Right, yes. I meant, you know, something else," Abby adds.

I chuckle as I take a seat. The bar area is much louder than the lounge where I was previously sitting with my colleagues. The TVs are on and it looks like preseason hockey is on most of the screens. It looks like Phoenix is playing, and I linger for a second on the screen. Bri and I went to a couple Phoenix hockey games when we were young. The brief memory makes me smile.

"It's fine. I'll grab some water for now."

The waitress pops over and the girls order some appetizers along with more drinks, and I put in my order for the water. When I first decided to stop drinking alcohol, I used to feel embarrassed when I'd be out with people. I don't mind that people ask questions about why I don't drink, but it's when they would talk down about it. I've dealt with that a handful of times, and I've since learned to be more direct in my response.

Thankfully there isn't even a question about it tonight.

"So, you moved in next to Liam. I can't believe he didn't tell us!" Mia takes a sip of a Shirley Temple.

"I may have mentioned it to the girls," Abby says, hunching her shoulders in her seat.

I smile. "It's fine. Actually, I'm surprised he didn't say anything. I mean, it isn't groundbreaking news but…"

"But he's obsessed with you so something like that is obviously eating him alive not being able to scream about it," Summer interjects as she dips a tortilla chip into the queso.

"He's a very good neighbor," I admit.

All three of them exchange looks, and it's painfully obvious they're trying to hold back smiles as Mia pulls her lips together, Abby's nearly biting a hole in her cheek, and Summer's hand is strategically placed over her mouth.

Sitting with the three of them makes me want to open up. Not anything crazy, but having girls to talk to about things again would probably be fun and I'd bet slightly therapeutic. I've never had more than quick conversations with them, but they feel so easy to be around.

"What?" I finally ask, tilting my head as I sip my water.

"Have you guys hung out or anything since you live so close?" Summer is the one to ask and even with just the little bit I know about the group, that feels on brand.

It'd be easy to say yes. Easy to just give them some tiny details because truthfully I'm dying to talk to someone about this.

"We've hung out…" I pause. "Yes." I smile down at the table, feeling their eyes on me.

"Liam's a really great guy," Mia says. Her eyes are soft and sincere as she smiles at me. "I know he gets kind of a bad rep sometimes because he can be wild and a little over the top. But he's Luke's godfather for a reason."

I didn't know Liam is godfather to one of her sons, and that small piece of information is enough to make me smile.

"Yeah, she's right," Abby adds. "For us, I think he's like that brother who really knows how to push our buttons. Right?" She shrugs her shoulders toward Mia. "He's like a sour patch kid with us."

The girls both chuckle, and I look at Summer who isn't laughing, but she does smile at me.

"He's one of the good ones. I know you didn't ask, and I have no knowledge of your personal life or your current intentions. Wow, I feel weird wording it that way." She blinks, holding her glass in her hand. "But I just really want him to be happy."

I've interviewed men about Liam as a football player many times. I've talked to coaches, owners, other reporters, and even event organizers. Every last one of them saying exceptional things about the person Liam is. All those people had a professional and vested interest in him. But words from the three women at this table with me mean more than any of it.

They're in his personal life. They know him on a level most people don't. Their lives are intertwined in more than just football, and I suddenly feel such an urge to talk to him.

Wanting Liam in the way I've grown to has been catching me by surprise. Sure, he's good company and I'm so comfortable being around him, but it's growing into something of a craving. And I have this thing about cravings.

My time with the girls goes by quickly, and I don't let too many more details about my time with Liam slip, aside from the fact that we've been working on the same puzzle for weeks even though I'm absolutely certain he could finish it in an hour without me.

I like your friends.

HOTSHOT QUARTERBACK

I like you.

His reply makes me blush as I read it walking through the lobby of our apartment building. It's almost ten o'clock at night and I honestly don't know the last time I was out this late if I wasn't working. I'm sleepy, but I really needed that.

Another notification dings when I'm heading into the elevator, and I smile at the message. Summer and I exchanged phone numbers before I left.

Summer Kincaid has added you to *GIRLS ONLY* chat.

SUMMER KINCAID

Hey Demi! We loved hanging out tonight, hope to do it again soon.

also, if Liam's ever annoying you this is where we lovingly vent about the guys so feel free to chime in at any time haha

I laugh at her second message, double clicking to add a heart to the first. I feel like I just made friends in the last two hours. Actual friends—and it makes my heart so happy.

CHAPTER THIRTY-FIVE

LIAM

"Ah, fuck this," Nate mutters as he's trying to tape his fingers.

"Why don't you let one of the trainers help with that?"

"Taping my own fingers shouldn't be the fucking puzzle it is." He tosses the tape to his side, standing.

I just shake my head. There's no talking to Nate when he's annoyed. Unless I'm five foot nothing and named Mia, he doesn't listen to anyone.

"Bring it in, boys," Chase announces as he starts walking into the center of the locker room.

Today's game should be a good one. I'm ready for it. Seeing my father on the other hand is something I could do without, but I do love seeing my brother. Something I haven't been able to do much of lately.

I hated the interview with Tess, but not as much as I thought I would. To be fair, she asked two questions about him—and more specifically, the questions were about his stats. I can talk about his stats all day long no problem, it's when things turn more sentimental. When a reporter thinks that talking about my father in the same breath as football is going to be touching or make me feel some kind of emotional nostalgia—when in reality, I can't get the dry, boring answer out fast enough.

"This game is a big fucking opportunity today, boys. Let's do what we know we're capable of and make sure that, after today, the league hasn't forgotten how fucking dangerous we are. I don't care about last week or next week. Focus on now. Today. Come on." Chase paces in the small circle we've created around him as he projects his voice.

I nod, hearing every word and knowing that this game means so fucking much to me. I already know my dad's up in some suite waiting to see how his former team is going to pummel through my line and get to me.

Once I'm introduced and make my way out onto the field, I hear the roar of the fans and the sound of the announcer echoes through the stadium. My teammates are all lined up as I trot to the sidelines, and I keep my head down as I make contact with my offensive coordinator. We've talked about the game plan a lot this week, which isn't anything out of the ordinary, but somehow I've kept feeling like I need the reminder. Our walkthrough the other day had me pumped—fucking amped for this game—and I can't explain how much of that is merely to shove things in my dad's face.

Demi's on the sidelines in the shaded area on the home side of the field. It's a beautiful day today too. Mid-seventies and kind of cloudy—a miracle mid-October. Her hair is up in a pony-tail with black shorts and a black blazer over a white top. I smile at her and she gives me a quick head nod as she sees me.

I just want to get through this game and spend time with her. Our schedules haven't synced up too much in the last week and I'm just missing her.

"I'll get you, keep running," one of Denver's defensive linemen says as he runs up to me just after I've thrown the ball. He braces his hands on my forearms, careful not to push me down and get a costly penalty for his team.

"I'll be here," I say, smiling as he jogs away.

My dad was right about Denver's defense being top notch. But I'm fucking proud to say so is my offensive line. The work these guys have been putting in at practice is translating to game days and I couldn't be more thankful. I don't think my body could handle another week of beatings.

"Let's go have some more fun," I say to the guys in the huddle as our offense takes the field to start the second half.

And I mean that, because today has been fun. I've been able to draw their defense offside twice in the last half, and it's always fun to get a free play out of it.

"Fuck off with your hard count, Evans," a Denver defensive player says to me as he lines up at the line of scrimmage.

"Why would I stop when they're so effective?" I tease, smiling through my helmet as I get under center.

He grumbles, and I take a peek at the game clock. Thirteen seconds.

"Blue 32, One, one, one." I pause my cadence. "Let's go, let's go," I shout, dragging the last word out. "White eighty. Boulder, Boulder, hut."

Cribley hikes me the ball, and I drop back quickly.

My eyes scan the field, lingering on the left, as Ford bolts down the sideline. For a tight end, he's one fast son of a bitch.

I can feel pressure to my right and know that they attempted a blitz on defense. Something my offensive line is doing well holding off with Nate helping to block, but I just need another second to make sure Ford has some separation from their safety.

He's practically stride for stride with Ford, but I decide to sling it downfield anyway.

All the pressure up front stops as the ball soars toward Ford. He's an easy thirty yards down the field, and I eagerly look on as Ford extends his hands, towering over the fast young safety and pulls the ball to his chest as he comes down with the catch.

The adrenaline when a play like that happens is instant. It's a mood and morale booster all around, and the fans erupt in cheers when Ford stands up and starts celebrating.

"Fuck yeah!" I shout as I run toward him.

"Nice throw, baby!" he says when we meet in the end zone.

I glance up, wondering where in the stadium my dad is, only to be caught completely off guard by Demi's reaction on the sidelines. It's subtle, but behind a stack of papers I catch her thumbs-up and tip my head at her, smiling.

Who the fuck cares where my dad is.

Demi's here.

The second half flies by, and thankfully we leave with the victory. I'm happy to win every single time, but today it feels even sweeter as I step out of the locker room and head toward the exit. I don't anticipate seeing anyone as I'm leaving since I'm one of the final few out of the stadium, but low and behold, my father is standing outside the double doors chatting with one of the athletic trainers.

My brother, Landyn, is nowhere to be found, which only irritates me as seeing him would've been the only reason I would've accepted a run-in with my father.

I say good night to the trainer, but my father's eyes meet mine, and I stop once I get to my truck. He no doubt weaseled his way into being allowed beyond the gate that's usually only for players and staff.

In the parking lot to the left, I see a couple of the production crew packing up and notice Demi standing outside of her black SUV chatting with one of her colleagues. Her heels from earlier nowhere in sight, just slippers on the pavement, and I fucking love to see it.

"Liam." My father's stern voice brings my attention back to him. "What'd I tell you about their defense, huh?"

"They were solid," I agree. "Thankfully, my guys were ready."

He shoves both hands in his pockets, and I stare at his body language. Smug. Arrogant. And I pray that, even though we share similar features, I look *nothing* like the man in front of me.

"Where's Landyn?" I ask.

"He's going to get a table at Lambert's."

I nod, knowing he wouldn't want any witnesses around when he starts insulting me at some point in this conversation.

"You're welcome to join us. Might be a good idea if you do."

"Why's that?"

"Well, you and I don't get out much together."

I scoff. "You mean we aren't photographed together enough for your image?" I open my door, tossing my bag into the truck.

I've showered and changed, but I still feel sweaty as I stand here. My jeans feel like they're clinging to every piece of my legs and I want to take off my hat and whip it across the parking lot. But it's him. He's making every fiber of my being feel like it's irritated. On fire. Like I'm an angry, upset teenager all over again.

"Watch your mouth, Liam. It's in bad taste to start running it."

I cock my head back with a laugh. I've learned over the years to take his verbal beatings, but something lately has me wanting to hit back.

"You thought I'd get slammed today. Hell, you were probably rooting for it."

"I'd never root for my son to get taken down. You had a good game." His compliment stuns me into silence until he keeps talking. "It proves how well I've taught you. Although if I had to guess your passer rating is around ninety-five."

"One twenty-four point six."

The voice is soft, but stern.

It's full of pride and compassion.

We both turn toward the fence. I know he's unable to fully see who it is, but I'd recognize that voice anywhere. I hear it in my head daily.

Demi is standing there, one hand propped on her hip, the other holding her phone. Slippers on her feet and her once perfectly bouncing ponytail now in a messier bun on the top of her head.

Her silhouette glows against the lights, brightening the parking lot around us.

"I'm sorry?" my dad questions, taking two steps before stopping.

"His passer rating," she calls. "It's not ninety-five. It's one hundred and twenty-four point six."

My chest swells with admiration for her.

"Huh." An amused sound comes from him as he looks down at his feet and then back up at me.

He scoffs and shakes his head. I don't get attaboys from him or good game compliments. So him taking a swing at my passer rating tonight comes as no shock, but the fact that he doesn't keep digging in is a surprise.

He's silent as he nods, paying no attention to Demi as if he doesn't even remember someone is on the other side of the fence. His stare is devilish, reminding me of being on the receiving end of it as a kid. Next would typically come the lash out. Ignoring everything I did right and focusing on anything I did wrong.

"Your throws were high," he finally says. "Guess it's good you have tall receivers."

And there it is.

I'm not giving him the satisfaction of a reply to that.

"I think it's best if you leave, Dad."

Stuffing his hands in his pockets, he pivots and walks back toward the door, and I watch it close behind him as he heads back into the stadium.

And when I glance over my shoulder, Demi's gone too.

CHAPTER THIRTY-SIX

DEMI

A wave of adrenaline came over me, causing me to jump in the middle of that conversation, but I saw no other choice. A fierce, protective urge had me stomping in my Halloween slippers over to the mesh covered fence once I heard Liam's voice and saw his father standing toe to toe with him.

I don't throw the word hate around often. I usually think no person is actually worth that much effort, but I just witnessed first-hand the shit that Liam shared with me. And seeing it up close and personal made me sick to my stomach.

Although it was so fucking satisfying to correct him. Something I'm sure nobody ever has the balls to do.

My walk up to my apartment is quiet. Thankfully, because I'm mentally exhausted after such a long day. I can't help but wonder if Landyn knew it was me behind the fence. I know there's a mesh covering, but only so many people are allowed in those back parking lots, and there are only so many female employees. Something I've been working to rectify, actually. Still, even if he would've seen me, it wouldn't have stopped me from speaking up.

No one deserves to be talked down to like that. And my soft

spot for Liam has only grown in the last few months—so shit like that in front of me just won't fly.

Once I'm finally settled on the couch with three chocolate chip cookies on a paper towel and my Netflix page loading, there's a soft knock on the door.

When I look through the peep hole, Liam's standing on the opposite side of the hallway against the wall. His head tilting back against the wall, eyes closed and both hands in the pockets of gray sweatpants.

"It's Liam," he roughly states. Although, it's a low tone, ragged even.

I pull open the door, noticing he isn't wearing his signature smile. There's no witty joke spilling from his lips or smirk covering his mouth.

"Hey, are you okay?" I ask.

He walks toward my door, stopping right at the threshold.

"You didn't have to do that tonight." His hazel eyes are blasting with more blue right now. "Thank you. I'm sorry if that jeopardizes anything for you."

"Come in," I say, taking his hand and pulling him into my apartment. "You don't have to thank me." We walk toward the couch, and I take a seat, moving my cookies from the cushion to the table. "And don't apologize. I made the choice to say some-thing to him."

He nods, looking around my apartment. I notice him cata-loging all the books on the floor against the wall and he smiles briefly.

"I wasn't expecting him to be out there, but I probably should've known," he says with a shake of his head. "What's with all the books on the floor?" His wave gestures to my moun-tain next to the television.

Liam takes a few steps, and I memorize his movements across my floor. The way he swiftly flows from one area to another.

"Well, I need another bookshelf." I stand, matching his body language as his hands land on his hips.

He glances down at me, bright eyes and takes a step closer, leaning down just a hair as his hand cups my neck.

"Want me to build you one?" he whispers against my lips, and I feel my insides begin to quiver.

"You have no idea how hot that just made you," I joke.

He brushes his lips against mine smoothly. It's soft. Cautious almost.

Kissing is something we've been doing in the heat of the moment or after some intense banter, rarely has he kissed me during a simple conversation before.

"I've wanted to kiss you all day. All week, actually."

"When we're here," I say, "or there"—I point to the wall where his apartment is—"we can do this as much as we want."

He nods, licking his lips as he takes a step back. "Right."

I know Liam wants more. And sometimes I think I could want more too. But I won't let myself get ahead of things. Right now this is working for me, and he did say we could do this on my terms.

At this moment, though, with the way Liam's looking at me it makes me want *everything*. His good mornings, his good nights, every in between of his day. I can't wrap my head around how quickly my emotions have latched onto him. His kindness and how much he cares for me is constantly on display. He goes out of his way all the time to make sure I'm safe and comfortable.

At first I figured he'd be somewhat of a distraction for me. Someone I can hang out with, who I know truly wants to hang out with me, where I'd feel very much in control of the situation.

If I've learned anything since spending time with Liam Evans, it's that as much as I think I have my emotions under control, my rapidly beating heart tells me otherwise.

"Liam." I reach for his hand, pulling him back toward me

and he closes the space between us, wrapping his arms around my waist.

"God, you smell good," he says as he inhales and pulls me closer to him.

I tilt my head, looking up into those dreamy eyes of his and feel my core tighten. His arms are strong around me, his chest is warm and firm, and he too smells so fucking good.

I'm not exactly bold in intimate settings. Or at least my track record says that. But Liam makes me feel like stripping naked right now without a worry or care in sight.

His fingers draw circles on my lower back as his hands are still wrapped around me, and I lean up toward his lips, not holding back as I press my mouth to his.

Liam's hands wander down my hips and he pulls me up in a sudden movement and holds me in place as my legs wrap around him. I rock my body against his, unable to stay still knowing what I want to happen. What I'm ready to have happen.

"Dem," he breathes against my lips as he breaks apart briefly, his eyes meeting mine and I nod.

Over and over, I nod, before the word "yes" breathlessly leaves my lips. Liam won't do anything I don't want to do—he's made that clear. And I respect him for it, but right now I need him to be the playboy. I want the Liam I've heard whispers about. The one I've briefly experienced—who knows what he's doing. And likes to do it again and again.

His mouth crashes to mine this time—hard and consuming. It's like he breathes life into me every time we kiss, and I keep coming back for more, afraid I might suffocate without him.

"Bedroom," I mutter against his lips mid-kiss, and he walks down the hall. Although we both get a chuckle realizing he hasn't actually been here enough to know which closed door is my room.

"Last one. Left," I say as I run my tongue along his lips.

"Fuck," he moans when I move my lips to his neck.

My back hits the mattress, and I take a look at him as he stands at the foot of my bed. My elbows prop me up and I just stare at him before me. He pulls his shirt off and tosses it on the floor, leaving him in those gray sweats, and I focus on the V-shape on his stomach. He's toned and lean and every bit of a fucking fantasy.

"So we're clear, I get tested yearly. Everything's all good," he assures me, and I lick my lips.

"I got tested after my divorce and I'm on the pill. But also I…" Hanging my head back slightly, I sigh. "I haven't been with anybody in well over a year."

"Dem." He runs a hand over his hair. "I haven't been with anyone since I found out you were divorced."

I pause. "That was…almost a year ago." My words are just above a whisper and filled with surprise.

He shrugs. "I know there's this narrative that I'm some playboy who dates around—and yeah, maybe that was true for a bit. I was trying to find you in any woman I spent time with, but from the second I found out you were divorced I haven't been with anyone since. I knew if anyone was *ever* dumb enough to lose you, I'd wait for my chance. And hope like hell to get one. I've always just been waiting for you."

God, this man. I've never felt wanted the way Liam wants me.

I can't find the words to say, pounding from my heart rings in my ears as I stare at him. His head tilts slightly, his jaw slacks just a bit before he speaks again.

"We can take it as slow as you need to. I can be tender." The left side of his lip pulls up and that earns a smile from me.

I avert my eyes down. "What if I don't want that?"

His eyes widen a little and he raises his eyebrows.

"I just mean, what if I don't want you to be gentle? Like I'm something fragile and breakable."

"I don't think you're fragile and breakable, Dem. But I do

think you're worth taking my time with." He kneels at the end of the bed and pulls me by the back of my knees closer to the edge.

His hands rest on top of my knees and he inches them up slightly every time he squeezes my legs. I'm seconds away from just ripping my shorts off myself as he slowly works his way up my thighs. I see what he's doing—the playfulness, the edging—but I've never wanted someone to tear a piece of clothing off me as badly as I do right now.

"Getting antsy?" he asks as I squirm again. My heart rate is rapidly increasing as I bring my eyes to follow his hands. "I remember what you taste like." He raises to his knees and leans in as he licks his lips.

Jesus, why is that hot?

He moves his hands up to my waistband, and I arch my back slightly, making it easier for him as he pulls my shorts and underwear completely off. Lying here bare in front of him feels empowering. Something I've never felt while being this exposed. But it's Liam. It's how he makes me feel and how he empowers me daily.

"Un-fucking-believable." He lowers his mouth just below my belly button, and I sharply inhale when I feel his breath against my skin.

I feel his finger slip between my thighs and I pant out. "Oh fuck."

My body jerks as he slides another finger in, pushing into me with the most amazing pressure before he brings them both to his lips and sucks.

He nods as he smirks, both fingers still in his mouth as he licks them clean. I watch as he lowers his head between my thighs and I feel his tongue run through me slowly.

Dragging. Painfully, deliciously slow.

"Jesus, Liam," I whimper. "Don't stop."

He brings his tongue through me again and again. Pulling

every moan and gasp from my chest as he does. It feels so good. *He* feels so good.

I feel his fingers spread me wider and his other hand opens up my legs as he pushes on my thigh. His tongue pulses on my clit slowly and my body bucks every time.

"Oh god, I won't last like this." My words are breathy.

Liam drags his tongue down while his thumb rubs slow circles over my clit, and I don't know which feeling to focus on more. He licks up and down, whispering "*fuck*" and "*I love this*" every time he pulls his mouth away. He pushes his fingers inside, and I gasp at the pressure, but desperately want more.

With his fingers he works in and out in strong motions as he brings his tongue back up to my clit. His movements aren't slow anymore, they're demanding and hard—exactly what I'm craving.

"Oh fuck, Liam. *Yes.*"

I feel his teeth as he nips, once and then twice and my back arches so far off the bed as he slams his tongue into me again and again, letting me ride out the best fucking orgasm while he doesn't let a single drop go to waste.

CHAPTER THIRTY-SEVEN

LIAM

"You have no idea what you do to me, honey."

Demi leans back on the bed, her chest panting up and down still. I had to will myself not to fucking lose myself during that for the second time. I can see her dimples from here as she smiles while lying back.

"Liam," she whispers my name, but her voice is raspy as she leans up to her elbows.

I stand and her eyes dart to my sweats where it couldn't be more obvious I'm turned on right now. I've never moved my way slowly through a bedroom before. There's been foreplay and then sex and it's finished. But with Demi all I want to do is take my time and hold all these moments close. I have no fucking idea how long this will last, if it were up to me we'd never stop. But I told her this was all on her terms. I can admit maybe I regret leaning so hard into that when I know how I feel about her.

"I want you." She sits up and reaches for my sweatpants, pulling them down to my ankles and I step out of them as I stand at the edge of her bed.

Her oversized band T-shirt is bunched up around her stomach, and I lean myself forward as I crawl over her on the bed, running my hand under the fabric.

My hand cups her breast. I knew she wasn't wearing a bra, and I smirk when she moans at the pressure of my palm.

I move my lips to the shell of her ear, lightly dragging my finger over her nipple, back and forth.

"Prove it," I say against her skin, taking my tongue to her neck.

She shudders, and I feel her hips nudge me as I'm leaning over her. She takes a moment, but her hand reaches for me, and I hiss at the way she delicately grips me from over my boxers.

I twitch at her touch. Holy fucking shit, this is not going to take long.

My lips find the spot below her ear, and she whimpers again. Demi spreads her legs even wider beneath me as she takes her hand and dips it into my boxers. I already know there's no going back once I feel her hand wrap around me.

I'll never feel this turned on by anyone else in my life.

"I have a condom in my wallet," I say as I pull myself away briefly.

My eyes linger on her as I grab it and pull my boxers down before sliding it over me. Her legs are wide open, and I have half a mind to just devour her again, but she pulls at my forearm.

"Come on, Twelve," she rasps, and I reach for her T-shirt.

She pulls both arms out, and I can't help but stare at the woman lying before me. She's stunning. Every inch, every curve, it's all I want. Now. Forever. But I don't say that out loud. The last thing I want to do is scare her away.

"What?" she asks when I don't immediately move.

"I'm just enjoying the view."

She smiles from where she's lying. Dark brown hair splayed over the pillows. Chocolate-coated eyes watching my every move as I bring myself even lower toward her. Her fingers feather my triceps as I'm hovering over her, and I bring my lips to hers.

Demi's hands grip onto my shoulders and she pulls me closer to her, the tip of my cock grazing her entrance as our kiss deepens.

Slowly, I edge myself in and feel her tense up the second I do.

"Oh fuck. You're so tight, Dem."

She lets out a gasp when I push harder, and I feel her fingers press into my back.

"Yes," I hear her whisper against my shoulder and pride swells in my chest. She feels so fucking good, I can't believe there's a chance I could've gone my whole life without this.

She inhales sharply when I push in again, pulling out slowly in hopes to help her get used to it. Her little moans and whimpers are enough to send me over the edge, and when I feel her nails digging into my back, pulling me closer, I know she wants more.

"You want all of it, Dem?"

I feel her nod through a moan, and I thrust into her. Her back arches and she cries out as I pull all the way out before thrusting in again. Harder this time.

"Oh fuck," she cries. Her hand reaches up to her breast, and I quickly move it out of the way and replace it with my mouth.

My teeth pull at her nipple as I keep thrusting into her. My movements slow, but I keep the pressure hard. Consistent. I know it's what she wants as her body moves in rhythm with mine.

"Keep going," she says against my ear.

And it's nothing but our bodies together and heavy panting from us both as we move together in a way I've never done before.

I've never been so goddamn in sync with someone sexually.

"Fuck, Dem," I pant out against her breast, feeling myself

almost bottom out inside her. I hold still, breathing against her skin and moving my lips up to hers.

"You're taking me so well," I whisper against her lips, my voice ragged as I pull out and then thrust back in. "I'm so fucking proud of you."

Another thrust.

Demi cries out a string of curses before she pulls my lips to hers. She sucks on my tongue, nipping at it as she starts to shake underneath me. I can feel her walls starting to crumble and know I'm just seconds behind her as I'm pushing in and out, over and over, until Demi completely falls apart under me.

Her hips wiggle and her heart looks like it might beat right out of her chest. She keeps her hands on the back of my neck, bringing her forehead to mine as she whispers "so good" against my lips, and I feel my body jerk at the warmth of her breath against my skin.

My stomach tightens and I growl out a mixture of whimpers and curses as I come harder than I've ever come before.

Demi Sanchez has fucking ruined me.

CHAPTER THIRTY-EIGHT

DEMI

That was—there are no words.

If I thought him kissing me was the part that was going to ruin me, I'm sorely mistaken. There's something about Liam right now when my eyes are connecting with his that's bringing me so much peace. He's lying on his side facing me—both of us completely bare. But there's an innocence in his gaze. Something so pure and hopeful, I just want to bottle up this moment—nay, these entire last couple months—and hold onto them forever just like this.

"You okay?" He reaches his hand up, tucking some hair behind my ear, and then pulls the blanket up to cover both of us.

"Mm-hmm," I hum, smiling at his touch. "You're different," I admit, trailing my fingers along his jaw. Feeling the stubble beneath my skin.

His eyebrows crease slightly. "Good different, or…" he asks, trailing off.

"Not bad at all. Just different than what I thought, I guess."

Liam's beautiful smile spreads across his face, holding steady in place for a few moments as we stare at each other.

"Yeah?" he finally says, placing his palm on the curve of my hip. His touch is warm and comforting.

"I didn't know you outside of the football field." I shrug, nestling closer to him. "I guess I just assumed that given your... um..." I pause, searching for the right word.

"Reputation?" His voice is rough as he says it.

I hesitantly nod. "You're not the womanizer I assumed I'd be getting as a neighbor. And I never would've pinned you for being as compassionate and caring as you are. I-I don't open up to people. Probably because I don't exactly have many people to open up to, but I've never *wanted* to, until you."

He pulls me closer to his chest, my arms snuggled into him as he wraps his around my body. I feel so protected with him. Being cared for the way Liam does for me makes me know with 100 percent certainty I wasn't properly cared for before.

"I've mentioned this before too, but even having the most incredible and accepting friends, it's rare I shared too much with them, at least not a lot of my deep shit. With you, it's just easy. I feel like I can rely on you, and I hope you feel that way with me too."

I nod against him, inhaling his rich scent. There are a lot of things I could say right now to myself about this current situation I'm in. And none of them are good enough to get me out of his arms. I feel like I belong here.

"I felt really empty after my divorce," I say in a hushed tone. It's so quiet in here, I can hear both of us breathing. "Like I was just kind of going through the motions on autopilot, not really enjoying anything. I smiled, showed up, did what was needed, and I think everyone assumed I was okay and happy." I pull my head back so I can see his face. "You didn't. You saw me exactly as I was. *Existing*. And slowly, you've been pulling me out of the numbness I was in. It's like the volume was at zero for so long and you've slowly been helping me turn it back up."

I feel his arms tighten around me. I wasn't expecting to say any of that tonight. Hell, I didn't even know I really felt that way until I said it. But it's all so fucking true. I couldn't have been happier to leave my marriage, but it was still hard. I had to learn how to be by myself again and relearn how to love the pieces of me that felt broken.

"I've been watching you for the last five years, Dem. Reading your body language and your facial expressions was all I had for so long. Keeping my distance from you when you were married was so goddamn hard. Even when you got divorced, the day I saw you on the sidelines when that article came out about him cheating—I could've beat him to a pulp that very instant. You were always just out of reach," he says with a chuckle. "I'm scared it'll happen again." His voice is soft. "And I think it might kill me."

My heart cracks at his admission. Liam's the most vulnerable man I've ever met, and I'd like to attribute a lot of that to him being in therapy—another thing most men won't do. But I also think it's just part of who he is. He's goofy and charismatic, fun and lighthearted—but there's so much depth to this man that I truly feel like I've only scratched the surface.

"I just know that right now I feel safe with you."

"Can I ask you something?" He rubs circles on my shoulder and I nod. "You've mentioned that you feel safe with me and around me—which, don't get me wrong, that's absolutely my goal with any woman honestly. I want you to know you're safe with me. But is the feeling of being safe a new one to you?"

Sharing about my ex-husband and every fight we would get into isn't how I want to round out this night with Liam. But I can shed some basic light on why it's such a hot topic for me.

"Brandon's temper would explode at any given moment. So many times our disagreements turned into arguments. When I'd bring something up hoping to talk about it, I'd always leave the conversation feeling worse than when we started. My soul liter- ally felt exhausted and my nervous system always felt on edge.

Like I couldn't ever be relaxed in my own home, and it made me tiptoe on how I responded to him sometimes. I guess I never felt safe to share my own emotions and feelings simply because I didn't know how he'd react. Again, it was never physical, but I was no stranger to a verbal lash out every now and then. I'm thankful he cheated, it gave me the push to leave."

"Jesus, Dem. I'm so sorry you had to go home to that for so long. He never fucking deserved you."

"Like I said, a lesson."

I'm not sure why I stayed so long. We didn't have kids, we both had good jobs—the reasons that couples so often stick it out when things are rough didn't apply to us. I used to tell myself he was just having a bad day. Because for a while, I think that's how it really was. His basketball career was beginning to see some real hurdles—he wasn't used to people not fawning over him. I think over time he began to resent me for not wanting kids, but looking at it now, I'm so glad I didn't make that man the father of my children.

"Well, what do you want to do now?" Liam wraps one of his legs behind mine, pulling me flush with his body.

"Oh my god, your foot is freezing, get it off me." I jerk back with a laugh.

He pulls me back to him, planting his lips on my forehead as he spins me on top of him.

"Warm me up," he teases with his lips on my shoulders. "What do you say, want a third orgasm of the night? You know, go to bed real nice and relaxed?"

"What I want to do and what we should do are very different right now. I have a big meeting tomorrow morning for the Girlhood Foundation and need to be bright eyed."

We're introducing a new scholarship opportunity this year—one I'm incredibly proud of. There are a ton of great options out there right now for girls, which is amazing. But this particular scholarship will be for Latina women interested in pursuing a job in a sports-related field. Having something like this will be huge, definitely something I wish would've been around when I was looking into colleges. But I'm so happy to be able to be part of this.

"You're gonna crush it," he says as I sit up, my legs straddle him for a brief moment before I slide completely off my bed and he sits up.

"I hope so. This scholarship program means a lot to me, and I really want to make it happen for girls interested in working in sports."

"I saw the post on the network's social media about the scholarship, it's a really great idea. I'm proud of you for being so passionate about it." He smiles when he reaches for his clothes.

"Thank you," I say, my cheeks blushing as I do.

Both of us back in our clothing, Liam leads me out of my bedroom and down the hallway.

"I'll let you get some rest. I hope you sleep well. Let me know how your meeting goes." He leans in, kissing my forehead.

My television went into sleep mode and the three cookies I had on the coffee table are still there—I'll be taking those to bed with me the second he leaves.

"You too." Our fingers intertwine as he opens the door, and I watch as he flicks the bottom lock before he exits.

"G'night, Dem."

I smile, tipping my head to him as he steps out into the hallway, and my heart could burst at the sight of him as he backs away.

CHAPTER THIRTY-NINE

LIAM

There's still a smile on my face when I wake up. The same one I had last night when I went to sleep. Everything with Demi last night was a fucking dream come true.

> I think I get it

FORD

> get what?

> what you've all been gushing about for the last few years.

NATE

> You'll have to be more specific… we talk about a lot of shit.

CHASE

> It sneaks up on you doesn't it?

> No, it snuck up on you because you fought that shit for too long lol I've been hopelessly wishing for this moment for five years

NATE

> are we talking about Demi?

FORD

yeah, he's talking about Demi.

CHASE

he's in love with Demi

you're all way too chill about this, I'm texting the girls.

FORD

DEMI!!!! YOU LOVE DEMI!!!

NATE

LIAM AND DEMI SITTING IN A TREE

CHASE

yeah, I'm not participating in that. But happy for you bro.

nice recovery.

My phone vibrates just after I close out of the chat with the guys and I see Summer's name pop up.

"Hey, did your boyfriend tell you to call me?" I ask as I answer.

"Chase doesn't tell me what to do," she says. "But he may have mentioned something that prompted me to call."

I laugh into the receiver.

"Yeah," I say.

"Did you tell her?"

"Hell no. I'm fucking terrified to tell her because I really don't think those are words she wants to hear. Even though I could easily see myself slipping and saying it." I run a hand through my hair.

Summer sighs, and I prop my feet up on my coffee table next to our unfinished puzzle. It's been forever since we started this one, yet I completed two alone last week. I'm not complaining, though.

"If we're being realistic, you're probably right. Having the first man you hang out with after your divorce drop the L-word might freak her out. But if we're being delusional…" she says in a sing-song tone. "You saying you're in love with Demi comes as a shock to absolutely no one, and telling her might be your opportunity to have everything you've wanted for the last five years."

"You and I live in delusion land sometimes, Summer. Doesn't mean everyone else does."

"Ugh, that's true." She sighs. "I wish everyone was on our same wavelength."

"No, you don't." I laugh, pulling the phone from my ear and tapping the speaker button. "You like being the only you, and if Chase was like you, you'd never be interested in him. Hence why you and I just wouldn't have worked out—so, sorry." I smirk, although she can't see me.

"Oh, right. Yes, *you* turned *me* down."

We both laugh, and I hear CeCe playing in the background. The television over there is always so fucking loud I swear I don't know how Chase doesn't go crazy.

"What are you up to today?" I ask, changing the subject to something that doesn't make me sweat.

"CeCe has a gymnastics meet downtown at two."

"Oh, right. I remember Chase mentioning CeCe's meet. Give her double high fives for me."

"I will," she says. "I'll let you go, but seriously I love that you're enjoying your time with Demi. We had such a nice time when she joined us the other night. She's cool as hell. And yeah, I don't exactly know how things are going to end up between the two of you, but I just want you to be happy."

"I know."

We end the call, and I toss my head back on the couch, closing my eyes. I'm exhausted. My conversation with my dad in the parking lot has been replaying in my mind for some fucking reason, and I slept like shit last night when I got home from

Demi's. I was close to texting her to see if maybe she was also struggling to fall asleep, but didn't want to wake her if she was already out.

I do know that last night solidified a lot of feelings I already knew were there. I know I love her. I've loved her since the day I met her, but being *in love* with her has happened over the last couple of months. Swiftly. Easily. Undeniably.

I have no idea where she stands. Not really. Am I a distraction for her? Something to pass the time while she heals? Does she even take me seriously? All the questions I've silently asked myself over the last couple of months. Because as much happiness as I exude around her and everyone else, I still sit home in silence and darkness—feeling everything so fucking deeply is draining me. But I want to know how Demi's early morning meeting went.

> I hope your meeting this morning went great. You're amazing.

GIRL OF MY DREAMS

> Can't wait to tell you about it. Later?

> Of course.

I smile at that. And then silence my phone and my mind to try and nap.

CHAPTER FORTY

DEMI

Not to sound needy or desperate, but I've texted Liam twice in the last hour and he hasn't replied. The man has never taken more than minutes to reply to me unless he was working. I open the sliding glass door, deciding some fresh air and a second coffee will do me good as I wait for his text. It's been a while since I've anxiously waited by my phone, excited to hear from someone. I suppose I could just go knock on his door, and maybe I will if I don't hear anything soon.

There's a lot of traffic today, I can hear the city below bustling, but I guess a Saturday during the fall makes sense. Horns honk as I take a beat, propping my feet up on the small table I put out here. It's still warm, although being higher up does have its advantages with the wind. My phone rings—which is odd, since no one ever calls me unless it's work related and even then, it's rare. But Liam's contact pops up and I do my best to rein in my smile.

"Hey," I answer with a grin.

"Hey, neighbor." His smooth voice floats through the phone. "I needed a nap and just woke up. Sorry I missed your texts."

"Oh, that's okay. Feeling rested?"

He hums and then I hear him yawn before he answers. "I'm all right, how'd the meeting go?"

"It was perfect." I'm beaming with pride over how excited I am about this opportunity. "There are a lot of I's that need to be dotted, T's crossed, things like that, but overall everything went great, and I'm just excited and so hopeful for the future of women in sports."

"You fucking did that," he says, and it's like I can picture his smile. All teeth, pure and authentic right through the phone.

I remember when I vaguely mentioned this to Brandon almost two years ago. He said "isn't there already a scholarship like that?" It made me feel small and made my contributions feel insignificant. The more time I spend around Liam the more sadness I harbor for the woman I was in my marriage. The one who begged for bare minimum, accepted mediocre, and truly couldn't tell if him saying "nice dress" was giving me a compliment or a sarcastic insult.

"I don't know if this is kind of forward, but what the hell… do you feel like celebrating? Maybe just dinner or—"

"Yes. Let's go grab dinner," he says, not missing a beat.

"I was thinking just at one of our apartments. I can cook or we can order takeout."

"Oh…" His voice dies down. "Right, right. Yeah, of course. Come over, I can order from anywhere you want."

I feel my shoulders fall slightly. Did he forget we shouldn't take our situation outside of this building? I heard his voice lose its pep when I corrected him and immediately felt like shit. But we agreed that this—whatever it is—stays here.

"Okay," I say quietly, hoping I didn't hurt his feelings. "I can be over within the hour if that works?"

"Absolutely. I'm taking a quick ice plunge in a few, but I won't be long. Come by whenever." As if he's rehearsed, he's back to his upbeat tone. And I should be happy he doesn't sound upset, but it's just a reminder of how he's had to learn how to bounce back quickly from feeling let down. And it stings.

"Sounds good." I pull open the door to head back inside as we end the call.

I give myself a glance in the mirror and contemplate if I should change my clothes or just stay in the comfortable bike shorts and T-shirt I'm currently in. But don't let myself dwell too long on a choice that doesn't matter.

After I've picked up a few things around my apartment, I head out and over to Liam's. He sent me a follow up text saying to just come in so I lightly knock, but then turn the knob to let myself in.

His apartment smells like apple pie. Apple pie and cinnamon rolls, and I feel my mouth watering. Is he baking? There's no fucking way. I peek my head in the kitchen and hear the sound of music coming from his patio, so I take that as an invitation to step outside.

"Knock, knock," I say as I slide the door open.

Liam's seated in the ice bath against the wall, head resting on the edge of the acrylic material. This thing is bigger than I was picturing, it's definitely not just your standard bathtub. Which makes sense since he's six foot two and probably doesn't comfortably fit in a regular tub.

"Hi." He opens his eyes and tips his head up.

I stare at his bare chest and my eyes trail his torso. Fuck. He looks too good.

"I have shorts on." He smirks as my eyes begin to wander but I narrow them at him after that remark.

"Good." I lift my chin, stepping closer to him.

His hair is wet, but not soaking. It's doing that messy thing in the front, and it makes me want to tangle my fingers in it to add to the chaos. Everything about Liam's shirtless chest dripping wet does exactly what one would think it does.

"You can join me." He extends his hand, and I back away.

"No, thank you," I say with a giggle.

"Come on, Dem." He tilts his head, giving me those annoyingly sweet puppy dog eyes paired with his lips curving up slightly. "I'll keep you warm."

My arms cross over my chest as I stare at him. I'd be lying if I said I wasn't the least bit curious about it.

"I didn't bring a change of clothes."

"Wear mine."

He has an answer for everything, doesn't he?

I roll my eyes as he stands, watching as the water sloshes in the tub, and I can't tear my eyes from his abdomen. The lines and ridges. I dart to his arms, the veins and the way his forearms flex. His thighs as he stands up straight, sopping wet and strong. God, I'm losing it. I'm about to cave and hop in the ice bath with this man, aren't I?

Liam extends his hands to me, licking his lips as he does. "We'll start slow." The words do more to me than they should.

"Fine." I exhale, slipping my feet out of the slides I was wearing.

Liam takes both of my hands into his and stands sturdy as I slowly—very slowly—dip one foot in.

I hiss the second my toes touch the water.

"Nope, don't back out, keep going, come on." There's no pity in his voice as I feel his hands pull me a little closer to him.

With one leg completely in, I stop for a moment, taking deep breaths.

"Bring your other leg in, and we're going to sit down together as soon as you're in. Got it?"

I nod as our eyes connect and lift my leg over the side and into the water. Liam spins me effortlessly in front of his body, my back flush with his chest. His hands hold my hips as he lowers both of us into the frigid water.

"Fuck, fuck, fuck, fuck, oh my god." I shudder. "What's the temperature?"

"About sixty degrees."

"I-I need to get out," I say, wiggling against him, but I feel the warmth of his breath against my ear.

"You can do this," he says. His tone is low, voice hushed as he wraps his arms around me. "Focus on me, honey. My voice. Got it?"

I tilt my head back into him and nod. How the hell am I ice cold, yet burning hot at the same time?

"I've been thinking about last night all day," he whispers into the shell of my ear. "You ruined me, Dem." I sharply inhale as his hand glides between my legs and rests on my upper thigh. "But you know that, don't you?" His lips feather kisses along my neck, and I'm completely under whatever spell Liam has placed on me as I close my eyes.

His hand squeezes my thigh, and I quietly moan at the touch.

"You like knowing how badly I want you." I feel his breath again on my neck.

The water moves as he sits us up more.

"I-I do," I admit. Because he's right. The way he wants me drives me wild. It pushes me to extremes—like this moment now. I wouldn't get into a freezing ice plunge for just anyone.

"Mmm." I feel his chest vibrate against my back. "Good."

I take a sharp breath in, counting to four, holding four, then releasing four as he holds me in place.

Barely another moment passes just as I'm getting comfortable and he moves his hand from my thigh, taps my hip and says, "Time's up."

I arch my neck, turning to face him as he rises to his feet, bringing me with him.

"What? That was it?"

He smirks. "That was three minutes. I already did ten before you got here."

"Oh. I guess that wasn't so bad." I step out and grab the towel he's holding out for me.

"Told you." He winks, and I roll my eyes.

Glad to see we're both in our usual form.

Liam lends me a pair of his shorts and a T-shirt to change into and as I'm stepping out of his bathroom, I quickly apologize.

"Oh shit, I'm sorry I didn't even think about you needing to change."

He's standing in his bedroom, completely naked, as if it's the most normal thing.

"Nothing to be sorry about." He pulls on his boxers and shorts, but opts to stay shirtless, and I'm internally cursing him while also loving the view.

"So, about dinner," he says. "Tell me what you want. Anything and it's yours."

My eyes linger on his chest and my mind wants to say, *you*.

CHAPTER FORTY-ONE

LIAM

Take-out containers occupy much of my counter space as Demi sits on a barstool and I stand across from her, leaning against the counter. A rack of baby back ribs is not what I thought she'd want for a celebratory dinner, but I'm not complaining.

I watch as she not so delicately tears apart the half rack on her plate, and I catch myself smiling as my eyes are on her.

"What?" she asks, wiping the corner of her mouth with a napkin.

Shaking my head, I stand up straight. "You're just beautiful. I can't stop looking at you." Casually, I walk around the island to where she's seated.

She turns to look at me, and I take her face in my hand, gripping gently, but leaving no room for guessing my next move.

My lips land on her. It's quick, but powerful. She tastes like sweet barbeque sauce and I loved every second of it.

"I've wanted to do that since you got here. Sorry it took me so long."

Demi licks her lips and pink coats her cheeks as she tries to hide a smile. "Forgiven."

Birdie starts yapping by Demi's ankles, and I half expect her to just ignore her completely, but to my surprise she doesn't.

"Can I give her a little piece of this?" She holds up some of the meat, and I shrug.

"Can cats have pork?"

"Well, they're carnivores by nature, right?" She pulls out her phone and does a quick search. "It says in moderation. So, here you go, Birdie." She takes a few small pieces from her plate and puts them on the floor.

"Great, now she's going to expect table scraps," I tease.

"Nothing wrong with letting her indulge in the good stuff every now and then," she says to me, but she's knelt down next to Birdie as she's breaking up a few more pieces.

My phone vibrates next to me on the counter, and I see it's an email from my agent. Only the subject and a quick preview shows, but it's definitely about my upcoming contract negotiations and I feel my stomach drop. I don't want to look at that right now.

This season has felt different. Not in a bad way, just uncertain, I suppose. It almost makes me wonder if there might not be a contract extension offer to even discuss, making me a free agent after this season. Although, I feel confident in my relationship with Coach Aarons, so we'll just have to see what happens. I've said time and again that playing anywhere else sounds absurd to me, but in reality, it happens all the fucking time. Great quarterbacks play for one team for a good chunk of their career before seasons shift and opportunities change.

At the end of the day, this league is a business. I'd love to stay in Tampa, but I do think I need to become okay with the idea of leaving.

"Want to try and finish that puzzle?" Demi's voice stirs me out of my daze.

She floats across my living room, wearing my shorts and T-shirt as she does and takes a seat on the floor in front of the coffee table. I really can't believe this puzzle still isn't done after all this time, but I'm milking every fucking second I have with her.

"Question for you," I say, taking a seat behind her on the couch, palming her shoulder as I squeeze.

"Go ahead." Demi grabs a couple pieces and attempts to work them together while I sit behind her, massaging her shoulders.

"Nate and Mia host a Friendsgiving every year. I know you don't want to be seen out in public, but they're my best friends. And they already know we've been spending time together. The piece in your right hand attaches to the black cat in the reindeer sweater," I say, trying to save her from another wrong attempt.

"Ah. Thanks."

"Would you feel comfortable coming with me? They're doing it early since they're going to Wisconsin for Thanksgiving this year."

She's quiet for a moment, and honestly I wasn't even sure I should ask her to come with me, but if it isn't abundantly clear to her by now, I'm so fucking serious about her.

"It wouldn't be weird for them?"

"Nothing is weird for them," I say on a laugh. "They'd love to have you."

"Okay," she says, turning her head to me.

I lean down and kiss her forehead, my chest exploding at the way her eyes are sparkling at me.

"Wow, that was highly scientific." I can't stop myself from laughing at the way Demi just explained—or tried to explain— the Big Bang.

"Listen, I went to school for communications, not physics. 'Boom' is the best I can do."

She waves her hand in the air, and I take it into my palm, kissing the back of her knuckles. We've paused the puzzle—again—and have spent the last hour talking about my "nerdy but hot" shirts. Her words, not mine. Although that's a compliment if I've ever heard one.

"I didn't study physics either." I stand, pulling her to her feet. "I was always more into chemistry." My hand wraps around her waist as I whisper my words into her ear.

She playfully tries to pull away, but then sways her body back into me. Her hand is cool as she places it against my bare chest. My heartbeat feels loud in my ears as the words I admitted to my friends recently play in my head on a loop.

"You've had the week off and haven't seemed antsy or bothered at all." She wraps her arms around my torso and leans back to look up at me.

"I've been with you, what's there to be antsy or bothered about?" I grin.

She leans forward, and I bring my lips down to hers, capturing her mouth against mine. Her lips are soft and sweet, sending a shock through my entire body. I simply can't get enough of this woman.

With my hands on her hips and our lips still tangled together, I gently push her backward, walking us toward my bedroom. Demi's eyes light up when she pulls back, her teeth pulling at her bottom lip as she stops halfway down the hall.

"I'm taking these off," she says, pulling at the drawstring of my shorts.

The hallway is dark and quiet. But I can see her eyes clear as day as she stands in front of me. They're blazing. I lift my hands up to my chest, signaling for her to take charge if that's what she's after tonight.

Demi pulls at the waistband, letting my shorts fall to the ground around my feet and she leans up to kiss me. Her tongue parts my lips immediately and her hand cups me through my boxers.

"Fuck," I breathe the word into her mouth.

She rubs against me with her hand, using her other to pull at the back of my neck as she kisses me. Her mouth is warm and hungry this time. Full of need and desire. I feel her hand slip into my boxers, and she touches my length with her fingers.

"Fuck, Dem. That's it," I whimper and feel my body shiver. The pad of her thumb smooths over the head and there's already precum at the tip.

My breaths are ragged as she kisses my chest, her hand still working my cock like a goddamn instrument. "I don't go first," I manage to say between breaths, and pull myself together long enough to scoop her up into my arms, stepping completely out of my shorts and boxers, walking us both to my room.

No words are exchanged between us as I pull the T-shirt off her body, her breasts bouncing the second they're free. Her taut nipples are the first thing I want, grabbing them in both hands as I bring my mouth to one, and roll the other between my fingers.

"Come here." My voice is heavy as I look at her.

She pulls her shorts down and follows me to the edge of the bed just before I lie back. I watch her eyes scan my body. She pauses her gaze on my cock, and I feel like even her just looking at me might make me combust.

I reach for her hand, pulling her closer to me. "Have a seat, honey," I say as she climbs onto the bed.

She straddles me, and the view I have of her right now is enough to send me to an early grave. She's completely bare and a goddamn masterpiece. There's a pink blush to her cheeks and when she smiles at me, her dimples come out to play.

"This view could kill me, but I meant to have a seat here." I point to my mouth. "I need to taste you again."

"Oh…" She hesitates, and I place both hands on her hips, pulling her up my body.

All I can think about is how badly I want to consume her.

I watch her body move up mine, her thighs hovering just over my chin as I give her one more tug toward me and pull her to my hungry lips.

My tongue finds her clit instantly and I feel her hips buck against me. I moan into her. Goddammit, she's sweet. My fingers dig into her ass and she swirls her hips. I fucking love that I can tell she's enjoying this. She's enjoying us. Her head tilts back, exposing her neck, and I see the smile playing out on her face as she moves back and forth against me.

I swipe my tongue up and down, sucking on her clit, letting my teeth nip a little more with each pass. Demi cries out, whimpering and moaning my name. She attempts to pull back as she whimpers, but I suck harder. I flick my tongue over her clit, back and forth, and hear her moans as her hips begin to pick up their pace.

"I think—*oh god*, Liam." Demi rides my face fast and rough. It's fucking messy and addictive. A lethal combination as I continue to devour her. "Oh my god," she says, trying to pull up, but I hold her legs in place, eating up everything she has to offer as I feel her fall over the edge.

My tongue sweeps and sucks, enjoying every fucking moment before she finally slows her movements. Her breathing evens out. I flick her clit one more time with my tongue as she settles, causing her to jerk back once more. And I smile as I lick my lips when she slowly pulls away and back down my body.

"That's all I'll ever need for the rest of my fucking life, Dem."

Demi stares at me. Naked, straddling my hips, with a sated look on that perfect face as she reaches her hand between my legs, taking my length in her hand again.

The pad of her thumb grazes the tip and she pulls it to her lips, tasting the precum that spilled while I was feasting on her. She sucks her thumb, and I feel my cock twitch.

"Can I feel you?" she asks as she moves down lower, placing me right at her entrance. "You said you get tested. I'm on the pill. I trust you."

"Are you sure?"

She nods, rubbing my cock a few times before wrapping her hand around it again. This time she sits up a little as she hovers over me, lining me up with her entrance.

"I might need to go slow before I'm used to all of you," she says, and I nod.

Demi lowers her body onto me, and I moan as soon as I feel her come down around me. My abs clench and my breath stutters. She's so fucking tight. But hell if it isn't the best feeling being inside of her.

She presses herself down a little more and then comes up again. Repeating that motion a couple of times before she finally sits herself completely on me. My back arches at the same time hers does, both of us feeling immense pleasure from the pressure.

"Holy shit," she breathes out as she smiles. "Holy shit, I feel so full. It's so good," she moans and begins to move her hips. She bounces once she starts to feel more comfortable, and I bring my hand up to her breast, feeling its fullness in my palm as she rides me.

"Goddamn. You feel good," I huff out, and take my free hand between her legs, playing with her clit.

Her body rocks and bounces, the only sounds are ones we're making together, and I could live like this for fucking ever. I'm a goner. Completely and undeniably so in love with this woman I can't even think straight. And it isn't even just because of what we have together physically—that's icing on the fucking cake. It's everything else. *Everything*.

I feel my lower abdomen start to tighten as she's on top of me. She cries out as her second orgasm rips through her, and I feel her walls pulsing around me as she does. The feeling sends everything I have combusting seconds later, spilling into her as she collapses on top of me, her chest meeting mine in deep labored breaths.

I hear her chuckle against my sweat soaked skin. And I wrap my arms around her body, pulling her tighter against me.

"Fuck, Dem. I love you," I blurt out in my orgasm induced stupor.

And my entire world stops.

CHAPTER FORTY-TWO

DEMI

No, no, no, no.

Please don't tell me he just said what I think he said. My body tenses against him. This is my fault. I led him on. I put us in this situation. My heart begins to race and I can't move. I can't speak. I don't even know what I'd say if I tried.

"I—*fuck*. I'm sorry if that made you uncomfortable."

Liam's hands hold the outside of my arms as I lean up and he tries to make eye contact with me. But I can't. I can't look him in the eye, knowing one look from him is going to break my fucking heart.

"That was an inside thought that should have stayed there. I got caught up in the moment." His explanation is hurried, and I sit up completely, bringing the blanket with me as I wrap it around my chest.

His hand grabs at his hair when he sits up, pulling through the dark brown strands.

I don't want to hurt him. But this isn't what this is. It *can't* be. It can't be love.

"Um, it's okay," I stutter, sounding so fucking stupid but I'm nearly paralyzed with guilt right now. "I just—I don't know what to say, Liam," I whisper.

The top sheet is up around his waist, but I still see his abdomen flex every time he moves. Which is a lot right now because this man can't seem to sit still when he's scrambling for words.

"Nothing. Say nothing. I shouldn't have even said it. I-I wasn't thinking straight and I take it back."

I shouldn't feel like I've just been gut punched by that statement. If anything, I'm the asshole here. I know that. But hearing him say he takes it back doesn't exactly feel any better than hearing him say it to begin with.

"Oh." My eyes dart to the door.

I have to leave. We can't have this conversation right after sex, our brains aren't working properly, and most importantly, I need time to process the last three fucking minutes and figure out what to do.

"I mean—" He pauses and sits up straighter. His eyes searching mine for understanding and hope. I see it so clearly. He's begging me not to hurt him, and I just don't know if I can live up to that expectation. "No." His arms cross over his chest. "No, I don't take it back."

"Liam, I'm not ready for...*that,* for this to be anything more than what it is." At least, I don't know if I am. I didn't picture myself spending time with someone again so soon, and I sure as hell didn't think it would end up being Liam.

"I'm not asking for you to say it back. I'm not asking for you to feel it. But it's how I feel." He stands from the bed, completely naked before grabbing his boxers and shorts, throwing them on.

I feel my shoulders sink and my stomach drops at how genuine he's being. I love spending time with him. I love talking to him. Kissing him. Texting him. Laughing with him. Having sex with him. But do I *love* him? I can't answer that right this second.

"Um…" I feel so fucking stupid right now. I can't put words together, or thoughts. I shouldn't have been so careless with his very clear feelings for me. I see that now.

He shakes his head and hands me my clothes from the floor. "You don't have to say anything. I'll let you get dressed." And he leaves his bedroom, closing his door behind him.

I've never rushed to the bathroom and gotten dressed so quickly in my life. And to top it off, I'm back in his clothes because mine are still soaking wet from the ice plunge. I smell like him. And I love it too much. There are too many things about my time with Liam that I do love, now that I'm forcing myself to think about it.

Exiting his bedroom, Birdie greets me with a tiny meow, and I let her rub against my ankle before I walk out to the kitchen and see Liam leaning against the counter.

"I'm really sorry about that," I say, jerking my thumb toward the bedroom as if that apology fixes things.

"Nothing to be sorry for, Dem."

"I should go." I reach for my clothes that he brought in from drying outside and grab my phone and keys from the counter.

Liam doesn't say anything, but he doesn't need to. He knows me well enough by now to know I need space. He follows me slowly to the door and then reaches his hand out in front of me to open it. But I pause.

"I noticed you always call me, Dem," I say after I step out into the hallway.

He leans against the doorframe, arms crossed over his chest, hair perfectly messy with just the right amount of stubble covering his jaw as he stares at me.

He gives me one steady nod. "I do."

"Everyone else calls me Demi."

His hand reaches up to the top of the door. Because of course he can touch it. His stomach flexes, and I feel a lump form in my throat when I watch him swallow, his Adam's Apple bobbing.

"Everyone calls you Demi because it's short for Demetria. I like being the only one who calls you Dem because it's short for Demi." He shrugs and there's something so authentic and tender about this moment it makes my heart ache. "You know I don't like to be like everyone else." He smiles, but I hardly believe the curve of his lips means that he's happy. "Have a good night," he says.

"You too."

I turn away just as his door is closing.

Back in my apartment, I throw myself on the bed. Not even bothering to shower or change my clothes. My head hits the pillow and I stare at the ceiling, watching my fan spin around and around.

I replay the last couple months in my head. None of it's a blur with Liam. I remember every second of us. Every beautiful, fleeting moment that brought me so much more happiness than I ever even knew I was missing.

But the reality is, this was supposed to be casual. And maybe I missed my opportunity to make that clearer to him. I got lost in the conversations and the warmth. The security I felt and the ease of being with him. I craved so much about Liam's entire presence that I was selfish with him.

My index fingers pick at the nail polish on my thumbs as I lie here. I should've been more careful with him and his feelings. Liam was so up front with me from the get-go, and I took that and ran with it because it made me feel safe and cared for. I hate myself for how I let things get so far away from me.

I feel my eyes sting as I reach for my phone and call my mom.

She answers on the second ring, and my emotions take over immediately. Tears well in my eyes and a sob builds in my chest the moment she asks how I'm doing. I didn't think at thirty-five I'd still be running to my mom for guy problems.

"Mija," she says softly into the phone as I rub my eyes before finally filling her in on every detail of the last couple months.

There's no lulls in our conversion. No moments where she's trying to convince me one way or another on things—except she does mention many times how handsome Liam is, and I agree every single time.

"Well." She sighs. And I can picture her right now. Out on the front porch in her rocking chair, looking out at the Arizona mountains across the street from the house I grew up in. "You know I will be the first one to tell you how special it is to love someone. I knew you seemed happier lately when we spoke, but I wanted to wait for you to tell me why. Or should I say, your father told me not to bother you with questions since you're a grown woman."

I laugh at that and envision their conversion over my love life and the ups and downs it's seen in the last year.

"I'm not telling you what to do, I know that's not why you called me. But I am going to say one thing, and I need you to listen." She clears her throat, and I know that means she wants me to really hear her. "You deserve a calm love. I know you've been working on moving forward, trusting again—and, my love, I think you did it without knowing. It happens like that sometimes. An ordinary dinner, a simple conversation, maybe in ways you wouldn't have pictured. Life won't feel so hard, things will slow down. You'll finally exhale."

I swallow the lump in my throat at her words.

"I'm not saying you love this man or don't love him, I'm simply saying that you're free."

My head nods up and down as she speaks, pivoting to comparing moving on to growing up. She does that sometimes.

And I smile to myself at the way she so seamlessly flows through conversations and subject changes.

Is she right, though? Did something happen without me even realizing it? Did I somehow let Liam in? The hotshot quarterback who's had his eyes on me for years. Would it be the worst thing in the world if I did love him? Could I?

"I just don't know what to do. I need time to think." I sigh.

"How is work?" she asks, switching gears, and I'm thankful for it. "Any word on that promotion?"

I should have led our conversation with that—but somehow that's not the most pressing thing happening in my life at the moment.

"Yeah, actually. I think it's a real possibility. My boss is great and really pushing for me, so we'll see."

My job is another thing to consider with all this Liam talk too. If I get this promotion, my home base can be anywhere. I'll travel with a network for prime-time games—and my association with Liam would be minimal, if at all, professionally.

She asks about the holidays, and we end our call shortly after that, but not before I thank her. Not just for the talk tonight, but always.

When I lost Bri, I thought I lost the only person I'd ever really share my secrets with. But, it turns out, when you're an adult your mom doesn't have to only be your mom, she can be your friend too.

CHAPTER FORTY-THREE

LIAM

I haven't seen Demi in two days. And I'm fucking sick about it. I can't sleep.

"So, you're worried you scared her off, huh?"

Chase props his feet up on the ottoman in his living room. My hand runs through my hair for the seventh time in the last few minutes, feeling anxious and worried, but still not regretting the words I let slip.

"Well, I was taught not to talk about emotions and feelings. That they're distracting, so you keep it all inside. And, you know, I've only been working on rewiring that part of my brain for a year now."

"Dana's got her work cut out with you," Chase jokes with a sly grin. "No, really, though, that's shit advice. Don't keep your feelings all bottled up."

"I don't have any regrets telling her I love her." I catch Summer walking out of CeCe's bedroom, and I continue as she takes a seat next to Chase. "But I know she didn't want to hear it. And I'm worried it's too much for her. Maybe *I'm* being too much for her."

"No," Summer says, nestling closer to Chase. "Don't let your mind convince you that expressing a feeling is being too much."

Summer's eyes flicker to Chase before she focuses them back on me.

"I've been getting really comfortable expressing myself," I say with my head down. I continue walking in fucking circles around their living room, and I can feel Chase's stare burning through me, telling me to sit the fuck down.

Summer nods. "You have been. I really am proud of you, and I honestly think Demi is part of the reason you've been able to start talking about your feelings more."

"Yeah." I sigh, shaking my head at myself.

"I'm serious, Liam." Summer pulls away from Chase and sits up, but her hand still rests on his knee.

I love their relationship. The whole dynamic. I loved watching them fall in love and become this little family.

"I really think Demi has helped you understand that all your emotions are allowed to co-exist. You don't always have to put on this happy face—no one is happy *all* the time and excited all the time. Even golden retrievers get sad sometimes."

"Are you comparing me to a dog? A dog like Hendrix?" I gape, but internally I'm okay with the comparison to Nate's dog. He's a good boy.

"Yes. You aim to please, you want everyone to be happy and never say no to a game of catch."

"Kincaid," Chase rumbles as he shakes his head.

"No, she's right." I nod, and Summer raises her hands in front of her chest. "About the Demi part." I glance her way with a smirk. "Being with Demi made me want to be vulnerable. It's why it was so fucking easy to tell her that I love her. It just came out of my mouth so naturally, like I've been saying it for years, like I'm *supposed* to be saying it forever."

Summer stands and meets me in the middle of the living room as I'm pacing. She brings her hands to my arms and gently holds them in place at the sides of my body, stopping me from moving.

"Rest, Liam. You don't have to keep moving at a million miles a minute. You don't have to keep running, unattached and uninterested." A lump forms in my throat. One I wasn't fucking expecting as Summer puts her arms around my middle and hugs me. "You aren't too much for her," she whispers the words against my chest as I hug her back.

"Can I cut in?" Chase's hand is on Summer's shoulder, and I move to back away, but it's Summer who squeezes my hand and walks down the hall into their bedroom.

"Sorry, I thought you meant—"

"Summer is unpredictable." Chase palms my shoulder, and I follow his lead into the kitchen, where we both take seats on the barstools. "She's outspoken and unapologetically herself. She dances in the grocery store when a song she likes starts playing over the speakers."

That pulls a smile from me. I know it's true, I've been in a 7-Eleven with her when Taylor Swift came on.

"I'm someone who wants routine and peace."

I feel my head nod, but don't really know where the hell he's going here.

"I need Summer's untamed spirit. I need her wild heart and her open mind. Demi and I are a lot alike in that regard." I dart my eyes to him. "She needs *you*."

Heart-to-hearts aren't something Chase and I often engage in. Sure, we share a thing or two here and there, but this is already deeper than most.

"I've never seen you as happy as you've been the last few months. Even though I haven't even seen you two together, I know it's fucking electric, man. I know it because I see you every day and I see your spirit, your goddamn contagious merriment, and the maturity you've shown. If I hadn't seen it with my own eyes, I honestly don't know that I would've believed it."

"That…means a lot. Thank you." I dip my head as I nod at him.

His mouth forms a firm line as he nods back. "Demi's happy with you too. I've noticed on the sidelines she's different. That's probably why she freaked out over what you said. Chances are, she didn't expect to feel it back."

"I'm not sure she does. Some days, I think she might, but then I wonder if it was just me thinking this was more than what it was. For her, it was casual. For me, though…it was the future."

"Have you talked to her since?" he asks.

I shake my head, stretching a hand behind my neck. "No, I was afraid to push her away. I thought maybe she needs space."

He shrugs. "She might. But I probably wouldn't assume she does. Maybe ask her?"

"Should I ask Summer's advice on this part?" I give him a half smile as I'm only half joking. Summer might need to come back to the kitchen for this part.

"Talk to her," he says, standing from the stool. His boots scuff their way toward me with his hand out. "If she wants space, she'll tell you."

"Thanks," I say, shaking his hand and heading for the front door.

I sent a text this morning to Demi, but it went unanswered. So instead of sending another, I thought it was more appropriate to talk face-to-face. Whether or not she'll slam the door on me is a thought that's only crossed my mind as I'm standing on the other side of it knocking.

I hear her on the other side, likely—hopefully—checking the peephole, and a moment later I hear the lock click and the door swings open.

Her eyes are heavy. Dark and alluring, and I feel like I can't read them. The one fucking time that would come in handy and I can't get a read on her simply by looking at her.

"Hi," I say roughly.

Her fingers fidget with the hem of her shirt as it hangs just over her hips.

"Hey." She stands there in the doorway, her phone in one hand and her other holding the door.

"We haven't talked in a couple of days, I just wanted to see how you're doing."

"I'm okay," she says, eyes darting around. "I know I look rough. I'm not sleeping great."

"You look perfect. But I'm also not sleeping great," I reply in a low voice.

"I—" she begins.

"We—" I say at the same time.

"Oh," we both say together then laugh.

"Go ahead," I say.

"I'm sorry. I'm just all over the place right now. And I— there's a lot to think about when it comes to us, Liam. I wasn't expecting to be in this situation."

I nod, trying to understand where she's coming from. She's done this before. She said those words to someone and it ended horribly. But god, I'm not him and I just want to show her all the ways I want to love her—ways I can love her that will show her what real love actually is.

"My job—I worked hard for respect in this field and I'm kind of caught between conflicting feelings right now. There's this promotion on the table and I can't risk—I just need to sort things out." She pulls the door closer to her, almost like she's ready to close it.

"I can give you space, Dem." Words I don't want to say, but I can tell she isn't looking for company tonight. I can't be selfish right now, even if I want to be. No one questioned her working in sports when she was married to a basketball player, because she didn't cover him directly. But I know the promotion she's speaking of—she mentioned it on our coffee date. It's big and it's important to her. I can't be the reason she doesn't get it.

All of this gets me thinking, but my train of thought is interrupted when she finally breaks the silence.

"Thank you. I'm sorry."

"Stop apologizing." I turn my head toward the hallway. I'm not annoyed at her. I'm annoyed that she's so conditioned to think she needs to apologize to me for expressing herself.

"I'll text you," she says, forcing a smile.

"Great."

Her door closes, and I turn away slowly. That didn't go how I'd hoped, but she answered and she spoke to me. And I'm okay with giving her space—hell, I'm really fucking good at giving Demi space. I've been practicing for five years.

CHAPTER FORTY-FOUR

DEMI

The moment I close my laptop after finishing a therapy session, there's a knock on my door. But it's one, then two more quick knocks, followed by another single one. Liam's signature knock.

I spent the last hour crying on and off to my therapist about Liam. After talking with my mom the other night, it got me thinking and spiraling. Because as much as I thought I loved Brandon, I'm realizing I may love Liam even more. And that's not something I was expecting. Or something I feel equipped to handle right now. It's taken me two days to even get comfortable saying that might be the case.

You're not supposed to fall in love with the next guy you meet after divorce, right? You're supposed to have a fun stage, a wild stage, a *this will show him* era, right? How'd I skip all of that and fall right into *love*? I shake my head out of the thoughts and walk toward the door.

Liam looks ridiculously handsome as I pull the door open. I'm afraid to open it too much because I might not be strong enough to close it with him on the other side if I do. And I *need* to allow myself the space to figure this out. To weigh everything potentially at stake and make sure I'm doing the right thing.

Because I thought I was doing the right thing once before, and I was humiliated.

His dark hair is tousled—I can only imagine from his hands raking through it. He's staring at me like he's desperately trying to read my mind, and I'm putting every ounce of a poker face I can into keeping my eyes unreadable.

I typed a reply no less than seven times to his text from earlier. Somehow unable to answer the question of "how are you?"

But it rolls off his lips again as he stands outside my door, and I feel my insides nearly melt at the sound of his voice. It's velvet. It's calming. It's like my favorite song that I haven't heard in days finally being played on the radio and I want to turn up the volume and close my eyes, smiling as I listen to it.

When he admits he hasn't been sleeping great, there's a pit that forms in my stomach. I feel guilty over any pain I'm causing him. But I'm also trying to do what's best for me. I promised myself. I promised I'd do that. And right now I just need a little more time to sort this out.

Our conversation is short and I hate that I believe him when he says he'll give me space—there's a look in his eyes telling me he's no stranger to it. But I believe Liam, I've always believed Liam.

At least I know I'm buying myself a couple more days since he's leaving tomorrow for an away game, and I'll be here, with all my thoughts and emotions to sort through so I can woman up and say exactly what I want.

GIRLS ONLY

MIA CAMPBELL

Do you girls feel like coming over for the game?

ABBY ANDERSON

Sure!

SUMMER KINCAID

Yeah want me to bring anything?

The chat with Liam's friends chimes as I'm driving to the studio for a work meeting. I'm surprised they're including me in this, to be honest, and it makes me wonder if Liam's even told them about the space we're taking. Maybe they don't realize I'm still in the chat. For the time being, I continue driving and ignore the messages.

My mind is bouncing between memories of the last ten years of my life doing this job—well, five here, but ten total.

The hurdles I had to jump over, people I had to prove wrong, and really just the sheer amount of absolute bullshit I've had to deal with to get where I am. To get to a place and a network where I feel respected and valued. It's not always easy, but I'm proud of the work I've done, the work I do, and what I know I can continue to bring. Who I may or may not be in love with should have no goddamn bearing on that. But even though it shouldn't, doesn't mean it won't.

MIA CAMPBELL

Demi, you in?

Another text chimes as I'm pulling into the parking lot. Okay, so they definitely didn't forget I'm here. And that kind of makes me smile. Maybe I could use a girls' night.

"This is the part where you say 'no, Summer, you don't look horrible in that dress.' Good lord, what kind of friends do I have?" Summer laughs into her margarita as she passes around her cell.

"You're obviously a ten. It's the dress, something is off about it." Abby shrugs and Mia points to her with an agreeing nod.

"Yeah, it's the dress."

All their eyes shoot to me as I'm sitting on the couch criss-crossed as the pregame is showing.

"Oh," I say, wiping the corner of my mouth. "The color isn't right. It's *really* teal. Maybe do a more subtle blue, like a light blue, or swing the opposite direction and go navy blue."

"That's how you help, ladies." Summer raises her eyebrows to her best friends as they sit spread out on this extra-large sectional.

Nate and Mia's home is beautiful. It's cozy, secluded, and filled with so much love. You can feel it as soon as you walk through the door. The pictures of the kids on the walls, the toys, the blankets, the smells—it's amazing.

When the game starts, they all sit back and watch, commentating on different plays and the calls from the refs. I've never done this—sat back and watched a game with girlfriends. I watch footage all the time, but it's usually in a room with other men, or by myself and I'm working; not exactly just watching for fun. And watching for fun is allowing me to focus on one player.

"Oh, come on!" Summer shoots to her feet.

"The baby is sleeping," Mia says, peeking at the monitor.

She mentioned the older two are doing a sleepover at her

sister's, and I guess going from three to one for a night is kind of like a mini vacation for parents.

"He looks so peaceful," Abby says as she looks over Mia's shoulder at the monitor.

Her brown hair falling over her shoulder, almost hitting the cushion with how long it is. She stares at the screen, even after Mia sets it down to meet Summer in the kitchen as they refill drinks. There's a look on her face of sadness. A longing in her eyes maybe, and she inhales a deep breath before she sighs and looks up, catching me staring at her.

"We've been trying for…a long time." She settles herself back in her seat.

"Oh." I swallow. "I-I'm sorry. I didn't know."

"Not exactly something Ford shouts in interviews."

"Right," I say.

Summer and Mia come back into the living room just as the second quarter is almost over.

"Come on, Liam," Summer softly says to herself. "What are you doing?" She sighs, shaking her head. Both of the girls seem to agree with her as we all watch him throw his third incomplete pass in a row.

"He's unsteady," I whisper as I'm staring at the screen, and I feel their eyes shoot to me.

I'm watching him scramble around the pocket, watching as he doesn't step into his throws. I know our situation is on his mind and that burns a hole in my chest, knowing he's off kilter because of it.

"Can you just get back together with him so he's not unsteady?" Summer playfully taps my shoulder. "I'm kidding, we don't do peer pressure here."

Since our hallway conversation, I haven't spoken with him. He's been giving me the space I asked for, and I've been cursing myself for asking for it. Because all I want to do is talk to him. But not until I know with certainty what I want. I can't keep stringing him along if I can't be in this the same way he is.

"How is he? Really." I bring myself to ask the question and brace for the answer.

Summer's head tilts as she looks up from her phone during the commercial break. Abby and Mia are both on their way upstairs since the baby started crying.

"Really?" She looks at me, a soft albeit sad smile on her lips. "He's a mess, Demi. He's going to smile and laugh for every single person because that's what he's been trained to do. He's really good at masking emotions if you haven't already noticed." There's a bite in her words. But she isn't being rude, she's being honest, protective over her friend. And I respect that. "He knows you have a lot to consider. But can I be honest?"

I nod.

"It's killing him." Her eyes water when she looks at me. "He doesn't want you to know it. But I can see it on his face, I hear it in his voice. The fear that he said something you aren't ready for. He wants to respect your request for space, and he is respecting it. He stayed on our couch the night before they left for the away game, did you know that?"

I shake my head, hurt covering my face.

Our jobs aside, there's something else that's been clawing at the back of my mind. I saw Liam with those kids at family day. I've seen glimpses of him with his friends' children, who he refers to as his family. He's made to be a father, I see it. And I can't be in the position again with someone where our wants don't align.

"There's just a lot to consider." My index fingers outline my thumbs nervously. "I-I don't want children," I blurt out, just as Abby and Mia come back down the stairs.

Tossing my head back, I let out a sigh. This wasn't the plan. Not tonight anyway.

"Oh. Okay. Well, that's okay," Summer says.

"It's a big choice. Not everyone wants to be a parent, there's nothing wrong with that," Mia adds.

I look over at Abby. My heart is aching for someone who so desperately wants to be a mother, while I'm here declaring that it's the last thing on my mind.

"It's okay to admit that, Demi. It's hard to live in a world where women are expected to become mothers. Some want it, others don't. Your hard just looks different than mine. It's okay," Abby says as she takes a seat.

"But he's so good with kids, he deserves to be a dad." I gesture to the screen where they've just shown Liam running back out on the field after halftime. "It'd be selfish of me to take that away from him."

"Have you told him you don't want kids?" I nod. "Okay, and did he say he wants to have kids?" Mia's tone is a little judgy—and I can't blame her.

"Well, no."

"Then you're taking that choice away from him. You're choosing for him by not giving him the chance to even tell you his thoughts." Summer's hand latches onto mine.

How did this conversation get here?

Because I just had to know how he's doing, that's how. Jesus, she's right, though. He knows I don't want kids, but it didn't change anything about how he treated me, how he cared for me, how he *loves* me.

I keep hearing my abuela's voice in my head telling me the same thing since I was fifteen.

Busca a alguien que te ame por lo que eres, no por lo que puedes hacer por ellos. Find someone who loves you for you, Demetria, not what you can do for them.

I feel so sure that Liam loves me for me. As I am.

Oh god, there's a lump in my throat. A racing in my chest, and if I was okay with crying in front of people I'd be sobbing right now. But I pull my lips together. My palms are sweaty and my whole body feels antsy. I need to take a walk or jump in a pool—anything.

"Liam said you like *Grey's Anatomy*." Mia grabs the remote, muting the television and then reaches for her phone.

I have no idea what the song is when it starts playing but all three of them are on their feet in their fuzzy matching socks—they had a pair waiting for me when I arrived too.

"You need to dance it out." Summer's hand extends to me.

My brows crease as I stand, a smile creeping up on my face, and I finally just let my body go.

CHAPTER FORTY-FIVE

LIAM

Last night's performance is one that should be buried and scrubbed from the internet. I don't need anyone replaying two interceptions and a shit passer rating.

I didn't bother with the text from my dad when I opened my eyes this morning. We were on a late flight home, and by the time I stumbled into my bed, I didn't even bother plugging in my phone. Hence the battery life sitting at 6 percent right now. A text from Kat, my agent, is the only one I read, and it simply says to call her when I can.

I'm certain it's about my contract. By this time there should be conversations happening, at least I can only hope that's the case. Deadlines are fast approaching.

"Hey, Kat," I say, twisting the charging cord between two fingers as I'm now tethered to where my phone is plugged in.

"Good morning. How are you feeling?"

I know she means how am I feeling after that shit game last night, and I answer honestly.

"Like I wish I could take a redo on the last twenty-four hours, how about you?"

Her laugh always makes me laugh. It's dry and always

sounds so forced, even when I've seen it in person and know it isn't.

"I'm good. I have some information I want to run by you. There have been some talks, and I've been holding firm at what you're asking for, because I without a doubt think you're worth it."

"I'm not going to chase money, Kat. I just want to play football."

"I know, I know. Heath sounds like they're willing to make this extension for you. But my question is actually about your plans for after football."

"Oh," I say.

My post-football plan hasn't changed since the day I came into the league.

I want to be part of the development for young players. At the high school and college level, if possible. A lot of kids grow up playing sports with their parent as their primary coach, and I know first-hand how fucking awful that can be. Some kids have it great, but I want to be there for the ones who don't.

"The owner's got wind of you wanting to be involved with the NFL's development programs. Is that still where you are looking toward in the future?"

"Yes." My back straightens as I perk up. "That's exactly what I want."

"Okay, I thought so but needed to make sure before I speak with the organization again. Like I said, it sounds like Heath is willing to make a deal with you for an extension. I don't think they are planning to franchise tag you, though. So if I got anything from another team…"

I pause, not getting franchise tagged means another team could potentially reach out.

"This is home," I say before my mind drifts to Demi.

She's here and I can't picture my life without her in it—even if it's not in the way I want.

"Say no more. I'll circle back with anything more, Liam. Get some rest."

"Thanks." I toss my head back against the pillow propped up on my bed.

I've loved working in the same circle as Demi all these years. It's how I met her, where I watched her, and ultimately the way I fell for her. But Demi's job means everything to her. I've watched her soar over the last five years. Opportunities have come her way, different brand deals, hosting events, she launched a podcast a couple of years ago. She speaks at Nate's foundation about her mental health struggles and pours every fucking ounce of her knowledge and love for this game right back into it for the future generations.

I can't help but fear that she may not be here next season because I told her I loved her. But still, I don't regret it. I've worked so fucking hard on myself over the years to be comfortable in my feelings and emotions. Saying it to her felt right. But just because I'm okay with saying it, doesn't mean she was okay with hearing it. And the thought of her potentially leaving so she doesn't risk her job is a small nugget of information stewing in the back of my mind.

Our time together wasn't nothing. I know that. It's whether or not she wants to ignore that fact—that's the question.

I've been replaying our conversations in my head, seeing every second as a movie flashing in my mind. The two months I spent in her presence were unlike anything I've ever experienced.

I've never opened up like that before. I've never given someone so much of my vulnerabilities—let someone see so far into my head and my heart. I can't see past the real possibility that this wasn't just some fling, something casual that can be tossed to the side.

I *miss* her. I miss her eye rolls and her heavy sighs. The way her dimples don't come out unless she *really* smiles. The way she talks about her mom. When she picks at her nail polish and twirls her hair. How her nose scrunches when she's trying to figure out where a puzzle piece goes. The sweet, flowery scent that follows her everywhere. Her eyes. Her hips. The sound of her laugh. God, I just miss her. And missing her is making me crazy.

Tampa is home. It has been for years. And I never thought I'd play anywhere else, or want to play anywhere else. But I want Demi more than I want to wear any specific jersey. I'm pathetically in love with this woman. I'll do anything, go anywhere I need to go if it means I even get a chance to be with her.

Football has been the longest relationship of life. The only thing I've ever really loved. But there will be a day I wake up without a meeting or a practice to make it to. No roaring crowds and grueling temperatures to play through. I won't suit up on Sundays or do Friday night walkthroughs. This will all be over. I know this isn't forever.

This career is fleeting. It's a blip of a time in my life—a time I've loved.

But when I wake up in twenty years with nowhere to rush off to, I want Demi to be the person I wake up next to.

I don't care where the fuck I play next season, because nowhere will actually feel like home without her.

My fingers can't move quick enough when I reach for my phone and go straight to my agent's contact.

> Hey Kat… if you do happen to get any other offers or even any whispers. Let me know before shooting it down.

KAT
> Got it.

The owners and managers won't lose much sleep over me saying I'm open to a trade. They'll look at it like a negotiation tactic—because maybe it usually is. But Coach Aarons deserves more from me. He's been good to me since I joined this team—treats me better than my own father, and the right thing to do is to give him a heads-up. Even if I can't share too much, simply implying that I'm not sure what my future looks like is better than blindsiding the man who has actually helped me become a better athlete.

Nate told me the girls—including Demi—were at his house last night watching the game and having a sleepover. I didn't actually think women still did that in their thirties, but who am I to place judgment? I just slept on my best friend's couch the other night.

But seeing Demi is on the top of my list today. I gave her space. We had our distance, and now my body feels like it physically can't be away from her any longer.

I'm going to talk to her today. Right after I talk to Coach.

CHAPTER FORTY-SIX

DEMI

Liam's off today. And as soon as I get home, I need to see him. I've had enough space, enough time to think, overthink, then rethink. If I don't just fucking tell him everything I'm feeling and everything I want, I might explode.

"Thanks for last night," I say to Summer as we're walking down Mia's ridiculously long driveway toward our cars.

"Of course." She smiles. "I'm sorry if I've been a little hot and cold with you. I guess I just know what it feels like to be in his shoes a little. Watching someone from a distance and wanting them to notice you." She shrugs. "He might be a little over the top sometimes, but his heart is pure."

I smile back at her.

"I like you Demi. And I think you two could be great together. He's different from your initial impression, isn't he?" she asks, pulling her car door open but she stands between the car and open door.

"He is." I nod. "He's nothing like I thought. I imagined he was as reckless as the media made him out to be, especially with women. Everything always just pointed to that."

"I know," she says, her head softly shaking back and forth with a laugh. "I thought the same thing when we first met. But it's an act. Or at least partially an act. Mostly a survival technique, I think. He's a naturally happy person who was never allowed to show anything but that growing up." She shakes her head. "His dad's a dick."

Understatement. I think of his father. How hard he was on him as a kid and how that made Liam feel as an adult. Acting happy all the time, masking the ways he's felt hurt with jokes and a flashy social life.

"Anyway, you're good for him. And I think he's good for you too. He needs to be reminded that you're allowed to have bad days. And I think you need the reminder that there are good ones."

She smiles at me, taking a seat in her car and pulls the door shut.

Being welcomed into this little close-knit family of theirs means something to me. Everyone talks about the closeness of teammates, the dependability, the tough love, the overall connection. But the women who support these men also have their own bond. A strong one, a fierce loyalty to the families they go on this journey with.

It's not easy being the spouse of a professional athlete. Hell, I know after being married to Brandon how difficult it can be.

I haven't felt this kind of closeness since I met Bri. And it's all I can think about on the drive back home.

Everyone in this friend group has their role, and they know it so well. Like a rehearsed play, but it's really just their life and how they live it.

Mia is everyone's little piece of comfort. She's sharp when she needs to be, but overall she's soft-spoken and supportive no matter what.

Abby reminds me of Bri in ways that send me back to our

moments together. The way she works to understand everyone's point of view. She makes everyone around her feel important and valued.

And Summer. She's lightning in a bottle. If looks could kill, she'd have a body count. I admire how graceful she is in her strength. She's feminine and soft, but stands up, no questions asked, for those she loves.

I see why Liam loves them. I see why they're so special to him. They're like the sisters he never had, and hearing how they speak about him only makes my admiration for them grow.

There's a text from Mia as I'm pulling into the parking garage. A reminder about Friendsgiving. I just hope Liam still wants me to come with him.

I quickly walk into the lobby, waving at Rob as I walk by in a hurry. I probably look like a crazy person right now, fuzzy socks with a pair of sneakers, leggings, and an old band shirt from at least ten years ago. But I don't care as I rush through to the double doors, entering my code and heading toward the elevators.

The thought of texting Liam crossed my mind, but I ended up deciding against it. Showing up at his door feels better. I know he got in late last night with how the away game travel works, but he's naturally an early riser. It's just past ten so he should definitely be awake.

Swinging my door open, I drop my bag on the floor and head right back out the door to his apartment.

When I raise my hand to knock, I stop myself briefly. Giving my mind just a moment to relax. My body takes a moment to calm down and my heart seconds to stop racing.

My knuckles tap on the door as I stand just outside, arms hugging my body. I shift on my feet, feeling anxious and excited at the same time. I knock again, a little louder this time.

What the hell?

At this point, I may as well text him to make sure he's home and not out somewhere. There's no chance he went anywhere last night when he got home and stayed out. I don't even let the thought linger.

I give it a couple of moments, but there's no reply. And no answer at the door. But I refuse to lose this burst of energy I have. This adrenaline. The need to see him.

I contemplate texting Summer, but before I resort to that I sift through our moments together. He's not home. But he's not at the facility.

The roof.

I spin on my heel, forcing one foot in front of the other as I make my way down the hall and toward the stairwell to get to the roof. I feel like I'm in a romantic comedy—rushing like a mad woman to get to the man she loves so she can tell him.

I take the steps two at a time, feeling like I definitely should start taking spin classes as my thighs burn after two flights, and I see sunlight coming from the small window of the door that opens up to the roof.

Without hesitating, my hand latches onto the lever and I swing the door open, crashing through it like I'm on fire.

And he's there.

Perfectly. Wholly. There.

"Dem," he says, a low rasp in his voice when he turns to face me. "What are you doing up here?" He takes a few steps closer, giving me a soft smile as he does.

I exhale a deep breath as I smile. "I was in the neighborhood."

He chuckles. A hearty sound coming from his chest as he stands just feet away from me. His beautiful hazel eyes admiring mine. A look I've seen on his face for years, but never gave a second thought to, is now the one look I long for. The way he sees me, wants me, craves me, is magnetic. I'm so drawn to him. So in love with him I can't see straight.

"I texted you," I say.

"Ah, sorry, my phone is on the charger. I just came up here to…sit." He shrugs, and I take a step forward.

"You love me," I say, sounding almost like a confirmation.

He runs a hand through his hair, pulling gently at the tips before he places his hands back in his pockets. The light gray T-shirt showing off every muscle on his chest and arms, dangerously close to distracting me.

He nods. "I do." His hand reaches for mine and I let him take it. "Yesterday, today, tomorrow. Forever, Dem. Even if you never love me a day in your life, I love you."

I feel his thumb caress the back of my hand, and I blink up at him.

"And if I do?"

There's a glimmer in his eye as he tilts his head. "If you what?" He inches closer, our bodies now touching and I could sink into the heat coming off him.

"What if I love you?" I whisper. "What if I can't stop thinking about all the ways you've loved me from a distance for years? What if when I can't sleep at night all I'm thinking about is you and the way you look at me?" My inhale is shaky as I look down, but I feel his hand on my chin, tipping it up. "What if I'm so madly in love with you that it makes me question *everything*? Makes me want to risk *everything*?"

"Dem," he says on an exhale.

His lips are on mine without a second thought, and I melt into his body against mine.

This. This. This.

It's where I belong. *He's* where I belong.

I knew it long before I wanted to admit it. My body tried to tell me, my nervous system kept finding solace in him. And I kept blowing past it. But no more. I've never felt more valued than I do when I'm standing next to Liam.

Liam's hand grips my jaw, the kiss breathing life into me,

and I feel my chest weaken. He pulls away slowly, his hand tracing down my neck as he does, holding it in place over my erratically beating heart.

"I know I love you." I lean my forehead against his chest, his hand sliding around my shoulders to pull me into him. "I didn't have anyone. And then…suddenly, there was you. And your friends. And this beautiful group of people around me. I-I think I forgot what it was like to have a person. Someone who wants to hear about my day because they genuinely care. Someone to run to, someone I can tell anything to." I sigh, and I feel his fingers making circles on my back. "I'd gone so long without it that it took me a while to realize it was *you*. You became all those things. Even when I was sure I didn't want to let anyone in, I always felt safe telling you anything."

"Dem, I will always be a safe space for you. Always. You broke through walls I had up too, and I'm so goddamn glad you did. I will always be in your corner. However you need me to be."

I nod against his chest. Because I believe him. And believing someone, trusting someone again isn't something I thought I'd be capable of for a long time. I was stuck after my divorce. Trapped in a bottle of jaded misery, and Liam was the piece that helped to wedge me out of it.

I think I'll always be grateful for him. He showed me a side of life that doesn't require too much thought. In a lot of ways, he taught me how to simply *be*. Be present. Say what I'm thinking, what I'm feeling.

There are a lot of things we need to figure out. A lot of moving parts involving our jobs that won't be easy to manage. But I don't want to be the bitter woman who holds one terrible relationship against every other man she meets. I don't want to push away the people who care.

I love what I do. I'm good at it, but I know that even if I had to leave where I'm at tomorrow, my time in this field wouldn't be over.

Entering the world as a divorced thirty-five-year-old came with a lot of mixed emotions. I went through hell. But I needed that rain. That storm in my personal life to realize how badly I needed the sun.

How badly I needed Liam.

CHAPTER FORTY-SEVEN

LIAM

The way Demi fits against my chest feels like the perfect catch. A well-placed spiral landing right into the arms of the receiver downfield. Except the boulder-sized lump in my throat doesn't happen when I score a touchdown. I feel every bit of emotion coursing through me right now. The hope, the love, the excitement, and even the fear. Because hearing Demi tell me she loves me is everything I've wanted to hear for years—but I know it's not something she's saying lightly.

"I knew waiting for you wasn't a waste of time," I say into her ear with a low laugh, and she shakes against my chest laughing too.

"I'm sorry I took so long." She pulls back, looking up at me.

"Forgiven." I smile.

Demi's fingers interlock with mine as she smiles back, but it slowly fades as she looks past me to the skyline.

I came up here to think. My world felt like it was spinning, and the need to get out into the open air was too strong to ignore. But I never would've expected Demi to come bursting through the door the way she did.

"You know, I've always admired you." She cocks an

eyebrow up at me and I nod. "For a million reasons, but over the last year I watched you become so damn resilient. You never faltered, at least not publicly."

She lowers her head, shaking it with a soft laugh.

"You're graceful in your resilience, Dem. A quiet strength you've shown that's inspiring as hell. You make me want to understand my emotions better, handle them better, *be* better."

Her thumb draws circles on the back of my hand slowly.

"There you go again," she says as she inhales. "Sweeping me off my already floating feet."

I feel her tense slightly against me before she clears her throat.

"I...I need to be clear, though. I meant it when I said I don't want to have kids," she says nervously.

And I never see her nervous. Overthinking, sure. Second guessing, yeah. But nervous? Like what she's saying could actually scare me away is a new one.

"I believe you."

"I-I've just been down this road before. And I'm not saying we're about to get married or *anything* like that. I'm just trying to be clear. So clear that there's no room for miscommunication."

My head nods and I pull my lips in, forming a firm line.

I've never been dead set on having kids or not having them. My first line of thought was always to find the woman I love and the rest—whatever that may be—will happen as it's supposed to. I'd be lying if I said I didn't have fears about becoming a parent and ending up like my father. Despite actively working to be nothing like him.

"And my job—it's important to me, and your career is important too. We've both worked hard. I'd hate for things with us to get in the way of that."

I take my hand and bring it to her cheek, gently cupping the side as I turn her to face me.

"I love you, Dem. I think you were made for me. Somehow,

someway—you and I were meant to find our way to one another. I'm so fucking certain of that. I don't need to have kids. It's never been a factor for me one way or another. I love kids, yeah, but I have a niece and some nephews. I'm with kids when I volunteer. I would never lie to you. I would never, ever put myself in a situation where I'd lose you. Because *you*, Demetria Sanchez, are enough. You are who I want. *You*."

She nods, placing her hand over mine resting on her cheek.

"And as far as *my* career?" I scoff playfully. "I won a Super Bowl. And I was named MVP. I hold the Knights record for most rush yards in a season for a quarterback. I've made the Pro Bowl, All Pro Team, and player of the week—many times. None of those accomplishments measure up when it's between you and football. It's not the most important part of my life anymore." Her dark eyes soften. "I already told Kat that I'm open to a trade. And Coach Aarons knows it's a possibility too—although he doesn't love it." I chuckle to myself. "But I won't let you risk your job here. I know you don't have news on the promotion yet, but I'm betting on you. I'll bet on you every damn time. But I don't need to play here. I just need you. If I could, I'd plaster how much I love you on every billboard in this goddamn city."

"What?" Her eyes widen and her lips stay apart. "You—you love playing in Tampa. This place was your dream, I read it on an interview sheet, Liam."

My head shakes back and forth as pink and purple colors sneak up in the sky.

"No," I whisper, bringing my other hand to her face as well. "You are. You're every dream I've ever had come true."

"Liam." I feel her knees weaken under her.

"Listen, Dem. I'm just getting the hang of sharing my emotions more openly, but I've never felt more sure about anything. I used to think that whatever bullshit I was going through in my head was something I had to ignore. Keep smiling through any pain or darkness. I never really…I don't know, let myself process any of it. But you made me feel like it was okay to sit in the dark for a minute. To feel what I'm feeling and get through it without letting it swallow me. Like I wasn't going to drown if I let myself show emotion. You helped me believe I could make it through any rough waters. You showed me how to build a boat."

"I love you," she whispers, eyes welling with tears. "I love you," she says again before bringing her lips up to mine.

It's sweet and soft. Warm and welcoming.

Home.

"My interview…" she says, shoulders pulled back in that confident way she does. "It's in two days, then I'll know within the week if I get it."

"And once you ace it, we'll know more about where we stand—publicly. For now, we can still do things on your terms. If we need to stay a secret, my lips are sealed. Ready to hold my hand in public? I'll grab yours first. I've waited for you. God, I've waited years for the way you're looking at me right now. I'll do anything you ask me to."

"I want to be with you." I feel her thumb brush my hand. "Everything else we'll figure out together. I just know I want to be with you."

I pull her hand to my lips, brushing her knuckles with a soft kiss.

"Last thing," she says, and I sling my arm over her shoulder as we walk toward the door.

"What's that?"

"I know you're doing something with my rent." Her eyes narrow my way. "And that stops now."

"I have no idea what you're talking about." I pull her closer, planting a kiss on the top of her head and I catch her eyes roll as she sighs with a smile.

A big fucking eye roll. And damn, I love to see it.

"Did we actually lose the last piece? I knew Birdie would eventually get sick of this puzzle all over the table and start swatting her cute orange paws at the pieces." Demi huffs as she looks under the couch.

We ended up finishing the puzzle over chocolate chip cookies and flan last night. Well, we didn't exactly finish it since there's one piece missing.

"How dare you?" I tease. "Birdie is offended."

"Ugh." Demi stands, rolling her eyes as she walks down the hall toward my bedroom.

I should probably tell her I see the piece next to the plant by the sliding glass door, although it's pretty hot seeing her all flustered over a missing puzzle piece.

"I can't believe we spent all of that time working on this puzzle and we aren't going to finish it." She pulls her purse over her shoulder.

"Dramatic, aren't we?"

She gapes at me. "Doesn't it bother you that the puzzle is unfinished?"

I just shrug, walking over to the door as Birdie meows at my feet. When I bend down to pick up the piece, I turn to face her.

"I found it," I say. "Want to do the honors?"

"Oh my god." Her hand flies to her hip. "We finished it."

"We did." I smile, placing the piece in its spot before taking her hand.

Her phone rings and she pulls it from her purse. I catch Greg's name on the caller ID.

"Oh god." She swallows. "I figured it was a no since I didn't hear anything."

"Answer it," I urge, silently praying for her dreams to come true.

Demi puts the phone to her ear, and I want to give her space so I back away slightly, but she reaches for my hand, holding it as she nods on the phone. She says very few words, most of them are "uh-huh," "okay," and "thank you"—really giving me nothing to go on.

When she hangs up and drops the phone back in her bag, her dark eyes connect with my patiently waiting stare.

"I got it," she whispers. "I got the promotion." Her eyes water and mine do too. I pull her into my arms, wrapping her body against mine.

"I knew it, Dem!" I celebrate. "God, I knew it. I'm so proud of you. Congratulations!"

She deserves every bit of this. Every good fucking thing that happens in her life, everything she works for and is passionate about. Even if things between the two of us never came to fruition, I'd still be shouting how proud I am of her.

"I can't believe it."

My lips land on the top of her head, pressing a hard kiss and inhaling the candy-like scent. "I can. Come on, let's go celebrate."

⊰⊱

"Happy Friendsgiving!" Mia shouts as Demi and I walk through the front door.

CeCe runs up and latches onto my leg for a brief moment, and I bend down, kissing her head. Nate and Mia's boys are nowhere in sight, but I definitely hear them running around somewhere.

"Hey, Clarky," I say, kissing Mia's cheek. "It smells good in here. Let's see what you've got going on."

"Uh-uh, you stay out of the kitchen." Summer comes up on my right, jabbing my bicep before giving Demi a hug.

"What? It's part of the tradition!" I yell as all three of them are already in another room of the house.

I notice Ford, Chase, and Nate out on the back patio, and I say a quick hello to Abby while she's on FaceTime with her mom, before heading out the sliding glass doors.

"Look who it is," Ford says, tipping his beer up at me.

"He's settled down now, so no more third-wheeling with Chase and Summer," Nate jokes as I take the seat between him and Ford.

"Ha-ha, very funny." I shake my head as Chase hands me a beer.

We cheers over the table, and I take in the scenery around me. Trying to commit every detail of this evening and these people to memory.

The girls come outside a few moments later, bringing appetizers, and I nudge Demi, knowing this is the perfect opportunity to share her news and the potential news of me playing elsewhere next year.

"Hey, while we're all out here, we need to make a toast. Demi worked her ass off for years—she put up with me for five of them," I say, earning a laugh. "And I thought you all should know you're looking at the new broadcast reporter for prime-time game coverage starting next season."

"No shit!" Ford shouts.

"Hell yeah," Summer says, nodding her head at Demi and raising her champagne glass.

Congratulations are heard around the table, and everyone takes a few moments to ask her some questions, some she can answer and others she can't.

"So what does this mean then? For you guys?" Chase asks, genuine hope on his face.

"Well," Demi says, bumping her shoulder into me. "I think he has some billboards he wants to put up." She smiles, and I can't fucking tear my eyes from her face when she does it. She's beautiful.

"Uh, one more thing." I clear my throat and the voices around me die down after laughter and conversation.

Summer takes a seat in Chase's lap, while Abby leans against Ford, his arm wrapping around her waist. And Mia stands with her palm on Nate's shoulder as Demi comes to my side.

"Before we knew what was going to happen, I did make it known that a trade wasn't completely off the table for me."

Nate's brow creases as he looks at me, but then softens when I see his focus move to Demi. He gets it. They all do.

"I love all of you. And I have loved playing this game with you. Every high and every low. When the lights are off and our time is up on the field, I know we left our mark. You guys made me love this game the way that I do. I know that football is a sport, but it means so much more than that. You're my family, and the thought of not getting to do this with you all forever is hard to process." I snap my gaze to the girls. "It's been an honor sitting back and watching my brothers fall in love. Seeing how beautifully your lives have turned out." Then I glance at Demi, and she smiles at me.

"Being along for the ride you each had to finding your better half was a fucking trip. One I don't think I'll ever forget. And if I don't end up playing here next season, I just need you all to know that this part of my life has been my favorite." I squeeze Demi's hand wrapped in mine. "I hope I'm here. But if I'm not, I'm okay with it. The game isn't forever, but this is—all of you are."

Everyone's eyes are wide, some are teary, but all are understanding.

My time with Demi was an unexpected blessing this year. Something I used to daydream about, never thinking it would be my reality. And now that she's standing next to me and our entire lives are before us, I feel the urge to protect it—protect her—at all costs.

Falling so deeply in love with her hit me fast. But it's not like

I didn't see it coming. I just didn't do a damn thing to stop it or slow it down. My feelings strengthened quicker than the snap of a football, the tick of a game clock, the blitz of a pass rush.

I'm in love. *Desperately. Undeniably.* In love. And I'm going to hold onto it as long as I can.

The guys nod, and Demi keeps her hand in mine as she rests her head on my arm. This has been the greatest adventure. It's changed me in every way possible. My life is infinitely better because of the people around this table, and I'll never be able to say thank you enough for the love they've given me.

I'm not 100 percent sure where the next season will take me. Maybe I'll stay here, maybe I won't—Demi's home base can be anywhere now. But it doesn't matter where I end up, because all I know for certain is she's who I want to end up with. Every day. Always.

I tip my head down, getting a quick glimpse of Demi. Dark brown eyes and curls sitting over her shoulders. She's beautiful and brilliant. And I'm so fucking lucky I get to call her mine. Every bit of my future lies with this woman—no matter where life takes me.

EPILOGUE

LIAM

"I've got the red cooler," I shout over to Nate as I'm loading up the boat.

The offseason came quickly, and while this time is often spent alone, I haven't had a day to myself since last November and I've never loved it more.

Demi's new role will officially start this upcoming season, and I'm so damn excited for her. She's part of the Monday night prime-time crew—so she'll cover any team playing during the season on Mondays. It's going to be so fucking cool to see her every week on TV doing what she was made to do.

The Knights and I did have a meeting about my contract—a couple, actually. The first thing I told Coach Aarons was how much I've appreciated his mentorship. And then I swiftly followed that up with telling him I understand this is a business and guys get traded every day. I was honest, telling him how much my personal life has changed, the happiness I've found. It turns out that was obvious to everyone around me. The uplift, the spark, the joy that seemed greater than my usual.

He was surprised when he found out Demi and I are together, but never judgmental. Never accusatory or off-putting. He had a couple questions, and I answered them with certainty, something I know he appreciated.

When our conversation shifted back to my contract, he chuckled, removing his thin-framed glasses from his face and placing them on the table.

"If you think you're playing anywhere other than this team, Evans, I'll tell you right now, I'll go to bat to have you stay."

His words made my breath hitch—I'm so used to being told that being vulnerable or my personal life might hinder my chances at longevity in this game.

I'm thankful we were able to find common ground and I can still call Tampa home for the next three seasons.

After last season ended, Demi and I took a trip to Arizona to visit her family. We spent two weeks out there, and I have to admit, although it was hot as hell, the no humidity thing is nice.

Her parents are amazing, and I found myself really enjoying my time with her dad. He isn't a Tampa fan, but I guess I wouldn't expect it living out west. Although he did wish me good luck next season, and Demi tells me that's a big leap from his previous comments about any team that isn't his.

I got to spend a lot of time with her mom and her abuela too. I can't count how many tostones I ate, but I know it was in the double digits. I also think I had the best empanadas I've ever had in my entire fucking life too.

Demi lit up around her family—her usual casual demeanor was lifted just a bit being around them. She smiled so much it made my chest pound every time I saw them interact. Her sweet abuela was trying to teach me some words in Spanish. I've been practicing every day, and I feel good about the prospect of being able to hold a decent conversation with her next time I'm visiting.

While out there, Demi and I had a long talk one night as we

sat in the bed of a truck on the side of a mountain. I was terrified we were going to be eaten by mountain lions, but she assured me she'd protect me if the situation arose.

I told her how free I've felt lately. How my life has felt so hopeful and exciting. After my contract was extended, I received a text from my father about how long it took for them to "want to keep me"—his words. And it was like the final straw I didn't realize he was on. My next session with Dana was one of the most emotional hours of my life. But I ended that afternoon blocking his phone number and deleting him from every social media app I have. Even going as far as sending text messages to my brother and my mom, letting them know how horribly our relationship had escalated and how I needed this break. My brother understood, no questions asked. My mom, not so much, but that didn't surprise me.

I don't know if I'll ever have a relationship with him again. Never say never, right? But right now, I breathe better without him.

"I'm not waiting much longer, ladies." I tap my watch as I wait for Summer and Abby to get on the boat.

"Liam Evans, if you would've left without us, I promise this would've been your last day on earth." Summer narrows her eyes at me once she steps on the dock and hops into the boat.

We're heading out to Bottle Island for the afternoon—finally, all eight of us are together again.

Demi's sitting in the back of the boat between Chase and Abby as Ford stands next to me, beer in his hand. Summer takes the tanning spot at the front, and, as usual, Nate and Mia are up ahead on the Jet Ski.

"Oh, shit," Ford says as he's glancing down at his phone. "Guess who just got traded?"

My brow creases as I shift my focus from the waves to him and back again. "On our team?"

He shakes his head and holds his phone screen up so I can see it.

"West?" I gasp, my jaw feeling slack as I stare at Ford wide eyed. "I'm fucking shocked."

"Listen to these fucking details." His head shakes again. "The Angels trade a lights-out pitcher for one first round, one fourth round pick, and centerfielder Danny Hule? That's one of the worst deals I've ever seen. Angels' front office fucked that up. They can't afford to lose West."

"Milwaukee won that trade, no contest. And teaming West up with Connor again is diabolical. I can't wait to watch them win a series."

Ford and I both shake our heads in disbelief over that lopsided trade.

As we pull up to Bottle Island, Chase and Ford hop out first to help pull the boat up to get situated on the sand. I do a quick scan of the perimeter, noticing only a handful of other boats out here, which is a nice surprise.

The girls head to the beach, blankets and bags in hand as Chase follows behind them with a small cooler to leave by their sides.

Days like today are extra special. I'm reminded just how fucking lucky I am. Six months ago, everything about my future felt unsure. My job, my relationship—if I could've even called it that back then. But now, looking at everything I have, I don't think I could've written it better. I'm so damn thankful for this group of people. I may not have come from the most supportive family, but the family I found—the one I chose—they mean everything to me.

"Quick touch game?" Nate tosses me the ball, and I put my beer down on Demi's blanket, bending down to plant a kiss on her forehead as I do.

She sure knows how to wear the fuck out of that swimsuit. I

might need to borrow Nate's Jet Ski at some point for some alone time with her and that white one-piece.

"Oh, how was your appointment?" Chase turns to Ford as the four of us are now huddled up in the sand.

Ford shrugs, glancing at Abby, and I don't miss how he swallows before clearing his throat to answer.

"We're not going to keep trying right now. Not like that anyway." His voice has a low rasp to it, and I feel my shoulders fall a little. "It's been really hard on her. Emotionally, physically. When we met with the specialist after the fifth failed round I could see how drained she was. It kills me that I can't give her what she wants so badly. It fucking *kills* me. We had a long talk, and she just said she needs a break from fertility treatments. I think all the failed rounds are really becoming too much—and who the fuck am I to question any of that? She's a damn warrior for what she's been putting herself through. I'm in awe of her every fucking day, and if she says she needs a break, she's getting a break. We both want to have a baby so badly, you know, but we talked about it—we've been talking about it for a while now, and if it's not part of our story then we'll have each other to help cope with that."

God, I've hated seeing them go through this for the last few years. They'd be the best parents.

"I'm holding hope for you guys," I say, extending my hand to his but pulling him into a hug at the last minute.

"Ah, thanks." He wipes his forehead, and I don't miss the redness forming in his watery eyes, but he blinks it away. "Let's play a game." He swats the ball from Nate's grip and it lands in the sand near his feet.

"Can we play?"

"Holy shit, you snuck up on us." Chase jerks back as Summer's at his side, icy blue eyes pleading at him. "You want to play instead of just lying out and yapping?"

"Yeah," Mia says as she snatches the ball from Nate after he just picked it up.

"Jesus," he says in a huff. "Can I not hold onto a ball anymore, what the fuck is wrong with me?"

"Girls versus boys, it'll be fun." Summer shrugs and runs her fingers along Chase's back. A distraction tactic I know they're all going to use if we agree.

"What do you say, Ab?" Chase calls over his shoulder to his sister, and I see both Abby and Demi stand, dusting sand from their hands onto their thighs.

"I'm in." Demi stands at my side, and I sling an arm over her shoulder as Abby agrees too.

"You guys can be on offense first," Summer offers, and I don't miss the small nod toward Demi.

"What was that?" I hook my finger into the upper thigh piece of Demi's swimsuit, holding her in place as I grin down at her makeup-free face.

"Nothing. Let's play, this will be fun." She smiles, and I lean my lips down to hers in a quick motion.

"You're so damn pretty," I whisper against her ear as she backs away, shaking her head.

We make a line in the sand and stand on opposite sides, everyone covering their partner in what's sure to be the most unserious game of football I've ever played. I'm excited to just have fun today, though. We've got nowhere to be, nothing hanging over our heads or causing us stress. It's fucking amazing how much can change in such a short period of time, but when I look at Demi, I know I'm looking at everything good in my life. It was a road to get here—but I wouldn't want to change any of it. Even the time I spent wishing she was mine. I think it helped mature me. It helped me realize that sometimes, the best things are worth the wait.

Demi's eyes shine when the sun hits them and she takes two casual steps closer to me as we're on opposite sides. She crosses her arms over her chest, and I make no attempt to hide the way I look her up and down, football in my hand.

She leans a little closer to me, her eyes staring at the football in my hand and climbing up to my eyes.

"Feeling good today, Twelve?" She licks her lips with a sultry smirk.

I take one hand and cup the side of her jaw as I look into the dark brown eyes I've been obsessed with since the second I saw them.

"Always good with you, baby."

The End

ACKNOWLEDGMENTS

The alpha/beta readers who helped fine tune this story. Wren, Emma, Kelsey, Lindsay, Abby, Isabella, Kayla, Kylee: I mean it when I say that this book is better because of you. Thank you for the endless excitement, support and brain power to help take this story to new heights. I'm so grateful.

My sensitivity readers, Carlina, Isabella, Ycel, Millie Perez and Ambar Cordova thank you for taking the time to read for Demi's background. I'm so grateful for all the feedback you provided to help make sure Demi's Dominican background was portrayed authentically and respectfully.

Indy Valentine and Cori Hamm thank you for the help you provided when it came to some of the mental health aspects of this book and the therapy session in Pass Rush. I'm so appreciative!

Samantha Brinn, thank you for being such a cheerleader and champion as you read Pass Rush. Your feedback was always so helpful and I'm so grateful for you.

The author friends who provided a safe space for my crash outs, brain dumps and overall vent sessions about anything and everything throughout this entire process, just know that you're loved and appreciated!

Cassie, Jenna, Kenz and Emma thank you for making my life ten thousand times less stressful by taking so much off my plate. I could cry if I think about it for too long. Between my newsletter, street team, graphics, reels and TikTok's, I never had to worry about dropping the ball on any of it because you all always had it covered. Thank you so much.

Caroline with Love and Edits, you've been with me since book one and I know we've both grown so much since then. Thank you for always working with me and my timelines, dealing with my voice memos and helping me get these books out into the world.

Mel with Mel D. Designs, you've taken every idea I've had and turned them into such perfect covers for this series. Thank you for everything you've done.

Cathryn Carter with Format by CC, your formatting is always one of my favorite pieces of the book. I appreciate how timely you are and how flexible you've been with my schedule throughout this entire series. Thank you for everything.

Hannah with April Editorial, thank you for working with me after so many timeline changes. Having a final set of eyes on things was so helpful! Thank you for being so kind and such a cheerleader for this story. I'm so grateful.

My mom, or as Instagram knows you, 'Nonna'. This book wouldn't exist without you. Well, maybe in about 2+ more years it would've seen the light of day, but it definitely wouldn't be releasing now without you. Thank you for the endless support and ways you show up to help, often without even being asked. You're the best.

My friends and family, your support always means the world to me. Even if you never actually read a word from any of these books, having you in my corner is everything.

K, I am so proud of you. I know you're tired of having to be the bigger person and having to be strong in situations that keep getting thrown your way, but you are graceful in your resilience. You are an example of growing and rising in environments that are tailored to pick you apart and wear you down. Love you forever.

To the readers, I wish I could hug each and every one of you. I genuinely mean it when I say you've changed my life for the better. Every conversation we've had, the comments, content made, posts, reviews-all of it. When Liam says in his final chapter that this has been his greatest adventure, it was me talking to you. I've loved being able to bring these characters to life. To talk about love, grief, mental health and so much more within the pages of these books. Thank you for taking a chance on me. Whether you're a new reader or have been around since the first book debuted, I'm grateful--so unbelievably grateful for you, sweet friends. I hope we get to go on a lot more adventures together in the future.

Until next time, xoxo
    Erin

ABOUT THE AUTHOR

Erin Mackenzie is from a small town in central Florida where she lives with her husband and children. Her love for reading started at a young age and then was rediscovered after she became a mom and wanted something that was just for her. When she isn't reading or writing, you can find her trying out new recipes to cook or bake, spending time outdoors or rooting on her favorite sports teams.